WINERY PEAK

WINERY PEAK

Chris Scott Graham

RAMBLE HOUSE

ISBN 13: 978-1-60543-340-0

ISBN 10: 1-60543-340-3

Cover Art: Gavin L. O'Keefe
Preparation: Fender Tucker

WINERY PEAK

CHAPTER ONE

THE HEADACHE pounded relentlessly against the back of his left eye, waking him again from a night that brought nothing other than troubled fits of sleep. With extreme effort and a low moan he partially opened his bloodshot eyes and then winced in response to the stabbing pain as the light hit his retina. Concentrating, although unable to fully focus, he desperately squinted across the room for the presence of his wife. Locating her soft outline near the doorway quieted his anxiety over being left alone. Another moment passed quietly until, with a tremendous expenditure of his dwindling energy, he lifted his head slightly from the soiled pillow and began to speak haltingly towards his children. Not knowing how to respond to this sudden display of attention, they continued to huddle anxiously against the wall next to the splintered packing crate that served as a makeshift table.

Tall and rangy, and usually clean-shaven with the exception of a dark black pencil thin mustache, he had always been admired among his friends as a strong and handsome man. A deep black stubble peppered with gray flecks now created shadows in shrunken cheeks, and his height even while prone served only to accentuate the spasms that racked his body with every phlegm filled cough. Amid his somewhat disjointed ramblings he continued to quietly repeat, over and over, the same phrase uttered in the urgent tones of a warning; "amargo . . . agua amargo . . ." Another cough triggered spasm racked his chest, further pressing him against sheets damp from a long night of fever induced sweat, and he fell silent. Still feeling weak, he partially rolled over onto his left side and motioned for more water to sip from a small partially cracked Peter Pan cup. The cup was the personal favorite of his six-year-old daughter. With the innocent love of her youth, upon the onset of his illness she had insisted that drinking from it would certainly make everything better.

When he was done drinking his wife carefully took the small plastic cup from his outstretched hand that shook as if with palsy. Although feeling confident in the strength of her prayers, her uneasiness continued to grow as she watched his strength persistently continue to diminish. Her husband had never been seriously ill in the 23 years of their marriage and she had nothing to compare to his present condition, which now included waves of searing heat alternating with bone numbing chills. As he slipped back into a disturbed sleep she drew his five children closer around the threadbare blankets that covered his makeshift bed.

The migrant fieldworker and his worried family were housed in a small building, located near the center of a haphazard cluster of tin sided sheds that made up the close community of vineyard laborers. Constructed in a style that existed throughout the Napa Valley wine growing region, but located out of sight of the well heeled tourist centers, the building consisted of two small rooms and was built using single wall construction. Sheets of metal were nailed to wood framing that was open and exposed on the inside of the building. Light from a small candle added to the light that managed to filter through the room's single dirty window. There was neither wiring for electricity nor any other heat source. Interior plumbing was also nonexistent. Although located in one of the wealthiest agricultural valleys in California, where large estates and spacious houses dotted the landscape amid picturesque vineyards that provided a favorite assignment for reporters and photographers from magazines throughout the world, among his own people poverty and sickness was not uncommon nor terribly unexpected. Every year many fell ill and died at ages that were far below the "national average."

Vineyard workers were almost always migrant farm workers as the more labor intensive agricultural practices in the valley did not require full crews on a year round basis.

Generally undereducated and most often underrepresented, they uniformly suffered from a complete lack of the basics in sanitary working conditions or housing, and generally experienced a consistent absence of any degree of interest from anyone outside their close-knit community. What was occurring at Winery Peak, however, was becoming impossible even for the outside community to ignore much longer. Over the last several weeks too many good workers had fallen critically ill, all of whom were displaying the same general symptoms, and the publicly available numbers of those affected had spiked upwards in the last three weeks. None of those suffering from the condition, however, had yet died from their illness. But the situation had become serious enough that the county health department had finally directed one overworked case worker to consider the possibility of the outbreak of an epidemic. The case worker had made the effort, on an already overbooked schedule, to drive out to the winery with the hope of conducting a few short preliminary interviews.

Although reaching the remote site where most of the cases were located would involve a drive clear across the valley from her last appointment, and she was sure that her department-issued car was going to break down as soon as she was well outside a reasonable walking distance of the town, the case worker rationalized that the exertion would be worthwhile if she could pull together enough information to write a report that would satisfy her immediate supervisor and push the matter to one of the county's two health inspectors charged with field investigations and ensuring compliance with temporary housing permits. An hour after reaching the small community she was back on the road, her half-hearted efforts to assess the situation unrewarded. The well intentioned attempts to interview the stricken fieldworkers and their families had been quietly rebuffed despite her attempts to explain to suspicious minds that she was not an investigator from the Bureau of Immigration and Naturalization.

The case worker had not been surprised by her lack of success and, as typical when making site visits, walked among the building in order to gather as much information as possible and left behind pamphlets in English and Spanish detailing the services offered by his department. Even though the economics of the wine growers in the valley, and the agricultural industry in general, were dependant on the lower wages that could be pressed on undocumented aliens, the "fueled by fear" politics of the state consistently identified illegal workers as a handy target during troubled economic times. For some time hospitals and clinics throughout the agricultural areas of the state had reported smaller numbers of patients as illegal aliens had avoided any situation were their status may come to the attention of the government, and her visit to the winery was not going to change the course of that troubling trend.

After the case worker left the small group of buildings that included the shed housing the stricken fieldworker his wife hurriedly returned from the doorway to her husband's side. She dipped a small square of cloth torn from the winery-issued bedding into a pan of cool water and gently wiped his forehead. After a time she paused to tiredly push a small graying strand that had fallen out the mass of her hair that she had clipped into a bun. Looking down at his body, each inch of which was so well known and loved, she was finally convinced that he would not respond without medical help. With a sigh she decided that the risk of involving strangers could not possibly outweigh the risk of losing him. Turning to her eldest son, who had been sitting on the threshold of the doorway looking sullenly out at the world in which his family was forced to live, she handed him the materials the caseworker from the county health department had left behind and instructed him to go and ask for help.

~ ~ ~ ~ ~

The dirt road wound its way across the hill and into the valley before again disappearing from sight around a sharp bend. Spring wildflowers crowding the sides and small plants growing along the center of the road attested to its general disuse. As the county health inspector paused at the top of the steep slope to catch his breath he turned and examined the view that stretched out behind him. From his current vantage point he could see the edge of the vineyards in the near distance. At this time of year the fields were a beehive of activity as the vines were checked and drip systems repaired. Lining the sides of the fields was an eclectic mixture of trucks and cars, parked haphazardly as the workers arrived that morning from their company housing at the far side of the winery. Although the inspector was now several hundred yards away from the edge of the fields, when the wind gusted the faint smell of commercial fertilizers rose unpleasantly to his face. The gusts also caught and swirled small dust clouds at his feet, leaving a fine grit lining on the edge of his clothes and a definite thirst on the top of his throat.

Tom Murphy had been a health inspector for the county for almost seven years and understood why ten years was considered the maximum before job burnout set in. The valley wineries historically paid its field labor subsistence wages, despite the highly publicized efforts of the labor unions during the past two decades, and "company housing" often consisted of thrown together shacks that lacked electricity or plumbing. Some families obtained water from centralized field wells when available, but many skimmed water from closer irrigation streams and ponds. From time to time union representatives would rouse themselves from their encampment in various dark and cool bars, where they could usually be found generously allocating the union dues to another round of drinks, and lodge a formal complaint with the responsible county authorities. Since the county was effectively controlled by the larger wineries, and the tax revenues that their profits generated, the complaints would be appropriately filed and ignored. A small number of the complaints were investigated from time to time, to make sure the system ran smoothly and to avoid involvement in the periodic claims for farm labor reform. The county health investigators learned how to handle their work discreetly, and quietly point out the more serious problem areas to the appropriate winery foremen for correction. Knowing how this game was played made Murphy a well-liked player among his friends in the department, but did little for his self-esteem.

Walking forward Murphy watched his boots kick little puffs of dust from the road, which consisted mostly of two well-worn tire ruts through a former meadow leading to an old long abandoned limestone quarry. Had he been paying attention, he probably would have enjoyed the pastoral setting of yellow and purple wildflowers amid tall grasses waving slowly in the light breeze. Murphy's mind, however, was still back at that hot tin shed with the feverish fieldworker and his distraught family. It had not taken Murphy long to realize that the farm worker could soon die without immediate medical attention, and he had exercised the full extent of his very limited authority by calling in a paramedic unit for assistance. The family had insisted, in a mixture of Spanish and halting English, that their family member had fallen ill after coming into contact with "bitter water" near the site of the old quarry. Although Murphy now half wished that he had simply returned to the county health offices and filed the appropriate report for handling by others, upon learning of the nature of the illnesses permeating the cluster of sheds he had concluded that he was not dealing with some semi-isolated form of viral outbreak that could be simply reassigned back to one of the department's overworked caseworkers. Spurred on by the knowledge that a simple report would merely lie fallow in someone's overstuffed in-box, and angered by the lack of care that allowed such conditions to exist, he felt compelled to spend the remaining time available that afternoon to search for the cause of the problem.

The quarry had been extensively mined in the early twenties, when limestone had been in great demand for the construction boom that was surging through the growing metropolis to the near south. Over the years the cost of running the operation had closed the mine as cheaper building materials had become available. Rainwater over time had gradually filled the great pit, and rusted the remaining pieces of heavy machinery that lay in broken jumbles around the site. Murphy rounded the bend in the road to be greeted by the sight of a rust-pitted crane that stood as a silent sentinel over the scene. He walked cautiously up to the cyclone fence that enclosed the quarry. A heavy padlock and steel link chain encircled the fencepost to the gate, which in turn rested on a large grate that had been designed during the heyday of the mining operations to keep the local dairy cows from wandering down the road and into the open pit when the gate was open. Without a second glance at the gate Murphy ducked through a large hole that had been torn in the side of the fence and returned to the road on the quarry side of the gate. Underfoot the loose dirt on the road gradually changed from a light brown to a dirty white from the powdered limestone residue, and the grasses that grew in the middle of the road thinned out and eventually stopped altogether. The road continued through a cut in the soft rock of the hillside and eventually wove its way up to a flat area near the low lip that separated the two sides of the pit.

During his questioning of the fieldworker's wife Murphy had learned that the fieldworker had been swimming with several of the other workers in the pit. According to her hesitant explanation, since their arrival at Winery Peak her husband had joined the other men on Saturdays evenings after the afternoon shift. The family had arrived approximately one month earlier for the spring season after harvesting winter crops from the fields near Palm Desert in Southern California. Since there was a lack of sufficient sanitation facilities at the housing sheds their activity was not unusual, and the pit was the only large source of freestanding water that the family had readily available other than the large pond that fed the field pumps. Murphy, thorough as his reputation led people to believe, had already checked the flow from the pumps to find that the draw from the pond and the wells was relatively clean. So he had decided that the quarry pit was also worth checking. This was a decision that seemed much more appropriate when he had parked his car at the farm worker's shed than now after the long dry hike up the hill.

From the top of the lip of the quarry the water looked turquoise green, and almost motionless since the steep sides of the pit protected the surface from any wind. From his position, with the sun generally overhead but now moving to the west slightly in front of him, the light glanced brightly off of water and into his eyes like a signal. With sweat trickling down the side of his face and under his arms Murphy could feel how the water must have beckoned to the sun-parched workers. Walking to the edge of the water Murphy kneeled down and removed a small glass vile from his pocket. Where the water was shallow he could see the bottom of the quarry as if he was looking through glass. Nothing grew on the bottom to obscure his vision, and the complete absence of any living thing in the water was vaguely unsettling. He unscrewed the top of the vial and blew gently inside to remove any traces of dust before placing it carefully underneath the surface of the water. His steady hand avoided rippling the water, as any turbulence could stir the muck that had settled to the bottom and queer his sample. A small gurgling sound paid quiet testament to the process as Murphy filled the vial from just below the still surface of the quarry basin. Two more containers filled as quickly and he snapped the caps into place to seal the contents. Murphy paused where he crouched before slowly standing and shaking the dust from his knees and drying his hands on the seat of his pants. Before turning away from the calm waters Murphy again peered deeply into the depths of the quarry. A thought crossed his mind, half formed but then lost, and he gently rubbed the sweat from his bare forehead before starting the long walk back down the hill to his car.

~ ~ ~ ~ ~

The late afternoon drive up to the old Napa Hotel must have been one of the most scenic drives in the entire Napa Valley. On either side on the roadway tall valley oaks majestically stood guard amid sun warmed splashes of bright yellow mustard and orange poppies.

As Dr. Peter Dickson drove along the winding two lane road he could not help but admire the view, although he had seen it almost every day for the past four years.

Dickson was the widely respected President and Winemaster of Winery Peak, a new start-up operation dedicated to the production of ultra-premium wines and varietals. Winery Peak was an operation that included both vineyards and a winery, and existed with the favorable financial backing of its multi-national corporate owner Wine House. A corporation that understood the world-wide wine trade and liquor business and was committed to play a dominant role in the industry through its ownership of several well established brands throughout California as well as the United States and Canada.

As he pulled up the long driveway to the hotel entrance Dickson continued to contentedly hum along to the tune on the radio. Flipping his keys to the parking attendant as he exited the car, Dickson paused briefly to admire the heavy adobe walls and supports made from massive oak timbers on the front of the old mission style structure that housed the original wing of the hotel. He could not have felt better, and this sense of well-being was reflected clearly on his lined and weathered face. Everything at the winery had been coming along on the schedule that he had outlined when the project had been first established, even if they were now projected at being slightly over budget by the time that the first vintage was shipped. The call from his liaison at Wine House, Tyler Klienman, to schedule this meeting could only mean further good news and congratulations. Glancing around the parking lot he recognized Klienman's blue convertible among the more exotic sports cars and Eurostyle sedans. With a strong sense of purpose Dickson turned from the parking lot and strode through the tall oak doors that framed the entrance leading to the central atrium and the registration desk. He was greeted warmly and then efficiently directed to a small conference room by an overly friendly desk manager who informed him that Klienman was already waiting. With a happy bounce to his stride Dickson traveled down the hallway of the historic building and, upon reaching the designated conference room, rapidly knocked and cheerfully walked through the doorway without waiting for a response.

Upon entering the room Dickson immediately sensed that his assumptions about the reasons for the meeting were significantly incorrect. Although the conference room was intimate in size Klienman sat defensively behind a large oak conference table as far across from the door as was possible. The table was completely empty except for a tall glass carafe of ice water bearing the logo of the hotel and a tray bearing several faux crystal goblets. Water beaded the sides of the carafe and created a small pool around its bottom, indicating that Klienman had arrived early to ensure that he would be waiting for Dickson instead of arriving at the same time. It was readily apparent from his body language that Klienman wanted to put as much space as possible between himself and Dickson. By Klienman's side sat a pretty young woman, known to Dickson as Klienman's own personal assistant, who self-consciously held a file in hand and a pencil in the other. On Dickson's side of the table was one empty chair.

"Sit down, Peter." Klienman began uncomfortably. "This is not going to be a lot of fun, so let me get right to the point."

He kept his eyes on Dickson and reached sideways to his assistant. In his hand she placed a single sheet of paper.

"You are being let go . . ."

Klienman's voice trailed off as he handed the paper across the table to Dickson. Dickson did not reach forward and it fluttered down onto the table.

"We want you to drive up to Winery Peak and tell the staff that you will no longer be working there."

Dickson stared and no one spoke. Finally finding his voice through the shock Dickson whispered harshly "And may I know why I am being fired?"

"It's your own fault," Klienman shot back and squirmed uncomfortably. "And you know that we are now having to face the threat of closure of operations because of the County's investigation."

Klienman's assistant cleared her throat in warning of saying too much. Earlier that week the County Health Department had contacted Winery Peak with the results of the lab analysis of the water in the quarry. Although subject to further testing and verification, the preliminary findings indicated the presence of large and dangerous levels of toxins. The analysis was labeled as "preliminary" and "inconclusive" as the findings pointed to the presence of chemical compounds typically used in the manufacture of nerve gas and the lab was hesitant to base its reputation on having found something that had no logical reason for being present at that location. The County had wasted no time sealing off the entire quarry behind reinforced cyclone fencing and in sending a large mobile lab to the site. The lab was made from a converted shipping container, mounted on the trailer bed of a truck and hitched to a cab-over Peterbilt. Testing wells were immediately sunk in the downhill slope to monitor for possible ground water plumes and soil samples were sent to Sacramento for processing to determine the extent of residual contamination levels.

"We both know that the chemicals the County located are not used at the winery," Dickson responded in turn, refusing to let up.

"And you know that the County's discovery of those chemicals in the old quarry has raised some difficult questions that you have not answered." Klienman rejoinder was flatly stated.

While Klienman spoke his assistant took notes to make sure that there was a "proper" record of the interview. When she paused expectantly Klienman looked past Dickson and continued with remarks that he had gone over carefully with the company's General Counsel before the meeting.

"While the investigation is pending we must make some hard decisions."

Understanding suddenly colored Dickson's face.

"You mean that Corporate thinks that the dumping of that shit was something I knew about?" He pressed both hands on the table palms down. "Winery Peak is my goddamn project. Why the hell would I pollute my own goddamn project?"

"Sorry, Peter."

Klienman, seeing the look on Dickson's face, realized that his response sounded too insincere and tried to placate Dickson with a different tactic.

"This is just how Corporate wants to deal with the problem."

The look on Dickson's face did not soften. Klienman tried to slide his chair back further away from Dickson's side of the room, only to encounter the far wall of the room against his back. Feeling cornered Klienman snapped out defensively at Dickson.

"And yelling at me about it ain't gonna change the fact that we have to let you go."

With surprisingly quick movements Dickson stepped around the table and grabbed Klienman by the arms, sending the carafe spinning to the floor in the process. Using both hands Dickson squeezed with the strength of a man who was used to long days working personally in the fields. Dickson struggled to maintain the last of his composure, his angry red face close enough to Klienman's that his breath fogged up the lens of Klienman's trendy tortoise shell glasses. As he fixated on the vein that furiously throbbed in Dickson's neck Klienman's world seemed suddenly filled with the thought that this approach had not been such a good idea. To his relief suddenly the grip on his arms loosened, but still did not completely let go.

"You aren't going to place the blame on me, you son of a bitch."

Klienman could not remember later whether Dickson had been talking to himself or not, so relived he was when Dickson finally let go of his arms. Without a further word Dickson turned and strode to the door, broken glass from the carafe crunching underfoot, and left. Klienman slumped back against the wall, all color drained from his face, and first stared mutely at the empty doorway and then at his assistant. She in turn quietly finished her notes of the interview and before looking down at the supine Klienman.

"He is going to cause trouble," she observed.

"No, he won't."

Klienman nervously picked himself off the floor and walked around the table carefully to avoid the pieces of glass. "He can't."

"Why not?"

"We have management prerogative and a contract that says we can fire him without having to give any reasons. We have to have a free hand to run our business, especially where high level managers are concerned. And there is not a jury anywhere that would see it different."

Klienman's assistant merely shrugged her response, which only served to anger Klienman.

"Well, what the hell do you think we should do?"

"I don't know, but I'm sure you have not heard the last of Dr. Dickson."

~~~~~

Press conferences tend to be very noisy affairs. Rooms are filled with reporters, each concerned primarily with making sure they are the first with a story. Too often any story will do, even though not necessarily the most accurate story. To the mind of many reporters, especially those who are struggling for recognition and the all important by-line, retractions can always be printed in small paragraphs on an inside page of the paper next to the obituaries. It is the byline, that small indication of authorship, that motivates and encourages members of the industry to manipulate events in return for a good story.

The members of the press were crammed into a room too small for the number present, as the room had been designed generally to hold the much smaller groups of reporters who covered the typical news stories that developed from time to
~~~~~

time on the winery beat. Stories that were usually found in the arts and leisure section of the newspaper. Most of the reporters milled around, checking out the competition, until a loud squeak from the amplification equipment announced the start of the conference. The entire crowd, as if on cue, quickly settled into their seats.

"I have a prepared statement."

The speaker in appearance was almost a caricature of a prototypical public relations spokeswoman. With naturally blond hair that fell gently off of her shoulders, she was cleancut and youthful, without appearing too much the model. Her suit was tastefully understated and included a light blue blouse, perfectly selected to better handle the strong white glare that reflected from the lights of the T.V. news cameras, of which there were several. She paused before continuing, while four efficient helpers in neat blue blazers handed out copies of the statement on cleanly typed sheets bearing the Wine House logo. Several reporters, who were experiencing the effects of their earlier decision to go wine tasting on their way to the press conference, eagerly snatched the statements for almost verbatim use during later calls to their editors.

"Wine House deeply regrets the recent discovery of a large concentration of toxic materials in the waters of a long abandoned quarry that is situated near the edge of the property at its newest winery—Winery Peak. Thankfully, there is no danger to the vines or the water sources in use for irrigation. Winery Peak was designed by the best in the industry to provide the finest wines using a combination of the most modern equipment and knowledge gained from our association with two of Europe's oldest wine families."

She smiled engagingly, without appearing to lessen the seriousness of the moment and paused to ensure that all of the reporters had time to note her words and inflection in the different portions of her presentation. When she was sure that they were ready for more information she continued with the prepared statement.

"In connection with the state and federal authorities we are working to address and clean up the site as quickly as possible and to deal with the responsible individual."

As she theatrically paused again, this time to replace her notes into a small red leather folder that sat out of sight on the ledge below the podium, several hands were raised and voices began to clamor for her attention. Questions were posed and hands were raised for acknowledgment, including one from a man sitting quietly near the middle of the room. In contrast to his neighbors, he was not wearing the otherwise ubiquitous white press pass. Although she was not done with her presentation she stopped to allow the entire room to focus. Then, with a gesture from the spokeswoman, the quietly possessed man stood and spoke loud enough for his voice to dominate the entire room.

"Was Dr. Dickson responsible for the chemicals that were discovered in the quarry?"

Other reporters, properly wearing the press passes that identified them with specific news organizations, picked up Dickson's name and repeated variations of the same question.

"I am not at liberty to disclose that information at this time. Dr. Dickson, however, has been released effective immediately from his position as the President and Winemaster of Winery Peak." As the reporters busily wrote down this new information the spokeswoman continued with her remarks as if she had not been interrupted. Turning to her left the crowd's attention was drawn to a large placard, which had been placed on a portable metal stand, as it was uncovered by one of her assistants. The placard set forth a complicated diagram, with particular attention drawn to the sum of $200,000 by means of bold red letters.

"We are setting up a trust fund to help the families of our employees at Winery Peak who have suffered through this tragedy. As you can see from this diagram, we have set aside two hundred thousand dollars to be administered to the people that have been impacted. And our crews have begun already to make sure that all contaminants have been removed."

Dickson's name was not again mentioned by the spokeswoman during the press conference. Most of the reporters present had already written, or at least thought out, their stories by the time they had left the winery. And in every paper the next morning Dickson's name appeared as the lead-in piece to the story.

CHAPTER TWO

WITH A SHARP NOD from the bailiff the court clerk buzzed the judge in his chambers, with that discordant sound advising him that all of the parties to the hearing were present and ready to proceed. Responding to this prearranged signal, the heavy door between the courtroom and the judge's chambers slowly swung open, and a stooped and wizened monk of a man scuttled up the short steps to the raised platform, on top of which sat a squat brown structure that consisted of a combination desk and table. This architecturally unredeeming focal point for the courtroom was referred to as the judge's "bench." As the door to the judge's chamber swung closed the bailiff rose and called out for all to stand as the honorable judge was now presiding.

The judge sat himself calmly behind the bench and adjusted his long black robe while the bailiff continued to fix the expectant group with his gaze and stared them into continued silence. Without more than a short glance at the small crowd waiting patiently before him, the judge began to leaf through a large stack of papers that had been placed on the bench earlier that day by the court clerk. Although the silence of the room was broken only by the swish of the ceiling fan as it slowly stirred the humid air hanging from the oak moldings that trimmed the ceiling, the judge gave no indication that he cared to proceed on anyone's timetable save his own. Long minutes passed until, finally satisfied that he had made the point that he was in supreme command of the courtroom, the judge glanced back to the bailiff who in bored but senatorial tones called the already still room to order.

As the process for calling the courtroom to order played out, Richard Magnus allowed his thoughts to wander slightly from the task at hand. He had always been impressed, in spite of the jaded attitudes of his fellow attorneys, with the general solemnity of courtrooms and in particular with the church-like rituals of the court personnel. When in court he sometimes recalled the cloudy memories of his youth, of long hours sitting next to his father and older brother during prayer sessions followed by serious and often animated philosophical discussions that were never fully resolved by the time that dinner's voice called them home. This particular courtroom strongly evoked those memories. In stark contrast to the utilitarian design of courtrooms built in the cold war atmosphere of the Fifties and early Sixties, the structure had been magnificently designed and constructed in the early 1920's to awe and inspire. Eighteen foot high ceilings seemed to stretch away endlessly, with layers upon layers of different colored moldings to frame murals depicting different attributes of the State during the early years of the century. Heavy wooden pew-like benches sat silently in multiple rows and continued the effect of creating a church-like atmosphere.

Immediately in front of the benches appeared a magnificently carved wooden rail, referred to as the "bar," eighteen inches round and supported by equally grand poles attached with an abundance of polished brass fittings. The bar, to Richard, did more than physically divide the room. When he had first been employed as a law clerk for an old-line San Francisco law firm, during the summer after his second year of law school, he had felt that the physical presence of the rail announced to the uninitiated that only those special individuals, the "priests" of this particular religion, could walk past the bar and thereby participate actively in the proceedings. Richard, now a licensed attorney, had inherent permission to enter the area in front of the bar and sit at one of the tables immediately before the judge's bench. These were the counsel tables; one for the plaintiff and one for the defendant, and their reassuring massiveness continued the theme of the room's near religious solemnity. They were both heavy pieces, impressive both in their size and time roughened age. On top of one of the tables, immediately in front of Richard, sat a thin leather notepad opened so that only a sliver of the long yellow notepaper inside could be seen.

"As there is but one witness left to be heard today . . ." The Assistant Deputy District Attorney began to talk rapidly, well aware of the judge's reputation for encouraging the parties to move quickly along in their presentations. He was no stranger to bored, but authoritarian, judges and wanted to take control of the proceedings in order to avoid this judge's displeasure. By preventing any of the other attorneys present from being the first to speak he knew that he had the best chance of directing the course of the afternoon.

". . . I suggest we immediately begin with the questioning of the next witness listed and then allow the parties to argue our respective positions on the pending motions for as long as possible this afternoon before breaking for the day."

As the Assistant Deputy District Attorney paused for the judge to consider his suggestion, the attorney to the left of Richard simultaneously stood and rapidly began talking. Significantly older and, with the help of his immaculately styled gray hair and Savile Row knockoff double-breasted suit, more distinguished looking than Richard, he was one of the many partners in the law firm where Richard worked. Between the two of them he was acting as the lead counsel for this hearing. To Richard's steady annoyance, his own role to date had essentially been limited to that of a glorified note taker while watching everyone else interact. Richard was restless to take a more active role, although he knew deep down that he would not have much of an opportunity to do so in this case. As was the typical practice in his office, he had been asked to help at the hearing in large part to add to a base of practical experience from which he could temper the ivory tower nature of his recent law school studies. He knew that he could only expect similar limited roles in the near future, at least until he could develop a client base of his own. Since his time was being billed to the client without deduction or write-down to reflect either his inexperience or the duplicative nature of his involvement, the firm was effectively making a profit on his training at the expense of the client. Nothing would change soon, he thought grumpily, as the client was unaware of how little he benefited from this practice and the firm had no real incentive to run its business any other way.

"First, your Honor, there are a number of procedural matters that we should go over before we commence with any examination and secondly . . ."

"Counsel, sit down and hold your comments." The judge interrupted the partner from Richard's firm irritably. "You had plenty of time to bring all 'procedural matters' to my attention before this afternoon and I want to get this matter resolved today."

"For the record . . ."

"No. No more delays, counsel. You can make whatever statements you want 'for the record' later. Right now, and not later, we are going to proceed with a witness. If you do not have another witness ready, then I will consider the presentation of evidence closed and we can proceed directly to your arguments. Your choice, and I want you to make it now!"

Richard muffled a grimace as the partner tried to sound as calm as possible in the face of the judge's pointed admonition. He knew that there were very few attorney's who were comfortable examining a witness that they had never spoken to or interviewed, but they were squarely faced with that situation. Now, to defeat the pending request for a receiver and restraining order, they had to take some gambles. One gamble was going to be the next witness, who had not only refused to talk to Richard before the hearing but had also made several derogatory comments about Richard's parentage during their one short telephone conversation earlier in the week.

Even though their client had fervently assured Richard that the testimony from this reticent witness would be favorable to his position, a subpoena still had to be used to compel the witness to come to the courthouse. If they could only get him testify on the stand consistently with what their client had described during his own earlier examination, then get him off the witness stand without too much damage and before the Assistant Deputy District Attorney could find some impeaching material to ask on cross-examination, Richard felt that the gamble was one worth taking. As if, he mentally shrugged, they now had a choice in the matter.

With a barely grunted "Proceed" from the judge both Richard and his client turned expectantly towards the back of the courtroom while the partner from Richard's firm continued to review their notes on this witness. As the bailiff marched to the twin doors to summon the witness from the hallway Richard began to take several deep breaths to center himself. In contrast to Richard's outward calm, his client was a study in heightened agitation. As his nervousness became more visible Richard quietly grasped his client's arm above the elbow and squeezed hard. Now was no time to fall apart and convey to the judge any lack of belief in the righteous nature of their position.

Within seconds of having disappeared into the hall the bailiff returned with the witness in tow. As he stepped out of the shadows of the hallway into the brightly lit courtroom the witness appeared as a man of medium height who moved cautiously down the worn carpet of the middle isle while nervously clasping and unclasping long fingers that seemed to unnaturally extend his work-scarred hands. As the witness came clearly into sight of all counsel and the judge the Assistant Deputy District Attorney hurriedly bent his head towards the police investigator, who stood next to him at the counsel table reserved for the prosecution. After a brief *sotto voce* conversation, the two exchanged half-smiles that went unnoticed by Richard as he tried unsuccessfully to catch the eye of the witness.

The witness reached the front of the courtroom and was quickly seated facing the court in the slightly elevated witness chair. The clerk picked up a small black leather bound bible and placed it on the small shelf in front of the witness.

With right hand raised, and eyes downcast, the witness mumbled his way through the swearing in process. There being nothing particular to make note of while the witness was sworn, Richard's mind slightly wandered from the moment at hand. At 26 years of age and steadfastly single, he was still easily distracted by the two most outstanding attributes of the court reporter, proudly but barely encased for easy viewing under a cobalt blue silk blouse. When she caught his eye and smiled he first blushed then cautiously grinned a suggestion in response. When she looked back at the transcription tape the moment passed. Then, tearing his mind back to the more immediate problem at hand, he listened carefully as the partner from his firm began to elicit the witness's background with short crisp questions. As each additional answer followed closely the notes that Richard had prepared during interviews with the client, a tempo to the process began to establish itself. Richard's confidence in his client's description of the events, as now being collaborated by the reluctant witness, grew. Even the Assistant Deputy District Attorney seemed to be cooperating by sitting still and refraining from making any distracting objections. The very fact of his cooperation, though, was in a manner that should have suggested the troubled waters that lay immediately ahead.

Richard had been advised on many occasions by the more senior members of the firm that a witness who intentionally lies on the stand, although always somewhat surprising, should never be a totally unexpected event. During one lunch meeting that doubled as a training session for the young associates, a particularly sarcastic partner of the firm had expressed his belief that no witness ever tells the complete truth. According to his experience, as he warned Richard and his colleagues, memory over time frequently changes the testimony of even the most honest person and serves as a handy excuse for inconsistent testimony from others. Now, suddenly faced with unexpected and simply unbelievable testimony from this witness, Richard tried not to express the surprise he felt even though he had never been given a reason to have trusted the veracity of this particular individual.

The problem started slowly enough when a relatively simple question elicited a response that did not fit with the information that an earlier witnesses had presented. The trouble then began to snowball as the witness began to get more inventive with the facts in a pathetically obvious attempt to help his friend. Acting as if the new revelations were reconcilable with the other testimony, and in fact a minor sidelight that did not really add any meaning to the dispute, the partner from Richard's firm tried to look stoic and glanced at the clock hanging above the bailiff's head as if to announce to all how truly bored he really was. The intent of these mannerisms, although well practiced, were lost on the judge who by now had begun to glare angrily around the courtroom as if trying to focus on the person responsible for bringing this mockery into his presence. The smile of the Assistant Deputy District Attorney was becoming quite noticeable. Knowing that his attempt to trivialize the damming statements through inattention was rapidly getting him nowhere the partner tried instead to look slowly puzzled, just as the judge began to focus his glare over black rimmed glasses that had been pushed down to the tip of his nose.

"I am concerned Counsel . . ." the judge began, the words formed slowly and almost delicately as if he had finally found something to interest him as the long afternoon ground on. "I am truly concerned and hope that you have an explanation that you would like to share with the court."

The Assistant Deputy District Attorney wisely decided to play invisible for the moment, letting his enjoyment show only to the extent of his poorly hidden but satisfied grin. At this point Richard knew the case was sinking fast and that their better option consisted of damage control. Which in this case meant getting out as quickly as possible with as much of the client's skin as possible.

"If it please the court . . ."

Richard stood and politely spoke for the first time in this hearing since stating his name for the record during the opening session, hoping that his sudden participation would distract everyone for a moment from the witness's creative recreation of the key events. He knew that the safest personal course would involve lying low while the hearing progressed and continuing to merely take notes, as someday down the road he surely would again appear before the same judge. The judge undoubtedly would remember during any future appearance anything that could be considered rude or without proper deference to the court, and could be relied upon to express his feelings to his brethren on the bench. But Richard was still bothered at the idea of having to play the demeaning role of the partner's bag carrier, rather than being allowed to take a more active role, and had long ago abandoned any pretense of "playing it safe" as a realistic alternative course of conduct when he was caught up in excitement and challenge of the moment. So, since he now had everyone's attention and before anyone could interrupt, he continued to address the court.

"There appears to be some confusion in the mind of the witness that we would like to address privately before we continue . . ."

His boss looked sharply over at Richard, silently communicating his keen displeasure at the impromptu interruption, but chose not to verbalize his feelings in light of the negative cast the testimony had placed on their position. This look and the judge's sudden attention caused Richard to stumble mid-sentence. Before he could continue the Assistant Deputy District Attorney interrupted the exchange before it could begin by gently clearing his throat. Richard decided to take the opportunity to keep quiet as the spotlight created by the judge's glare shifted slightly, but the respite was short as the Assistant Deputy District Attorney's remained quiet, his interest in interrupting Richard's tactic wilted when eyeballed by the judge.

"Excuse me, counsel," the judge responded politely to Richard's unfinished comment in a manner that did nothing to outwardly convey his thoughts, but suddenly brought to Richard's mind the picture of a cat beginning to play with a mouse "but are you suggesting that we should simply interrupt this witness as he testifies because he is 'confused'?"

"Yes, your Honor. I think that we can clear up this problem quickly if . . ."

The Assistant District Attorney nervously broke in to the colloquy as soon as could, his indecision at interrupting having faded as the suggestion of a break seemed suddenly to hang pregnant in the air.

"Your Honor, the People object to any interruption. If he is 'confused' or simply lying we should all find that out together."

The judge smiled to himself as if remembering a funny story and then, suddenly irritated by the exchange, snapped at Richard.

"No counselor, and you should know better than interrupt someone else. If he is truly confused we can all find out right here and right now. There is clearly a problem with this witness that I will not let ripen into grounds for an appeal. Now, all of you, sit down."

The judge understood Richard's motivation, but did not like anyone to make suggestions of that type in his courtroom as they just created problems and arguments down the road which added nothing to his view of the successful and fair resolution of the case, and was not hesitant to let people know his feelings. Turning to the hapless witness the judge continued evenly but with growing irritation at the thought of this witness creating problems in the record that might result in one of his decisions being challenged on appeal. He had a fairly unblemished record, was proud that his decisions were consistently upheld by the Courts of Appeal, and he wanted it to stay that way.

"However, we will now break long enough for the witness to make arrangements to get your own attorney. Half an hour. And I do strongly suggest you do get your own attorney as I am inclined to refer your conduct today to the District Attorney's office to review for recommendation on a charge of perjury. And the bailiff will join you while you make your calls. In the meantime I do not want either side having any discussions with the witness."

With dawning awareness of the seriousness of his predicament the witness watched the Assistant Deputy District Attorney interact with Richard and the judge. To the witness, isolated on the witness chair as the bailiff approached, they all seemed comfortable in their respective roles and alarmingly unconcerned with his needs. As the bailiff motioned for him to step down from the front of the courtroom, the witness watched the Assistant Deputy District Attorney motion to Richard and his boss, both of whom in turned leaned over to close the space between the two tables. After a few murmured comments each side nodded in agreement and looked away from one another as if trying to avoid any body language that would indicate agreement. The witness could see, with helpless realization, that all of the anger and moral indignation that had just been displayed was mostly on the surface of all of the counsel. What he did not know, and would never be privy to, was the unspoken acknowledgement by both sides of the danger of becoming too personally involved in the underlying dispute.

Richard and his boss huddled for a few moments more and, after whispering in the ear of their client, the partner leaned back to the prosecutor and confirmed one last point. Knowing that they were merely buying time that would not be needed and probably could not be used even if ultimately required, at the direction of his boss Richard cleared his throat and again addressed the judge.

"In light of the nature of the break suggested by your Honor, perhaps it would serve the interests of justice, and expedite the proceedings, if we were to break for the day to allow discussions between the parties and begin again on Monday."

The Assistant Deputy District Attorney, with the understanding that Richard had secured his client's agreement to the general terms of the proposal, happily nodded his agreement. The judge added his assent to the suggestion with appreciation. He had in fact made the same type of suggestion many times over the years, during his otherwise undistinguished former position with the Public Defender's office. Twenty minutes or so worth of discussion in the hallway later the case was resolved to the general satisfaction of both Richard's client and the Assistant Deputy District Attorney and they returned to the courtroom where a consent decree was entered on the record. Moments later, with his client's continued protestations of innocence still fresh in his ears, Richard began the short drive back to his office from the courthouse. By the time he pulled into the office's parking lot the case had already been mentally assigned to dead storage.

~~~~~

Richard woke up feeling dead tired. The darkness outside reflected his habit, drilled into his core in college by an anal but noisy roommate who liked to run at dawn, to begin the day as early as reasonably possible. Arriving at the office at 6:30 A.M. was not uncommon, although more and more difficult as the years began to pass by. Since, however, this particular morning held no special promise, and nothing on his weekly calendar called out for immediate attention, he did not even wake up until his alarm went off at 7:00 A.M.

After hitting the snooze switch on the alarm for the third and final time Richard swung into his early morning ritual. He eased out of his king-sized bed to avoid waking Woody, a two year old golden retriever that Richard had received as a graduation present from his former girlfriend. Richard had happily accepted the gift and ignored her none to subtle hint that he should settle down now that law school was behind him. The bed was much larger than he needed, as he often slept alone, and dominated the bedroom by comparison. He and his former fiancée had purchased it, along with all of the bedroom furnishing, right after college in anticipation of a marriage that fell apart by mutual agreement shortly before the wedding ceremony. She had not wanted to endure the life of living as a student for another three years while he
~~~~~

was in law school, and Richard had been unwilling to give up his dream of—someday—being a trial lawyer. The floral patterns that she had selected, that he had disliked so intensely at first, had over the intervening years turned out to have the hidden bonus of being constantly mistaken by his female guests as a reflection of otherwise hidden sensitivities.

He walked quietly through the house, the popping of the hardwood floor shifting beneath his weight providing the only sound. With a flick of his thumb Richard hit the TV remote to catch the morning's sound bites while doing twenty minutes worth of penance on his stationary exercise bike. After the quick workout and a hot shower, during which Woody bothered to get up and tried to join the fun by sticking his head into the shower enclosure to bite the stream of water, Richard grabbed a fistful of cereal for himself and placed another in a bowl for Woody. By this time Woody was ready to go outside for his own morning ritual, and the two headed out the front door together.

With only two years of practicing law behind him Richard was already a veteran of knowing how to create the proper appearance to get ahead. In sharp contrast to his favorite weekend attire of sweats and rugby shirts, his business suits were understated in a Brooks Brothers fashion, with properly muted ties that he even wore on every day other than dress down Fridays when he joined the rest of the staff in wearing everything from sports jackets to khakis and polo shirts. He had learned the hard way that his former law school preference for jeans and baggy sweaters, although more comfortable than the standard attorney wear, was frowned upon by most judges when it came to appearing in their courtrooms. On that occasion a client had requested an immediate restraining order against his ex-wife before she could make good on her threat to sell their Mercedes coupe to the pool man for $1000. In a flurry of activity Richard had prepared the papers and run over to court, only to be lectured for ten excruciating minutes on courtroom protocol and decorum. Richard had been successful in obtaining the order, but had never forgotten the speech, or the snickers from the older lawyers that had witnessed the judge's diatribe. From then on, by watching and observing how both clients and judges reacted to lawyers who looked the part, and by obliging them in this small matter, Richard rapidly gained a reputation in his office as someone who could be counted on to handle any situation at a moment's notice.

Upon arriving at work Richard headed first to the coffee station nearest his personal office. By rote he proceeded to make the first of the many pots of industrial strength coffee that would sustain the office during the day, using coffee grounds prepackaged in two single pot sized bags. The coffee stations could be found at evenly placed locations throughout the floor, and freely provided caffeine in many forms that included tea, cola and even caffeine tablets. Throughout the day an office staffer had the specific responsibility to circulate the coffee stations and fill any empty pots of coffee. The drawer below the coffeemaker also contained various medical supplies and displayed a proud cornucopia of headache and stomach remedies. In his first year of practice Richard had initially been impressed with the largess of the partners to provide these essentials to the associates and staff without charge. In every law firm the combination of caffeine and aspirin, laced occasionally with Maalox, was indeed essential to the successful ability to deal with the stress and workflow. As his first year with the firm went by, however, Richard learned that the largess was provided simply as a means of making sure that productivity remained as high as possible throughout the day. Once, upon making this observation to one of the other associates, Richard had received the cynical response that electric prods would have been used by the partners to increase productivity if the accounting department could demonstrate that there would be enough of an increase in billable hours to offset the capital investment.

Without waiting for the pot to fill Richard placed his mug under the spout and, as soon as it was full, added half of a packet of Sweet & Low and a plastic stirrer. Before the coffee could begin to cool, Richard slurped back half of the mug and then refilled it before turning from the coffee station to his office. Once in his office he sat down, waited for the caffeine to kick in, and stared with resignation at his desk. A large number of faxes had already begun to pile up, even though he had not left the night before until well after 8:00 P.M. "Goddamn New Yorkers . . ." he muttered, thinking briefly that the three hour difference had already given his east coast opposition a head start on the day's game-playing of fax and email tag.

The faxes were already curling at the edges as if to express the urgency of their messages. Although the partners at the firm prided themselves on having a technologically advanced office, they did not want to replace any machines until absolutely necessary. Which was long ago in Richard's mind when it came to dealing with thermal fax paper before caffeine jolt started. To make matters worse, the message light on his phone was blinking nonstop, reminding Richard of the many calls he should return before 9:00 A.M. From a trick learned from one of the senior associates, if he returned the calls before 9:00 A.M. or during the lunch hour he knew that he could avoid having to actually talk to most of the callers and be able to honestly claim that he had promptly returned their calls.

As a junior level associate, Richard only rated a window office of roughly equal size to the remaining twenty-three associates in the firm. While the window was nice, and the office large enough to fit a desk and client chair combination, it was substantially smaller than the offices of the seven litigation partners. He didn't care. One of the attributes that would help in his elevation up to the partnership track, and hopefully to admittance to the partnership in four or five more years, was his political skills in dealing with the sometimes enormous egos of the senior partners. Although most were strong technical attorneys, and generally billed an average of eighteen hundred hours a year, only a few could be legitimately characterized as "superstars." Yet each demanded to be treated as such, as if their individual contribution to the firm was the sole reason for its continued success and profitability. In turn, since being implicitly recognized as an emerging "superstar" himself, Richard was often struck by the change in conduct displayed towards him by the staff and especially by the other associates. Where before he had merely considered himself one among many, that relationship was subtly changing to one of deference from the office staff. Although he understood on a logical level that they were simply doing the politically correct thing to their future "boss," on an emotional level he knew that he would soon miss the camaraderie shared by the other junior associate level attorneys with the staff employees.

Richard's personal office, while not a picture of efficiency, was not a disaster area either. Nothing appeared on his walls, not even a diploma or painting. When asked occasionally why he had not decorated in a style befitting a lawyer in such a prestigious law firm, Richard would shrug and provide some meaningless response calculated to satisfy the person's curiosity. But the truth be told, Richard simply looked at his office as a place to work and nothing more. Decorating his office seemed to Richard as appropriate as hanging an oil painting over the workbench in his garage and just as much of a waste of money.

Although no one tended to describe Richard's office as messy, files appeared on almost every flat surface, including a substantial portion of the carpeted floor. Richard's desk was also buried, as usual, beneath a large number of projects. Each project, represented by a different color code on the file, was ranked in urgency by its closeness to the top of a pile. On the top of his desk sat two concessions to his reluctance to individualize the office, a satin covered squeeze ball and an oversized coffee cup emblazoned by the slogan "Legal Beagle." The squeeze ball actually was a replacement for a gift from his secretary soon after he had been hired. She had handed it to him with the instruction to squeeze tightly during periods of stress and with the gentle reminder that his change of status from law student to associate was merely an exchange of one set of problems for another. Taking a liking to the relaxing feel of the ball during telephone conferences, he had learned that the ball's ability to resist pressure was a result of being filled with silicon gel, which had leaked over the desk one day after being squeezed too hard during one particularly acrimonious conversation. The coffee cup had a more mysterious background, at least to his friends in the office. He kept to himself the fact that it was also a present, and kept especially quiet the name of the person who had given the gift. Inside the cup, however, at the bottom, was a perfectly fashioned beagle that stared upward out of the cup. Richard used the cup to hold pens and pencils, and the beagle was therefore unknown to others and hidden from sight. His little private joke. Knowing that it was there, unseen, always gave Richard a lift.

As was his custom Richard left the lights off while he began his day, preferring instead the purer light of the early morning sun as it poured through his large and untinted window. Although the owners of the building had modernized the air conditioning in an effort to justify the rents that were already above market, he also knew that he would have to shortly pull the shades to avoid being cooked as the sun's intensity increased throughout the day. Finally digging into the stack of work on his desk Richard began to fidget under the effects of the extra strength caffeine. But before an hour had passed he had cranked out responses to all of the faxes and was well into answering most of his emails and voicemails. And all the while the rest of the office around him began its own morning wakeup routine.

~ ~ ~ ~ ~

With the smooth opening of the elevator doors signaling his entrance the receptionist looked quickly up from her morning crossword puzzle. Displaying a practiced smile after sizing up the approaching figure, she waited until he reached the expansive reach of the marble topped reception desk before speaking.

"Good morning . . . How can I help you?"

She knew that her opening line worked well on most men, and mouthed the words in a way that made them sound perky and inviting. It did not take a close visual examination to reveal that she had been hired for her physical attributes instead of her mental powers. Which was especially apparent when the conversation lasted more than two or three sentences.

"I hope I can help you" she added after a brief pause, the smile widened enticingly.

"I want to talk to Richard Magnus," Dickson tightly answered, uninterested in responding to the friendly opening.

"May I tell him the nature of your business?"

Brushing aside her question with a wave of his hand, Dickson turned on his heel and strode down the hall in the direction of Richard's office.

"Come on in Peter." Richard called out with a practiced grin when he caught sight of Dickson outside of his office door. "I was wondering what had happened to you after our lunch last week. I thought you were going to follow-up on that bottling contract we had been looking at."

"Bullshit," Dickson stated crossly, throwing himself into a chair in front of Richard's desk. "The only thing you were wondering about that day was whether you were going to get a phone number from that blond at the table next to you."

Richard ignored the harshness in which Dickson stated what normally would have been considered a friendly accusation by turning and moving a bulging file that was sitting on an armchair at his side to the top of the stack on his desk. There was sure to be, he figured, a reason behind the terseness of Dickson's comment.

"I have a problem," Dickson continued somewhat hesitantly, draping himself into the chair as his restless energy quickly faded. "And unless we can provide a response quickly I am going to be history in the wine business in short order."

Richard looked expectantly at Dickson after this somewhat dramatic statement, waiting for more information while Dickson gathered himself. Before Richard could do more than merely look interested, Dickson tossed a short stack of newspapers onto the top of the desk.

"To save you the time of going through the fine print," he continued while Richard looked at the papers, "you should know that I am being set up as the fall guy for the fact that some major amounts of toxic chemicals have been discovered on the winery property."

"What the hell are you talking about?"

Richard sat back, mind at complete attention, struck by the seriousness of the charge. When Dickson merely waved at the newspapers he then reached for the top of the stack. On the front page, in large black print, Dickson's name appeared followed closely by the unmistakable assertion that he alone was the person responsible for the illegal use of various banned chemical agents at Winery Peak.

"It seems that, somehow, chemicals have gotten into the water source that feeds a pond located in an old abandoned quarry behind Winery Peak. Three vineyard workers, at least at last count, have now been hospitalized from exposure to the chemicals. And now I'm being blamed."

"Blamed by who?"

"Wine House. The newspapers. Everybody. Blamed and now fired."

Dickson reached inside of his coat and with distaste took out a piece of paper, which he placed with care on the desk on top of the pile of newspapers. The letterhead of Wine House stood out, prominently indicating its origin. It was a copy of the single sheet letter of termination handed to Dickson during his afternoon meeting with Klienman.

"They gave me this and then gave their damn press conference the very next afternoon."

Richard glanced at the sparsely worded letter of termination and then picked up the entire stack of newspapers and began to leaf through the various editions. Both to get a better handle on what had been said by the press as well as to buy some time to think through Dickson's news. All of the stories contained the same basic information, which was slim in content but had in common the central theme that a environmental crime with significant consequences had been committed to the wine growing region, "allegedly" by world renowned winemaker Dr. Peter Dickson. In some of the editions appeared companion articles that detailed the spectrum of Dickson's background including such trivial and irrelevant items as the fact of his divorce twelve years earlier and his decoration for valor earned while flying combat missions during the Korean conflict.

As he leafed through the papers Richard thought back on what he knew about Dickson. They had first met a year or so before through a mutual friend who had personally found a way to invite into his life more than one person's share of trouble. Richard had been the most junior member of the trial team responsible for pulling off a noteworthy settlement for the individual only two days before what would have been a difficult and complicated trial, resulting in a victory party being thrown at which Dickson had conducted a private wine tasting event. Like most people who live in Napa, especially attorneys, Richard wanted to be knowledgeable about wines and happily developed a modest friendship with Dickson, who was regarded by many as one of the world's foremost winemaking authorities. The situation now facing Dickson, and the fact that Dickson had felt comfortable enough with Richard to bring the problem directly to his attention, presented Richard with his first real opportunity to handle a significant matter for a client without having to act as a second chair to a senior member of the firm. In fact, given the nature of the statements made about Dickson to the press, Richard almost could say that he had the fate of Dickson's personal and professional reputation in his hands. This would be quite a responsibility, even more so as Dickson had never questioned him closely about the number of cases that he had personally tried before a jury—which was none—or about any other aspect of his expertise. Of course, he rationalized, Dickson had seen him in action and that should be sufficient disclosure. In any event, he thought as the concern was pushed from his mind, these cases usually settled before trial and he could always ask one of the partners in the firm to assist him in the remote chance that an actual jury trial was necessary.

Through the open door of his office Richard flagged down his secretary, Jo, who in turn gave him an exasperated frown and headed over with her steno pad.

"Yes?"

"Peter just made the papers. I want you to read the first article. Aloud, please."

As she began to read from the paper Richard tried to assess how Dickson would do on a witness stand should he actually authorize the filing of a lawsuit. An enigmatic person, after graduating with a doctorate in enology and viticulture from the University of California at Davis in 1979, Dickson had continually astounded the scientific community by receiving a new plant patent on aspects of cellular biology on almost a yearly basis. Yet he was not one to spend every day in the laboratory. Tall yet muscular, with a shock of gray tinged hair, Dickson seemed to revel in the unconventional and was as much at home playing his saxophone in an impromptu jazz session as he was discussing plant cell patterns and root stock selections with his colleagues.

As was the situation with all overly intelligent witnesses, Richard knew that he would have his hands full keeping Dickson in line during his pretrial deposition, not to mention how he would perform in front of strangers on the witness stand. Like most people testifying, Dickson would be in unfamiliar surroundings and would eventually have to answer questions from someone whose sole purpose would be to make him look like an asshole or liar, or both if at all possible. To make matters worse, Richard knew that Dickson would have a hard time being passive on the stand during cross examination. From early in their careers doctors tend to believe that they are the mortal equivalent of the right hand of god, and PhDs are not terribly different from any other type of doctor. Dickson, like most of his fellow scientists, would likely attempt to show the jury how much smarter he was than the cross-examining attorney and—if his adversary's counsel was a capable questioner—thereby unintentionally allow his own words to be twisted, created the false impression of what an asshole he could sometimes be. Breaking out of this train of thought, Richard began to watch Dickson's demeanor as Jo carefully enunciated each word in the article.

". . . 'and sources have confirmed that Dr. Peter Dickson, noted scientist and winemaker, was terminated because of his alleged role in the illegal use at Winery Peak of large quantities of highly toxic chemicals.' "

Jo glanced up and paused nervously. "My god! They don't waste much time convicting you in the paper."

Dickson did not respond, but stared intensely at Richard as if daring him to believe the statements.

"You're going to have to look a little less hostile than that."

"How would you feel?"

"Doesn't matter how I feel, or even how you feel. What matters most is making sure we jump on this for damage control."

"What do you mean?"

"Simple. If you do nothing to respond then you can be sure everyone will forget the word 'alleged' in those stories. And even if the State Water Resources Control Board does not convince the Attorney General to initiate criminal proceedings you better figure out some other way to make a living."

"What do you suggest?"

"I suggest that you allow me to put together a pre-emptive strike. That we immediately file a lawsuit for wrongful termination and defamation, and try the case in the press as well as in the courts."

Dickson sat back and worriedly rubbed his hand through his hair. Which made it stand up in back and gave him the appearance of the classic mad scientist.

"And are we going to prove that the newspapers lied?"

"No, Peter. Taking on the papers is not where the pressure points are and they are not the ones who fired you or held a press conference to announce it. Besides, they have way too many 'allegedlies' in their stories for us to win that case, as well as the First Amendment to hide behind. We have got to go directly after Wine House."

Dickson sat still. Though his eyes remained only partially focused on the papers on the desk, Richard knew that Dickson was rapidly trying to calculate his position. He waited patiently and within a few short moments was rewarded as Dickson's eyes snapped sharply back into focus.

"All right, Richard. Let's do it !"

~ ~ ~ ~ ~

By late in the afternoon Richard had temporarily pushed Dickson's problems out of his mind. Shortly after walking Dickson to the elevator, and telling him to relax and avoid talking to anyone about the situation until he could do some background checks on Wine House and research some recent cases on wrongful termination, Richard had turned to other matters that had been pending when Dickson had arrived unannounced that morning. Predominant in his mind was an expensive dispute that was rapidly turning ugly between a local Chinese restaurant and one of the firm's clients whose business specialized in the importation of fancy oriental delicacies.

The restaurant had ordered a full shipment of thousand year eggs from Hong Kong, and the owner and his head chef were now claiming that the eggs had spoiled before they had accepted delivery.

Richard's client, on the other hand, took an hour explaining in heavily accented English that the eggs, although known as "thousand year eggs," were actually specially aged and prepared by soaking in salt brine and were supposed to look grayish black and smell pungent. Because the United States Customs Department was refusing entry of the shipment into the United States, the dispute had to be resolved quickly or the eggs would indeed spoil on the container ship as it sat in dock. Understanding the complexities of this matter alone took up so much of Richard's time that he had even skipped his usual practice of immediately dictating a memo of his meeting with Dickson, feeling as the day wore on that he could do so at the very end of the day or early the following morning.

As the afternoon rapidly approached 5:00 P.M. Richard could see the office slowly wind down as the secretarial staff completed working on the last of the more critical crisis of the day and faxed or emailed off the last of the afternoon's missives. Before the advent of the various forms of electronic delivery systems lawyers often had to resort to the use of personal messengers, who would pick up documents in time to deliver them to opposing counsel as close to 4:59 P.M. as possible. As long as a document was delivered before the "close of business," typically considered 5:00 P.M., the sender could then include that "business day" in calculating the time in which the recipient could have responded. Under this system advance planning was all important, especially where out-of-town counsel were concerned, and a document or letter would have to be sent out a day or so in advance to a local messenger service in order that it could be delivered at the last possible second. The use of fax machines and the ability to attach large files to emails changed the dynamics of the game, and greatly increased the ability to send last minute self-serving statements written in a way that implied agreement and consent unless a reply was immediately forthcoming. Rather than becoming known as labor saving devices, however, these tools were considered a royal pain in the ass as they undercut those time tested reasons that justified a failure to provide a same day response. But these were devices that no law firm of consequence could now do without.

Richard turned to his desk to make sure that he had properly noted all of the things that he had to do the following day. After checking his handwritten list, and noting at the bottom two more legal research items that one of the partners in the corporate department had requested during the afternoon, he pulled a time log out of the side drawer. The log was used to keep track of time spent on each matter for purposes of properly billing the firm's clients. Like almost all law firms, time was the main commodity and clients were billed based on the number of hours it took to handle their problems. Results were neither guaranteed nor a condition of payment, although the firm's standard form retainer agreement allowed permitted "value billing" clients based on results. Richard, like most lawyers, hated to keep contemporaneous track of the precise time spent during the day and tended to wait until the end of the afternoon to fill out the log. The unfortunate consequence of this practice, however, was the seeming loss of an ability to accurately track how much time was actually spent on each activity. On average he spent ten to twelve hours a day at the office, or on client matters out of the office, yet he could rarely seem to account for more than eight or nine. Today was certainly no different, especially since he had a personal rule not to bill clients for the first interview on a new matter. Meaning that Dickson would not be charged for the time spent during today's meeting. The firm partners disagreed with this approach, and had pointedly made their position known to Richard. He did not change his personal rule, however, but merely kept his practice to himself. As a result he was forced to work longer hours to make up for the loss in billable hours, but the emotional satisfaction was worth the price. Although Richard liked the support that came from working in a large office with other attorneys, he wished at times that firm policies were not so tightly controlled by economic considerations. Early in his career he had developed a personal philosophy that a client should feel comfortable to call or come by the office to discuss whether there was a case to even consider pursuing, without worrying about being charged for the pleasure. As time went by this long term approach to client development seemed to be paying off, as there was now a growing steam of return clients and referrals that knew Richard would not nickel and dime them for every phone call or quick drop-in visit.

After completing the time log for the day's activities, and noting with satisfaction that he had still been productive in terms of overall billable time, Richard turned back to his handwritten notes from his meeting with Dickson. Checking to make sure that he had captured the salient points, he then grabbed the newspapers off of the stack of manila files where Jo had left them and began to systematically search for and then cut out the articles on Winery Peak, even if Dickson was not mentioned. The process took another half-hour, interrupted finally by Richard's growling stomach. When done with the most recent articles he stood and stretched, and was in the middle of deciding whether to break for the night when the ringing of the phone interrupted his thoughts.

Richard did not immediately pick up the receiver, as habit long ingrained cautioned him to first look down at the caller id display on the face of the phone. The small digital readout confirmed that the call had been placed from an outside line to his direct dial number and had therefore bypassed the receptionist. This meant that the call was from one of the few people that knew his private number, a group that included his partners and a few of his more intimate friends. Crossing his fingers against the possibility that the call was from one of his partners asking for assistance on an all-night project, Richard reluctantly hit the "hands-free" button and simultaneously lowered his voice in what he hoped would sound either sexy or profound, depending on the perspective and interest of the caller.

"This is Richard Magnus."

"Hello stranger . . ."

Richard smiled eagerly, his willingness to take the call rewarded by the husky tones of Lynn Schaber, a petite blond who had helped him through the rigors of law school in ways that just don't appear on the published curriculum. After law school they had gone their separate ways, motivated by the jobs they each obtained in different parts of the country was well as the unspoken recognition that their law school experience was one best savored as an amazing interlude and not spoiled through critical self-examination. Over the three years of law school they remained strong friends even after knowing each other more intimately, a feat itself when compared to the condition of the majority of Richard's other past relationships. In fact, although women were often attracted to Richard because of the gentleness that existed beneath his competitive façade, most tended to believe in retrospect that their failure to tame him was a reflection of a bad attitude towards relationships rather than the simple fact that Richard had no intention of being tamed.

"Hey kiddo. Where are you calling from?"

"Close enough to drive up in an hour to meet you for a drink . . . I'm in San Francisco for a few days to document the sale of an operating subsidiary and could use a quick break."

"You could use a 'quickie' what?"

"Nice try guy. 'Quick,' not 'quickie,' and you need to buy me some of that great Napa wine before you try out any more of those smooth lines."

"Sorry, Lynn," Richard responded grinning, "I'm a little out of practice with the one-liners. But I can definitely break free if you can."

"Great! I'll meet you in about an hour at L'Auberge. And don't worry. Since you are out of practice this time I'll pay."

Richard chuckled and said goodbye with a tired grin on his face. Lynn was a knock-out, pure and simple, with a mind sharper than most of his colleagues. Best of all, she was one of the few people that Richard could feel completely relaxed around. Someone who didn't want something for nothing or have a hidden agenda. Whistling to himself he grabbed the phonebook and wrote down the number for L'Auberge. He figured that he would call from his truck, which would give him enough time to race home and get cleaned up before Lynn was expected to arrive. And to clean up the house in case he got lucky. Not all friendships, after all, have to remain completely platonic. Ten minutes later Richard was out the door of his office. Before leaving he had glanced down again at the remaining pile of materials concerning Dickson and wavered. He knew that the best course dictated memorializing his thoughts so far on the factual issues and possible procedural moves available. That would have been the more responsible thing to do. But after Lynn's call Richard was of two minds and, as usual, the lower mind won.

CHAPTER THREE

WIPING THE SWEAT that threatened to drip down his dusty forehead into his eyes, Dickson looked up from his work to see a long white van pulling slowly up the gravel driveway toward the house. Like many of his contemporaries, Dickson had grafted several different hybrid vines to the root stock that grew around his house as a part of ongoing experiments to develop different and unique grape strains. He had been trimming the vines all morning and the unexpected intrusion momentarily provided a welcome respite from his efforts.

As the van pulled closer he could make out the stylized logo of Channel 6, one of the two local television stations, and his pleasure at having a break from his efforts quickly grew to irritation. Although Richard had told him to say nothing to the press, he stopped what he was doing, carefully wiped off the hand shears before placing them in his rear pocket and stood his ground to wait for the van to stop and the television crew to get out. With an eruption of activity the side door of the van sprung open even before the wheels stopped turning. The familiar face of Rico Martinez emerged from the front passenger seat followed closely by a handycam solidly attached to the shoulder of the cameraman and a soundboom carried gingerly by the sound woman. Dickson had worked with Martinez on prior occasions, the most recent during the grape boycott two years before, and therefore decided to at least listen to the questions Martinez would inevitably ask before telling him that he was not going to provide a formal interview. Dickson figured that Richard would not mind, seeing how Martinez was not a stranger who might twist what was said between friends merely to make a story. After all, he could always avoid responding to any particular question if he thought that Richard would not have wanted him to provide an answer.

"Morning Dr. Dickson."

Still twenty yards away, Martinez's voice easily carried across the distance as his feet rapidly closed the space between them. Martinez had taken advantage of the glaring absence of Hispanic reporters in the early 1980's to obtain a series of featured assignments with the local station. Once started, he had rapidly made his reputation as a hardworking professional. Recent cutbacks in the number of reporters overall, coupled with the large influx of Hispanics throughout the industry, weakened his uniqueness as well as his ethics. He knew from watching the fate of other minorities that to survive he would have to produce more stories than others in his position. Even if production meant using techniques historically reserved for the tabloid press. As Martinez reached Dickson he tried to smile compassionately, his youthful face set in a welcoming, friendly manner.

"I sure was sorry to hear about all of the problems at Winery Peak."

"Thanks Rico. What can I do for you?"

"Well, let me get right to the point. We wanted to hear if you had any response to the allegation that you are responsible for the decision to use banned chemicals at Winery Peak."

Points of color flashed to Dickson's cheeks and as quickly faded as he struggled to maintain his composure.

"Yes, chemicals were found dumped in the old quarry on Winery Peak property. And I hope that they string up the bastards who did it."

"Were you fired because of the discovery of the chemicals?"

"All I know is what I was told when they handed me the letter of termination."

"Which was . . .?"

Dickson paused for breath, the memory of that afternoon still sharply painful.

"I recall words to the effect of quote 'Because of the investigation and the threat of closure it's my own fault.' Close quote. Nice bunch of people, don't you think?"

"Can you give me a full interview?"

"No, I really shouldn't say anything."

"Well please let me know. Sometimes I am allowed to put together an in-depth piece . . . you know, to tell the whole story from both sides, budget permitting of course."

"Sorry, Rico. I just can't help."

Rico turned back towards the van and silently motioned his cameraman to take a wide angle shot of the house before getting back into the van. Turning back to Dickson he stuck out his hand and the two men shook silently.

~ ~ ~ ~ ~

He was ignoring the evening newscast. Too tired to get up to turn on the lamp, he was trying instead to read by the flickering gray light emitted from the television when he caught out of the corner of his eye a picture of Dickson projected behind the newscaster. With a quick flick of the remote the sound came flooding back into the semi-darkened room.

". . . at the home of Dr. Peter Dickson, world renowned winemaker and target of the investigation at Winery Peak. During the interview Dr. Dickson had the following comments."

The screen cut away to a tight camera shot of Dickson standing next to Martinez. Superimposed across the bottom of the screen in bold yellow letters ran the legend "exclusive live interview." Richard groaned to himself and quickly hit the record button on his DVR.

" . . . you are responsible for the decision to use banned chemicals at Winery Peak?"

"Yes, chemicals were found dumped in the old quarry on Winery Peak property."

"Were you fired because of the discovery of the illegal chemicals?"

"Because of the investigation and the threat of closure . . ."

"Can you give me a full interview?"

"Sorry . . ." shrugging. "I just can't help."

The brief but jerky segment cut back to the studio were the anchorman commented briefly that the investigation by county officials was still continuing, and then segued smoothly into the sports and weather reports. Richard turned off the DVR and pressed the mute button before sinking back deeply into the overstuffed cushions of his coach. Staring blankly in disbelief at the set Richard cursed Dickson's naivety silently and thoroughly. His immediate reaction was that the case was over, stillborn and killed by another client who could not follow the simplest of directions. Even if he could be successful in blocking any attempts by the attorneys for Wine House in getting the footage into evidence during a trial, a result that he was not the least bit confident of, he could rest assured that most of the potential jurors in the Valley would either remember having seen the footage or—worse yet—remember exaggerated versions of the interview by the time jury selection had begun.

Groaning with the effort Richard got off of the sofa and grabbed his dishes on the way to the kitchen. He tried to shut his mind off to the case and concentrated instead on the process of cleaning up from his late dinner. Although he normally kept the house fairly clean, at least clean enough to be livable between the twice monthly visits from an older woman who cleaned the house while sternly lecturing him on his pathetic attempts at keeping things in order, his present efforts reflected his agitation and went far beyond his normal practice of merely wiping off the plates and glasses before tossing them into the dishwasher. He even reached under the sink for the liquid soap to scrub down the counter, an act reflective in a Freudian sense of his desire to cleanse himself of this new problem. In the middle of pouring the soap carefully on the sponge Richard stopped short, hit strongly by an idea, and then abandoned his efforts at cleaning without a further thought or attempt at putting away any of the cleaning materials.

With a glance at the clock that now showed 11:23 P.M. Richard pulled on some sweats, grabbed his keys and headed out the door. He practically jumped into to his truck, a four wheel drive pickup that he had bought four days after learning that he had passed the California Bar Examination. Throughout the three years of law school he had promised himself a Porsche 911 immediately upon becoming a licensed attorney and a member of the State Bar. A poster of the racing version of the 911 had even graced the space above his study desk. The poster, and the promise it reflected, acted as a means of self-motivation, principally on those long and lonely Friday and Saturday nights in the law school library. The day after receiving the news that he had passed the bar examination he had wasted no time in heading to the dealership. Finances of a recent graduate being what they were, and given his love of skiing but hatred of installing chains in the snow, after indulging his fantasies one last time he had compromised on the pickup as a reasonable alternative.

Sliding behind the wheel Richard's mind continued to race with ideas and game plans. He backed out of the driveway and headed down the street in the direction of the office without a thought to what he was physically doing. With one hand on the steering wheel he reached across to the passenger seat for a pad of notepaper and began to jot down in numbered order his thoughts so as not to forget all of them by the time he reached the office. Pulling into the parking lot of his office some fifteen minutes later Richard tossed aside the notepad and steered the truck into his reserved space. One of the minor perks he had received upon being hired by the firm. The headlights flashed across his name, appearing in reflective paint on a small strip of metal that had been attached to the wall to create an appearance of permanency. Richard grinned and nodded to the small white and black strip, happily having forgotten his darker mood of just an hour earlier. Stepping out of the truck he reached over to the pad and carefully tore off the two sheets that he had covered with his thoughts on the drive over to the office. Although most of what he had written would have been difficult for anyone else to read under the best of circumstances, given the difficulty of writing at night in a truck that was being at driven well over the posted speed, the unrecognizable scrawl also reflected Richard's growing excitement at the thought of a possible strategy for dealing with this new development.

The white-haired security guard barely looked up from his paper to nod and sip his coffee as Richard crossed through the lobby on his way to the bank of elevators located at the center of the building. The security guard was a fixture at the building, having been at his post near the front desk every night long before Richard had joined the firm. Richard knew better than to expect more than a passing nod, as the guard had simply seen too many people step on and off the elevators at strange hours to be impressed by another late night visit by a junior associate.

The original owners of the building, in the mid-thirties, had framed the elevator doors in fancy hardwoods that could not be replaced without incurring the wrath of save-the rainforests environmentalists. This excess of improvements, matched by the polished marble floors and the neoclassical style of the ceiling designs, reflected an interest by the original owners in style and substance, and were used by the current owners to support their position that the above market rents were justified by the obvious class of the building.

Stepping onto the floor that the firm leased, Richard walked down the hallway before flicking the main switch to illuminate the entire north wing. The main door to the firm library was almost directly across the hall from his office, and Richard went straight to the stacks after dropping his handwritten notes on his desk. The library was considered to be one of the best private collections in the entire county, and librarians from the other local firms could be often found in the stacks looking on behalf of their attorneys for some of the more obscure cases or statutes that popped up from time to time. Not surprisingly, however, the library was deserted and silent at this time of night. Richard walked straight to a series of books that summarized California law and quickly pulled two well worn volumes off the shelf. The table of contents of first one then the other was skimmed and, with a fist punch in the air and a quiet "yea!," Richard moved over to the long series of dusty volumes that contained every opinion written by every appellate court in California since the State was first voted into existence. Grabbing several different volumes under one arm, Richard transferred the books to one of the three long tables that sat in the center of the room. To make some space he brushed aside one law clerk's research in progress and sat down to work. Flipping through the books in logical order Richard made more careful notes, keeping some of the volumes and as quickly discarding others.

Several hours later Richard looked up from his notes and realized that the office was starting to stir around him. By reflex he stood and stretched, and immediately went over to the nearby coffee station. Grabbing a fresh cup, thankfully made by someone else for a change, he returned to the library table to grab his notes before ducking back into his office to contemplate at the draft of the complaint that he had spent half the night preparing. Just as he sat down in front of his computer Jo marched businesslike into his office without, as usual, bothering to knock.

"You look horrible! What have you done . . . spent the whole bloody night here?"

"Thanks and a good morning to you as well." Richard smiled, feeling upbeat about what he had been able to accomplish.

"Well . . . you are going to make a fine sight this morning wearing sweats and not shaving all day."

Jo grabbed the dictation tapes and the interoffice memos from Richard's overflowing out box on the credenza behind his desk.

"Okay, okay. Don't look so disapproving. I'm going home to change. But before I get back, could you please get the complaint I just did for Dickson cleaned up and ready to file." He thought for a moment, then added decisively "and call Wolfe at Channel 3 and tell him I've got Dickson and a good story, but don't tell too much. I want to get him interested."

"Should I call Dr. Dickson?"

"No. . . . Wait, call him and tell him to stay the hell away from the damn reporters. And tell him I'll call him later today."

Whistling the melody from The Allman Brother's "Rambling Man," Richard quickly stepped around her and walked out to the elevator.

~ ~ ~ ~ ~

By midmorning Richard had showered, shaved and dressed in the fashion that he usually saved for his most important court appearances. The entire outfit including a dark blue pin-striped suit, white button-down shirt and a deep red power tie. As he drove back towards the center of town his mind raced with an exciting jumble of ideas. Jo, in her usual efficient manner, had scheduled an appointment with John Wolfe that same morning. Wolfe was the station manager for Channel 3 and the one most likely to see a good story as a means of increasing the number of viewers and the station's market share. An increased market share would mean that he could justify raising advertising rates, which was the lifeblood for the station. Richard knew that he would have to come up with some angle to entice Wolfe into asking him to give a live interview, and a local scandal was always a sure seller to the voyeuristic mentality of the average viewer.

Pulling sharply into the station's parking lot Richard finally decided that the best strategy would be the appearance that he had a major disclosure to make soon, but had to temporarily hold off for tactical reasons that he could not disclose. He would let Wolfe pry, and allow himself to be convinced by Wolfe to grant an exclusive as soon as the time was right for disclosure. In this manner he could buy some time and with luck actually have the interview aired that much closer in time to the trial. With his game plan set and mind at ease he grabbed his briefcase and headed into the building.

Inside the station he was surprised by the blur of activity. A number of people came and went in a fashion that appeared chaotic to his casual observation. The pace was accentuated by the number of framed proclamations and wooden plaques that lined the walls, reflecting awards and recognitions from the various local charities and nonprofit organizations that the station had to support in order to avoid adverse public comment. Even though it was a network affiliate, and therefore received a portion of the advertising dollars earned by the network, a substantial portion of its revenues were still generated from advertising from the local merchants and business community.

Richard stood immediately inside the main door for a moment, gathering his thoughts while he watched for an orderly pattern to appear from the chaos. Then, tightly gripping his briefcase, he had just started towards the receptionist when he felt a hand on his sleeve slow his progress.

"Hello Richard."

Wolfe spoke quietly but firmly, with a voice trained in the diplomatic art of selling the station both publicly and privately. Richard turned and looked down at the familiar face. Although he was only five feet two inches tall, Wolfe refused to let his physical stature hold him back. As a reaction to the perception of the focus groups hired by the marketing department that the male newscasters should be tall as well as handsome, he had insisted for years on personally doing the public service announcements that aired several times a week. And, as he had privately intended, the announcements had made him into a minor local celebrity that he in turn used to bed any woman who was taller than he was.

"Hello, John. You talked to my secretary?"

"Yes. Thank you for having her call. British, isn't she?"

"Don't try it, John. She is definitely not your type. Besides, I can't really allow you to have an inside source at my office, now can I?"

"All right then," John laughed and allowed his not so subtle suggestion to be easily deflected, "let's go into my office and you can tell me why you wanted to see me."

Directing Richard past the reception desk, he nodded to the receptionist who buzzed them past the door to the interior working area. Steering Richard into his office Wolfe quickly motioned Richard to sit down. At the same time with a practiced reach he grabbed a reporter's pad from his desk and came around to sit next to Richard on the couch. Wolfe was no slouch when it came to developing a story line, and Richard could see the shift in intensity as evidenced by the slight tightening around the eyes and lips.

"Soooo, Richard, I hope you have something interesting."

"I'll let you make up your own mind." Richard slipped open his briefcase and pulled out the draft of the complaint. "We are going to be filing this against Wine House and I thought you would want a little informal advance notice."

Wolfe was silent as he quickly flipped through the several pages of the complaint. Richard knew better than to disturb him while he absorbed the information and sat quietly until he reached the last page. Wolfe, as Richard had expected, spoke first to break the silence.

"So what? So Dickson is going to sue Wine House for wrongful termination. Doesn't he have a slight problem with having allowed that chemical shit to get into the old quarry in the first place?"

Wolfe looked expectantly at Richard, having hoped to provoke a response that would provide more information by which to analyze the possibilities that Richard's complaint would create. Richard did not bite at John's attempt to bait him, but he knew that John would not wait forever to hear the angle and quickly obliged him.

"Now why would Dr. Dickson put his reputation on the line and sue for wrongful termination if he did what they are claiming? Dr. Dickson swears that he did not authorize or even know about the stuff that they found in the quarry. Besides, this is the perfect follow-up to Martinez's interview last night on Channel 6. Which, by the way, appears to have been a skillful job of 'editing'."

"Meaning what?"

Wolfe liked the sound of that last comment, which had the ring of dirt, and wanted to hear more.

"Meaning Dickson told me that Martinez recorded a lot of supposedly off the record comments and then freely edited them out of context in a cut and paste job to make a story."

Wolfe sat back in his chair and thoughtfully chewed on the end of his pencil. He knew if he played this correctly he would have a good local story no matter what the outcome of Dickson's problem. Either Dickson would prove that he had been wrongly accused by Wine House, in which case his station would have been the first to break the story, or Dickson would be found to have participated in the decision to use banned chemicals, in which case he could have both a great human interest story as well as the beginning of a great editorial on the failings of the American legal system.

"Well Richard," he began slowly, wanting to see exactly what would be expected of the station, "exactly what do you suggest we do here at the station?"

"Just play a short piece on the news tonight under the heading `further developments' and credit the information to unnamed sources. We will be filing later this afternoon, well before your broadcast time and I'll leave the copy of the complaint for your story boys to use for the intro."

"Sounds interesting, but you got to promise me an exclusive on the rest of the story, including an interview with the Doc."

Richard smiled inwardly, knowing that an acceptable deal had been made. Outwardly he paused in apparent introspection and after a short moment nodded his head in agreement. Wolfe stood up to signify the meeting was over.

"And you will keep me posted on what happens?"

"Don't worry, John . . . I know well how we are counting on each other."

They both smiled, each happy to have achieved a good result and knowing that they were bound only as long as each could help the other. Not the basis for a great friendship perhaps, but at least the basis for a good working arrangement.

~ ~ ~ ~ ~

" . . . and in a further development in the investigation of the use of toxic chemicals at Winery Peak, a lawsuit has been filed by Dr. Peter Dickson against Wine House, the owner of Winery Peak. The suit claims that Dr. Dickson was wrongfully terminated from his position as President and Winemaster of Winery Peak as a part of a scheme to divert the attention of the wine buying public from the fact that chemicals had in fact been found on the property at the winery. Winery Peak has advertised itself as a maker of super premium wines, and had intended to release its first vintage this fall."

Dickson looked over admiringly at Richard who was too busy sitting at his living room table jotting down more notes to pay close attention to the newscast. Although Richard had told him that he would try to counter the perception problem that Dickson had created by talking to Martinez, he was still surprised that Richard had been able to move quickly enough to get their version of the story on the six o'clock news. Before he could express his satisfaction Richard looked up from his seemingly endless notes to pick up where they stopped when the news came on.

"Okay, Peter. We have now drawn the proverbial 'line in the sand.' With this press there is not likely to be any settlement of this case, because Wine House knows that the industry will characterize anything less than a complete victory as a total failure and will construe any agreement as a public apology."

"You are right on that point. And if I know anything about those in charge at Wine House, an apology of any type for sure will never happen."

"Well, we do not have to worry much about that possibility. Wine House just has too much exposure as it is from the situation with the regulatory agencies, and even if the EPA doesn't care about you Wine House still needs its public scapegoat."

"So where do we go from here?"

"Not 'we.' You go nowhere and speak to no one!" Richard shook his head and tried to take the sharpness out of his voice. "You have got to stick with the program Peter. We have a lot of work ahead of us and it will be a lot easier to pull this off if you just keep a low profile while we pull all of the facts together."

"Okay, Richard, but remember that I'm the one that got screwed."

"I know, I know. But you just remember that when the evidence has been placed before the jury, and the jury goes into a room by themselves to deliberate, they will have only heard just a small portion of what really went on at Winery Peak. I just don't want their thoughts garbled by the hack reporting of some reporter that wants to use you as a ticket to the big time."

~ ~ ~ ~ ~

Klienman gingerly put down the phone and gently massaged his left ear. He had just finished some twenty minutes on the losing end of a long distance shouting match with his boss, who had been calling from the corporate headquarters of Wine House in New York City. Wine House had been served earlier that day with the summons and complaint prepared by Richard, and the news departments from all three major networks had jumped on the newest development in what was developing into a story that did not seem to want to go away after its initial news cycle. What had started out as a minor problem with one of the smaller wineries owned by Wine House was rapidly becoming a major embarrassment.

The call had ended with very specific instructions for Klienman: handle the problem now and make it go away. No particular details were provided on how to accomplish that goal but, as his boss so bluntly pointed out, he was being paid over six figures a year to figure out exactly how to handle these types of problems. He sat and stewed, mad that he had been put into this position in the first place. It had not been his idea to fire Dickson, and now it sure looked like he would be set up as the next fall guy within the company if the problem with Dickson did not go away quietly and quickly.

He picked the phone back up and hit one of the speed dial numbers. First things first, he thought, and that meant getting local counsel on board to respond to the complaint. And to file a cross-complaint if at all possible. Something to put more pressure on Dickson in the hope that he would just fade away without more attention. After three long rings a voice came on the line and announced, in disgustingly patrician tones, the name of one of the largest law firms in the country that specialized in this type of law. Klienman mentioned both the company's and his name to the receptionist and was pleased with the immediate attention borne from the name recognition. Truthfully, he had not expected a different response given the fact that Wine House employed thousands of workers throughout the United States and was constantly calling for advice on how to handle problems with its workers. Just the type of institutional client that law firms love and prosper by. After next asking for Patrick Stucky he then waited impatiently during the very few minutes that passed while the call was transferred and was ultimately rewarded by the quick response.

"Hello, Tyler. Heard that you are having a little trouble up in Napa. What can we do for you?"

Stucky, who liked to consider himself as a master of the understatement, was located on the twenty-fourth floor of the Post Street Tower in the San Francisco financial district, which resulted in Napa being 'up there' from Stucky's perspective. Klienman did not care much for the display of rhetorical wit, and responded in a way to clarify that he had no time for idle small talk.

"You have got to jump on this one quick, Patrick. Dickson has no right to sue us for wrongful termination!"

"Whoa! Slow down Tyler. Lets get the facts first before we decide who has the right to do anything "

Stucky did not like to be hurried, especially by a panic stricken client. Too often the client would forget some essential detail, or exaggerate another in the excitement. Klienman, however, was not listening.

"But our contract says we get to fire him without cause anytime we want to! Besides, we had damn good reasons to shit-can him if he was the one that approved the use of those chemicals."

"What do you mean by 'if he was the one'? From what I've read in the papers he all but admitted to doing it."

"Ya, well, whatever works. I'm faxing you a copy of the complaint. Just make sure this bullshit gets handled, and handled quickly. And more importantly, make sure it happens quietly. We don't need any more publicity about that damn spill eating into our market share for wine sales."

"You mean that you want me to see if Dickson will agree to a quick deal to go away?"

"No fucking way! We paid him his goddamn severance payment exactly as spelled out in his contract and we aren't paying a penny more."

Klienman paused to take a breath and get his emotions under control.

"I want you to tell that lawyer he hired that we will be suing the both of them for malicious prosecution if they don't immediately dismiss the lawsuit with prejudice."

Stucky tried to placate Klienman, to knock some of the panic out of his voice. "I think I got the picture, Tyler, even if your suggested strategy may need some fine tuning."

"I hope you do. We pay your firm a lot of money every year and now I'm calling on you to get some results . . . and quick!"

"All right, Tyler, all right. We will send them a letter demanding a dismissal of the case. But don't hold your breath on that one. We will also get our side of the case ready and try to help the feds wrap up their investigation before the trial starts. If we can get the feds to come out with a public statement that concludes that Dickson had something to do with those chemicals then there is no jury in heaven or hell that will find that the termination was wrongful. Okay?"

"All right, all right. Sounds like a plan. Just make it work, and let me know what happens before it happens."

With a click Klienman hung up, leaving Stucky to stare at the phone in silent amusement.

CHAPTER FOUR

THE WINDING DRIVE up the hill to Winery Peak looked over some of the most beautiful wine country in the world. Acres upon acres of chardonnay, cabernet and zinfandel vines stretched to the horizon, covering almost every available piece of ground for miles. The rolling hills that surrounded the valley were also striped by the green rows of vines alternating with the light brown dirt. Where the vines reached the steeper slopes of the taller peaks the rows stopped abruptly, as if carefully cut with a giant knife, leaving a straight line that marked the boundary of each field. Early each morning in the spring and summer, before the breezes began to blow off of the upper reaches of the nearby San Francisco Bay and through the funnel shaped valley, hot air balloons would lift off when weather permitted and dot the sky with a matrix of colors. By midmorning each spring the balloons would often be replaced by long thin clouds resting high overhead without the promise of rain, and in summer by clear sky so blue that the eyes of visitors to the valley marveled at its intensity.

As Terri Davis drove the windy road to the top of Winery Peak she was oblivious to the natural splendors surrounding her on every side. From behind reflective aviator sunglasses her eyes instead concentrated alternatively on the road and on the several vineyard workers dotting the nearby fields. Bypassing the main building complex, she slowed and turned her car onto the side road that eventually led up to the quarry. Even at a severely reduced speed the tires on her car immediately kicked up a noticeable cloud of dust. Rather than take the risk of drawing attention to herself, she soon pulled off of the track and parked her light green Mustang between a small scrub oak and a large bush of glistening poison oak. In the near distance, partially obscured by a large clump of Manzanita, sat an old rusting Quonset hut.

Terri had been an private investigator for as long as she cared to remember. Which too often nowadays felt like a very long time. She specialized in working up background materials for lawyers, but accepted jobs from anyone who was nosey enough about someone else to pay $85 an hour for her services. In the last two years since the first time that she had worked with Richard, he had asked her to perform a number of investigations. Most of the assignments involved locating information that could be used to damage the reputation or credibility of a witness in front of a jury. Her resources were many, and included the ability to obtain background information in ways that Richard did not want to know anything about. Her work was also helpful in evaluating the economics of a case. If someone claimed that they had no money to satisfy a claim or judgment Terri could usually verify net worth quicker than the IRS, and with substantially better results at obtaining payment.

To be successful in her chosen profession one had to present a fairly nondescript appearance and Terri was as forgettable as they came. Her work clothes ran the gamut from dull browns to light grays, and her physical characteristics would be best described as medium age, height and weight with sandy brown shoulder length hair and pale brown eyes. For this job she was dressed true to form, and as she stood from the car she pulled a dusky brown work jacket free from the cluttered backseat and draped it loosely around her shoulders.

Walking away from her car Terri pulled a thick notepad with pen attached from her side pocket. She kept meticulous notes of every step in her investigations as insurance against the opposing attorneys that constantly tried to trip her up on cross-examination. Terri knew that memory can play strange games, especially when she was involved in several investigations simultaneously, so at a minimum she constantly jotted down arrival and departure times to orient herself should she be called upon—weeks or months later—to testify about her activities. Turning to the most recent entry, she reviewed again her tortured scrawl from the previous night's meeting with Richard.

Breaking from the traditional custom of meeting in his office to discuss the case, they had instead met for a quick beer at Henri's, a downtown microbrewery favored mostly by the yuppie set who could and would pay significantly more for a beer than the $2.00 commanded by a Budweiser at any of the several older bars along the edge of town. Set on the edge of the Napa river as it flowed near the center of the downtown area, Henri's had been established in an long abandoned stucco building that had served countless years before as the town livery stable. The current owners of the building, stymied in their attempts to redevelop the old structure because of its designation as a historic landmark, had finally decided to use the building's history as the basis for the restaurant's theme. Now decorations matched the period of its original glory, with worn leather harnesses and traces on the walls complementing the bright cooper vats in which the brew was made. While neither Terri nor Richard especially identified with the somewhat pretentious clientele, they enjoyed the relaxing atmosphere, the sawdust floors and were both particularly partial to the thick red ales that were rapidly become a local institution.

During their short meeting, measured later in Terri's bemused recollection by the amount of ale consumed rather than the precise amount of elapsed time, Richard had outlined the history of Dickson's predicament and the need to locate some background information relating to the types and amounts of chemicals used at Winery Peak. Richard had previously sent Wine House a formal written demand to produce any documents reflecting the same general information, but had received nothing apart from the stony response that no such documents had ever existed at the winery. Dickson knew differently, and in his precise handwriting had sketched a detailed map of the physical operations, indicating in several locations where helpful documents might still be located. Terri had been given a copy of both the map and the demand for documents to assist her efforts.

She walked the last several hundred yards to the hut, which served as a makeshift storage container, located as described by Dickson next to the heavy equipment yard. Several tractors in various stages of disrepair sat haphazardly amid empty 55-gallon drums that once contained different grades of fuel and machinery oil for use during the development stage of the winery's limited history. Near the back of the yard two large pieces of equipment loomed over the top of the hut. From top of each appeared a menacing snout, tipped with large metal teeth perpendicular to the tip of the boom. This equipment had been used to dig the large caves out of the living rock of the hillsides during the initial construction phase. The caves had been architecturally designed for, and now served as, storage facilities for the large oak barrels that had been filled in the last several years with slowly aging wines. The rock walls of the remaining hillside provided essential temperature control for a fraction of the cost of a standalone facility, as well as security from theft or tampering. Covering 40,000 square feet of enclosed space, the caves were only filled with a fraction of the wine that would exist as soon as all of the young vines began to prove themselves.

Alongside the rusting walls of the Quonset hut tall grasses grew as a testament to its general lack of use. Glancing around the area, Terri could not see any signs of recent visitors near or around the front of the hut. She took hold of the old doorknob and opened carefully the side door. After grudgingly opening a foot or so the door caught on something that she could not see and held fast against her tugging. Peering into the dark interior, she was greeted by the overwhelmingly sour odor of pack rats. As she yanked the door it suddenly opened further, though not all of the way, and from the light that crept over her shoulder she could see jumbled stacks of boxes scattered throughout the hut. Most were still intact, but from the ones that had fallen over she could see documents and records Dickson described spread loosely on the floor. From the corner came the sound of scrabbling, which stopped completely as soon as Terri rapped her fist twice sharply against the doorframe. Pack rats are generally shy, she assured herself, and these apparently would be content to wait until their visitor had left before continuing to go about their business.

Terri stood back on her heels and surveyed the work ahead. Even billing her time at $85 an hour, she felt at times like this that the job just wasn't worth the money. With a shrug she entered the room, and turned towards the far end of the storage area. As she reached down into the first box of documents to inspect the records she felt her hand lightly brushed. As she withdrew her hand into the light two large hairy brown spiders dropped off her sleeve onto the dirt covered floor. With a grimace Terri squashed them under her heel, leaving a long dark smear in the dirt. "Got ya," she swore under her breath with satisfaction. She went back to work quickly, knowing that she could be arrested for trespassing or even burglary if she was caught inside the structure. One by one she skimmed through the files, discarding those that looked unrelated to her investigation and stuffing into her large knapsack anything that looked even remotely interesting.

Forty-five minutes passed methodically and uneventfully. She had gone through almost all of the boxes that Dickson had described when the sound of footsteps crunching on the gravel outside the hut stung her into silence. Terri froze and, as the sound from the steps continued to come closer to the partially open door, looked quickly around the single room building. There was clearly nowhere to hide inside the building and too much open ground outside of the building to make a run for cover. With deliberate calm Terri opened her knapsack and removed all of the files that she had just selected from the boxes of records. Better to be found empty handed and claim that she was just snooping than to be accused of actually stealing something. She remembered a friend of hers in the same business who had been caught taking pages from a desk calendar. Although he had argued that the pages had no value since they were for days long gone by, the judge had disagreed and suspended his investigator's license in addition to two years probation. Terri opened one of the boxes and placed half of the records in the middle of the files already in the box, and repeated the process with a different box and the other half of the records. At least she could preserve the time she had already spent selecting the individual pages by placing them together where they would be easy to find if an opportunity later presented itself. Moving quietly she then placed the two boxes on the dirt floor and covered them with several other boxes of assorted files. With the appearance of more boldness than she felt, Terri slung her dun colored daypack over her shoulder and walked the length of the building to the door opposite the boxes that held the files she had selected. Taking a deep breath for confidence, she pushed the door open just as the knob was turning from the outside.

"Tommy! What are you doing here!?"

Waves of relief rolled over Terri as she immediately recognized Tom Murphy, clipboard in hand, squinting from the sunlight as he tried to peer into the gloom of the building. Terri had long made it a point to know—at least by sight—every one of the County employees, as she never knew who might be handy to hit on for a favor or two. Murphy, however, was more than just a passing acquaintance. They had gone to school together at Napa High School more years ago than either of them generally cared to admit.

"I should ask the same about you, only I know better." He replied with a grin. "You're gonna get into trouble one of these days, snooping around, and you aren't gonna have someone who knows you arrive in time to bail you out."

"Give me a break. And give me a hand. I'm trying to tie up a few loose ends and get the hell out of here."

"Why? What are you looking for?"

"I really shouldn't say, but I guess I owe you to keep this quiet. I'm trying to figure out some background for an attorney named Richard Magnus. He's defending the guy the papers say caused the toxics to end up in the old quarry."

"Think he did it?"

"No." She responded thinly, knowing better than to ever admit guilt—for herself or others—even when directly caught in the act. "And neither does Magnus or he wouldn't have taken the case." She paused and looked Murphy squarely in the eyes.

"Why are you here, Tommy? And why so many questions?"

"Hey! Back off, Terri . . . You're the one who should be explaining, not me. And I don't need to be peppered with questions from you—I'm not the one after your guy. I'm just the one that was unlucky enough to have made the initial investigation that led to the testing of the water at the quarry. So I'm the one who gets to spent the afternoon looking through old and dusty boxes of records to see when and how much of the stuff was used."

"Well, good luck."

"What do you mean by 'well, good luck'?"

"Now who is sounding defensive?" She asked with a slight grin. "I found the records you are looking for and there's nothing listed that you wouldn't find being used in all of the wineries in this valley. Certainly not what you guys found up at the quarry."

She walked Murphy across the inside of the Quonset hut to the stack of boxes. Handing him the knapsack, as she did not want any unnecessary surprises when she got home like more of those hairy brown spiders, she reached down and with a few quick movements lifted clear the two boxes that now contained the files she had set aside. Handing him a loose pile of files that bulged with assorted papers, she motioned for him to open the top folder to a series of pages that she had clipped together.

"Here, look for yourself and tell me what you think."

Murphy sat down on the boxes, creating a small cloud of dust that they both ignored, and began to read. After flipping through the first few pages he reached out and removed the computer printouts that had been clipped to his clipboard. Terri quietly watched his eyes flip back and forth from the files to his notes. One of her best traits was patience, to allow the information to come at its own time at its own pace. She could always follow-up with questions, and knew from learning the hard way how easy it can be to chase away information by being overly eager.

"You're right." He confirmed finally, reaching up for a hand to stand. "Nothing unusual here."

Murphy began to hand the files back to Terri, only to be stopped half way by her hand outstretched with palm up like a traffic cop. He smiled, recognizing the look on her face as both thoughtful as well as the one that usually preceded a request for a favor.

"Tommy . . . if you had to testify right now, what would you say?"

"Well, I guess I would say that the records at Winery Peak indicate that nothing improper was used. And . . . hmmm, I guess I could say that there is no mention of the chemicals we found when we tested the waters at the quarry."

"And that Dickson didn't use the stuff."

"No way, Terri, I can't go that far." He could not help reacting to the disappointed look on her face. "But you know I'll do what I can."

"Well, can you at least take those files so somebody doesn't add to them?"

"Sure. After all, I was given permission to look around. I guess that means I can hold on to these as part of my investigation."

"Thanks, Tommy. That helps with a chain of custody problem that would have occurred if I had taken them. Now let's get out of here before I get us both in trouble."

~ ~ ~ ~ ~

The Chief Investigator for the Federal Environmental Protection Agency, California Division, did not have a fancy office by the standards of his contemporaries in private industry. Just a small windowed office in a gray nondescript low-rise building in downtown Sacramento. But the power he wielded by reason of his position made the officers and directors of many companies pale with the thought that their operations might come under his scrutiny. He was a career civil servant and, in addition to the power that he held by through the nature of the Agency's operations, he rested comfortably in the knowledge that there was little that could happen to jeopardize his tenured employment. Against this backdrop of power and arrogance few dared to tread. His secretary of the last seven years knew this to be a truism, and was therefore surprised when he had cancelled a very important meeting at the Capitol Building to accept a previously unscheduled conference call that was supposed to take place in a few minutes. Like most professional secretaries, however, she knew better than ask or even intimate that she thought something was out of the ordinary. So when the call finally came through the conference call operator she dutifully buzzed her boss on the intercom and, when he picked up, discreetly disconnected her extension from the call.

The Chief waited until the conference call operator had signed off, after having confirmed that all of the conferees were on the line, before taking the initiative.

"I hope this call is important. I cancelled a meeting with the Speaker of the Assembly to take this call . . ."

"Quiet."

The fact that the voice on the other end of the line was barely audible did little to conceal the tremendous force of will behind the words. As intended and expected, the Chief immediately stopped talking.

"We all have important things to do."

The caller paused again, allowing the silence explain better than words the seriousness of the call.

"I know you are wondering why this is a conference call, and who is on the other line. This information is not of your concern."

"What do you mean 'not of my . . ." the Chief growled, only to be cut off in mid-sentence.

"Not of your concern. Correct. And do not waste any more time on the subject." The finality in his voice was clear, and the Chief decided wisely not to push the issue. "You are aware of the illegal use of chemicals at a winery in Napa County?"

"Yes. You mean Winery Peak. One of my best men is monitoring the local investigation."

The Chief quickly selected a pencil from a drawer in his desk and jotted a note to assign someone to oversee the investigation starting the next morning.

"We understand that the person who authorized the use of those chemicals has been identified."

"Well . . . uh, not exactly. In fact the newspapers picked up on some rumor that the president of the winery involved had something to do with it, but nothing has been substantiated."

Ignoring the interruption, the caller repeated himself, making it clear that he was making a statement and not asking a question. "We understand that the person who authorized the use of those chemicals has been identified."

"You mean the winery president?"

"And you are taking steps to accelerate the investigation."

"Look, I just told you that we are monitoring the locals . . ."

"I had hoped that you would not forget your 'obligations.' And I do not like to repeat myself."

The Chief shivered involuntarily at the thinly concealed threat. Although the caller was far too smooth to make anything other than the occasional oblique reference, both remembered well the control the caller had over the Chief. Several years before, when the Chief was considered a rising star within the Agency, his fondness for late nights and easy women came to the attention of the Division of Environmental Compliance.

A small and generally unnoticed group of senior managers at Wine House, the Division was responsible for overseeing the labyrinth of environmental regulations that faced large corporations. Regulations that, in this instance, governed the manner in which Wine House dealt with its waste products and the various hazardous materials used in the course of its operations including how it processed the chemicals used in the process of making the wines and other spirits and the toxic byproducts from those processes. Regulations that tended to add huge sums to the operating expenses of the various manufacturing and production divisions of Wine House—at least when there was compliance with the regulations.

The Division had carefully cultivated the Chief. First, slowly, by making sure certain "ladies" were available at certain times and in certain places. These women were discreet but expensive, both in their hourly price for "favors" as well in the cost of entertaining them before and after. The Chief, with his slim government salary as a division assistant, could hardly afford the continuing cost of this entertainment, but found himself as addicted to the continued liaisons as others would be to the use of the strongest narcotic. Wine House patiently watched and waited. And when it became clear that he had overstepped his ability to possibly pay off the large amount of money borrowed to service his cravings, and could not withstand public disclosure of his habits, he was approached.

Among other matters, at the time he had been in charge of a small cleanup involving some fairly benign materials. The operators of a commercial landfill, although licensed to handle the type of chemical residue in question, unfortunately had an onsite spill that resulted in a small waterborne plume. Concerned citizens living nearby, fearful that the runoff contained carcinogens in health threatening quantities, had called the EPA to handle the investigation. Before his written recommendations for remedial measures were issued, he was offered and accepted a small sum to make minor modifications to the report. Modifications that were almost completely innocuous, except for the fact that they were a result of a request from an interested party instead of as a result of the finding of his own staff. The spill was cleaned up, the concerned citizens went on to fight for their next cause, and the two versions of the remediation report made their way into a locked file cabinet on the twenty-third floor of the corporate headquarters of Wine House. As the years went by additional requests were made, additional favors granted and additional sums changed hands. At first the Chief justified his actions on the fact that he was acting on behalf of a friend who just happened to work at Wine House, and later on his view of the parsimonious nature of a Democratically-controlled Congress who was more likely to give money away to welfare cheats than the honest federal workers who deserved a fair salary. By the time he had earned the long sought civil service promotion to Chief Investigator for the California Division, the file at Wine House had grown to three thick volumes. Volumes that the Chief now regretfully knew to exist.

"All right, all right. I get your point. As usual. I'll do what I can to get the local boys to turn up the heat on the investigation." Sensing an interruption, the Chief quickly continued. ". . . But I can't just muscle in and take over the investigation. Doing it that way would step on too many toes and result in too many questions being asked. And I can get the same results doing it this way."

The Chief tried to sound positive, at least more positive than he felt.

"Well, how you proceed is your decision," the voice came across the line thin and cold, "just as long as you make sure that you don't drop the ball."

With a dull click the line went dead. The Chief's initial reaction of anger was quickly replaced by the overwhelming fear that someone might have overheard the conversation. After glancing at his secretary through the cracked open door of his office to confirm that no one had been within earshot, the tension in his shoulders relaxed somewhat as he played the conversation back in his mind. He finally convinced himself that he had said nothing to implicate himself and, after slight hesitation, reached over to his rolodex and rifled through the cards until he came to the number for the Napa County Health Department. Although past interactions between the two departments had reflected the type of resentful competition that typically exists between local and federal agencies, the Chief had long mastered the political type of maneuvers necessary for an individual to advance to any level of authority within the civil service ranks. These maneuvers included the art of delicately handling the local ranks to achieve the broader goals as defined by federal policy wonks in Washington D.C.

His telephone call was rapidly put through to the head of the Napa County Health Department. Ten minutes worth of conversation later, including a gentle reminder that the federal grant of matching funds for environmental controls was up soon for renewal, the Chief was rewarded by a firm commitment to have the investigation wrapped up by the end of the month at the latest. And was also able to extract an implicit commitment that the investigation would support a reasonable conclusion that the recent past-president of Winery Peak had been aware of, if not directly responsible for, the ongoing use of certain chemicals that had been banned from commercial use in California.

~ ~ ~ ~ ~

"Buenos Dias, my friend."

Dickson turned from his work and looked up into weathered eyes that sat deep in a craggy face. Manuel Lopez was an old friend, tied together in a common bond that had formed over the many years that they had spent together in the industry. Nearly four decades had passed since the young field hand had been assigned to assist the similarly young summer intern. The intern, although green, had immediately recognized a kindred spirit as well as the field hand's instinctive capabilities. Throughout the many promotions and changes in his employment over the years, the former intern had always made a point of finding the former field hand a nearby position were they could work together.

Rocking back on his heels Dickson smiled a welcome and absently waved towards a small cooler that sat in the nearby shade of an olive tree. He knew from long experience that Lopez would not turn down a can of his favorite refreshment, and Lopez did not disappoint him. Lopez was very deliberate, almost reverent, in his actions as he drew a silvery can out of the ice and slowly flicked the beads of water into the air with a heavily callused thumb. Grasping the top of the can in one hand with the tips of his fingers, he hooked the pull top with the opposite index finger and with a quiet hiss slowly released the built up pressure. Both men sat in silence as Lopez emptied the can in one long pull. Dickson knew from watching this ritual on many occasions that he could not hurry Lopez into a discussion—or anything else for that matter. But Lopez was thorough and thoughtful, a man to be reckoned with in his community, and these traits more than made up for the lack of urgency as expressed by his physical movements.

"I am concerned my friend."

"You have not been one to worry before, Manuel. Do not worry now. My lawyer will take care of this problem."

"You misunderstand me. There are many in the camp that are unhappy with what has happened."

"You mean the workers in the housing units?"

"Si. The younger men, the ones who do not know you. They listen to the reports from the new manager. And they blame you for the troubles."

"They will have to get in line."

Dickson tried to make his comment sound like a joke, but deep inside he only felt sorely hollow at what Lopez had to say. One of his pet projects over the years had been to vigorously support uniform improvements in the living conditions of the fieldworkers. While his motives were not altogether altruistic, they had been the direct beneficiaries of his efforts. To avoid the possibility of unionization, and the increased expense to winery operations, he had realized that he would have to gain their individual cooperation. To gain their cooperation he had to first improve their living conditions. His activities had angered the local union organizers, who cared more for increasing the ranks of their members than the conditions of their constituency and who consistently had tried to fan the flames of their passions by casting

Dickson as the enemy of the working man. These attempts to create disharmony mattered little to the older workers, who paid more attention to the individual needs of their families than high minded slogans, but it served as a rallying point for the younger workers who had never even suffered the far worse conditions experienced by their predecessors in years past.

"You must take this matter seriously. These young men—these boys—talk of vengeance, and they have too much idle time."

"Do not worry, my friend. I will try to be careful. After all, it is not like I have a reason to go out to work in the fields these days."

Lopez frowned at the afternoon sky and Dickson could see that his attempt to make light of the situation was not working.

"Seriously, I appreciate your coming over to tell me this information."

Dickson stood and helped himself to the cooler after offering another ice cold can to Lopez.

"But now, my friend, let us talk of other things."

~ ~ ~ ~ ~

Murphy walked into his boss's office, carefully brushing the dirt off his pants before he entered. Even though the interior was strictly government issue, from the laminated furniture to the cheap prints that graced the walls, the entire staff had long ago learned that the office should be treated with the degree of care normally reserved for the Sistine Chapel. While they considered this mania for cleanliness and order unusual, notwithstanding the type of business they were in, all respected the unwritten rule.

Sitting down in front of the desk, Murphy considered the deeply drawn lines that appeared across the face of his boss. Not normally a worrier, there clearly was something gnawing at him. Murphy felt like they had a good working relationship, although they were not particularly close friends, and thought that he should try to open the conversation by offering a sympathetic ear.

"Bad day?"

The head of the department looked up wearily, took a deep breath, and without further preamble quietly ripped into Murphy.

"Bad enough, Murphy. And you are not helping anything with letting that goddamn winery investigation drag on as long as it has."

"Whoa! Hold on. Nobody ever said anything about fast tracking this investigation. I have over a dozen other active . . ."

"And the rest of us are just sitting here on our collective goddamn asses while Thomas Murphy does all of the work. Is that it?"

Murphy did not like the sound of that challenge and, knowing that it was not justified, decided not to reply at all. His boss paused and reached for a cigarette, studiously ignoring the countywide no smoking policy. With practiced ease he flicked his thumbnail against the tip of a blue tip match and applied the flaring head to the end of the cigarette. The first drag seemed to consume the first inch before disappearing into a cloud of smoke. Consistent with his obsession for cleanliness, he carefully tapped the ashes into a small marble ashtray before continuing. For a moment the department head appeared to relax as smoke spiraled off of the end of the cigarette, and they both silently watched the trail rise straight into the air where it eventually dissipated. Murphy's boss then laid the cigarette carefully against the ashtray, where it continued to burn by itself for a moment, and finally stubbed it out. When he had finished this little ritual he looked up at Murphy with a calmer expression on his face.

"Look, Tom, you are generally a good worker, but I just got the word that this has to be wrapped up and quickly."

The head of the department kicked himself for letting that slip, but Murphy appeared to have missed the implications of this remark. He decided to change pace and further softened his tone.

"You know who is responsible for authorizing the use of those chemicals. You know the nature and extent of the concentrations in the quarry. You should be able to get a report together within a day and I can kick this over to the District Attorney where it belongs."

To emphasis his point, he walked over the open window and waved at the criminal courts annex across the street. In contrast with most of their investigations, which they could handle informally with the offending party, the notoriety that the spill had created in the press and then with local environmentalists had insured that the matter would have to be referred over to the district attorney to review for potential criminal violations and prosecution. As with previous cases that had been referred for prosecution, the staff officer would normally act closely with one of the lead attorneys for the prosecution, with the tacit understanding that the Health Department would get its share of any fines. The system resulted in a significant conflict of interest, as it had the tendency to encourage preliminary finding by the Department that would support large criminal and civil fines. This conflict, as with most conflicts, was generally ignored and the relationship even appeared in the Department's annual budget as an income line item.

"And just who do I think is 'responsible' for authorizing the use of the stuff we found in that quarry?"

"Don't play cute with me, Tom. I have scanned through the preliminary reports from the chemical analysis department. The only one at Winery Peak who could have known about all of the different chemicals in that soup was that Dickson guy. Unless you think that there could have been someone outside Winery Peak that had something to do with this mess."

As a matter of fact I do, Murphy thought to himself. But he knew better than to further rile the boss when something or someone had so clearly put him on edge.

"Okay, boss. I'll do what I can to get the report to you A.S.A.P."

"See that you do, Tom . . . see that you do."

Murphy had not even walked all of the way out the door before he decided to call Terri and fill her in on his new orders. Although he could stall the report for at least a week, he knew that the information uncovered to date could be easily manipulated by the District Attorney to get a grand jury indictment against Dickson. And he could not afford to directly refuse to prepare the report along the lines suggested by his boss in the absence of further information unless he wanted to put his own job at risk. At least by tipping her off, he reasoned to himself, he would be doing the right thing. Where it went from there would not be his responsibility.

~ ~ ~ ~ ~

The phone sat on a separate stand, framed neatly by the oak trim of a large bay window that looked out across Manhattan from the forty-seventh floor of the Central Bank Building. After two rings, which sounded as low steady tones, Lynn took off her reading glasses and absentmindedly reached across the desk for the receiver. With her other hand she rubbed the bridge of her nose where the heavy glasses had chaffed the skin to a dull red. "This is Lynn." Although she spoke the words automatically, they still came out with quiet authority.

"It's Richard."

He spoke softly to measure the reaction. He was not disappointed. "Richard! Where are you?"

The full force of her concentration snapped back to the present and away from the complexities of the public offering prospectus that she had been poring over during the last several days.

"I hope that I'm not bothering you. But I have to be in New York soon to take a deposition in that winery case I told you about. And I was hoping you could check out a few things for me."

"Sure thing. What have you got in mind?"

Richard smiled, then decided against making a cute, but way too predictable, one-liner in response. He could picture in his mind's eye Lynn's exact movements on hearing that he needed help and he did not want to make light of the situation. Lynn had been the one student in their law school class that always had precise and accurate notes of the lectures, no matter how difficult the professor was to understand. She had an almost unfailing ability of having a pen and pad of paper at hand on all occasions when the need arose, and was the first to begin writing notes whenever it was important to record the information. Richard's mental picture was in fact accurate, as Lynn had automatically reached for a fresh legal pad even as she had picked up the receiver.

"I would like you to dig up whatever you can on Wine House. I get the feeling that there may be more to this case than meets the eye."

"What do you mean?"

Richard paused before answering, weighing the need for help against his natural inclination to hold his opinions close to the vest. He trusted her implicitly, at least as much as he trusted anyone, but his suspicions were too tenuous to lay them out completely. Deciding to minimize the exposure while enlisting her help, he continued with an abbreviated version of the facts of the case as he knew them. Subconsciously Richard lowered his voice while relating what he had just learned from Terri.

"I just get the feeling that there is an agenda underlying Wine House's position—an agenda that is far removed from a mere disagreement over management styles, or even the need to blame Dickson in an attempt to shift the public's attention from the discovery of the chemicals in the first place. I just don't know how far this case may go."

"Why?"

"Because Wine House fired Dickson too quickly to make real sense. They could not possibly have believed that they could look good on the issue simply by firing Dickson. Neither the negative publicity from the chemicals being in the water nor the results from the official investigation required that type of immediate action. And Dickson swears that the chemicals identified by the County were never used or stored at the winery. No, Lynn. Something else is going on."

"Do you mean that you are going to expand your case to include more than suing Wine House for wrongful termination?"

"I don't know. But we may have to. I originally thought that we would get a quick offer to settle. Even a lowball offer from which we could negotiate and then make an announcement that the case had settled. Dickson felt that he could at least have preserved some portion of his reputation in the industry. But nothing, zip, nada. Not a word."

"Well . . . I don't know what I can do to help on this kind of thing, but I'll see what I can do."

"Unless we get something on these guys soon, we are going to have to go to trial on this case."

"Hey! That's great, Richard. That means you will get your first jury trial."

"Don't you think that I haven't thought about that. Nothing like a closely watched case in which to start."

"Does Dickson know that this will be your first solo?"

"No, but I don't want to bring one of the senior guys in or they will end up taking the case over. I have worked this case up, and I really know it best. I figure that I'll tell Dickson later and if he is uncomfortable we can change then. But I know that I can win this case, and it's important that I check ever angle."

"Sounds like you need my help, Richard. I will make some calls right away."

"And Lynn . . ."

"Yes?"

"One other thing . . ."

"Yes?"

"I owe you one."

"I know, Richard, I know."

CHAPTER FIVE

NEW YORK CITY from an air approach is always breathtaking. From the towering buildings silently standing guard over the financial powerhouses of lower Manhattan, to the large natural expanses of waterways that encircle the island. Stucky looked down from the safety of the airplane, glad to be removed from the street level grime and what he considered to be the sometimes insufferable attitude of the typical New Yorker.

The increasingly loud whine from the engines immediately outside of his window signaled the last stage of their decent into Kennedy Airport. Stucky chugged the dregs of his third in-flight cocktail, ignoring the probability that the alcoholic buzz would distract him from the job ahead. He hated to travel cross-country in the best of times, and depositions on the road were not the best of times. Not even close. A few drinks made the trip passable, even if they did lessen his concentration. Much earlier in his career he would have avoided anything that might have an effect on his edge, but years of trying cases in courtrooms throughout the country coupled with the financial rewards of being a senior partner in a large law firm had dulled his formally strong interest in self-sacrifice when exercised merely in the name of his competitive spirit.

"You need to bring your seat back to its upright position and be ready to land . . ."

Stucky turned his head to see the long legged stewardess that he had been flirting with—so far unsuccessfully—throughout the flight.

"Always ready," he replied with a lopsided grin. He had been using that line, with increasingly poor results, seemingly since sometime around high school. When she smiled mechanically, and kept moving on to other passengers, he mentally kicked himself for not thinking up a better line.

All around him people began to push their belongings into a variety of carry-on bags. With annoyance Stucky watched them pull themselves together, as if being the first one off of the plane when it reached the gate really meant something other than the privilege of standing inches apart while the plane was secured. Although the airline regulations permitted two small bags per person, as a convenience to those individuals traveling lightly, the allowance was conveniently ignored by most of the passengers. Armed with the unshakable belief that there was a substantial probability of lost or misdirected luggage, items were constantly brought aboard that could never fit adequately into the overhead compartments, much less below the seats. All of this activity surrounded Stucky, who was too tired simply to ignore the indignity he felt at being constantly jostled.

Stucky tried to sit still and took the time to review again the notes he had penned in outline form during the last hour of the flight. He had many cases that begged his attention, and clients that did not care about the impact that cross-country travel had on his ability to meet deadlines. As a result, he had worked on two separate lawsuits during the flight. The time in the air was also separately billed to Wine House at his hourly rate of eight hundred seventy dollars an hour even though he had also watched, but not enjoyed, an edited version of a third rate film that had come out on video six months earlier. As a result, Stucky was able to bill a total of seven hours work for a five hour flight. On the return flight Stucky knew that he could bill a similar amount of time and, taking advantage of the change in time zones between New York and San Francisco, could even exceed twenty-four hours billed for a single day's entry.

His notes, all sixteen pages, were the beginnings of his outline to prepare for his defense of the deposition Richard had requested of the Chairman of Wine House. Pages of possible subject areas that Richard might want to explore, to prepare for the inevitable process of questions designed by

Richard not only to elicit information, but to trick and trap the witness. Stucky knew that Richard was good, if—in Stucky's opinion—somewhat green, and that Richard intended to first punish the witness, the deponent, through hours of mind numbing minutia. Details dissected to the nth degree until the witness was sufficiently worn down to change from warily giving answers to saying anything to get the damn deposition over with. Stucky was determined to avoid this result through a careful preparation and practice session with the Chairman before the deposition started.

As the plane lurched to a stop at the gate almost all of the passengers jumped as one to their feet and stepped into a packed queue in the center aisle. They then stood motionless, cramped in place for the next ten minutes, as the plane was secured at the gate. Which created one last opportunity for Stucky as the stewardess made her way slowly down the plane in his direction.

"It looks like you had a busy flight . . ."

Stucky paused and hoped this line, reflecting commiseration rather than plain horniness, would work better. The Alan Alda school of hitting on women. Not receiving a discouraging response, he tentatively continued to explore the situation.

" . . . I hope you at least get a chance to catch your breath before heading back."

He decided to look serious, yet tired, as if they already shared a common misery. And misery loves company. Her response was encouraging.

"Why thank you. I noticed that you also worked through most of the flight. Will you get a chance to relax before your business in New York?"

"I hope so," he responded, then added boldly "and I hope with your company."

Turning slightly, in anticipation of the needs of the other passengers, she hesitated and then quickly nodded her agreement. As she walked back up the isle to the front of the plane Stucky relaxed outwardly and mentally reorganized his schedule. He knew that he had several more hours of work to do before the deposition. Work that included reviewing files and files of premarked and tabbed documents. Work that also included reviewing testimony previously given by other witnesses. Work that would now have to wait until early tomorrow morning.

With the center aisle now clearing Stucky began walking towards the exit. Like most of the other experienced business travelers, he liked to avoid the lines at the baggage carousel and carried all of his luggage and his laptop computer in two carry-on bags. All of the files and documents, filling two large boxes, had been sent the day before to his hotel via Federal Express. For the time being they were now out of sight, out of mind. As the other passengers continued to disembark he passed his new companion standing near the cockpit. She motioned with a smile for him to remain at the passenger area inside the terminal. Stucky waved, making sure to catch her name—Linda—from her name tag as he went by.

The terminal area was typical for most urban airports. Seemingly planned by experts in discomfort, from the overly bright florescence to the rows of orthopedically improper chairs. The whole effect, coupled with the surly security guards that patrolled the concourse, appeared to be designed in a pre-9/11 era to discourage the ranks of homeless from taking up residence during the winter months in the heated terminals. No experienced passenger would intentionally make the mistake of a long layover here. At the far end of the passenger area, immediately past the security gates, stood a number of uniformed limousine drivers. Each, in a manner that clearly proclaimed their boredom, superiority and indifference, held up a small board. On each board appeared a name. The name of a passenger. On one board appeared Stucky's name. In most cities he would have skipped the extra expense of a limousine, opting instead for a taxi or a rental. New York is not most cities, and the expense could easily be added to the bill to Wine House as one cost item among several others. And tonight, with Linda just emerging into the terminal from the airplane, he already felt that the incrementally larger expense had been doubly worth the price.

Stucky handed his bags to the driver just as Linda stepped to his side and into the harsh florescent glare. His feelings of regret, for making the personal time commitment when the deposition was first thing in the morning, were soon gone. Even under the unflattering glare of the overhead lights Linda's beauty stood out, from the gentle curve of her slender neck to the well toned calves that peeked out from beneath the regulation navy blue uniform. Stucky mentally shrugged, secure in the belief that he could handle an upstart like Richard. And Linda's reaction of being clearly pleased by the presence of a limousine driver made certain that at least part of him in the morning would not criticize his decision. Besides, he knew that all self-recriminations are best suited for analysis in the daytime.

~~~~~

Morning broke coldly in the form of the 5:30 A.M. wake-up call Stucky had requested from the hotel concierge desk upon checking in the night before. He rolled back over and gently slapped the exposed rear of the body next to him and again promised himself never to drink on cross-country flights. It was still too early for any other promises. He rose, quietly made his toilet and dressed. Now fully awake, and head clearing steadily from the drinks the night before, he knew that it was time to get his competitive nature to reassert itself. There was a lot of work to do before his meetings, and not a great deal of time in which to become fully organized. After ordering coffee from room service he pulled the sheets off of Linda in his none too subtle way of encouraging her to get moving. When she responded by pulling the covers back over her head, he picked her up in his arms and moments later one sleepy stewardess was quietly deposited into the shower.

"You bastard!" The shout came out loud and clear over the stream of water. "What the hell are you doing?"
~~~~~

"Look Linda, I've got two hours to read all of this shit and get moving. No offense, but you have to get moving too."

Taken aback by his brusque response her tone immediately softened. "Just please order me coffee and . . ."

"They can get you coffee downstairs."

The finality in his voice firmly suggested that any further argument would be unavailing. In fact, Stucky's mind was now definitely in gear and churning ideas for the day's battle. If he felt any remorse, it was for not having her leave late last night as she had devoutly promised to do during the long ride in from the airport. She stepped out of the shower, grabbed a small towel and stood in the doorway to the suite. Seductively bending over and away from him, she tried one last time to get his attention. To no avail. Mentally he was already light years away and partially buried amid the stacks of documents that he would be using during the day's session. With a sigh she gave up. Fifteen minutes later she was gone. Stucky barely noticed but did not care. He knew that his responsibility to Wine House left him with no time for further personal pleasures or distractions.

~ ~ ~ ~ ~

The elevator ride up to the sixty-third floor of the glass and steel cylinder made him nervous. Even though he knew that New York was not prone to earthquakes, as a native Californian Richard could not help but subconsciously analyze every structure over ten floors for how it would handle itself should the earth suddenly decide to move. And being sandwiched between way too many people in the small confines of the express elevator didn't help the feeling that this particular structure would not perform very well in a big one. He had just arrived straight from the airport, having taken the red eye directly out of San Francisco. Although Dickson had agreed to front the entire out of pocket costs being incurred, including airfare and lodging, Richard had decided before he left that he should do all that was possible to keep the costs to a minimum. Now he wondered about the impact of false economies, having been kept awake all night next to an obnoxious salesperson who thought that their close physical proximity gave him a right to ask for free legal advice about his pending divorce.

With relief Richard felt the express elevator slow as it reached the floors it was programmed to access. Mumbling "excuse me" indistinctly, as he heeded the conventional West Coast superstition that one should never display weakness by being too polite to anyone on the East Coast, he shouldered his way sideways from the back of the elevator amid hostile stares as the other passengers had to squeeze further together to make room for him to pass. Breaking free, he stepped out into an open and elegant foyer.

Entering the corporate headquarters of Wine House Richard couldn't help but be impressed by the spaciousness of the surroundings. Although millions were spent every year in advertising to create the appearance of a small and friendly maker of wines for drinking with friends and family during those "special" moments, Wine House was actually one of the industry's largest producers and marketers of both wines and spirits. In addition to its fine wine division, its labels included some of the best known whiskeys down to the least expensive "fortified" wines. Which were produced under a wholly owned subsidiary and were consumed by those down on their luck in almost every city from coast to coast.

Approaching the receptionist Richard admired the marble floors, the mahogany woodwork and the oil paintings that clearly avoided any attempt at modesty. As he was ushered into a nearby conference room he thought fleetingly how nice it would be to have a typically conservative Napa County juror view this ostentatious display of wealth. Twenty minutes later, after draining three cups of coffee to keep from falling asleep in the small and colorless room, he was still sitting alone with the certified shorthand reporter. Richard began to get annoyed, his lack of sleep getting the better of his normal good humor. Upon arrival the receptionist had taken his name and then immediately relayed the information over the phone to some unknown individual.

Without a further glance she resumed working reviewing a lengthy email on the monitor in front of her while an administrative aide appeared and efficiently directed him to the conference room. Someone at Wine House was clearly trying to impress upon him the company's belief that he was a mere nuisance. One that would be attended to after the more immediate and important business of the day had been handled.

With irritation he finally stood and walked past the wall-to-ceiling windows and stuck his head out the door. At first he had to walk gingerly. He had been sitting for so long in one place that his left leg had gone to sleep, and each step caused tingling shocks to race up his calf. Down the hall numerous secretaries and well dressed junior executive types hurried about self-importantly as if all of the problems of the world was their special responsibility to solve. The classic New York City superiority complex, Richard thought, held even by those recent transplants from the farm belts of Iowa and Indiana. After three ignored attempts to gain someone's attention Richard decided to take matters into his own hands. Starting off down the long corridor he stuck his head into the first open office that presented itself. Inside three typists worked away busily on workstations, imputing reams of information into the computer database. His request for a list of internal telephone extension numbers was satisfied without a glance. As he expected, he was simply taken to be one of the many ubiquitous employees that came and went on an endless basis in every large corporation. Richard skimmed the list of four digit extensions that made up the in-house directory and noted with satisfaction that the number for the president of Wine House was listed.

Turning to an unoccupied desk Richard picked up the phone and dialed the extension number. To his surprise the call was answered within two rings by an older sounding no nonsense female voice. In retrospect he should have anticipated that the president would not personally answer a phone that had a published extension number. She quickly confirmed in a voice laden with undercurrents of disapproval that the president was in a conference in his office and had left specific instructions not to be disturbed. By the time she asked for his name and the nature of his call Richard had recovered from his misstep and quietly pressed down on the disconnect switch and replaced the handset. Within a minute he was back into the conference room.

"Are we still on?"

The shorthand reporter looked up from her reading and asked the question in a completely disinterested tone. A tone that Richard immediately adopted with a flash of intuition.

"Yup. They want us to take the deposition in his personal office. So grab your stuff and let's go on up there."

The hell with them, thought Richard. If they want me to wait, then we will wait in their face.

The shorthand reporter efficiently packed her transcription machine and followed Richard out the door. Upon reaching the central reception area Richard played a hunch, stopped and put on his best smile for the receptionist. Who looked up and returned his smile.

"I've been told to go to the president's office. Should I get someone to show me the way?"

"No problem, honey."

The receptionist was an older heavyset black woman overqualified for the position and eager to show off her initiative.

"This is a map of the building. All you have to do is go up these stairs two floors and follow this line. You need to go up the stairs behind me because the elevators don't stop on that floor. I'll tell Mary, she's the receptionist up there, to keep an eye out for you."

Richard stretched his smile in thanks and motioned for the reporter to follow him through the fire door to the stairwell. The internal stairs were designed for internal traffic. Large enough for four people to walk abreast and heavily carpeted. As they ascended, they were met and passed by a number of office messengers and clerks too preoccupied by the urgency of their own errands to even smile a greeting as they passed, much less take note of their presence. On reaching the proper floor Richard simply bypassed the receptionist, who was busy ignoring an impatient Federal Express deliveryman, and walked to the opposite end of the building. Using the directions that he had been given, Richard located a solid mahogany door that identified itself in ten inch high brass letters as the entrance to the office of Montgomery Arthur Alexander III. President and Chief Executive Officer of Wine House. Without a pause or bothering to knock Richard opened the door and held it open for the reporter to enter. He then entered behind her and found himself in an exterior office in front of a face that matched in appearance the voice he had heard upon dialing the president's extension.

"You have an appointment?"

Although phrased as a question, the eyes made clear that it was meant as an accusation in anticipation of the negative response that she knew was forthcoming. Richard did not even bother to answer and instead grabbed and turned with one hand the large brass door handle attached to another oversized mahogany door at the other side of the office foyer. With the other hand he reached back and encircled the wrist of the reporter to make sure that she followed.

"Who the hell are you?"

The question shot across the room from a distinguished looking man in a dark blue suit, standing next to a table covered with charts and graphs. The question was answered quietly for Richard by one of the two other men in the room, both of whom were wearing similar dark blue suits and sitting on an overstuffed coach in front of faux stone fireplace.

"It's Mr. Magnus."

Richard looked over and immediately recognized Stucky. "Hello, Patrick. Thought we should get started."

"Okay, Richard. You made your point."

He stood and motioned for Alexander's executive secretary to lead Richard out. No attempt was made to introduce the other two men in the room.

"There is a conference room next door. We will join you in a minute."

Richard nodded, first to Alexander and then to Stucky. Confident that the point had been made that he was not the type of person to sit meekly and wait, whether here or at trial, there was no need to further press the issue at the moment. As he turned from the room he called over his shoulder "five minutes" and went smiling to the conference room.

Three minutes later Stucky and Alexander filed somberly into the conference room. Richard mentally noted that the third person from the meeting did not join them and jotted down a reminder to ask Alexander who he was. Richard was sure that he had seen him somewhere before. Whether or not they had met on a personal basis was an open question, but Richard had a good memory for faces developed during his first year as a lawyer. During that time, before he had made the switch to private practice and joined his current firm as an associate, he had been an entry level attorney with the District Attorney's office. Most of that time, it now seemed, had been spent with investigatory services looking at books of mug shots with crime victims. Using a habit that was now hard to break, Richard mentally stored the face in his memory to consider later at his leisure.

In response to the expectant look from the shorthand reporter Richard nodded for her to begin. They were starting nearly an hour after the time originally scheduled for commencement of the deposition and had a lot of ground to cover if they were going to be able to finish in one day. Although he had the right to continue from day to day until done, the last thing he wanted was to burn another working day unless there was an indication of helpful information that justified spending the additional time. With her right hand raised the reporter administered the oath to Alexander. As soon as Alexander finished repeating the words Richard glanced at his watch. He noted out loud for the record that it was almost ten o'clock and mentally changed his strategy to respond to the implicit attempt by Stucky to make Richard hurry through the proceedings in order to complete the questions by the end of a single day. With his expression completely hiding his thoughts the questioning began.

~ ~ ~ ~ ~

Nothing softens a person's resistance to answering questions more than making them believe that they can hurry the process only by volunteering information. After three hours of reviewing in great detail and depth Alexander's educational and employment history, and ignoring Stucky's increasingly adamant objections to the relevance of the questions, Richard was still on the first page of his thick deposition outline. Responding to a pointed look by Alexander at his gold Rolex, Richard flipped casually to the last page of the outline as if to confirm some point that he wanted to cover. And made sure that both Alexander and Stucky could see that the page was numbered "43" and was covered with questions, single spaced, in the same fashion as the first 42 pages. Flipping back to the first page, Richard calmly continued.

~ ~ ~ ~ ~

Once he hit the street Richard felt free for the balance of the trip. Although it was close to seven o'clock at night the sidewalks were packed with people hurrying to a thousand different destinations. The weather was softly warm and perfectly matched the dusky pastels of the early evening sky. Looking around to get oriented, Richard now found himself in midtown Manhattan, some forty blocks away from his hotel room at the Ritz Carlton at Battery Park. With time on his hands until he was supposed to meet Lynn for dinner, the sights and sounds of the City convinced him to skip a cab and walk in the direction of his hotel. As he moved along the crowded streets, he was amazed by the sheer number of people outside and on the streets. Hawkers on all four corners of each intersection, selling food of every type imaginable from boxes of fresh fruits and vegetables to mini-braziers on which kebabs of questionable meat sizzled. Goods of almost every size and description were laid out for inspection and sale. Items including "Gucci" wallets for twenty dollars and

"Rolexes" for as little as thirty dollars were displayed and haggled over. With instinctive distrust and wary of being hustled Richard managed to avoid making eye contact with anyone who appeared to have anything for sale. Including two sparsely clad women that boldly asked him if he wanted a "date."

Finally reaching the chaos of Grand Central Station was a satisfactory accomplishment. The street energy had momentarily made him forget the length of the day, or how tired he was. He paused and looked around for a place to get a drink of water. Between the distance walked and the energy level that surrounded and pulsated through the City, Richard realized that he had actually worked up a slight sweat and was tiring fast. After a moment of looking around without results, he decided that the public water fountains were out of the question. Those that were not busted or vandalized were surrounded by kids who looked like they had dressed for bit parts in a remake of Night Of The Living Dead. Nothing being immediately available, Richard decided that the walk was enough exercise for the day and with a look that he hoped would be taken for supreme indifference, so he might be mistaken for a native, he entered a sloping walkway leading further underground to one of the subway platforms. He had ridden the commuter trains in California on many occasions, but had often heard horror stories about the New York subway. Looking around at the people headed in his direction towards the platform failed to show any need for major concern, and it was hard to believe that the crowded section of subway between Grand Central Station and the station at Bowling Green would hold any dangers as long as he kept to himself.

As if the large signs on the walls of the tunnel to the subway platform were not enough to send the message, the row of green and chrome turnstiles at the end of the tunnel clearly indicated on the top of each that a subway token was required. Feeling foolish, as he had no idea how much a token cost, Richard joined a short line in front of the cashier's booth. The booth was enclosed in what looked like bullet-proof glass with a small circular opening at the bottom to facilitate the exchange of money for tokens. Typical for New York there was no sign immediately available to indicate the cost of a token. Although Richard tried to divine the cost by paying close attention to the people in line before him, the individual transactions moved so quickly that they seemed to Richard to have been conducted in a foreign language. Not wanting to appear as a complete out-of-towner, Richard decided that the ride couldn't possibly cost more than a couple of bucks and calmly pulled a five dollar bill out of his wallet and pushed it through the hole under the bullet-proof glass. Without a glance at Richard the operator took the bill and promptly rewarded Richard with a huge fistful of change and tokens. Using both hands, with briefcase between his feet, he scooped the mixture up and nervously jammed the entire amount into his pockets without bothering to see if he had been shortchanged. Notwithstanding his attempt at quick and unobtrusive action, Richard had already become the object of attention for the small group of homeless men who had staked out this section of the underground passageways as their private territory to work. Two of the more aggressive panhandlers nonchalantly approached with Styrofoam cups in outstretched hands.

"Hey man. Spare some of that change man."

"Yea bro. We got to get home and still need a couple of bucks."

Richard knew better than to even acknowledge the requests and stepped immediately towards the turnstiles while groping in his pocket among the large combination of change to find one of the tokens. Amid growing concern at spilling the entire pocket of change on the ground, he finally located the one he was looking for and rapidly deposited the token into the slotted opening to pass through to the other side of the turnstiles. He still didn't know how much the damn trip was going to cost but was already beginning to regret the adventure. This setup was clearly not as well run as BART of the San Francisco Bay Area, or even Boston's more civilized "T" system. So when a subway train finally pulled up to the landing Richard wasted no time in getting aboard and sitting down as far out of the way of the other riders as possible. The doors promptly hissed shut and the train rapidly gained speed as it pulled out of the station.

Relaxing somewhat, Richard placed his briefcase under his legs and surreptitiously looked around at his fellow passengers. Mostly Hispanic, with a few Asians scattered in small groups at the far end of the car. He noticed only two men in suits, but on closer inspection in the dim light also noticed that the quality of the suits was what could only be described as bargain basement. Clean, but definitely bargain basement. The subway car itself was relatively new with only the ubiquitous gang symbols spray painted across the walls and ceiling to mar its cleanliness. No one looked his way and, knowing enough to mind his own business, he finally leaned back against his seat. After a few minutes, lulled by the swaying action of the car as it moved rapidly down the tracks, Richard's eyes began to droop and he even began to relax enough to congratulate himself on the adventure.

As the train roared through two stations without slowing, much less stopping to pickup additional passengers, Richard slowly came to the unhappy conclusion that he may have mistakenly boarded one of the express trains to some destination unknown. Armed with the firm belief that discretion is the better part of valor, he realized that he better take whatever action was necessary to confirm the next stop on this ride. Across the aisle on the wall of the car was a poster map of the entire metro system. It was the type of map engineers love but everyone else hates. Drawn as a schematic in the fashion of a layout of an electrical grid system, no details other than station names were provided to orient oneself to the layout of the City, or to the Tri-Borough Area in general. After several minutes spent in a vain attempt to understand the map in relation to his current position, from the information readable where the graffiti had not obscured the station names Richard came to the startling realization that he was heading in a direction that was completely opposite from where he had intended. Worse yet, he was headed directly for the Bronx, and he knew that was not a good idea. As he tried to think of the best way out of the situation the doors at the end of the car was opened and a number of leather jacket clad teenagers pushed and shoved each other into the car. They stood together for a moment, playfully hassling each other, before one of them tripped over a shopping bag that an elderly Chinese lady had placed on the floor near her feet. The youth immediately jumped to his feet, amid the razzing of his friends and kicked the overturned shopping bag. The laughter of his friends was joined by the shouts of the lady in Mandarin. When he ignored her curses she grabbed the arm of his jacket. With a movement too quick to be seen clearly he swung her around and slammed her down into the seat. Without thinking about what he was doing, Richard jumped forward help her just as a transit authority officer entered the car at the far end. One of the gang was squaring up to meet Richard's charge when he first saw the officer and hollered at his friends to get their attention. They now ignored Richard and bolted in a confused mass for the opposite door with the officer close on their heels. The remaining passengers watched them go, and one of the other Chinese ladies helped her friend sit up and collect the shopping items from where they had landed across the floor. Seemingly seconds later a loud hiss of the air brakes announced that the train was making one of its few remaining stops before leaving Manhattan proper. Richard was quick on his feet, the adrenalin still furiously pumping through his veins, grabbed his briefcase and headed straight through the doors as they opened. He was on the station's platform almost before anyone else had even left their seats. Without worrying about appearances, Richard jogged up the steps and into the now chilly night air. Stepping off of the curb, mindful that the gang had probably also taken the opportunity to leave the train, he flagged down and stepped into the relative safety of a yellow cab that he would have killed for if anyone had stood in his way.

After twenty minutes of cross-town driving by a maniac taxi driver whose name he could not pronounce, Richard was back in the protective comfort of his $255 per night hotel room. Sitting down on the edge of the bed he quickly popped the tab on a can of Heiniken grabbed from the in room mini-bar. $7.75 may be a lot for a can of beer, but the hotel management knew that the expense accounts who usually booked the room never complained too long or loudly. Tonight, still thinking about the ride and the chances that he had recklessly taken, neither would Richard.

~~~~~

"Just explain to me where the hell is this case going! And why the hell haven't you been able to control it."

Stucky flinched visibly, and silently wondered for the hundredth time why he took so much shit from Alexander. And for the hundred and first time remembered that it was because of the money. Alexander was as angry as Stucky could ever remember seeing him. Anger which was somewhat understandable considering they had just spent almost nine hours in a deposition that should have taken four and during which Richard had explored a great deal of information that Alexander strongly considered both personal and private.

"Look Montgomery, there is only so much we can do to hinder his ability to conduct discovery and prepare his case."

Alexander rose purposely from one of the supple brown leather chairs that encircled the conference room table. Walking over to the end of the table where Stucky was sitting he thrust his face within inches from Stucky's. The smell of stale cigars and the garlic from their lunch wafted up to Stucky's nose. He hoped that his eyes wouldn't water, and that his grimace would appear to Alexander to be a look of utmost seriousness. But from such close range all he could concentrate on was the huge pores that dotted Alexander's nose. Stucky shook his head to clear his mind. A motion that Alexander immediately misinterpreted.
~~~~~

"What the hell do you mean by 'no'? If you can't find a way to get the case kicked out of court I'll find a way to make sure they at least lose interest in this goddamn case."

"I don't understand." Stucky answered wearily. "Do you mean you would offer them some money to settle?"

"Hell no! If we settle then the trade papers will kill us—those hacks will see that as an admission of wrongdoing. No, we need to discourage them my way, the business way, and you just get back to California and figure out a way to tie them up from getting any more information as long as possible. And I want you to push out the date of the trial . . ." Alexander paused ominously, then quietly added to himself ". . . if it even gets that far."

~ ~ ~ ~

A great restaurant is more than great food, Richard told himself. A great restaurant acts and feels the part. And tonight, when he really needed it, Lynn had picked out a great restaurant. The waiters all wore crisp tuxedos, and there was enough silver on the tables to finance the overthrow of a small country. The wine list was heavy of French wines and was presented as a separate book by a haughty sommelier, who had looked pained when Richard insisted—over his recommendation—on selecting a California chardonnay. Looking across the table at Lynn he wondered again why his luck insisted on their working on opposite ends of the continent. Too much work and too much drive to succeed would rapidly bring him alone to middle age if he was not careful enough to pay attention to life outside of the courtroom. A singularly depressing thought.

"You don't look so happy. Deposition go bad?"

As usual Lynn perceptively picked up on his mood. Deciding that being maudlin would be a quick turnoff to the conversation, he took her question instead as a lead-in to discuss the case.

"It did not really go especially good or bad. At a minimum I was able to establish the corporate controls and systems for

Wine House. I got Alexander to admit that he knew exactly what was going on at Winery Peak, at least so far as the financial end was concerned. For the head of a multinational corporation, he sure knew a lot about the operations of what has to be considered as a relatively small division. I think I will be able to show the jury that Wine House is a heavily integrated structure—throughout all of the separate divisions—to counter their claim that Dickson had complete autonomy in running the local winery operations."

"Sounds like you got what you wanted."

"I did, I guess. But something keeps bugging me. At the beginning of the day I saw the head of Wine House talking to someone I know that I have seen before. I just can't remember who he is or where I saw him."

"Why is that important?"

"During the deposition, when I asked Alexander to identify the guy, he got very nervous. When I pushed for the information Stucky kept interrupting and finally took the position that they would not answer the question."

"Can't you get the court to order them to answer?"

"Maybe. But not till I get back to Napa to make a motion to compel the information. And then there is no guarantee that the answer will be true. If they just make up someone's name there is no real way for me to prove it is a lie."

"Well, you sure are ruffling someone's feathers."

"What do you mean?"

"I asked around like you wanted. One of the lawyers in the local bar association has some contacts among the inhouse lawyers who work in the office of the Wine House General Counsel."

"And?"

"And you better be careful, sweetie. Word is that this case has been given high priority. But no one wants to, or can, talk about it. Seems like a lot of fuss for a wrongful termination case."

"Don't worry, kiddo, I'll be okay."

He gave his best swashbuckling grin and lifted his wine glass in a mock toast. But a concerned frown was all that he got in return for his bravado.

"Richard, either you just don't understand what's going on or you are simply not paying attention. You are talking big time money flowing through this industry. And these types generally play for keeps. Honey, I'm talking about your safety."

"And does the condemned man get a last wish?"

"All right, fine . . . I give up."

Wiping her mouth angrily in frustration at his stubbornness she looked up, caught his look and the unmistakable suggestion in his eyes.

"And as to that 'wish'," she added in a more playful tone, "I think I know what you want. But remember, it was your decision to stay behind in California, not mine. You could easily have joined me out here at any of a dozen firms. Nope," she added cheerfully, "I think you may just have to die an unhappy man."

Richard, signaling the waiter for the check, shrugged good naturedly.

"Well, you can't blame me for trying. Even if it would ruin one of the best friendships I have."

Lynn jabbed him playfully in the arm, signaling that all was forgiven. "Right here and now, probably one of the only friends you have."

~ ~ ~ ~ ~

He never saw them coming.

Walking out of the hardware store, arms weighed down with various lengths of white PVC piping that he intended on using to extend his automatic sprinkler system, Dickson was concentrating on locating his keys without dropping his load. Though the parking lot was not busy, and in retrospect he would wonder how he could have been surprised by their presence, he suddenly found himself surrounded by six seemingly hostile young men. They wore similar outfits, in the gang type fashion of a uniform, of gray pants worn low off of the waist and bagged at the knees and ankles, along with untucked flannel shirts buttoned at the collar and open at the waist. He stood silent for a moment, the lights from passing cars casting shadows across faces only dimly lit from the parking lot light poles. Two of the younger men, standing near the back of the others, grinned nervously while the others stared down hard at Dickson as if daring him to make an abrupt move. Suddenly, one near the front with a blue bandanna pulled low over his forehead broke the silence that separated them.

"Que pasa, essa. Who you staring at, man?"

Dickson fought the immediate urge to avert his eyes in response. He had managed too many men for too long to allow this one to gain the upper hand so easily. Instead he looked directly back into his eyes.

"Is there a problem, my friend?"

Dickson spoke quietly, but forcefully, and imperceptibly shifted the weight of the load from his right arm to his left.

"We are not your 'friend,' senor. No, no you are not a friend of ours."

Dickson shrugged, as if merely to take in this new information, and began to move sideways to his left towards a gap between a 1978 F-100 pickup and a small yellow sedan. Before he could take more than two steps, however, he felt and almost simultaneously heard a zing against his right ear. One of the group had flicked a penny like a missile at his head, using a snapping motion between thumb and index finger. It stung like hell where it had glanced off the side of Dickson's head, but did not inflict any real damage. Unfortunately, Dickson turned towards the source of the missile, only to see the grins of the group. Distracted by their response, Dickson failed to notice that he had been flanked and his line of exit past the truck had been blocked. An unexpected shove against his left arm almost caused him to stumble and fall, and he staggered to regain his balance.

"You poisoned our brothers man, now you gonna pay."

This time Dickson sensed the oncoming blow and was able to throw up his right arm in time to partially deflect an object that briefly reflected the lights of the parking lot. He felt a sharp pain across his forearm, which quickly gave way to a feeling of boiling red haze across his eyes.

Without further conscious thought he dropped one of the two bags and with the free hand whipped a four foot length of pipe out of the remaining bundle of PVC. With no concern for the consequences he slashed out and across with the PVC in the direction of the blow, the tip traveling near face level at a speed that was accelerated by the springy nature of the material. For Dickson it seemed like time had slowed in its progress, allowing him to participate in the moment with crystal clarity. With blood lust enjoyment he noted the look of surprise on his attacker's face as the tip of the pipe connected solidly just above his ear and behind the temple. The attacker dropped like a stone to his knees, his hands unable to stem the fountain of red erupting from the side of his head. Dickson spun around and slashed at the next one in the group, the blood lust now high in his throat and the weeks of frustration pumping adrenalin into the accelerating ferocity of his response. This time the length of pipe connecting against the arm of his antagonist with a loud crack, which was joined quickly with a sharp howl of pain. In a flash the rest of the group scattered, followed almost as quickly by the two Dickson had struck.

Several moments passed while Dickson stood on the balls of his feet, ready and hoping for their return. When he was convinced that they were not likely to come back for more, with deliberate effort of will he loosened his grip on the pipe. His grasp had been so tight that his fingers were actually numb from the restricted flow of blood.

As his senses slowed his range of hearing seemed to change, allowing him to hear once again the background noises from the street traffic and from the stores behind him. Bending at the knees instead of the waist, in order to keep his head up and his lines of sight clear, with one hand he grabbed the two bundles. Walking quickly to his truck he threw the bundles into the passenger seat and keyed the ignition. When the engine kicked over the adrenalin surge kicked out, leaving him feeling somewhat hollow and extremely tired. Grabbing the wheel to steady himself against a sudden feeling of nausea, Dickson suddenly felt a searing stab of pain and realized with surprise that he had been cut threw his heavy jacket and into the muscle of his forearm. Blood was beginning to flow freely, and with an effort Dickson took his jacket off and placed it on the floor. Then, taking his belt off, he wound it around his arm as a tourniquet to staunch the flow, wondering the entire time about how he would explain this one to his wife.

CHAPTER SIX

WHEN SHE DID NOT APPEAR at his office for her scheduled appointment, to discuss her involvement with Winery Peak, he did not give it much thought. In the week since returning from New York he had been too buried by the various problems that existed in his other cases to dwell upon one witness. And witnesses, especially those that do not have a stake in the outcome of a trial, are often reluctant or "simply forget" to come to meetings with lawyers. When she failed to return any of his follow-up phone calls over the next several days, however, Richard started to get worried.

Rebecca Stewart had been the in-house manager of public-relations for Wine House for over twenty years. For the last three years, since leaving Wine House, she had run her own independent public relations and marketing firm. But one of her biggest accounts was still Wine House. Richard had originally contacted Stewart after seeing her name appear in some of the documents that Terri had pilfered from the files of Winery Peak the week after Dickson was fired. Not being one to leave loose ends, Richard had instructed Terri to serve Stewart with a trial subpoena even though the trial was not set to start for more than two months. The subpoena commanded Stewart's appearance at the first day of the trial, and had the power to keep her waiting in the courthouse hallway for days on end until it would be her turn on the witness stand. Along with the subpoena, Richard had included a short note that apologized for the inconvenience. The note further suggested that she give him a call to arrange some type of schedule to minimize the disruption on her business. This was a sometimes successful tactic with people who were self-employed or who ran their own business, and Richard was not surprised when she had called the very same day that she was served. He had politely refused to discuss the details of an accommodation over the phone, leading to an agreement to meet at his office. The time for that meeting, however, had now come and gone.

Not being one to stand on ceremony, Richard decided to drive to Stewart's office unannounced and remind her in person of the fact that she would have to testify, willing or not. Almost an hour later Richard pulled out of traffic and into the hilly streets that typify San Francisco. He turned his wheels sharply against the curb to ensure against the possibility, however remote, that his car would suddenly decide to slip the parking brake and head down the hill and into one of the chic shops that line Union Street. After double checking the address that he had hurriedly scribbled on the back of an old Lotto ticket, he found himself outside of a restored Victorian that Stewart had cleverly converted into a design and advertising studio. From the outside the two story building was truly magnificent, with ornate and flowery carpentry on the turrets and gables. Freshly painted, the white porch gleamed with country blue and dust rose accents. A hand carved redwood sign, posted prominently on the front of the building, proclaimed the nature of the establishment in old English script consistent with the style of the building.

Walking up the short stairway, Richard peered inside the large leaded glass windows and could see a half dozen well dressed women, including one very attractive woman in a stylish, yet somewhat risqué, short black leather skirt and tight fitting cowl neck sweater, busily working at desks and drawing tables. As he reached the front door he had to refrain from the instinct to knock politely, reminding himself that this was a business and not a private residence. Shifting his briefcase to his left hand, he opened the door with his right so that he would be able to immediately shake hands without bumbling around. From experience he felt that he could disarm a potentially hostile welcome quicker if he could make at least some immediate physical contact. And if the contact was with the one in the short black skirt, so much the better.

The doorway opened immediately into the middle of what once was the hallway outside of the living room. Richard suddenly found himself to be the center of attention as heads swung in his direction. Turning to the nearest desk he quickly introduced himself and asked if Stewart was available. After asking the nature of his business, the woman behind the desk stood to tell Stewart that he was here, and not unexpectedly asked Richard to wait while Stewart decided whether to come down to talk to him. To his satisfaction and relief the woman returned immediately and instructed him to go up the stairs to the offices on the second floor. Richard quickly complied, grateful that Stewart had decided against trying to play some type of power game by making him wait downstairs the entire morning.

Reaching the top of the stairs Richard was greeted by a very attractive woman who appeared to be in her late thirties, although Richard knew from his investigation into her background that she was actually closer to fifty. And also knew that he had to make a favorable impression quickly or run the risk that she would simply call Stucky and ask him to run some type of interference.

"I want to apologize for not calling first . . ."

"It is I who should apologize Mr. Magnus. It was terribly rude of me to miss our appointment."

She spoke the words very graciously. Years of employment in the field of public relations had polished and honed her presentation to the level of a career diplomat. Which meant, to Richard, that he could not completely rely on anything she might say.

"That is quite all right, Ms. Stewart. I had business downtown and just thought that I would stop on the way to see if you might have a moment to talk."

Richard also knew how to play the "politeness game." Even if she tried to go south on him, and testify favorably to Wine House, he still had enough material in the documents Terri had located to impeach her testimony to the extent of showing the fiscal reasons for her bias. But to have her testify favorably to Dickson could have a terrific impact on the jury. She indicated her willingness to let him talk further with a slight nod of her head.

"I appreciate, Ms. Stewart, your busy schedule and your willingness to spend some time discussing your involvement at the trial. But before we discuss when your testimony will be required, I want you to know that you are doing the right thing. And we subpoenaed you so—if asked—you can honestly tell Wine House that you were not a willing participant against them."

"Thank you, Mr. Magnus. But as I mentioned over the phone, I have my own reasons for what I do. I will testify, but it is not something that I will look forward to."

"Then I won't waste your time further with unnecessary preliminaries."

Stewart again simply nodded her agreement to the arrangement and led him to the second floor foyer. With a series of graceful movements she sat down on the short sofa that guarded the hallway to the remaining offices, and continued to wait patiently while Richard stood next to her, no other chairs recommending themselves to his attention. With a gentle smile and pointed wave of a delicate hand she motioned for Richard to seat himself next to her on the sofa. Once situated, although uncomfortably perched on the edge to avoid sinking into the overstuffed cushions, Richard felt that prudence dictated an immediate plunge into the issues before the interview could take any further turns to the intimate.

"Please tell me in your own words again what you know. I don't want to put words in your mouth, so as you talk I am going to jot down questions to fit with your information. Your testimony at trial will then flow naturally."

"Good. I am not going to elaborate unnecessarily or say what I do not really know. But I was asked to put together the press campaign to show how much money Wine House had set aside to be used for the workers who had suffered from toxic poisoning, and I put my reputation on the line when I contacted my friends with the press and advised them that the distribution of those monies had already begun."

"And?"

"And them I found out that no monies have been distributed to anyone."

"What!? After all that hoopla, nobody has gotten anything?" Richard found himself leaning forward to take even greater notice of what she was saying. She mistook his intentions and conspiratorially placed her hand gently on his leg slightly above the knee. Richard tried not to notice, as long as the information kept coming.

"That is correct, Mr. Magnus—Richard. And I now doubt that anyone is going to get anything from the program. After we put together the trust fund and held the photo sessions for the networks to show our mobilization, nothing, absolutely nothing, happened. And what makes me even more upset is the fact that the whole program was transferred back east to Corporate for handling as soon as the news lost interest in the victims."

"You think the whole program was a setup for favorable press coverage."

He phrased the question as a statement.

"Of course. It happens all the time. I just don't plan on being the setup person on this one."

He decided to leave alone what she meant by "this one" and jotted down the gist of what she had said on a long yellow pad of legal paper. If what she was saying was true or, even if difficult to substantiate as true, could at least be presented to the jury as her well founded opinion, he could use it to color the minds of the jurors as to the corporate character of Wine House.

"I need you to tell the jury what you know. Otherwise, once word gets out from some other source during the trial you may get blamed for the cover-up."

"Look, Mr. Magnus . . ." Her eyes flared briefly before she collected herself. "I know how the game is played. Do not give me this 'some other source' routine. I will be there."

She abruptly stood and Richard wisely took the not so subtle hint that the interview was over.

~ ~ ~ ~ ~

The papers and stacks of open law books scattered around his office played a silent testament to the amount of effort that Richard was putting into Dickson's case. Thankfully, Richard had help from several other lawyers, also associates of the firm, who were available to monitor and fill in with the rest of his caseload. With their help he could be free to concentrate on the problems existing in Dickson's case. Problems that included having to face the general rule that Wine House had the right to hire and fire its upper level managers, including Dickson, with a great deal of latitude. As long as the reasons for firing Dickson were based in part on some reasonable business reason, Wine House had colorable justification for its conduct. Richard had to find and then present enough evidence to convince the jury that the reason was pre-textual, and that Wine House had been predatory in its dealings with Dickson.

From time to time one associate or another would pop into his office with a question about strategy or tactics on one of Richard's other cases, or with a letter prepared for his signature to maintain the illusion that he was personally working on every aspect of every one of his cases. He welcomed these short intrusions, as long as they were kept short, and the camaraderie that arose between lawyers working on the same side of a case. When he stopped long enough to think about it, he was most thankful for the interference that Jo ran for him. She unfailingly managed to stop most of the nonessential interruptions that would otherwise take up all of his time. But in the middle of trying to decide how to present the order of witnesses the phone ringingly jangled, the blinking light indicating an interoffice line from Jo's desk. With irritation Richard punched the hands-free button on the telephone.

"Yep?"

"I'm sorry Richard, but I have someone on line two who says it's urgent but he won't give his name or business."

"You know better, Jo. I don't like anonymous callers."

"I know, but something about this guy's voice made me think I should interrupt you."

Richard stretched with resignation. "All right, put him through."

The phone went quiet for a moment, followed by a short crackle that indicated that the call had been transferred to his extension. The silence was then broken by a voice that sounded like gravel sliding down a metal chute.

"Mr. Magnus?"

"Yes. To whom am I speaking?"

"Doesn't matter." From the slight distortion Richard could tell that the call was on a long-distance line. "Please take me off the speaker."

"Well, Mr. Doesn't Matter, what can I do for you?"

"No, Mr. Magnus, it's what I am doing for you. You're getting involved with people who aren't very happy with what you are doing. They are going to warn you in unpleasant ways if you continue to go after Wine House. And believe me, you don't want to be warned by these people."

The line went dead so quickly that Richard had a hard time believing what he had heard. Ten minutes later, when Jo brought in the morning mail, Richard was still staring at the phone in disbelief.

~~~~~

"I assume that you have a good reason for asking to have this hearing on such short notice. You know I don't like *ex parte* hearings."

Judge Marwick leaned back in his chair, the tie around his neck loosened to accommodate the heat of the late afternoon. He sat facing Richard, who stood rigidly to his left, and Stucky, who sat intently on the judge's sofa to his right. As with all *ex parte* matters, proceedings that were not set on the court's normal hearing calendar because of the need for quick resolution, the Judge took counsel into his chambers alone. No court reporter, clients or other spectators were invited or allowed. Judge Marwick, who as presiding judge of
~~~~~

the Napa County Superior Court fielded the responsibility of court administration, learned long ago that the absence of an audience helped the attorneys get to the heart of a problem without all of their usual rhetoric.

"We need to immediately advance the trial date, Judge . . ."

"NO WAY, JUDGE! This is preposterous . . ." Stucky jumped to his feet shouting, to be hit head on with a steely glare from Marwick that stopped him in his tracks.

"There is no reporter here, Mr. Stucky, and I will assume that you will be opposed to EVERYTHING that Mr. Magnus has to say. SO SIT DOWN!"

"Thank you, Judge." Richard continued without a glance over at Stucky. "You know that I wouldn't make a request like this lightly. But this morning I received a serious threat should we continue with the case."

Richard went on to recount the telephone conversation from the morning. As he spoke, Marwick pulled out a gnarled briarwood pipe and calmly began to stuff the bowl with a moist clump of dark smelling tobacco from a worn leather pouch on his desktop. As Richard finished the story the Judge fished into his pocket and withdrew a silver plated lighter, which he clicked open with his thumb and spun the metal against the flint in an easy, practiced, motion until the wick ignited. The wick first flared away the excess lighter fluid and then shrank to an even burning flame. The yellow tip of the flame was carefully lowered to the bowl, hand stopping far enough away that the flame was just out of reach of the first layer of tobacco. Then, with a slow and steady draw on the pipestem, Marwick allowed the flame to first heat and then curl the top layer of tobacco before drawing deeply down to ignite the entire bowl.

Throughout this ritual Stucky sat in quiet agitation. Although it was against his nature to sit silently, he knew better than to anger the Judge twice in one hearing. Finally, Marwick's eyes focused through the smoke at Stucky, and with a curt nod Marwick indicated approval for Stucky to state his position.

"This is OUTRAGEOUS!"

Stucky roared without thinking to his feet, releasing too quickly the frustration of having had to sit quietly.

"There is NO reason to reset the trial date on an expedited basis. For GOD's sake, your Honor, all he received was one damn telephone call from some nut."

"First, Mr. Stucky, SIT DOWN. Second, you control yourself or I'll have you wearing a French bit when you appear before me! Third, you swear one more time in my presence and it will cost you fifty bucks. Do we understand each other?"

"Yes, your Honor."

"Good. I don't need histrionics inside my office, or for that matter anywhere in my courthouse. And although I would normally deny a request to advance a trial date when based solely on one crank call, I think that there is a way to accommodate both of you so that there is no prejudice to the defendant in this case. You've got your special setting, Mr. Magnus, and trial will start in six weeks."

Richard nodded, and jotted down the information on his notepad.

"And Mr. Magnus . . ."

"Yes, your Honor?"

"You had better be ready to proceed on that date. I'm putting a note in the file that no continuances will be granted unless there is a death in the family . . . Yours."

"I understand, your Honor. Thank you."

Richard hustled out of Marwick's chambers before anything could be said or done to mar his victory. As he walked briskly towards the central stairwell of the Courthouse Stucky caught up and walked beside him. They strode together in step down the hallway in silence until Stucky stopped a quarter step in front of Richard, causing him to pull up involuntarily.

"Did you really get a call . . . "

Richard bristled his response. "Are you saying I was in there lying to the court?"

"Sorry Richard. I did not mean it that way. It just sounded so . . . I don't know . . . unusual in any case, much less one like this. But I was not suggesting that you just made it all up. Anyway, do you really think you will be ready in six weeks?"

"I guess I don't have a choice, unless Wine House wants to resolve this matter."

"The only way Wine House will 'resolve' this case is if Dickson dismisses his claims with prejudice."

"Ya, well, I guess we are going to trial." Stucky shook his head in exasperation. "I don't know what case you think you've got, but there is nothing there. And even if you do win, which will never happen unless the jury totally goes sideways, Wine House has told me that we will appeal through the Supreme Court if necessary."

"Then I guess we will be seeing a lot of one another for years to come."

Stucky stopped and reached out for Richard's arm.

"You know, Richard, I asked around about you and about your firm. Just about everyone was highly complimentary, even if you have a reputation for being somewhat stubborn, but no one can figure out why you took such a loser of a case."

Richard turned to face Stucky directly, but paused to consider his response. He knew that Stucky thought him to be wet behind the ears, but that did not make it any easier to be talked down to. Since a well considered comment concerning the merits of the lawsuit would be lost on Stucky's closed mind, Richard elected instead to simply terminate the conversation with a statement that would do nothing to convey anything les than his complete belief in Dickson's position. Looking Stucky squarely in the eyes Richard spoke slowly and carefully, as if each word had a special meaning, and was rewarded by the uncertain look in Stucky's face.

"Why did we take it on? Why else would someone like me take this type of case? Because my grandfather taught me to believe in honesty, integrity, and fairness. That's why."

~~~~~

"We have problems."

Stucky had wasted no time in using the courthouse telephone to give Alexander the news about the expedited trial date.

"What happened, Patrick?"

Before Stucky answered Alexander quietly put the call on the speaker phone. In his office two other businessmen stared intently at the small metal speaker while Stucky rehashed the hearing and the Judge's decision. When he finished Alexander took the phone off the speaker before answering.

"Don't worry about it, Patrick."

The response did little to reflect the feelings of the listeners.

"I am sure that you did all that you could do. Just let me know when you have further information. All right?"

"Certainly. We will continue to focus on preparing for the trial."

"That will be fine. Goodnight, Patrick."

Stucky hung the phone up and stared blankly in puzzlement at the wall. He had expected Alexander to go through the roof. Alexander must have something up his sleeve and, Stucky decided, sometimes it is better not to know what.

On the other end of the line Alexander looked at his two guests and waited patiently. He knew from long experience that he could often get the results that he wanted by sitting silently until the proper suggestion was made by others. Which could then be approved by a mere gesture, such as slightly raising an eyebrow, and allow his the benefit of plausible deniability. In that fashion no one could say that he ever expressly authorized any improper or illegal activity. Alexander did not have to wait long. And in response to a few quiet suggestions the eyebrow went up.

~~~~~

Back at his office Richard wasted no time in asking Jo to call Dickson and tell him to drive down to the office for some brainstorming. They would have to make several decisions quickly, and Richard was going to have to rely heavily on Dickson to do some of the legwork. Normally Richard hated to rely on a client for anything related to fact gathering, as they did not know enough about chain of custody issues to protect the usability of the information, and he at least made sure that he would not have to rely completely on what Dickson might be able to develop without some backup in mind. Clients had a way of screwing things up, to Richard's way of thinking, which is why they needed lawyers in the first place. Most also had a nasty habit of then blaming the lawyer for the screw-up, even when they had insisted on helping in the first place. Dickson, however, was different than most clients. Richard could not remember when he had met a client that gave him as much confidence. Or who, with the proper coaching and practice, was sure to do as well on the stand. Dickson, to Richard's pleasant surprise, quite possibly could be made into a natural born witness.

During the time it took Dickson to drive downtown to Richard's office, Jo and Gayle had already joined Richard in his office and were listening intently while Richard dictated a long list of things that seemingly had to be done yesterday. A witness list had to be drawn up, to be served on Wine House, and the witnesses on the list had to be contacted and advised of the new trial date. Careful thought went into the witness list, as the failure to identify the witnesses before trial could result in the exclusion of the witness from testifying at trial. Although rebuttal witnesses did not have to be included on the list, by not including their name Richard would be taking the calculated risk that there would first be some testimony for a non-listed witness to rebut. Richard also had to post jury fees with the court or Dickson would lose the right to trial by jury. This errand, although simple to execute, was critically important. If Richard's strategy for the trial was to succeed, the story had to be heard by a jury of Dickson's peers. A judge acting alone as the trier of fact was too much of a risk, as most judges acted as if they had heard it all by the time they ascended the bench, or at least believed they had, and were hard to impress with stories that would shock a lay audience.

When Richard paused for breath, Gayle took over and began to recite the items on a list that she had prepared immediately before the meeting. She had been the lead paralegal in at least a dozen major trials, and was a true professional. In fact, when Richard had burst excitedly into her office with the news of the rapidly approaching trial date, she had merely nodded and marked where she was in the project in front of her before taking a fresh pad of paper. Without pause she began to outline the projects that she would have to make sure were done to get Richard's case ready for trial. As she now spoke Richard listened carefully and made an occasional comment or correction. Although he deferred to her judgment on most of the items, some decisions were just too critical to allow someone else to make the final judgment call. When she finished with her list Richard sat quietly for a second or two and then added three more things for her to take care of on his behalf. She nodded her agreement, made one last scribble on her pad, and left the office to parcel out the assignments to the paralegal assistants.

Turning to his calendar, a notebook size week-at-a-glance, Richard flipped ahead six weeks. And then flipped through two more weeks. He reached over to the beagle coffee mug and withdrew a red felt tip pen. He was in the process of drawing a red line through each day of the two weeks when Dickson walked in.

"Red pen," he commented dourly. "Must be important."

"I've got great news, Peter. Trial starts in only in six weeks!"

"Six weeks! You have got to be kidding! You said last week that it could be four months or more before we would actually get into the courtroom."

"Well, that was the good news. Now let me tell you about why I was able to get you such an early trial date."

Richard quickly recounted the events of the day, placing special emphasis on the way in which he had deftly played the hearing. Dickson was suitably impressed by the quick action in having the *ex parte* hearing and the special setting, but appeared unconcerned by the description of the telephone call.

"Sounds like some guy with too much time on his hands and an overactive imagination."

"Could be Peter, but make sure you let me know if anything funny happens in the next couple of weeks. I don't want anything to happen to you, and I really don't want the news to get wind of this."

"All right already. You've made me eat the 'interview' with Martinez enough times." Dickson grinned sheepishly. "I promise that I will not talk to the press."

"Okay, okay. Nuff said. Let's get down to business."

For the next four hours Richard and Dickson went over the case issue by issue. On points that needed clarification in Richard's mind he led Dickson through mock cross-examination, and constantly jotted down notes on four separate pads. One pad that would be used to outline Dickson's testimony at trial. One that listed points for cross-examination of potential defense witnesses. One to make reminders of ideas that came to Richard as they talked, some not even connected to what they were talking about. And the last one for a list of Dickson's responsibilities, those legwork items that Dickson would have to do, and do correctly, in order for the case to have the best chance of success.

By the time they were done the office was quiet and empty. It was nearly 9:00 P.M. and the general office staff had long since gone home. After copying Dickson's sheet of to-do items, they walked together in silence to the elevator. Richard reached out to press the down button and they both stared mutely at the door. A loud bell signaled the elevator's arrival, and as the doors slid quietly open Richard turned to Dickson and noted the worry lines that were highlighted by the soft light from the wall sconces. He softly grabbed Dickson's arm and grinned his best "let's go-gettem" grin.

"We got a hell of a lot done tonight, Peter. The next six weeks are going to be long and hard. Physically, mentally and emotionally. Make sure that you take care of yourself. In eight weeks we will sit down and be able to talk about how we kicked their butts! Okay?"

"Thanks, Richard. Sure has been a long day though."

Dickson stepped into the elevator. Just as the doors closed he grinned back at Richard, his confidence momentarily restored. Richard stared a moment at the closed doors, and with a tired sigh turned back to his office to continue with what would surely be another all-nighter.

~ ~ ~ ~ ~

Dickson eased into the driver's seat of his Chevy Blazer that he had parked on the street outside of Richard's office. Rain had been drizzling earlier, and the wet streets still reflected the orange glow from the low pressure sodium streetlamps that lined the streets of downtown Napa. Dickson grinned with the memory of the salesman who had pestered him for weeks to buy several dozen of the streetlamps for the long driveway up to wines caves at Winery Peak. The salesman, who in the end had not been successful, had kept repeating like some demented mantra the phrase "less pressure, more light." Recognizing the unlikelihood that any salespeople would be contacting him any time in the near future, he shifted his attention back to the problems of the present. Dickson flicked his wipers once, to clear the last few drops of water that clung to his windshield, and then listened to the engine start with its characteristically distant sounding roar. Easing out of the parking space into traffic, his mind continued to churn even as the day's events and the work with Richard began to take a strong mental toll.

Some twenty minutes later Dickson pulled off of the highway and turned down the county access road that lead to his property. The gentle whine of tires on rain slicked asphalt was replaced by the crunch of gravel, and the harsh white backlighting from streetlights installed by the County was replaced by the softer silvery light reflected off of a quarter moon. Dickson loved living in the Napa Valley for this very reason. Notwithstanding all of the development that constantly threatened to pave over everything green in California, and in particular the always growing influx of tourists into the area, he was still able to be deep in the countryside within a half hour of leaving the congestion of downtown.

Pulling into his driveway the headlights splashed the front of his house in bright yellow light. Built in the early Spanish mission style, the structure had a low roofline that allowed the red adobe pavers on the entryway to reach up in a continuous flow to the red adobe tiles on the roof. Bougainvillea climbed white trellises from the ground in a riot of purple, white and yellow flowers, framing the wooden arches that led to the cool interior courtyard. Dickson shut the engine off and listened for a minute to the metal make a quiet tinkling sound as it cooled in the night air. Breaking out of his reverie he glanced up and around into the shadow darkened bushes that lined the driveway and immediate grounds.

Opening the door of his truck Dickson whistled loudly, a puzzled look on his face. He was the proud owner of two champion Labradors, one chocolate brown and the other mustard yellow. They were smart dogs that absolutely worshipped Dickson. Although they were not much for barking, they usually were quick to greet the Blazer and seemed to recognize its sound from the sound of other cars. Dickson did not believe in chaining his dogs, not out here in the country, and as they did roam from time to time he could not cancel out completely the idea that they might be out having some good old dog type fun. Something in the back of his mind, however, bothered Dickson as he climbed out of the truck. He stood still, and quietly turned his head to take in the 180 degree view available from the concrete apron that led immediately from the driveway to the garage. Behind him slight wisps of steam rose gently from the hood as the engine continued to cool in the moist night air. With a jerk born of nervous premonition he began to walk forward, slowly placing one foot in front of the other as he moved.

As his mind focused on the sounds of the night he could discern the difference between the constant chirping of the cicadas from low rumble of the bullfrogs near the stream at the edge of the property. These sounds generally formed background white noise for the area, and were noticed by Dickson about as often as a city dweller notices the sounds of buses as they travel on their route or sirens echoing in the distance. With nerves already stretched tight from the recent events tonight was different, and his ears strained for something, anything, that would give him direction. A hundred feet from the Blazer his ears were rewarded by a slight scratching sound, clearly out of the ordinary from the local night sounds. Dickson paused, then hurried forward and around a leafy corner that was created by a large juniper that had grow tight against two medium sized sugar pines.

"Oh shit!"

Dickson whispered under his breath at the sight. A pained series of whimpers greeted Dickson in response, along with a tail that wagged twice and then lay silent in apparent exhaustion. In the hollow created by the intersecting roots of the pines lay the two dogs. The yellow Labrador tried to lift her head to greet Dickson, and then dropped it heavily back down into the moist dirt with a soft thud. Whitish-green foam dripped from the lining of her mouth, which was forced open by a tongue swollen to twice its normal size. Dickson flung himself to his knees and gently scooped her head onto his chest. She trembled quietly at his touch, all of her energy seemingly directed towards drawing air into laboring lungs. Dickson stroked her head for a minute to settle her down, speaking quiet thoughts into her ear. When her breathing settled, he then turned to the chocolate Labrador, a large male of three years with muscles that rippled under a gleaming coat.

Dickson knew immediate that the chocolate Labrador was dead. His tongue lolled darkly out of his mouth, swollen grotesquely like the yellow's. Dickson closed his eyes tightly and took a very deep breath. The events of the last several weeks, broken loose by the sharpness of this tragedy, washed over him in paralyzing waves.

He probably would have stayed there all night, wallowing in the self-doubt that threatened to completely overwhelm him, when a whimper from the yellow Labrador snapped him back into the present. Gently placing the chocolate down into the depth of the hollow, he reached over to pick the remaining Labrador up into his arms. Great strides took him back to the Blazer, where he lay her down on the floor of the backseat on top of his suit jacket in order to insure her warmth and comfort. Dashing into the house he quickly informed his wife of the situation. In minutes he had the Blazer started and was roaring down the driveway back to the main road and town.

Even though the drive into the far end of town usually took him from twenty-five to forty minutes, depending on traffic and weather conditions, he was able to pull up to the veterinarian hospital in closer to fifteen. The lack of late night traffic was a help, and probably a blessing to anyone that might have been unlucky enough to have been traveling in the opposite direction. His wife had phoned ahead to the hospital and alerted the staff, and as he pulled up the veterinarian was already waiting expectantly outside with a gurney. Dickson threw the truck into park in front of the entrance, even before he had come to a complete stop, almost jolting himself forward into the dashboard. With a single motion he was out the door, the lab slung limply in his arms, and was through the double doors of the building followed immediately by the veterinarian.

Almost an hour later Dickson was still waiting anxiously in the sterile waiting room when the vet came in to announce that the yellow Lab was seriously weak, but should survive.

CHAPTER SEVEN

"I THINK you're gonna kill yourself by taking this case too damn personally."

Richard looked up to see his mentor, one of the firm's senior litigation partners, standing in the doorway. With the trial starting in only six days Richard was practically living full time in the office. The last five weeks had passed by in a blur of concentrated activity. After Judge Marwick had agreed to set the early trial date, Stucky had instituted a campaign of activities designed to inundate Richard and prevent him from having enough time to prepare his own side of the case.

Stucky had immediately demanded the right to take Dickson's deposition. After two days and twelve long hours of probing into areas that had nothing to do with the central issues in the case, Richard had finally objected and walked out of the deposition with Dickson in tow. To Stucky's consternation, Judge Marwick had agreed with Richard that the pace of the deposition seemed primarily designed to delay and harass. But, over Richard's objections, Judge Marwick had allowed Stucky four additional hours to complete his questioning.

The day after the deposition Stucky's office then hand delivered a thick set of interrogatories, detailed written questions that had to be answered by Dickson under penalty of perjury. Stucky also retained his own investigator to interview potential witnesses as to Dickson's character and personal finances. Richard constantly had to be on top of the contacts, to the extent he could learn about them, and debrief the witnesses to hear what they might say at trial should Stucky serve them with subpoenas to appear. At the same time he was fighting off Stucky, Richard was trying to line up his own witnesses and also prepare for the numerous aspects and details that go into preparing for a lengthy jury trial. Now, with tired eyes blinking, Richard looked away from his mentor and out the window towards the east and the reddish-yellow light of the early morning sun before turning to grumpily answer.

"Morning, Michael. Since when do you get in this early?"

"Since I heard that you stopped going home at night. I wanted to see it for myself if the rumors were true. And by the way, you look like shit."

"Thanks a lot."

Richard put down his pen and tried to relax. Michael Shaw was the best lawyer in the firm and enjoyed being recognized as one of the more accomplished trial lawyers in the state. He had made his reputation in the late 1970's prosecuting gang members in Oakland before turning to the more lucrative and less dangerous civil practice. Although considerably grayer than the days when he represented the People of the State of California, at 6'2" and trim Shaw still cut an impressive figure in the courtroom as well as across the negotiating table. Richard had been assigned to assist him on a contentious partnership dissolution soon after joining the firm and wasted no time in recognizing that his advice was definitely worth listening to.

"This case, why don't you settle it?"

"Lots of reasons, Mike. First, Dickson is being screwed. Second, these guys got some agenda that they are using this case for. Their attorney has told me that they're not going to offer a damn nickel, so at least I don't have to worry whether or not we should take their offer. Anyway, Dickson doesn't have the ability to hire someone else to handle this case if I cut him loose."

Almost feeling before seeing the frown form on Michael's face, Richard hurriedly continued.

"Don't worry. I have run the numbers on the damages we can present to the jury. When we win this case our fee will be one third of a whole lot of money."

"You mean you took this case on a contingency?"

Shaw sat down heavily in the chair in front of Richard's desk, a look of disbelief on his face. With a sweeping arm he angrily gestured around the room.

"How the hell do you think the firm is going to be able to pay for all this and your secretary on a third of nothing? And you know that all contingency fee cases have to be approved by the partners before they are accepted."

"Look, Mike, this case is important . . ."

"All of our cases are important. Don't you forget that. You just haven't thought this through. Wine House's attorneys have already buried you with discovery requests and have yanked you around on scheduling. They have the money to buy the best experts to testify at trial. They will hire a jury selection expert and even someone to pick out their goddamn clothes on the first day of trial! Even before you get this case to trial we are going to spend tens of thousands to line up the most basic of experts to testify to the fact that Dickson's reputation in the industry has suffered and someone else to say how much. And who is going to pay all the costs? You have already been to depositions, both here and in New York. Who is paying for the plane, the hotel, the court reporter? And you know that Allen is going to shit purple when he hears of this."

Shaw paused, seeing the misery taking its toll in the form of Richard's slumped position in his chair. Although Allen Rose was not the most highly respected of lawyers in the local legal community for his technical skills, he had been appointed the head of operations for the firm that year and acted like he was one of the founding members. This situation was easily explained by the fact that his father was in the position to send a large amount of work to the firm every year for a long time to come, and had already done so for the last two years. In the absence of this support, the associates consoled themselves that Allen would probably find himself out of a job in a heartbeat.

Allen tended towards the stiff side, walked as if he had a stick up his backside and, although he would never stand tall in the face of an angry opponent, had a propensity to draft stinging and vitriolic letters from the relative safety of his office. On more than one occasion suggestions had been made that, as a child, he had been the routine subject of attention of the schoolyard bullies. This explanation was commonly offered whenever he demonstrated his propensity to exercise to the fullest extent possible the authority and power that he gleaned from the fact that he was a licensed attorney. In another life, others suggested, he must have been a petty bureaucrat of the type that would have insisted to the end on the proper use and placement of deck chairs on the Titanic.

Allen also had a special dislike for Richard. Unfortunately for Richard, this dislike was easily explained by the fact that Richard has been a witness at Allen's two most notorious moments. Both events had occurred during a time when both Allen and Richard were employed with the office of the District Attorney. Allen had been substantially senior, as Richard had been a lowly intern at the time. During the first situation Allen had been lead attorney on a case involving a grand theft charge. They had been in a settlement conference in the chambers of the judge who would ultimately try the case if necessary, and Allen had stubbornly been resisting the pointed suggestions of the judge to accept a plea on a lesser included charge and wrap the case before trial. As the comments from the judge grew increasingly hostile to Allen legal theories, Allen's position grew more entrenched. At that time he had political aspirations, and longed for a reputation as a "hard nosed defender of the People." Tempers had finally flared, to Richard's secret amusement, and with a show of bravado Allen had leap to his feet without leave from the judge. Flinging open the door at his elbow, Allen had stomped out of the judge's chambers and crashed the door behind himself to shocked silence. To Allen's everlasting chagrin, the moment of silence was quickly replaced by peals of laughter from the judge. Soon all in the room joined in the merriment as the judge shared the fact that Allen had stomped off accidentally into the judge's private toilet. The second situation had not been much better for Allen's self-esteem. Richard had been assisting Allen in a trial on a bank robbery charge against two would-be folk heroes. The police had arrested one of the two defendants a few blocks from the bank, and the other one an hour later, but could not get a positive identification on either from any of the bank customers as both robbers had worn masks during the holdup. The key evidence against both of the defendants was almost entirely circumstantial, based on the fact that the two robbers had been described as wearing the same type of cowboy boots that the defendants had been wearing.

The trial had gone badly for Allen, in part because the view from his narrow world caused him to ignore Richard's suggestion that he not underestimate the popularity and generally availability of those boots. To make matters worse, both defendants were fairly clean cut and lacked either prior criminal records or any particularly strong motivation for committing the crime as charged. During closing argument Allen had emphasized the only real physical evidence that he had—the cowboy boots—by waving one of the boots high over his head like some demented madman from a shoe store going out of business sale. Suddenly, in the middle of what he considered to be an impassioned speech to the jury, a wad of dollar bills sprayed from the boot and into the startled faces of the jury. One of the defendants apparently had stuffed a number of the bills in the pointed toe of the boot, where it had remained wedged throughout the arrest and trial. The judge had not been amused, and called a mistrial. Within a few short days of the trial Allen had found himself no longer with the office of the District Attorney. Allen Rose Sr. was not the type of father to let his son roam aimlessly, even for a long weekend, and quickly arranged a position with the firm. The senior partners at the firm understood the true nature of the relationship, and in record time Allen became a partner, although without equity voting rights, in the firm. In his quest for full equity partnership, he had seized upon the role of rule enforcer within the firm.

"Look, Richard. What's done is done. And the trial is too close to worry about Allen now. I will run that interference for you. Just remember we didn't make the facts, we just present them in the best light possible to the jury. Nor are we responsible for what ultimately happens to our clients. Stay detached. Stay objective and just give him the best case you can consistent with our fee arrangement."

"You mean the cheapest case possible."

"No, Richard, that is not what I meant. The best case this matter deserves. And no more."

Shaw stood up and leaned back against the wall, eyeballing Richard for signs of strain.

"Remember what that guy at the public defenders' office said last year when his client was sentenced to death in the gas chamber? As the judge read the sentence his client turned towards him and asked in hushed tones what came next. As I heard it, the public defender simply closed his briefcase before responding, 'I don't know about you . . . but I think I'll go have some lunch.' "

Shaw smiled briefly as soon as Richard realized that he was merely trying to make a joke, and then leaned forward conspiratorially.

"Seriously, Richard, this is just another case. Don't let it get to you. Lose your objectivity and you are a large step towards losing the case"

As Shaw walked off Richard leaned back in his chair and tried to empty his mind. On a business level he knew that his boss was right. To be truly effective he had to maintain a certain level of professional detachment, maintain the ability to honestly weigh the information gathered and estimate its impact on a jury and be able to tell the client when to compromise and settle or even just walk away even though the other side may be totally in the wrong. Justice in America simply worked that way. In his mind the logic was unassailable. In his gut he knew it could be so much bullshit when a wrong had been committed.

~~~~~

"You have a call on line two."
~~~~~

"Jo, I asked you to hold my calls. I've got too much to do before trial to be talking to everyone."

"I think you better take this one. Its your friend, Frank Walsh from the D.A.'s office. And he says it's pretty important."

Picking up the receiver Richard wondered what could be so important that his former law school classmate, and current advocate for the People of the State of California, would interrupt his pretrial preparation. Nothing possibly good, of that he was sure.

"Hey, Frank, what's up?"

"I'm okay, Rich. But I wanted to slip you the word before it became general knowledge . . ."

"Thanks. I'll owe you another. What have you got?"

"One of the vineyard workers from Winery Peak died this morning. The autopsy is tomorrow morning. The boss here said in our staff meeting that he may go for an indictment against your guy for manslaughter—or even homicide since the death took place in connection with an illegal activity."

"Shit, Frank, Dickson didn't do the dumping. That's why we are starting trial in three days against Wine House."

"Yea, well, that's what I told the old man. He thinks, though, that you filed the case to take the offensive just in case this very thing happened. He knows you have handled your fair share of criminal matters, both for our office and now for the bad guys, to know how that game is played. And he didn't believe me when I said you couldn't possibly be that smart."

"Thanks a lot, pal."

"Not a problem. But I did convince him to lay off until you had finished your trial. I know you don't need either the jury hearing the publicity or having your guy's cage rattled, and I told the old man that he would be better off seeing how your guy did before making a big play in the press. Hell, that's all that guy thinks about is the press . . . especially in an election year."

"Thanks, Frank. I really do owe ya one. But do me a favor and steer clear for now. I promise we will cooperate with any investigation after the trial."

"Oh don't worry old buddy . . . We who but merely live to serve the public know where you high-flying private lawyer types work."

"Ya, and your mother, pal. See ya and thanks."

Hanging up, Richard took a deep breath. When he first changed employment from the District Attorney's office to private practice the firm had assigned him to all criminal matters for their institutional clients in addition to assisting the more senior partners with the civil cases. These criminal matters included everything from driving under the influence to major penal violations involving company employees. He had been getting away from defending the criminal cases over the last several months because of the added stress involved. In civil cases a win or loss merely meant the exchange of money. A mere redistribution of wealth. He often cautioned his civil clients to look at a settlement from the sole perspective of whether it made sense to the client and to disregard whether it was a good deal for the other side. Litigation of principles is often the most expensive type of litigation, as even the "winner" usually takes home a bitter taste when it is all over. But at least both sides, winner and loser, gets to go home when a civil action is over. Criminal defense lawyers, on the other hand, take on a higher level of responsibility as the cases involve an individual's life or liberty. A heavy experience at best, and one that could be unbearable in the rare cases in which the client was actually innocent. He had been told in law school that the role of the criminal defense lawyer is to act essentially as a safeguard on the abuse of the police power in society. A check and balance, with the result that the criminal cases that actually go to trial often involved an accused who is actually guilty. Knowing this, however, rarely made it easier for Richard to represent someone who is facing a long period of time as a guest of the criminal justice system.

Standing up from his desk Richard walked over to the window to gather his thoughts. To tell Dickson of the conversation would be the morally correct thing to do, but the worst thing possible from the standpoint of Dickson's confidence and demeanor on the witness stand. All he could do is hold the information inside and pray that the District Attorney would not leak the story to an overly eager press over the weekend.

~ ~ ~ ~ ~

"Thanks for the call, Doc."

"No problem, Peter. I just didn't want to talk to you about this over the phone."

"Why? What did you find?"

Dickson came around to the side of the stainless steel counter where the veterinarian stood, a large glass vial in one hand and a clipboard with a well-marked chart in the other. The vial held a murky and foul smelling fluid that coated the glass as the veterinarian swirled the vial in a lazy circle to agitate the mixture. Although the autopsy on the chocolate Labrador had been finished earlier in the day, and the body parts all neatly disposed of in a heavy vinyl body bag, the room held on to the rank smell that comes from an open body cavity. Dickson tried hard not to notice the pungent odor. He had killed his share of deer and other game over the years, and had shared too often in the chore of cleaning and preparing the carcasses to be overly squeamish about dead animals. This smell, however, bothered him because of the knowledge that it was not merely from some dead animal, but from a companion and friend.

"Your dog died of chemical poisoning."

"What?!"

"That's right. When I opened the stomach I found fairly large quantities of organophosphates."

"What the hell?"

"Its an old type of insecticide derived from World War II nerve gas."

"I know what the hell it is," Dickson snapped, grabbing the clipboard out of his hand. "I know people who used to use it into the 50's before it was banned."

"Well, it sure isn't seen around nowadays."

"Of course not. It isn't used anymore because it has such a high acute toxicity. But that's not the problem."

"Why? What are you talking about?"

"That's the same stuff the Board of Health found in that old quarry."

~ ~ ~ ~ ~

Walking down the street Richard tried to collect his thoughts before returning towards the courthouse. The pressures of the last few weeks had run him ragged, and he knew that the strain was starting to show. Earlier that morning he had almost taken Jo's head off when she took too long in finding one of the trial briefs that he was to submit later in the day. He knew that he had overreacted, although he had later explained to Jo the risk of running afoul of the court's rule that all trial papers must be filed no later than the third business day before trial. To make matters worse, Jo had found the brief right on top of his desk, exactly where she had placed it yesterday afternoon as he had requested. At least she had refrained from saying anything, given her right to do so, but had merely handed it to him in her usual competent British manner.

Since it was 4:17 P.M., according to the clock tower in the Courthouse square, he decided to walk the documents over to the courthouse himself to file before the clerk's office closed at 5:00 P.M. His office was located in a building that sat four short blocks from the courthouse, close enough to walk over for the morning calendar, which was precisely why it had been selected by the firm. Usually the job of court runs, for filing papers and similar activities, were handled by a number of runners that the firm employed from the local junior college. He never could keep any of their names straight, as the turnover was quite high, fluctuating mostly in tandem with the beginning and end of the school semesters. Today, however, he decided to handle the filing himself on the assumption that the short walk in the open air would do him good and help to clear his mind from some of the crazy scenarios that he kept conjuring up from too little sleep and a too fertile imagination.

The decision turned out to have been a good one, with the weather cooperating as it can only in Northern California. The navy blue jacket, made of summer weight wool, lay lightly across his shoulders and after two blocks Richard felt like a new man. In fact, he felt actually buoyed, as if he was playing hooky from school, which was not a completely unexplainable feeling since he had not been outside at that time of the day in several weeks. With one block to go, and with plenty of time to spare, Richard impulsively turned into Cafe Sophia to grab a quick espresso to further clear his head. He opened the door and slid past the mixed bag of customers waiting in line. Some of whom were standing and staring at the selections written in different colors on a chalkboard behind the counter, others with heads buried in parts of several different newspapers while sipping the high octane mixture from thick ceramic mugs. With a short nod Richard gained the attention of one of the trendy looking young servers behind the counter and quietly stated his order. He pulled from his hip pocket a well worn eel skin wallet, received as a Christmas present several years ago from a former girlfriend who had not lasted long enough to have her picture included in one of the inside pockets. As he was counting out some bills to hand to the cashier he heard the bell on the door ring as the door was opened and his name being called out.

"Hello, Debby. How are you?" Richard responded to her greeting with faint enthusiasm, and tried to drum up some interest while hoping his coffee would arrive in a hurry. He felt that he could be polite at least, especially since she was pushing a baby carriage. A sure sign that a long conversation was coming. One that would require all sorts of questions about friends and family, goings on and doings that at the moment he cared nothing about. Fulfilling his unwanted prophecy, Debby stopped the carriage right in front of him, clearly expecting the proper sounds of amazement, including oos and ahhs, as if her baby was the first and only baby ever born—if not at least the most beautiful.

"Hey there, Richie." He winced visibly, hating the diminutive. "Whatcha doin?"

"Just getting by Debby. Just getting by. Got a trial starting Monday and wanted to stretch my legs."

Debby reached down into the carriage to straighten the receiving blanket, oblivious to his answer and anything else for that matter except her baby. And from her manner she clearly expected everyone else to feel the same way too.

"Would you like to hold her?"

Richard groaned inwardly and looked for the quickest way to extricate himself from the conversation. A typical bachelor, he was neither comfortable holding babies nor knew what to say about them when asked for his opinion by always too proud parents. As Debby held the baby out for him to hold he almost bit his lip. The little girl had to be the ugliest baby that he had ever seen. Not that he had seen too many up close. But from her splotched complexion to her overlarge ears there simply wasn't a thing that he could think to say that would sound like a compliment. He stalled, and made a guttural sound that he hoped passed for an appreciative murmur. The effort did not satisfy convention, and Debby continued to wait expectantly.

Knowing that he had to say something, in desperation Richard suddenly blurted out "Wellll . . . now THAT'S a baby!" causing an instant reaction in the form of a startled look from the child, followed by a quick intake of breath and an ear piercing shriek. Debby merely smiled and immediately hugged the little one to her chest. The baby, instinctively knowing that she was in the right location to feed, began to root against Debby's breasts. Debby cooed back. Richard, taking his cue, quickly muttered "nice to see ya . . ." and headed out the door. Debby hardly noticed he was gone.

Walking down the street back to the courthouse Richard downed his coffee in two long swallows and immediately felt raring to go. Even apart from the lift from the caffeine, just being out made him feel up and congratulated himself for his quick wit and selection of just the right thing to say to Debby and the baby. Taking the moment as an omen, and a good one at that, Richard marched up the courthouse stairs with renewed vigor and a relaxed but focused mind.

Back from the courthouse Richard stepped out of the office elevator and immediately spied Dickson pacing across the far side of the reception area. Dickson, in turn, looked across to see Richard and quickly closed the gap between them. The worried look on Dickson's face immediately wiped out any benefit Richard had obtained from his short walk. Without a word he motioned for them to head down the hall into Richard's office. Once inside Richard closed the door before turning to face Dickson.

"That look could only mean bad news. Well?"

Dickson did not answer immediately, but instead chewed his lip silently. With a short sigh he looked Richard directly into the eyes.

"When you hear what I have to say, I won't blame you for telling me that you don't want to continue with the case."

"Hold on, Peter." Richard raised his hands as if to ward off any further comments of that type. "Do not start making those type of decisions for me. Just tell me what is going on."

"My dogs somehow worked their way into my well house behind the garage. They chewed through some sacks that contained the same type of pesticides that the County found in those water samples from the quarry."

"What?!"

"Jesus, Richard. I haven't ever used that stuff. Not on the winery grapes, and certainly not on my own garden."

"Then how did it get in your well house?"

"I don't have any idea how those bags got there or how long they have been in there. One of my dogs died from having licked some off of one the bags. The other dog . . ."

"Wait, Peter. Hold on. Who knows about this?"

"The vet analyzed what the poison was. But I didn't find it in the well house until after I left the vet's."

Richard leaned forward, mind racing at the impact of Dickson's news and their limited options. All lawyers had heard at one time or another horror stories about other lawyers who had failed to turn evidence over to the other side when it was legitimately requested. One attorney had even been brought up on criminal charges for spoilation of evidence when it had come to light through a disgruntled assistant paralegal that the attorney had shredded some documents instead of producing the copies as requested. The fact that this attorney's client may have faced millions in potential damages had he produced the documents had hurt, rather than helped, his position. Although criminal charges had not been pursued, the State Bar had moved quickly and very publicly in terminating the attorney's license to practice. Richard's mind also flashed on the many one-sided discussions that he had endured with his grandfather over the concept of fighting a "fair" fight.

His grandfather had been an All-State collegiate wrestler in the 1920's, and lived by the credo that he would always treat his adversaries with respect and dignity, and never take advantage in a fight of someone who was down. Richard had grown up in awe of his grandfather, considered by most of his own contemporaries to be a larger than life figure even before his untimely death, and for the most part Richard tried to emulate him. On the issue of a "fair" fight, however, their philosophies had one day diverged. Growing up in a middle class California suburb did not lend itself to substantial exposure to the type of lifestyles endured by those living in the "across the track" households. Even the advent of busing in his high school did not create much diversity in the predominantly white school body. Disputes between the students were generally resolved out behind the gym or the practice field next to the running track. One student might "call" another "out," and they would march to the field often trailing a number of supporters and onlookers simply interested in watching a fight. The fights generally did not last long, and seemed to follow a loose pattern. A quick round of name calling or similar insults would occur first. Then one person or the other, seeing an opening, would charge in swinging. If a punch connected solidly the fight typically would end quickly. If the initial punches failed to land squarely the fight usually degenerated into a wrestling match as the protagonists maneuvered for position. Once one of the fighters pinned the other, the fight was typically over and the winner could stand and glare down at the vanquished before walking off to the praises of his old and new supporters. Although the rules were unspoken, fight after fight followed generally accepted notions of fairness. No one used knives or other weapons, and kicking was definitely considered to be a form of "dirty fighting."

Richard had experienced several fights of this type as he grew up, as both a participant and as an observer. He had won most of his battles and reached a point where he was rarely challenged. None of his fights had resulted in serious injury, with the worse consisting of a black eye and split lip to a boy who had deserved what he got, and he generally ignored the fights among the other students. But one afternoon Richard noticed a rowdier than normal group headed past the gym. He turned in that direction, and reached the fringe of the onlookers just as the first swings were ineffectually exchanged. One of the fighters was an athletic looking boy who had been in one of Richard's classes the prior semester, but he did not recognize the antagonist who looked several years older and stood with his back protected by four other boys.

This dispute clearly had a different tone and feel than the ones Richard was used to, as if the stakes were substantially higher. The boy from Richard's class moved to gain the early advantage and blood began to flow down the other boy's nose. The boy reached up to wipe his face and, seeing the bright red blood on the back of his hand, seemed to grow more agitated. Swinging first with his left as a feint, he allowed Richard's classmate to react with an attempted block before striking through to the now exposed throat with his right fist. Richard's classmate immediately went down to one knee, gasping for breath. As he was about to get back up, one of the older boys stepped forward and kicked him in the ribs with a steel toed boot. Richard jumped forward through the crowd, and tried to intercede before being grabbed from behind by one of the larger boys who pinned his arms to his sides. Richard struggled out of his grasp and whirled around to help his classmate, shouting that they were not fighting fairly. The older boy merely stood by until it was clear that the fight was over, and then spat contemptuously in Richard's direction before sneering that fights were made to be won and not fought fair.

Richard had discussed that fight with his grandfather, who had strongly suggested that Richard had done the right thing in insisting on a fair fight, and used the event to illustrate how in all aspects of life one should fight fairly regardless of what the other side may do. For a long time Richard had tried to reconcile his grandfather's beliefs with his own experiences before finally reaching in his own mind a compromise. As long as the other side fought fairly so would he—but one step out of line by his opponent and he would just worry about winning. He would always avoid doing anything that was illegal or unethical, but neither would he give out any breaks or favors. With these thoughts dancing through his head he reached a decision, and knew that the stakes had been unalterably changed. With this philosophy in mind Richard calmly turned to counsel Dickson.

"Peter, you have no choice but to get that stuff out of your well house now."

"What do you mean? Why should I have to act like I'm guilty of something? Shouldn't we tell someone that we found this stuff in my well house?"

"Look Peter. It's just too much of a coincidence for that stuff to 'suddenly' show up in your well house. Somebody must have put it there to be 'discovered', and I do not consider that to be "evidence" of anything other than the fact that someone is trying to screw you. Somebody who surely knows enough about what they are doing to avoid leaving anything behind to suggest that the stuff is not yours. Should any reporters catch wind of this before the trial starts you are dead in the water. If you didn't put it there its just not evidence."

Richard straightened up and tried to stretch away the stress that was quickly building up in his shoulders while Dickson mulled over his comments.

"Well, Richard, I wouldn't worry about the vet. He is an old friend of mine . . . he will keep quiet."

"Shit, Peter, if you don't get that stuff out of there now, and the District Attorney ties it to you, you are going to have a lot more to worry about than this civil trial."

Richard motioned for Dickson to get up and then practically pushed him towards the door, damning silently Dickson's stubborn streak. He almost had gone into his discussion with Frank, and he surely did not need to open that can on worms now.

"Just trust me on this, Peter. You hired me for my advice. Now is the time when you should be smart enough to take what you have been paying me for."

"All right, Counselor. And how do you suggest I get rid of two large sacks of highly toxic chemicals?"

"In any way that can be done quietly. And quickly."

Promising to call as soon as the job was finished, Dickson promptly left the office.

~ ~ ~ ~ ~

Like most small town police departments, the pace at the City of Napa Police Department is slow and regular, not hectic from chronic understaffing or continuous crime sprees. With a low crime rate for serious offenses, the focus of the tiny police force reflected a tendency to concentrate on the need for traffic control, brought on by the ever-expanding tourist groups thirsty to taste the wares of the multitude of local wineries. During the spring and summer months the main stretch of road through town bottles up at each of the three stoplights, and particularly on late weekend afternoons patrol cars are in force to keep an eye on the few tourists whose driving reflects having consumed more than their fair share of samples.

Sergeant Ronald Bondi had been a member of the force for twenty-seven years. Although he had enough years under his belt to request any assignment, he especially liked to head the weekend command desk. Apart from the fact that he would not be interrupted by the Lieutenant, whom Bondi thought was an alright guy if he didn't always want to talk about golf as if were a religion, Bondi truly liked to be available to handle the frequent calls from weekend visitors needing information. He was proud of his city and liked to think of himself as one of its frontline goodwill ambassadors.

Bondi's family had been living in the Napa area for almost ninety years, since his great-grandfather had immigrated to the United States at the turn of the century. Unlike many immigrants to California, who spent years living on the east coast before making the journey west, his great-grandfather had known exactly where he was headed the moment his feet hit the soil of the eastern seaboard. With a small stake of savings, hoarded from years of working for others doing jobs he could barely stand, he managed to find a small parcel of fertile land to farm in the Napa Valley. The chalky soil was perfect for grape vines, and he quickly began the process of planting vines and developing a modest winery. The initial vision took him almost a decade to complete, and by then he had six boys who would grow to help him expand the operation eventually into a decent producer of hearty red table wines. Along with several other local families of Italian descent, Bondi's family had dominated the local wine industry until the years of prohibition had forced them to turn to other endeavors while the banks took back farmlands and vineyards that could not support their mortgages on the sale of medicinal wines and unfermented grape juice. As a result, Bondi's family had developed a well ingrained dislike and distrust of financial institutions and viewed as an extension of those faceless entities the large corporate wineries who now owned under one roof many of the old family holdings.

As long as he could remember Bondi had been told by his elders, who tried to wear the most serious of expressions, that winemaking causes a subtle change in the body's chemistry. According to his late grandfather, a proud man who had spent a lifetime studying the art and industry of winemaking, after a while the veins of a true winemaker no longer carry just blood, but also a rich mixture of cabernets, merlots and zinfindels. Bondi knew that his family was no different. Slowly over the years after prohibition they had acquired an acre here, some farmland there, until enough had been amassed to once again operate as an acceptable commercial vineyard. There were insufficient jobs in the downsized operation to employ all of the patriarch's progeny, and Bondi had entered the police academy upon graduating with a degree in criminal science from Sonoma State College. He had never considered working somewhere other than Napa, and a combination of his family background and a naturally outgoing personality ensured that over the years he would come to know almost everyone in the industry including Dickson. So when the phone call had come in from an unknown junior investigator at the Sacramento office of the E.P.A., strongly advising of the type of action that the Napa Police Department should be taking immediately in connection with the workup into the illegal aspects of the chemicals being dumped, Bondi did not feel any ethical, legal or moral impediment to calling Richard and advising him that a search of Dickson's house was about to take place. And, after agreeing with Richard's suggestion that it might be best if he would personally handle the investigation, grabbed his hat and cheerfully headed out the door.

~ ~ ~ ~ ~

"I think that you have some very well connected 'friends'."

Bondi dryly called out this observation by way of greeting as Richard yanked himself out of the driver's seat. Bondi had arrived five minutes earlier and had waited outside by his patrol car until Richard had pulled his truck up to the carport at Dickson's house. Two of his uniformed officers had already commenced a walk around the yard, noting anything that looked out of place. Richard watched the officers as they disappeared around the corner of the house towards the rear yard and, being ever the lawyer, decided to appear ignorant of Bondi's ominous comment in the hopes of getting more information.

"What's this all about, Ron? Not that I don't appreciate the call."

"It's not everyday the E.P.A. cares enough about a local matter to request the direct involvement of a local police investigations unit."

"What do you mean by that?"

Richard cleared his mind to concentrate on Bondi's comments.

"What 'investigations unit'? When you called I assumed that this search was at the request of the District Attorney's office."

"Oh, don't worry, they should be joining us here shortly."

Bondi paused and walked Richard towards the rear yard where he could watch his officers at work.

"But the D.A. wasn't the one who suggested this friendly little get together. Someone who identified himself as an investigator at the E.P.A. called—completely out of the blue—and said that we should be able to find information here connecting Dr. Dickson to the situation at Winery Peak."

Richard nodded and reached inside his coat pocket for a pen and piece of paper. On the paper he wrote the word "situation" and then placed the paper back into his pocket. It seemed that the people that were friendly to either Dickson or himself referred to what had happened at the quarry as a "situation." In contrast, those people that wanted to hold Dickson responsible for what had happened used the phrase "illegal chemicals" or some other type of pejorative term. Because the jury would be receiving almost all of the information audibly, he would have to be very careful in his word choice at trial to make sure his created the proper picture in the jury's mind. While he made his note, Bondi was respectful enough to make only one covert glance at what Richard had scrawled down on the pad, but was unable to read the scrawl from his upside-down perspective.

"Where is Dr. Dickson?" Richard asked, aware that Dickson's truck was gone and hoping that Dickson had figured out what to do with the bags of chemicals. "And what information is the E.P.A. talking about?"

"I don't know and he didn't say. And I don't like being told what to do by some junior achiever with the Feds who thinks he is some kind of 'super-cop'. Especially where a standup guy like Dr. Dickson is concerned."

"Thanks, Ron. I'll let him know you said that. He could use some moral support."

"No problem. My family has known him too long for me to believe that he would have done what they say he did. A man like that . . . Well, even if he isn't Italian, he has too much respect for the vines, the grapes, to poison the land like that."

"And I just hope that I can get twelve jurors like you."

The two uniformed officers returned to the front of the house as Frank Walsh pulled up in a tan four door sedan that had been assigned to him on the anniversary of his second year with the Napa County District Attorney's Office. He and Richard often joked about the car, especially in light of Frank's often stated goal in their law school days of driving a red Mercedes 450 SEL to court. But one look at Frank's face through the windshield convinced Richard that today would not be a good day to further razz him about his choice of transportation. Even Bondi straightened up, and withheld all further comment until Frank and the uniformed officers joined them in the center of the driveway.

"Nothing unusual in the carport, the back porch or the well house."

The senior uniformed officer made her report to Bondi in clipped sentences and then waited, her manner polished and professional. Richard squinted at the officer to control his nervousness at the nature of the police search, and then shifted his attention to his old classmate.

"I don't know what's going on, Frank. And I don't like the idea that someone is trying to screw with my trial preparation or my client's mind by phoning in a bogus search request."

Frank gave Richard a withering look.

"Don't even start with me. There isn't anybody here right now that is against you or your client. We all got our problems and I do not need you starting to stand on a goddamn soapbox."

"I just need to get this trial over without any shenanigans. Then, as I promised already, I will make sure that Dr. Dickson cooperates with you fully to get to the bottom of this entire mess."

Frank waved Bondi and the officers off and taking Richard by the arm walked him to the edge of the gravel driveway.

"Richard, if it is any help to your piece of mind, I think that this 'tip' or whatever from the E.P.A. makes your guy's position even more believable."

"How so?"

"I am starting to agree with your half baked idea that Dickson would not be getting all of this attention unless something else was up. But you just make sure you get this trial started next week. I don't know how long I can keep my publicity hungry boss happy."

They turned back towards their cars and the officers. Bondi waited until the gap had closed and then walked forward to join them. The two uniformed officers stood at a respectful distance, waiting for further orders.

"Well, Frank, I guess we are at your disposal."

While Bondi was not, technically, under Frank's authority during investigations, he knew how to diplomatically handle the chain of authority situation. And Frank knew that as well.

"Thanks, Ron. I think we better get out of here before Richard starts to use us as a reason for having such a hard time next week." Turning to Richard he continued. "Seriously, though, if you need any 'unofficial' help this weekend give me a call." And with a quick handshake he was back in his car and gone.

The dust kicked up from the gravel by Frank's car hung in the stillness of the air as Richard considered Frank's remark about negative pretrial publicity. One way to unfairly skew the results of the trial would involve convincing the press to air pieces negative to Dickson, such as a report on the search of his house. Even though nothing was found, the story hungry reporters would merely report the fact of the "raid" and let the viewers draw their own, generally negative, conclusions. And although he couldn't stop the press from reporting on what had already taken place, he could at least ask Judge Marwick to issue a gag order to prevent Wine House from issuing any further statements that would add further fuel to the fire.

Waving his goodbyes to Bondi and the other officers Richard headed back to his office. First he had to prepare a short written brief and then advise Stucky that he would be meeting with Judge Marwick that afternoon.

~ ~ ~ ~ ~

"Well, Mr. Magnus, I hope you aren't planning on making it a habit on coming down to my courthouse on such short notice to Mr. Stucky."

"With the trial to start Monday, your Honor, operating on such shortened notice really shouldn't be a continuing problem."

"All right, all right. Just tell me what is so important."

"I would like to have you issue an order that all parties refrain from making any statements to the press until after the trial is over."

The Judge looked over at Stucky and cocked a bushy gray eyebrow in anticipation of an explosion of protest. Stucky, however, had learned his lesson and decided to wait in silence until Richard had finished his request. Pleased that there would be no inappropriate interruption, the Judge turned back to Richard.

"And may I know why you think that it is so important to restrain the First Amendment rights of Mr. Stucky's client?"

"I have reason to believe that someone at Wine House is trying to set Dr. Dickson up." Before Stucky could come unglued at that accusation Richard hastily continued. "Although I don't have any reason to believe that Mr. Stucky personally knew anything about what is going on."

"I would hope you can do more than tell me that you 'have reason to believe' that the Defendant may be doing something that it should not. If you have some verifiable basis for this serious charge . . . well, then, I am willing to entertain your request."

"I will need some time to pull something more formal together Judge . . ."

"Look, Richard," Judge Marwick interrupted in a friendly tone and with a pointed glance at Stucky. "No one wants to do anything to taint the trial. I know Mr. Stucky will tell his client to use good judgment. And in case you can put something together that supports a formal order I am assigning this specific request to be heard by retired Judge McDonald. You have until tomorrow morning to make your showing directly to him. He can then make his recommendation to me for a final order."

Stucky began to stand, but did not get a chance to speak before the Judge continued.

"There is nothing for you to add, Mr. Stucky. Unless you would like me to grant Mr. Magnus' request right now?"

Stucky, not willing to further cross the Judge, mutely nodded his head from side to side.

~~~~~

The videotape library at Channel 3 was extensive, filling a large storage facility separate from the station's main studio building. Wolfe had listened cautiously to Richard's request for help and, finding an opportunity for the station, had bar-
~~~~~

tered the use of the library in exchange for an exclusive post-trial interview with Dickson. Which would take place, Richard promised, regardless of the outcome of the trial.

The library held more than the camera footage that was actually televised. Raw footage from remote interviews and press conferences were also stored in the reels and cassettes that lined the dusty shelves that lined the wall from floor to ceiling. Richard felt that he would obtain the best result from Judge McDonald, in his effort to stop Wine House's media manipulation, if he could put together a chronological history of the unusually heavy press coverage that the case had already generated. To that end he had made his deal with Wolfe and sent Gayle to the library to pull all applicable tapes. She could then review the applicable portions and select the most inflammatory footage, to maximize the impact of his application to the Judge. The rest of the coverage would not be actually shown to the Judge, but would be identified in the written chronological listing that Richard would present in support of his application.

For three hours Gayle cross-referenced the station's index of footage against the material that actually appeared on the shelf. The process took longer than she anticipated, as the station did not reference the unused footage in its computerized database, but haphazardly indexed the entries in an old black ledger. The extensive effort was rewarded with a disappointingly small pile of four cassettes. The incident at Winery Peak had probably generated more space in the newspapers, Gayle thought, and was glad that Terri had agreed to take that part of the workup. Crossing the last line item off of her photocopies of the station's index, Gayle gladly arched her stiffening shoulders, grabbed the pile of tapes and headed back to the office to screen them with Richard.

~ ~ ~ ~ ~

Terri had beaten Gayle back to the office with the results of her search, so that on Gayle's arrival she was waved to one of the empty chairs while Richard finished his review of the newspaper clippings. With each one he would first circle the date and then glance briefly through the text. Some of the articles went in a pile to be included in the material to be sent to the Judge. The rest were simply tossed on the floor. The rejects were few, however, as Terri knew from long experience what to pull when making the original selection. Gayle did not have to wait long. Richard of necessity had to move fast. He still had a lot to do in the two days before the start of trial, and the task in front of him was distracting him from that end.

"What you got?"

"Not much, Richard. The station did not pay much attention after the news broke. One filler piece on the testing equipment at the quarry, one 'investigative' piece on the use of pesticides on grapes, the Winery Peak press conference and the announcement you engineered about the filing of our lawsuit."

"Let's look at that press conference tape. I still have the copy I made on the DVD-R of the 'interview' that Peter gave to Martinez at Channel 6 last spring went this whole thing started. We can look at that next."

They walked in silence from his office down the hall to the main conference room. Inside the room, hidden behind flush mounted wall panels, sat a video center that would make any technician envious. Included in the setup were three 32-inch color monitors that dominated the wall, flanked by two digital recorders, a dubbing unit and an editing display. As Gayle took a seat in one of the plush leather conference chairs Richard placed the first DVD in the console. Too tense to sit still, Richard ignored the remote control unit and continued to stand next to the wall unit after punching the play button. The screen stayed gray blank for a minute before the sound came tumbling out of the two oversized speakers, positioned at the opposite end of the conference room. A jumble of voices came out, then faded to background noise as the sound technician's count test took over. "This must be the unedited version."

Gayle added her comment unnecessarily as they waited and Richard did not bother to answer. Then, with sharp clarity, the press conference was called to order. Richard stepped back from the wall and sat in one of the chairs. He stared intently at the center monitor while the conference proceeded onscreen, trying to focus his mind on how the recording could best be used. He then froze, eyes wide at the screen. Grabbing for the remote Richard put the recording on pause and stared incredulously.

"What? What do you see?"

Gayle thought that she had been looking hard at the screen, but had seen nothing that justified Richard's startled reaction.

"See that guy who just asked the question about Dickson?"

"Yeah . . ." she answered hesitantly, trying to remember what the man on the screen had just said before the recording was paused and then thinking over the question in her mind. "It did not sound like he really cared what the answer was."

"I've seen him before."

"Where?"

"Remember when I told you about the deposition in New York? He was the guy in Alexander's office."

"You mean the guy that they wouldn't identify during the deposition?"

"That's the one."

Richard thought back to the deposition. He had asked Alexander to state the name of the businessman had been conferring with Alexander and Stucky in Alexander's office. Alexander had hesitated while looking very uncomfortable, and had glanced over at Stucky for support. Stucky filled the silence by objecting that Alexander's business associations were irrelevant to the case. Richard pressed the issue, turning to Alexander for a response. Stucky responded in his place by instructing Alexander not to answer the question. Richard had countered the instruction by arguing that the name of an individual was not privileged information.

Stucky had merely shrugged his shoulders, and told him to move on and ask the next question. Too far from the Napa courts to do anything about the stalemate at the time, Richard had dropped the issue in favor of examining Alexander on other areas. Once the deposition was over more important problems vied for his attention and, until now, he had forgotten about the dispute.

"We may have something here. If this guy is somehow working for or with Wine House on this thing, and it looks like he is, then we may be able to show an attempt to use Dickson as more than just a fall guy for some corporate screw-up."

"What are you getting at?"

"Wine House is not going to go to all the trouble of putting a shill at a press conference unless someone is worried about more than getting caught with their corporate pants down. There has to be something larger than this that Wine House is trying to direct attention from."

Richard's mind began to crank, taking the jumble of information and trying to place it in logical order. Along with the strange phone call and the bags of chemicals that had surfaced at Dickson's well house, the press conference setup convinced him that Dickson had nothing to do with the chemicals at the quarry. The unfortunate problem was the sorry truth that this information would never be heard by the jury, as it created too many tangential questions that would surely confuse the issue of the wrongful treatment of Dickson. At least he could follow-up with this lead, and see if it could turn into something to present during the trial.

"Look, Gayle, get a still photo of the guy off the recording and give it to Terri to use to identify this guy. And Terri, I need you to bust ass. We don't have much time to hit him with a subpoena to appear at trial."

CHAPTER EIGHT

RETIRED JUDGE DENNIS MCDONALD was a fixture at the Napa County Courthouse. He had been appointed to the bench many years before by some long forgotten governor, and had remained an active judge for as long as any of the courthouse regulars could remember. Which was too long, according to many attorneys who, in the last few years, had experienced the misfortune of having their disputes referred to his attention for resolution. Although everyone was courteous to his face, his detractors now referred to him derisively as "Old McDonald".

In another time, and another place, McDonald's wisdom and legal acumen had been well respected and widely sought out. After graduating from Yale Law School near the top of his class, he had quickly tired of the wood-paneled benevolence that permeated the legal establishment on the eastern seaboard and had instead sought his fame and fortune in the less civilized west. Several years practicing law in the small city of prewar San Francisco left him bored and disheartened of the prospect of reaching his goal of participating in more of a frontier style, and less polished type, of justice. When friends had suggested that the area around the headlands of the Sonoma coast would offer more of the adventure that he was seeking, little time had been wasted in packing his belongings to head up the coast.

A heightened ability for sharp legal reckoning, coupled with a willingness to stand a round of whiskeys, had made his election to the bench the surest political bet west of Tammany Hall. From there the decades seemed to just roll by. And though the forces of time and postwar population growth radically shaped and changed the San Francisco Bay Area, Judge McDonald continued to preside and hand down decisions based on the same public policies and ideals that existed when he first was sworn as a judicial officer. Although the knowledge that a judge existed who still "knew the meaning of justice" was heartening to some, an increasingly growing and vocal minority had their concerns satisfied when Judge McDonald was finally persuaded to retire.

To obtain his consent to retirement, and avoid a political battle wanted by none, Judge McDonald had been asked to assume the role of "senior status" and to continue to handle special overflow assignments from the Presiding Judge. These assignments included disputes that revolved around the ability of parties to conduct discovery into the positions held by their adversaries, and to assist in settlement negotiations before trial. Although the assignments never took more than a few hours a week, they were enough to satisfy McDonald's sizable ego as well as his desire to stay involved in the legal system.

Like most of the lawyers that practiced on a regular and ongoing basis in Napa, Richard had mixed emotions concerning the continued use of Judge McDonald. On the one hand, McDonald was far more flexible in his hours and availability than the active judges on the Superior Court who were, after all, underpaid civil servants and could not be fairly expected to put in large amounts of unpaid overtime. On the other hand, McDonald was draconian in his views on discovery, having practiced at a time when lawyers first learned about their opponents' cases while listening to opposing counsel make their opening presentation to the jury. He had no real choice in the matter now, however, as the timing on his request and the unavailability of any other judges made McDonald better than nothing. With these thoughts in mind Richard waited outside the courthouse for McDonald to arrive. Around him the square was empty and quiet, as befitting a lazy Saturday. Because of the limitations on his time, he had barely reviewed and not corrected or changed the memorandum that Gayle had finally put together towards midnight the night before. She had also edited together segments of the video recordings into a five minute presentation that Richard would show on the video equipment that still sat in his car.

"Good morning, Mr. Magnus."

Richard whirled around to see Stucky's young associate, a recent Stanford Law School graduate who had been peppering Richard throughout the last five weeks with various requests for information. The requests, though superficially seeking legitimate information, were propounded with the primary goal of keeping Richard too busy to work up his own portion of the case. A goal that had not succeeded as Richard had merely assigned to Gayle the task of responding in his place.

"Well, Roger . . . I see that you finally get to do more than merely carry Patrick's bags."

Richard found it dryly amusing to be greeted as "Mr." by someone only a few years younger than himself, but he couldn't help but needle Roger, especially after getting only four hours sleep the night before.

"Don't tell me that you guys are actually going to oppose this request?"

"Well, Mr. Magnus, if we on behalf of Wine House truly understood the reasons and rationale behind your request, we could see if an accommodation would be possible or appropriate."

Richard turned away, disgusted with the sheer amount of words used to pitch so little bullshit. Too bad Roger wasn't trying the case before the jury instead of Stucky, Richard thought, as they wouldn't understand a point he was trying to make. Richard knew, however, that Stucky was much savvier than Roger and understood how to modify the words and phrases used during trial to match the type of jurors selected. Stucky was also smart enough to have a client with a substantial enough financial strength to be able to afford several lawyers on one case. This allowed Stucky the luxury, compared to Richard, of having his associate handle this hearing when time was at its most precious. While Richard was fighting what many would consider a minor and distracting skirmish, Stucky would be able to concentrate on big picture issues. But to Richard, and to those who largely practice in small communities throughout rural California, control of adverse press coverage from the local papers immediately before and during a long trial is critical. No matter how many times the trial judge may admonish the jurors to refrain from talking to anyone about the case before being told to deliberate amongst themselves, practical experience had long established that most people who sit on a jury discuss the case as soon as being selected to serve. If not with their friends or fellow jurors, then at least with their husbands and wives. Even good people who would otherwise follow the judge's admonition had different opinions, shaped by their own experiences and perceptions. Richard merely wanted to avoid the possibility that Wine House would continue its attempts to shape those opinions improperly through the press.

They continued to stand together yet apart in the sunshine in front of the courthouse for another interminable fifteen minutes. Neither bothered to say anything more, as Richard felt that he could accomplish nothing by engaging in further conversation with someone who Stucky himself considered to be but a lackey. To alleviate his tension, Richard began pacing back and forth between the sidewalk and the main entrance to the courthouse. Counting first the number of cracks in the concrete sidewalk and then the number of steps he could take without seeing a crack, he let his mind relax and wander. Anything to keep his thoughts from dwelling on the use he could otherwise make of the time he was wasting here waiting for McDonald to show up. Anything but the present, Richard thought as he again glanced at his watch, or he would soon go out of his mind with the aggravation of waiting. Finally, the shuffling appearance of Judge McDonald a block away drove from his mind all thoughts other than the need for this specific hearing and he mentally girded for immediate battle.

~~~~~
~~~~~

The darkroom was an oppressively tiny cubicle of a room, attached as an add-on to the rest of the building by a narrow windowless corridor. In the winter it was heated by a small kerosene fired stove that had to be vented to the outside through a hole hacked out of the gypsum wallboard long ago with a hand held axe. Without the heat from the stove the toner and wash used to fix the prints would be useless in the winter cold. In the summer the stove had to be physically moved to one side and replaced with a shallow electric fan which spun the stale air around and out of the hole, creating with the draft a false but welcome impression of fresh air. But with all of the physical limitations on comfort, it served its purpose well enough by allowing private onsite development of often sensitive film from Terri's inquisitive camera.

Terri achingly arched her back and straightened up from the wide metal trays that contained the pungent mix of chemical agents used in the developing process. Shrugging her shoulders to relieve the cramp that had developed over the last half hour, she again wondered whether her continued insistence on using film over digital was simply too Luddite. Reaching down she picked up the enlarged negative taken from a portion of the original tape from the press conference recording. She desperately wanted a smoke, could feel the nicotine craving begin to tighten in her chest, but had to wait until she was clear of the chemicals. Weariness made the red light dangling from the overhead fixture seem too low, and she kept having to duck her head lest she bump it as she worked.

For three hours she had been trying to glean any information from the videotape that would indicate the identity of the mysterious stranger. She had been sure, before starting the process, that the task would be an easy one. Taking information off of an enlargement from a videotape did not require any special expertise, as long as there was information to locate. First she would make a reverse negative from the tape, and then use the negative to make a series of blow-ups. The blown up prints would be analyzed for the sought after information, with the interesting portion of the print enlarged again. She even had a digital enhancer to recreate through computer-generated digital enhancements portions of the picture that did not translate well to the expanded version. And on occasion had further boasted that she could recreate any image regardless of the quality of the original print, with the sole catch that there had to be something, anything, on the negative which to use as the basis for enlargement and enhancement.

Too many hours into the process went by without any success. She was beginning to wonder whether there was anything significant to enhance. Methodical as always, Terri had first looked at whether the stranger was holding something that would carry his name. But he was not carrying any documents, notepad or a briefcase. She next looked for his press pass. The passes generally were in the form of a white rectangle that announced the name of the trade publication followed by the name of the participant, sealed in clear plastic with a metal clip attached. Nothing appeared clipped to the front pocket or the lapel of his sports jacket in the places usually favored by the older reporters for displaying their press passes. Nothing was attached to the belt in the manner of fashion favored by younger reporters trying to look cool. Further time was spent, to no avail, as she searched the tape for the clean shots of him standing against the crowd with his jacket opened, in the hope that he clipped the small white pass to his shirt pocket. Or anywhere else that would provide a clean shot of the face of the pass.

For a moment she thought that she had something to go on. As he stood up against the crowd the front of his jacket opened and parted to reveal a contrasting square of color against the shiny gray inside jacket lining. With renewed vigor she hastily created the negative and then the blowups. But she was quickly disappointed with the realization that the square of color merely identified the owner as one of the few hundred thousand who consider themselves upper crust individuals simply because they wear clothes designed by Ralph Lauren. “Goddamn clothes horse,” Terri muttered in disgust and tossed the blowup on top of a discouragingly large stack of rejects.

With disappointment Terri shut off the videotape machine and grabbed a crumpled pack of smokes from the inside pocket of her non-designer jacket. Careful to first check that the negatives were safe and the chemicals stored, she opened the darkroom door and headed down the corridor to the fresher air of the adjoining office.

"Any luck?"

Terri's secretary looked up hopefully from her typing as Terri entered the office.

"Nope."

"What happened?"

"Nothing. They didn't even bother to give him even a bogus press pass. He must have just walked in the conference room at the last moment. The tape doesn't show him talking to anyone before the conference started, and he only asked that one damn question before taking off as soon as the conference was over."

"What did he look like?'

"Cute as hell. I've got to admit that. Even if he does dress a little too fancy for my tastes."

"What do you mean?"

"One of those Polo guys. You know. Ralph Lauren. Expensive country casual . . ."

"And . . . ?"

Terri's secretary looked expectantly at her boss, who had stopped talking in mid-sentence. This type of one sided conversation was not unusual. Terri often went straight from an intense conversation into solo travel to another universe when an idea struck her.

"Did you think of something?"

"Goddamn right. It isn't likely that he would be wearing a three hundred dollar sport coat and pricey slacks without wearing a Polo shirt."

"So?"

"So, when you show off by wearing a Polo shirt there's a good chance that it's a monogrammed Polo shirt. I bet his damn initials will be monogrammed right over his shirt pocket."

Terri took one last long drag that burned through half of the cigarette before rubbing the ash tipped end against the side of the gray metal wastebasket. That same drag, a moment later, came back out as a thin trail of blue gray smoke that followed Terri as she went down the hall and into the darkroom. Moments later found her with the videotape machine on, all thoughts in favor of her hunch playing out successfully. With great delicacy and renewed interest Terri analyzed the tape, frame by painstakingly slow frame, where the camera had focused on the area that happened to include the stranger. Paying special attention to the frame numbers previously noted on a now slightly soiled piece of paper, including the precise number of frames that contained shots of his shirt where exposed by the unbuttoned coat, she slowly eliminated the possibilities. "Gotcha . . ." Terri muttered to herself with satisfaction when the tape displayed a contrasting mark set somewhat indistinctly above the shirt pocket.

Again Terri began the careful process of preparing the reverse negatives from the tape. This time her efforts reflected the additional energy that always seems to appear when the answer is near. The negatives took a little time to finish, and Terri then jumped immediately into the process of preparing the blowups and placing then into the chemical bath. While they were floating in the metal trays she leaned back against the workbench for a moment to relax, and thought with satisfaction about the bonus she could legitimately ask from Richard for such keen detective work.

The buzz from the small oven timer used to time the processing brought her out of the quiet reverie. She reached down with great expectation to pick the enlarged print out of the chemical bath. Although still somewhat indistinct, it confirmed her read of the tape. There definitely was some type of marking over the shirt pocket. One that still had to be enhanced digitally to make out the individual initials. With care she wiped the remaining chemical wash off of the print and placed it on the glass of the digital enhancer. Ten minutes later the enhanced print slid out of the computer into Terri's eager hands. Her eyes squinted to focus on the print, then widened.

"Shit, shit, shit . . ." she breathed through clenched teeth. For the mark above the pocket had materialized into a small rider on horseback, polo mallet in hand. The trademark for the Polo line of clothes. And no initials after all.

~ ~ ~ ~ ~

"Mr. Magnus. Good afternoon."

"Good afternoon, your Honor."

Richard was both pleased that Judge McDonald recognized him, and still somewhat put out with the Judge's unwillingness to meet with them earlier in the morning. "No, no, Mr. Magnus," the Judge had said the day before when Richard had telephoned after leaving Judge Marwick's chambers to set a time for the meeting. "I'm afraid that I have to prepare for the judging of the annual camellia festival. Has to be around the noon hour." Not much that Richard could do about it, except press upon the Judge the need to meet as soon as possible. In return the Judge promised to come over to the courthouse straight after the judging was over, " . . . around 11:30 or so."

Forcing a smile he did not feel, Richard tried to wait patiently while the Judge fumbled in his briefcase for his copy of the keys to the courthouse. With great deliberation of movement, that reflected the infirmities of age more than anything else, the keys were produced. They were an awesome collection on a large steel ring. Little wonder, thought Richard tangentially, that he carries them in his briefcase. In due course the proper key was selected from the jangling ring, matched to the lock, and the three of them walked into the great hall of the ground floor of the courthouse. The courthouse was quiet but for their footsteps off of the faux marble tiles, which echoed up from the ground floor to bounce against the open rotunda.

Even though Judge McDonald no longer rated the privilege of being assigned to his own courtroom and chambers, especially given the shortness of available space for full time judges, he had taken over one of the small conference rooms on the ground floor and turned it into his own personal office. The room was small and had window frames that had been painted so many times with industrial strength white paint that it was now quite impossible to open the windows. But, as the Judge often liked to joke, ". . . it's home."

"All right, Richard," the Judge began as he maneuvered his ample frame into the high-backed chair behind the weathered desk, "if I correctly remember what you said over the phone yesterday, you are going to begin trial over whether your client had the right to dump toxic waste into the old quarry east of Highway 29. Can't say I think you have much reason to be suing about that."

"No, your Honor. That is not what the case is about."

Shit, thought Richard, this guy doesn't have a clue what's going on and can't even remember what he is told from one day to the next. Worse yet, Roger sat smugly across the room enjoying the Judge's misperception. He had to just ignore Roger and get on with it.

"We are suing Wine House for terminating Dr. Dickson wrongfully. Wine House has claimed that it was justified in terminating Dr. Dickson based on its unfounded claim that he had some involvement with the chemicals found in the old quarry."

"All right then, why don't you tell me what today's hearing is all about."

"Simple, your Honor."

Richard raised his voice and spoke louder than usual. He could not tell from this vantage point whether the Judge had remembered to wear his hearing aid. Michael had mentioned that he tended to forget to bring the small device, and in fact kept insisting that there was nothing wrong with his hearing. Richard had to be careful, as he remembered how the Judge had angrily treated one of Richard's colleagues who had suggested politely that the Judge had misunderstood an argument because he could not completely hear the attorneys voice their positions.

"We want to make sure that our trial beginning Monday goes on fairly. By that I mean an order telling the parties not to argue their cases in the press before or during the trial."

"Well, Richard, if I understand you correctly, you want me to prevent your opponent from exercising his constitutional right to free speech."

"No, your Honor, that's not it at all."

The response came through clenched teeth. Richard desperately held back from snapping out the words, knowing that the accumulated lack of sleep was beginning to stretch his nerves, but he was disturbed and angry at the Judge's complete lack of understanding. Now was no time to be a shrinking violet, and pushing the issue was his only realistic option.

"There is no First Amendment issue at stake, none at all. We just want to make sure that the jury does not begin to form its opinions before they fairly hear all of the evidence—not rumor and misinformation—and are told to deliberate. And I have brought a short video to show you the types of publicity stunts that Wine House has tried to pull."

The Judge frowned, waved off the offer to show the video and turned to Roger, who had been sitting quietly, almost beatifically, during the exchange.

"Well, young man. You having been waiting very politely. What do you think."

Give me a goddamn break, Richard said to himself. Mr. Sweet and Innocent.

"Thank you, your Honor."

Roger pulled a sheet of paper from a manila file and glanced quickly at his notes.

"I agree with you completely. There are fundamental First Amendment issues at stake. Prior restraint and censorship. Not that Wine House intends to try its case in the press. Wine House is confident of its case and that a jury will reach the proper result. We just don't think what Mr. Magnus is trying to do to our Constitutional rights is correct."

Give me a double goddamn break, Richard said to himself. Must be awful crowded in there with your head up your ass. He could not simply sit there quietly while Roger wrapped himself and Wine House in the flag.

"Look, your Honor." Richard interjected. "There is no 'prior restraint' or any other constitutional problem here. I just want to make sure that we can pick a jury that does not have preconceived notions about the case."

"Well, Richard, I agree that I don't need to address the constitutional issues here. I think that you are a capable enough attorney to deal with any negative press—should it even happen. Although . . ." turning in his seat to face Roger as well as Richard, "I think that everyone here knows better than to make inopportune statements to the press. Your request, Richard, is denied."

Richard stared at McDonald to voice with his eyes the keen displeasure he felt at the decision. But he knew that nothing more would change McDonald's mind and it was better not to say anything now in anger or frustration that would come back to haunt him should he appear again before McDonald. Without a word he stood to face the Judge, and forced himself to state before leaving the cramped office the closing comment that all attorneys, winning or losing, must ritualistically say out of professional courtesy at the close of a hearing.

"Thank you, your Honor."

~ ~ ~ ~ ~

The iron circled back slowly until it reached the end of the arc. It then hung motionless for the smallest fraction of a second before smoothly dropping forward with ever increasing speed. As the tip reached the bottom of the arc it seemed to hesitate briefly, an illusion caused by the fact that the tip actually jumped forward in increased speed for the carry through. Passing through the object of its intention, the iron continued forward and then upwards and outwards before slowing at a point that was almost a full circle from the point of its beginning.

"Damn, damn and double damn."

Richard watched the range ball fly forward on a straight line for the first hundred yards before hooking savagely to disappear with a splash into the pond that bordered the driving range. Dickson smiled and turned away lest Richard think Dickson was laughing at his attempts. Not that Dickson's stroke was any better. Richard would have described Dickson's game as the "army method" of playing golf. "Left, right, left, right." First a hook, then a slice. Another hook, another slice. One thing was certain. They had both needed time outdoors and away from the case. At least for a few hours to cool off their minds and get their bearings back. And nothing was better for that purpose than golf. Even if they just had time for a bucket of balls on the driving range, no one, according to Richard, could concentrate on anything else when that little dimpled white ball is sitting there laughing at you.

Dickson looked around at the other golfers that were beginning to straggle over to the range. Most squinted into the early morning sun as it peaked over the low-lying hills that bracketed the course. Some clearly nursed hangovers from the night before, as evidenced by the breakfast beers and bloody marys clutched in slightly trembling hands. He and Richard were almost done with the large bucket of balls that they had grabbed upon arriving an hour ago. They had beaten most of the golfers on to the driving range, except those that had the 6:15 A.M. tee off time. Dickson turned to point out to Richard a trio of particularly hung-over golfers, but stopped short upon seeing the look in Richard's eyes. The look was similar to the eyes of a born politician intent on playing the crowd. Alert and inquisitive without appearing to stare too long in any particular direction. Following the general line of sight from Richard's eyes he noticed an individual approaching an empty space next to them on the tee off line, golf clubs slung easily over one shoulder.

"Good morning, Richard. I didn't know you to be a golfer."

"Judge Marwick! Good morning. I would like to introduce you to Dr. Dickson."

Marwick nodded pleasantly to Dickson and turned slightly to place his clubs against the club stand. Richard immediately motioned for Dickson to leave them alone to talk. Dickson stepped back over to his golf bag, selected a driver, and began to take practice swings.

"How do we stand on getting a courtroom tomorrow?"

"Oh, don't worry, Richard, we will be able to get you a courtroom. Both Judges Lewis and Jamison are available. And I well remember six weeks ago when I promised that you would start tomorrow."

Think fast, thought Richard. Judge Jamison may have a reputation as an unyielding hard ass, but from personal experience Richard knew that Lewis was a downright fool. Worse yet, Lewis had no experience in this type of law, and would lose the subtle distinctions Richard was going to make to get by the general legal advantages Wine House had on the existing law in this area. And Richard needed someone who could at least follow the law if he was to have any chance of success.

"That's terrific, Judge. Either one would be great. But . . ." Marwick threw a sharp glance at Richard.

"But what?"

"Judge Lewis is still acting as the special settlement judge in that big trade secret case my office is handling." Marwick looked skeptically at Richard, who added lamely "Well, I'd just hate to deal with some later claim of preference."

"Well, Richard . . . You know that you don't get to pick and choose. But . . ." he added without a smile, "I'll give it some thought."

Richard thanked the Judge, commented briefly on the condition of the course and quickly took his leave. He motioned for Dickson to also pack his clubs and follow. Dickson had the common sense to remain quiet until they had reached the parking lot, where their spikes clacking on the asphalt made the only noise. As they changed out of their golfing shoes Richard finally recapped for Dickson's benefit his conversation with the Presiding Judge.

"Well, Richard," Dickson spoke reverently, "it sure was a lucky coincidence that we happened to be at the driving range at the same time as Judge Marwick."

Richard paused before answering, then figured with a smile that a short response that conveyed the essence of his efforts and planning could do no harm.

"What makes you think that I would leave a detail that important to mere luck?"

~ ~ ~ ~ ~

Only force of habit long ingrained convinced Terri that she should clean the darkroom. After her hard work went so completely unrewarded, she merely wanted to take a long drive in the open air and get away from this case. Instead, immediately upon concluding that her attempt to divine the stranger's identity from the video was fruitless, she began to systematically index her work product in the off chance that it may be of use in some future project. Two of the cleaner prints, one showing the stranger's face and the other a full length shot, she placed in her binder with the vague idea that—time ever permitting—she could show them to former Winery Peak employees and ask if anyone knew his name or function.

As she stepped into the office and closed the hallway door to the darkroom the prints slid out of the binder and spilled across the floor. Terri's secretary reached over to help and picked up one of the two prints. Her eyebrows arched and she automatically voiced her opinion with a low long whistle.

"Wow. Bet he has a nice butt under those slacks!"

"Great. You are truly a lot of help. I can't get a read on his identity off of the tape and you can only think of him out of his clothes."

"What happened to the idea about the monogram?"

"Nothing. Dead end. All he had was that dumb polo rider on his shirt."

"What about above his cuffs?"

Terri stopped short and grabbed back the prints. Too many hours in a small airless room was turning her mind to mush, she thought. She should have been thinking that most people that wear emblem shirts, with the designer's emblem over the shirt pocket, often have their initials monogrammed at the end of the cuffs. She opened the desk drawer and pulled out a large magnifying glass. Putting the glass near the surface of the print, she skimmed the portion where the shirt sleeves peeked out of the jacket. Then, without another word to her secretary, Terri practically flew back into the darkroom and began the process anew. And was rewarded twenty minutes later with a print showing clearly the sleeve where it displayed the stranger's three initials.

CHAPTER NINE

FOG ROLLED PAST the windshield, heavy, thick and gray with moisture. Its pure physical presence blocked the early morning sun, keeping visibility down to less than thirty yards. During this time of year the morning tule fog, hugging the tops of the long open fields that defined the valley, could be intense. For the next several months, when the saturated mist was the heaviest and most persistent, fender benders became a commonplace occurrence. Most of the accidents every year involved tourists, unfamiliar with the local driving conditions, coming into contact with local trucks as they lumbered directly onto the road from the fields. Bright yellow warning signs had been put in place at strategic locations by the well-intentioned members of the Napa Elks Club, indicating the possibility of seasonal cross traffic, but these precautions did not seem to slow the operators of rental cars moving faster than the prevailing conditions or common sense dictated. Although Richard did not personally handle "whippers," as the legal trade referred to traffic accident plaintiffs because of the generally asserted claims of whiplash and soft tissue injury, every year the fog related accidents alone appeared sufficient to support the local personal injury section of the Napa County Bar Association.

Richard drove with careful but absentminded intensity. Even though his present state of attention did not include direct concentration on what the car was doing, he subconsciously kept his eyes focused on the double yellow lines to insure that the car remained on his side of the two lane expressway that he favored over the use of the freeway bypass. The physical mechanics of driving were fortunately being taken care by learned muscle memory. Although he was not terrifically hungry, his stomach felt light and empty, caused by a combination of nervousness and excitement in a form of "pre-game" jitters, and seemed to float somewhere above his belt. When a truck roared out of the mist and safely passed in the opposite direction he snapped his attention into the present and unnecessarily jerked the steering wheel towards the shoulder. Both hands now white-knuckled tight on the steering wheel, Richard accelerated back towards the center of his lane and simultaneously tried to maintain his internal equilibrium. His thoughts were tightly focused on his responsibility to Dickson, and whether he should disclose the limited extent of his courtroom experience. In his attempt at rationalization, he considered the fact that he had handled several court trials on his own before, where the judge alone acted as the trier of fact, but for the most part the disputes had involved relatively minor matters. In fact, he had never been lead trial counsel in a large civil case before a jury, although he had twice been the second chair in support of one of the senior partners of the firm. Richard was well aware of the difference between taking the lead position at trial and assisting someone else.

No matter how much responsibility the second chair attorney was given or voluntarily assumed, the lead attorney was still ultimately responsible for the resulting verdict. The difference in pressure could be staggering in a long or complex case, for the lead attorney had to be on top of all issues, facts and potential problems, whereas the second chair attorney generally could relax by comparison and focus on the particular matters that constituted his assignment for the trial. Now, for the first time, Richard was to act as lead counsel in a fairly long and complex jury trial, the outcome of which would have a significant effect on a person's life. He felt confident enough to try the case alone, with only a few nagging self-doubts, but could not shake the feeling that Dickson would want someone else with more experience if he knew the truth. Richard wanted the trial, knew that the experience was a golden opportunity, and the benefit to him personally only made him feel worse about the possibility that Dickson would feel that he had been deceived if the trial did not turn out favorably.

Michael Shaw had given Richard plenty of advice and encouragement over the last several weeks, involving the nuances of trying a complex case to a jury. During the course of their discussions, Richard had developed the distinct feeling that a credible presentation to the jury, although itself important, was secondary in the mind of the Firm to the goal of achieving a successful result financially. Michael, seemingly able to read Richard's thoughts on this matter, had attempted to relieve some of the pressure to win by reassuring Richard that the Firm was simply looking at the case as a training experience for Richard. But Richard knew the true situation, at least as it impacted on aspects of internal firm politics, was far different. This case would play a large role in how he would be perceived by the other partners, including his position on the track to an offer to join the partnership. In addition, the immediate economics of this case had become something of a divisive issue within the Firm itself.

As he drove Richard thought back to a discussion that he had with Michael some three months before, shortly after the case had come up during the review of existing business at one of the quarterly partnership meetings. At that time a trial date had not been set, and the economics of continuing to handle the case on a contingency basis had developed in to a subject of sharply divided opinions amongst the various partners. The Firm was weathering the recession better than most law firms in Northern California, due to its strong ties to some of the better established businesses in the area, but was still suffering stagnant profits from the impact of a tight economy. Not only was there an overall decrease in the amount of legal services being sought by the general public, including some of the otherwise longstanding clients of the Firm, but the client base as a whole was much slower in paying their bills. Though no slower in demanding immediate response to their legal needs. Because his billable hours on Dickson's behalf were not being invoiced to Dickson on a monthly basis, the time Richard was not spending on other pending client matters was further cutting into the cash flow of the Firm.

Even in the boom years of the late 1990's, when the economy had been robust and legal services in greater demand than available supply, the Firm had looked askance at contingency fee cases as not in keeping with the history or culture of the Firm. The concept of taking cases on contingency was simply inapposite to the general business practice of the Firm of billing for the high quality legal services on an hourly basis. When the partners had learned that Richard had accepted the case on a contingency basis, and would not receive any payment for services unless there was a judgment in Dickson's favor, and then possibly not until after many years and the exhaustion of all possible appeals, many voices were raised to state their displeasure. Not surprisingly, Allen Rose had been one of the most vocal in opposition to the contingency fee arrangement, insisting that the Firm withdraw from its representation of Dickson unless he would agree to pay for the legal services on the basis of the standard hourly rate. Michael, unwilling to allow his protégé to stand alone, had interceded on Richard's behalf and explained that he had approved the arrangement after learning about the case. Allen had responded to the entire situation badly, as if Michael's position was actually meant as a vehicle for challenging Allen's systematic process of creating a power base within the Firm. When Allen's attempt to rally support from the other partners failed to sufficiently materialize, he had backed away from his demands. Not satisfied with letting the issue completely disappear from sight, he made clear that he would undertake as his personal responsibility a review of the time being spent on the case to ensure that the cost of proceeding did not outweigh the potential benefits that may materialize. Later, in private, Michael had spelled the situation out in precise detail, including the potential impact the case could have on Richard's future with the Firm. Richard had remained resolute, refused to either transfer Dickson's case to another law firm or change the fee agreement, and stubbornly accepted the risk of an adverse result.

Richard's thoughts were brought back to the present as the top of the Courthouse cupola peaked through the fog. As he drove closer, the fog parted and gave way to a view of the Courthouse square, where to Richard's amazement several dozen people haphazardly gathered in what appeared to be the early stages of a demonstration. Although he normally would have parked in his assigned space in the lot adjacent to the office four blocks away, to get a better view of what was happening he instead slipped his car into a curbside space on the street within a long block of the Courthouse and in sight of the demonstrators.

At the turn of the century the Courthouse did not yet exist and the square had functioned as a parade ground for the local militia. As the years passed, one and two story buildings were built facing in towards the square, storefronts connected by a narrow wooden walkway that spanned the oozing gray-brown mud during the wet winter months. As time passed the town continued to grow and prosper in spurts. Trees were planted along the sides of the square and over time grew tall to provide shade over areas where men once marched in direct sunlight. Finally, as the county seat became established, a single story stone courthouse was built from large squares of granite and limestone mined locally in great quantities. During the Roosevelt Administration, the WPA added another story to the Courthouse. The second story was made out of wood, and reached upwards sharply from the original structure. At the end of World War II, the local chapter of the VFW built a redwood bandstand on the lawn in front of the Courthouse. For the next fifty years the bandstand had served the community well, hosting band concerts, Fourth of July celebrations, junior league picnics and, increasingly over the years, demonstrations.

The demonstrators down the street from Richard appeared generally as a mixed group. Some of the younger individuals, bunched around the foot of a large oak tree, were dressed in what Richard could only describe as "Grateful Dead chic." Among these demonstrators tie die shirts in an assortment of bright colors were favored as well as an equally eclectic assortment of hats that did little to contain wildly long hair. Complementing this group were a larger number of people that proclaimed on picket signs affiliation with various environmental groups ranging from the benign to the militant including the Sierra Club, Greenpeace, and Earth First! Although several Napa City police officers were standing nearby in discreet observation, the mixed crowd was generally quiet and well-behaved. Several smaller clusters of apparently "independent" demonstrators chatted quietly together, while others sipped hot drinks and coffee poured from small thermoses.

Richard watched the demonstrators with quiet assessment for a moment until a picket sign became visible and with a bang of realization he understood that the demonstration was for, or rather against, Dickson. As he continued to watch, the white Channel 6 news van pulled up to the sidewalk in front of the demonstrators. Martinez was the first to get out, a plastic smile on his face and microphone in hand, followed quickly by his assistant and a cameraman. A number of the demonstrators greeted his arrival with a spirited jostling of their picket signs, which slowed quickly to a desultory wave and then stopped altogether when they realized that the cameraman had not begun to shoot the scene. One of the members of a larger group, a fiftyish woman dressed in Patagonians and Birkenstocks, stepped apart from the others and walked towards Martinez, who waved a greeting in apparent recognition. The two quickly bent heads together in collaboration while Martinez's assistant walked through the crowd looking for human interest pieces. Richard knew that he had to think fast. He had to get in touch with Dickson and Gayle, and warn then about the demonstration awaiting Dickson's arrival. He turned the key in the ignition and clenched his teeth as the engine caught. No one from down the street paid him any attention, however, and he eased the car away from the Courthouse and headed directly towards his office.

Stucky was sure to disavow any responsibility for the demonstrators, Richard thought, making another complaint to the judge a meaningless gesture. Richard did not mind the fact that the trial would be reported in the press, and in fact welcomed the exposure he would receive. He simply did not want a confrontation between Dickson and the demonstrators on the Courthouse steps with an opportunistic reporter like Martinez at his back. This type of mike-in-the-face confrontation would get more exposure on the fifteen second T.V. news sound bite than his own statements. Richard knew that the crowd would remain relatively well-mannered until Dickson should arrive, when they would be sure to break into a preprogrammed bout of "spontaneous demonstration" as soon as the cameras began to film the events. While these thoughts floated through his head Richard pulled into the parking lot for his building. He recognized with relief Dickson's truck was already in a visitor parking stall and, as he locked the car, Richard flashed on an idea for how to deal with the demonstrators.

~ ~ ~ ~ ~

Dumpster diving was definitely not her favorite method for collecting information. Every time a case called for a midnight trip to a target's trash container Terri was reminded of how ruthlessly she had been hazed during her first year as a rookie investigator. Fresh out of college with a political science degree and no real employment prospects, she had reluctantly accepted a position as a secretary in a large investigations firm dominated by deeply chauvinistic former military types. For two long years she had typed reports, followed orders and observed carefully as the investigators around her displayed a number of techniques for obtaining information. Terri had asked questions, at first shyly and unobtrusively and with time more directly, until one day an opportunity presented itself.

A telephone call from a small biotech company came in during the lunch hour. Terri was on duty and was the only one in the office at the time. The company had routinely used the firm to run background checks on new employees, as some of their work was performed under contract to the

Department of Defense, and the repeat business was an important source of revenue for the investigations firm. When she took the call, to her surprise the personnel manager specifically requested that the matter be assigned to a female investigator. Terri automatically said she would make sure the job was properly assigned and thanked the caller for the assignment. As soon as she hung up the phone, however, Terri remembered that the single female investigator on staff could not possibly handle the assignment for several weeks due to other commitments. With a combination of trepidation and excitement, Terri decided to handle the job herself. Pulling a file that contained a similar project for the same company, she proceeded to work on the background check. When she finished later that same afternoon, she placed both the telephone message and the typed report on the desk of the office manager before returning to her own desk in the reception area. An explosion of sound ten minutes later signaled the fact that the office manager had read the report and realized who had performed the work. Before he could have the satisfaction of summarily summoning her into his office, she walked straight in without knocking and announced her desire to work as an investigator.

For the next six months Terri worked directly with the office manager, learning in detail the paperwork side of investigations. Long dull hours reading data files and drawers full of aged information for leads to other drawers full of equally aged information until the one helpful piece could be located. At the end of that probationary period she was finally assigned for six months as an assistant to a senior investigator doing field work. During that time she was his to do with as he pleased, and had been assigned all of the grunge jobs, including dumpster dives, even on files otherwise assigned to the other male rookies. These outings often involved mucking around in all types of refuse for a clue, a lead or a piece of a larger puzzle that she generally was not considered senior enough to know about. Added to the indignity of the hours spent knee high in garbage was the perception held by most security guards, who disliked private investigators to begin with, that the trash was still the inviolate personal property of the target being investigated. They simply did not seem to know or care that the courts had long held that there is no legitimate expectation of privacy in items voluntarily thrown into the trash. The security guards were often simply bored by their jobs and many were not above the distracting excitement of beating on investigators caught trespassing in the bins.

As the availability of information on computer databases became more accessible during the last several years, Terri had made a concerted effort to further diversify her sources of information by learning as much as she could about computer hacking. With the help of a series of consultations from a friend who taught basic programming at the community college, Terri had quickly learned the fundamentals of tapping into the large and diverse areas of information contained on databases throughout the country. The ease of access, coupled with the fact that the task could be performed from the comfort of her own office, made the database search one of her first steps for uncovering information in many investigations. She became so proficient in tapping the keyboard that her six months as an assistant was cut short and she was soon given direct responsibility for her own caseload and client relationships. Her specialty became civil litigation, due to the abundance of financial information available through the Internet, and several local law firms depended on her services.

When Richard had first described his conundrum, Terri had tried to locate information on the mystery man by logging into the human resources files on the local network at Winery Peak. When her search indicated no matches for the initials she that had identified from the digitalized pictures of his shirt, she logged off and transferred to the network in the New York offices of Wine House. To her more immediate satisfaction, she was able to quickly find a match between the initials and a name in the personnel records in the human resources department. Her satisfaction was blunted, however, by the seemingly sanitized nature of the file contents.

From the printout, it was almost as if Wine House wanted to acknowledge only enough information to be able to account for the fact that he was on the payroll, and not provide any information concerning his job functions other than a notation that he was designated as a "special assistant" to the Chairman of Wine House. The file alone simply did not provide enough information to lead Richard to a reasonable and justifiable complaint to the Judge about the failure of Wine House to identify the individual during the discovery phase of the pretrial proceedings. In addition, Terri could not simply print the screens and hand the printed information to Richard for his use. In fact, she knew that she could not even tell Richard exactly where she had obtained her information. Apart from the ethical problems Richard would face in using the information, she knew that her access was—without question—against the law. At the very least Wine House would be able to quash the use of the materials, and could also make a good argument that she and Richard should be criminally prosecuted for the illegal hacking.

Knowing that time was rapidly running out on the ability to implement different long term surveillance activities in order to assist Richard's demand that the mystery man be produced at trial, Terri reluctantly came to the conclusion that a "low tech" workup was required to supplement her "high tech" findings. A series of dumpster dives was the quickest means of trying to secure confirming and possibly incriminating information. Fortunately, during her search through the electronic files of Winery Peak, Terri had also accessed the electronic mail of the secretary to the Acting President of Winery Peak. In one of the electronic "letters" she noticed a confirmation for reservations at the Lodge at Napa Valley for Stucky and a senior manager from Wine House to be used during the duration of the trial. Stucky had apparently decided against using the facilities at Winery Peak, which was an understandable decision given the long drive from the guest facilities at the high elevation winery building to the Courthouse at the floor of the valley.

Within a half hour Terri had made her way to the Lodge. Knowing that the hotel manager would not willingly tip her off to Stucky's room number, she instead crossed the open lobby to an attached atrium filled with overstuffed chairs set amid lush banks of well-tended ferns. On a small writing table next to one of the chairs sat a small white princess phone. The phone did not have a dial, as it was intended solely for in-house calls, and connected the caller directly to the hotel operator. Terri looked around quickly and, comfortable that no one was in listening range, picked up the receiver. After a short series of rings the operator came on the line. Without hesitation Terri asked if any deliveries had yet arrived for the Stucky party. The operator went off line to check, and then returned to confirm that nothing had arrived recently. Terri crisply advised the operator that several packages were expected, and asked if the staff could make and bring them directly to the room as soon as they were received. To Terri's satisfaction the operator confirmed the request by noting that everything would be brought promptly to Room 240. Terri thanked the operator for the assistance and hung up the phone.

Now, armed with knowledge of the number of Stucky's room, Terri hoped that she could minimize the amount of time she would have to spend locating the trash from his room. Trash that could prove invaluable to Richard if it contained any of the working materials used by Stucky in preparing the case for Wine House. She walked quickly over to the receptionist desk and asked if there was an available room that she could take for the next week. The receptionist on duty, a bouncy twenty-year-old, smilingly informed her that she could have her pick of locations until the following Friday as the Lodge had already booked a large tour group from Japan. Terri gravely considered the options that this information provided and then asked for a room on the second floor that would be down at the opposite end of the hall from the rooms Stucky had reserved.

After getting situated in her room, Terri glanced at her watch and, somewhat reluctantly, confirmed to herself that she had plenty of time to drive to Winery Peak and rummage through the accumulation of refuse from the office operations. There simply was nothing more that she could count on accomplishing at the Lodge that night. She would have to wait until midmorning, when Stucky and his staff would have cleared out for the day. At that point the cleaning service would have had its opportunity to make up and clean the room and, most importantly, remove anything placed in the small wastepaper containers. Depending on the maid, for she knew some well enough to approach them without fear of being confronted by management, Terri would either be able to strike a deal for the maid to separate and deliver to her room all of the garbage from Stucky's room, or she would just have to wait until the maid had cleaned the room and then grab this trash after it was placed with the rest of the garbage from the group of rooms that made up the south wing of the Lodge. Even if she missed the maid, Terri could still look for the garbage when it was transferred to the outside bin.

Whatever else happened, Terri knew better than to personally set foot into the room. Should she be caught, even with the best of intentions, she could be charged with burglary and certainly would not be able to count on Richard to do anything more than to post her bail. With one more reluctant look around her room, particularly at the very inviting queen sized bed that would go unused, Terri closed her door and headed back to her car and work.

~~~~~

"DA's office."

Frank Walsh had a trademark way of answering the phone that simultaneously communicated intensity and overwork. His clipped greeting also had the secondary benefit of prompting new callers to get to the point immediately. Like most of Frank's friends, Richard had long since become used to his terse approach to salutations, but knew better to needle
~~~~~

Frank about the level of his public demeanor during office hours.

"It's Richard."

"Rich! Hey ol' buddy." His rapid change in tone pleasantly marked Richard's good standing. "I thought that you had a big day in court ahead of you this morning. What's with the social calls?"

"Wish this was a social call."

Richard hesitated momentarily, trying to find the best way to describe the problem, only to be interrupted by Frank.

"Sounds like you need a favor. Boy, you have always been way too easy to read. As long as I have known you there has been that hitch in your swing when you are going to ask for something."

"Well, this is obviously not an official call, but I need your help."

Richard quickly sketched out the new situation at the Courthouse, including the gathering demonstration and the problem with having the local newscast give him a bad feature on their 6:00 o'clock broadcast the first day of trial. As he began to describe in detail the adverse impact from the demonstration Frank peremptorily cut him off.

"What do you want me to do, Richard? I can't interfere with the demonstration. I can just imagine the headlines now—'District Attorney's office rousts peaceful demonstrators to help personal friends.' Even if I had the power to get the police to sweep the area, my boss would kill me."

"Ya, I know all that, but you could get Dickson into the courthouse without him being seen by either the demonstrators or the camera crews. We could go through the Pen."

"Oh! Right! I could probably work that out."

"And what the demonstrators don't know won't hurt them or—more importantly—us."

~~~~~

The "Pen" was the nickname for the security holding area in the basement of the courtroom annex. It was connected to
~~~~~

the main courthouse through a long underground passage, through which the sheriff's department could transport prisoners for arrangements and trial without the risk of escape. Dickson would be able to park behind the annex, where he would be escorted down to the Pen and then through the underground passage to the courthouse, where Richard would be waiting. Richard knew that Dickson would not like the symbolism of arriving in court through the same passage used by criminal defendants, and would balk at the thought of being described as too embarrassed to face the crowd. But he did not need to add to his problems by providing an opportunity for Martinez to ambush Dickson in front of a crowd eager to be on TV, resulting in another story that could influence the jury against Dickson.

~~~~~

Terri drove slowly, thinking about the job ahead. The degree of difficulty she would face in searching through the trash at Winery Peak depended on the extent to which its head of operations cared enough to have its refuse sorted prior to being collected by the County sanitation department. Some business went to great lengths in their efforts to be "green" and had separate containers set aside for "dry" garbage, containing everything collected from the administration offices, and used other bins for the "wet" garbage used to hold the discards from the rest of the facilities including the field operations and the employees' cafeteria. If her luck was bad, and with this type of job her track record was nothing to brag about, the bins would not be segregated between the different aspects of the winery operations. If her luck was very bad, the office garbage would be at the very bottom of the mixed bins. Since there was nothing that she could do about the situation, however, she simply had put it out of her mind as she drove along the county roads.

At least the night was good for the task ahead. The moon, which was rising slowly behind her as she drove uphill, appeared as a fat yellow crescent in the evening sky. It gave off just enough illumination that Terri would be able to avoid
~~~~~

using her flashlight until she was inside of one of the bins. If the moon had been new, and the night lit only by the stars, Terri would have had to take the chance of using her flashlight to negotiate around the site. Against the deep black of the moonless night, the beam would have stood out like a beacon, potentially attracting the otherwise bored security guard like a moth to a flame. A full moon, on the other hand, would simply create other problems by throwing too much light and could leave Terri visible to the casual glance.

Exercising extreme caution, Terri pulled off the road and coasted to a stop, parking her car well away from the main gate that stood in front of the complex of winery buildings. She stepped from the car and closed the door carefully, so it would not make a sound as it latched, before taking the time to thoroughly stretch her back and leg muscles. The distance from the gate to the main office building was still at least good half mile up a decent grade, but Terri knew that the noise of her car in this area could carry too far and loud in the cool night air to drive closer. With plenty of time to complete the task at hand, Terri did not mind the trade-off in the energy needed to walk the distance in return for the stealth of this approach. Before moving toward the gate, Terri opened the trunk and reached deeply into the black well. She had previously removed the bulb from the trunk light, to avoid having her activities noticed by some passing good Samaritan who might mistake the scene for car trouble and stop to offer unwanted assistance. The contents of the trunk were well known and location of equipment familiar enough that the lack of light posed her no impediment. With a smile she pulled out a small red rectangular box. From the box Terri withdrew a new pair of jet black running shoes, which she quickly exchanged for the hiking boots that she had been wearing. Should she have to move in a hurry, Terri wanted to be light on her feet. The running shoes also had the benefit of being extremely quiet to walk in, at least compared to the stone crunching sounds from the waffle patterned soles of her boots.

Fortunately for Terri, the winery was not yet large enough to justify a night crew to operate production. The bottling operations had been recently added, in the form of a fancy Italian bottling machine that first cleaned the bottles, loaded each with wine, withdrew surplus air, added the cork and lead foil cap and then glued in place the front and rear labels in a series of highly synchronized steps. In the first few years of wine production, Winery Peak had simply shipped half of its wine in bulk lots to other wineries for use in blends and hired one of the local mobile bottlers to cork the balance of the harvest. These mobile bottlers catered to the smaller operations, ones that could not afford the large capital outlay to have the expensive equipment permanently installed onsite, or who sold the majority of their wines in bulk lots to the midlevel market producers, retaining enough of the reserve wines to produce upper end library selections to retail at inflated prices. The mobile bottlers generally housed their equipment in customized truck trailers, which then could be hauled from site to site as the need demanded. In order to maximize the ability to process orders from the largest number of wineries during the fairly short bottling season, the mobile units tended to operate several shifts every day while onsite. This would have greatly increased the chances that someone would bump into Terri during her investigation, had Winery Peak been in the process of bottling with any of the mobile operators, and she was pleased to confirm the absence of any trailers as she approached the main complex.

Terri approached slowly, the dusty pea gravel from the parking lot crunching softly beneath her feet. She was able to walk with the assurance that she was heading in the right direction, having scouted the entire site shortly after her original conversation with Richard about the case. Terri had learned that the best way to orient herself with the subject of an investigation involved exposure to their physical environment. Armed with a mental picture of the site, Terri could envision how the subject may think or act. This knowledge tended to help throughout an assignment. When circumstances made it difficult for her to personally view a site, and she had to rely on someone's description of the local conditions, inevitably her perception would be different in material respects from the actual layout. These differences could mean much more than merely success or failure in locating information. They often related directly to Terri's ability to disappear quietly from a scene should the need arise. For this case Terri had conducted her original recognizance late on a Saturday afternoon. She had driven the long winding road to the tasting rooms behind a charter tour bus loaded with eager tasters, already full of samples from the wineries visited at the beginning of the tour. The bus had emptied quickly after pulling to a stop, and Terri simply mingled into the boisterous crowd as it besieged the somewhat bored but generally bemused tasting room employees. After an appropriate amount of time had passed, and joined by a small number of the tourists who needed the break for a dose of fresh air, Terri had actively wandered around, taking mental notes of the layout before walking slowly back to her car and driving off without drawing attention from anyone.

As she now walked near the center of the complex of buildings, the tasting room door opened, spilling yellow light across the parking lot. Terri slowed abruptly then simply paused in place. She knew that with eyes acclimated to the dark she could see into the room and the people inside would not be able to discern her presence in the shadows. Ignoring the open door, and the light that was eating away at her night vision, she looked across the open space. She could make out the outlines of the administration offices next to the tasting room, and the loggia that connected the two. The loggia was made from poles salvaged from old growth redwood trunks that had been cleared years before in construction of the original buildings on the property. These beautiful columns supported an equally impressive redwood lattice, which was in turn covered by the fragrant white flowers of star anise and several wild trumpet vines.

Terri had moved quickly towards the relative safety of the loggia and was almost halfway across the open space when two men stepped out of the tasting room and began to walk in her general direction. Although terribly exposed in her current position, a plastic picnic table was the only available cover and she quickly crouched down behind the bench seat. The two workers continued in her direction talking quietly and carrying a large barrel shaped object between them. When they were not more than a few feet away she realized that the closer of the two was talking in Spanish about the buildings that they would have to finish before they could go get a couple of cold beers and hopefully some hot women. The second, and apparently older, man swore good-naturedly in response and suggested that the younger man's wife may have something to say about his bold suggestions. Terri's shoulders relaxed involuntarily with the deduction that the two were merely part of the cleaning crew and not a part of the security staff. Even if spotted by the two they were unlikely to do or say anything immediately. Most of the Mexican nationals in the local workforce simply avoid involvement in any matters outside of their work even when they were in the country legally, and were instead disposed to do their jobs quietly and unobtrusively as a form of self-protection for themselves and their families.

The two men continued to walk over to a large enclosure, attached to the far end of the loggia, which housed several garbage bins. With a loud clang the younger man threw open the lid of the second bin. That type of noise would be something for her to avoid at all costs when looking into the bins. The two men then lifted the barrel over the edge of the enclosure and emptied the contents in one fluid motion. Although she could not see clearly from her vantage point, the easy in which they had hefted and then emptied the barrel indicated that it had been full of paper and other office type refuse instead of the heavier garbage from other aspects of the winery operations. If her luck held out it would only have been collected from the administrative offices. Hopefully she could comb through the mess quickly and be soon gone from this place.

As they left the immediate area she noted with satisfaction that they closed but did not lock the enclosure. Joking as they walked away, the men only took a few minutes to retrace their steps across the open space and return to the tasting room, closing the door behind them on their way inside. The light previously flooding out from the tasting room door snapped off as the door clicked shut, leaving Terri once again in relative darkness and silence. Blinking quickly to regain her full night vision, she rose from her hiding place next to the bench and stepped cautiously forward, only to be met by a stinging sensation in her right leg where the foot had gone to sleep from being kept motionless for too long in a bent position. Standing on her left foot she tried to maintain her balance while shaking the other foot to get the blood to circulate. Gingerly she placed her weight on her right foot and was greeted by a distinct lack of feeling other than the unpleasant tingling of pins and needles. The lack of feeling made her misjudge the weight she was placing on her foot and caused her to stumble into the bench, knocking down the sun umbrella with a loud clatter. Terri again froze. Glancing around nervously she quickly moved away from the table and towards the bins. The sound must have seemed louder than it actually was, for there was no response. Even so, Terri stayed close to the side of the loggia for a few extra moments until she was satisfied that no one was going to investigate the noise.

Slipping through the gate in front of the bins Terri pulled two black cotton gloves from the pocket of her jacket. The gloves were made of very thin material to avoid interfering with her manual dexterity, but were thick enough to avoid leaving prints. Inside the enclosure sat four squat bins, each five foot wide and painted a uniform gray. On the front of each appeared the markings of the local waste management company, and Terri made a quick note of this information. From her right pocket she then withdrew a small penlight and flicked on the tight yellow beam. Lifting the heavy metal lid of the first bin with one hand was difficult, so she gripped the penlight between her teeth and grabbed the lid with both hands while the beam from the penlight danced on the walls of the enclosure. Peering inside the bin she was able to make out Styrofoam packing material, plastic bubble wrap and broken down cardboard boxes. Materials used to ship individual bottles and marketing merchandise to retailers. At the bottom were piles of Styrofoam popcorn, in places mounding several feet deep. Grabbing a piece of the cardboard she stirred the mounds, poking and prodding in an attempt to make sure she was not missing anything of interest. With nothing uncovered she closed the lid and moved to the next bin. Within seconds of cracking the lid her nose was assaulted by a noxious wave of smells. A quick glance inside gave her enough of a view to discern the wet remains of the slop from the cafeteria which had been decomposing for too long in the bin, and she dropped the lid in her haste to close the bin. The lid dropped into place with a loud clang. Terri froze in place, damning her own sensitivities and wondering for the first time whether she was getting too old and soft for this type of duty. Already tonight alone she had made several mistakes that would have caused her significant trouble if the winery used a more sophisticated security system. Maybe it was time to hire someone to train for the field work, while she spent more time on analysis of information. Minutes that seemed like hours passed while these thoughts danced through her head, but not response greeted the noise. Fortunately too there were no dogs about, for the clanging would surely have set off a lively round of barking.

Knowing that she had already taken far too much time at the site Terri moved to the third bin and lifted its lid. Flashing the light inside revealed a much more interesting sight. Included among the mounded piles of loose paperwork were two large bags of shredded documents. Pay dirt, as far as Terri was concerned, since documents are not usually shredded as a matter of course in most businesses unless they contain information of importance. With an effort Terri pulled herself up and over the lip of the bin and reached inside. The two bags were lifted out of the bin and placed by her feet on the ground. She knew that piecing together the shredded documents meant a long night stretched ahead, and the sooner she started the better. Before leaving she glanced quickly at the remaining loose documents in the bin, to make sure she was not overlooking anything helpful, and then closed the lid. In each hand she grabbed a bag of the shredded documents and, carefully looking around, silently made her way back to her car.

CHAPTER TEN

AFTER ENTERING the Courthouse through the main entrance on the first floor Richard swung down the stairs that lead to the basement to meet Dickson. Although the situation involving their arrival now felt somewhat anticlimactic, he was still relieved by the ease in which he had been able to outmaneuver the crowd waiting outside. Martinez had looked directly at him as he walked up to the main entrance to the Courthouse and mounted the wide steps fronting the old stone facade. Apparently satisfied that Richard was entering alone, Martinez had merely acknowledged his presence with a nod and then looked away. Richard was not the story that interested Martinez. Dickson was really not the story either, at least to what Martinez had in mind. The story for the news broadcast would be the crowd, when and if they came to life, and the fact that a demonstration would act as a good backdrop for a segment on the six o'clock news. Without some reaction from the crowd to make the scene more dramatic, Martinez could have easily made the report from the confines of the sound stage in the station's studio.

As was typical for a Monday morning, Judge Marwick's courtroom was full of attorneys waiting on various different matters for their respective clients. The first order of business would be a call of the calendar by the Judge's clerk, essentially a list of all of the trials that were set to begin that day. When their matter was called by the clerk, the attorneys on the selected case would state their appearances for the court reporter, who was busy taking down the official record, and they would then quickly describe the status of their case. If any of the cases had settled over the weekend, and there usually were quite a few, the Judge would ask those attorneys to return at 10:00 A.M. to read the settlement agreement to the court for the official record. One by one Judge Marwick would then hear the attorneys on the remaining cases represent whether they were ready to proceed to trial and, if not, the reasons for the delay. If a case was not ready, even if according to only one of the sides present, the parties would be excused if the reasons were interesting or fair and the trial reset for a later date. If the case was not reset, the attorneys would be asked to wait until all other matters on the calendar had been resolved. Assuming that there were no other judges available to conduct the trial, then the side requesting a continuance would get one by default. If a courtroom and judge was available, however, then they would be immediately sent out to trial whether or not they were ready to proceed. For those attorneys who truly needed a continuance, to locate and subpoena a reluctant witness or for any other legitimate reason that may or may not convince the Judge, the wait until the end of the calendar could be extremely nerve-wracking.

Richard quietly said hello to a few of the attorneys that he knew from other cases and tried to keep his mind clear and body relaxed. A continuance could mean a delay for months, as the cases that did not go out for lack of enough judges or courtrooms were generally set over for at least ninety days. Since the court clerk was constantly setting trial dates for cases moving through the system, the new dates had to be set out far enough in the future to alleviate the congestion that would occur if the older cases were merely set over to return the following Monday. With nearly ninety percent of all cases settling before trial, and many cases that did not settle taking longer or shorter to actually try than the early time estimates given by counsel, there was simply no other way of managing the limited resources of the few available judges.

After spending close to an hour dealing with the settled cases and the first round of excuses from those attorneys who were not ready to proceed, Marwick stopped to check his notes and brusquely announced a ten minute recess. His apparent lack of good humor had not been helped by one young attorney sitting near the front row of the courtroom. The clueless neophyte to the scene had fidgeted continuously during the first half hour of the calendar call, to the irritation of those in his immediate vicinity and to the distraction of the Judge. When Marwick finally could ignore the young man any longer, as it appeared that he was going to twitch all morning, the Judge abruptly interrupted in the middle of a lengthy explanation on various constitutional imperatives from the attorney who was standing directly before him. Addressing himself directly to the young man, the Judge asked if there was a problem of which he should be made aware. The following few seconds of silence were deafening, broken finally by a small voice that timidly asked to have his case called out of order so he could go to the bathroom. With mock seriousness and decorum that stifled any possible thought of outright laughter the Judge assured him that he would not call his matter until he could relieve himself. With neck reddened beyond belief the young man left the courtroom, wishing he never had to return.

As soon as Marwick called the break everyone immediately stood until he left the bench and, as soon as he had passed through the doorway beside the bench into his chambers, the sound level in the courtroom increased dramatically. Ten minutes would quickly stretch to twenty, to the surprise of no one who was familiar with "lawyer time." Most of the more experienced attorneys knew that they had plenty of time, and left the courtroom to grab a cup of coffee in the small cafeteria down on the floor below. Richard, feeling the anticipation of trial creep through his chest, leaned over to Dickson and told him to stay put while he got up to recheck the number of matters posted. Dickson's case was listed as number 5, but Richard knew that the mere numerical listing had little to do with which case went out and in what order. Some cases were assigned to particular judges depending on the types of cases and the anticipated length of trial. Of the judges that were still available, Judge Grey had a reputation for requesting "short cause" matters—those that could be tried in under a week—and Judge Takori who was well known for his dislike of personal injury and medical malpractice cases. Which still left Judge Jamison as the only other judge free for assignment.

Richard did not really care what the posting said, as it would have no impact on what he would be doing while waiting for Marwick to come back out to the bench, but he wanted some physical activity to deal with the buildup of nervous energy. Although on a logical level he knew that he would be fine once he was in action, he could not help but feel antsy during the wait. It did not help matters to see Stucky sitting quietly on the other side of the courtroom reading a copy of the *Napa Register*. Richard did not know how many cases Stucky had tried, but in this setting he was acutely aware of the fact that it did not have to be many to equal or exceed the number he had under his belt.

Richard shoved the thoughts of Stucky aside and moved back to where Dickson was sitting as the bailiff again asked the courtroom to come to order. Marwick did not waste any time upon his return, and quickly announced that he had only three judges that remained available for civil trials. Reading off the balance of the calendar, Marwick first called a case that resulted in a loud clamor as almost a dozen attorneys stood and approached the counsel tables at the same time. A multiparty construction dispute, this case was sure to take several weeks and the likelihood of settlement had been exhaustively reviewed and finally rejected as impossible to achieve. Instead of sending the case to one of the waiting trial judges, however, Marwick made some pointed comments about the waste of judicial resources and the stubbornness of the parties. The attorneys involved all took the comments quietly, eager to get out of the range of Marwick's displeasure and on with the laborious process of trying the case. Marwick knew better than they how to play the game, however, and he personally felt that he would be damned if he would let them clog up his courthouse while other cases waited. He did not express these feelings aloud, and after a brief moment advised them that he would reconsider the availability of courtrooms for their case at the end of the morning's calendar.

The second matter was quickly sent out to trial in Judge Grey's courtroom, with the admonition that they would trail behind a case that was currently in the last stages and which should be over by the afternoon. As Marwick announced the third and final case to be assigned Richard began to stand until he realized with a shock that the Judge had not called Dickson's case. Richard sat back down amazed. After their brief meeting on the golf course he had assumed that the Judge would be sure to send him out to a courtroom. Dickson looked over at Richard, question marks in his eyes. Richard ignored him, calculating quickly how he would deal with the fact that the case would now be reset to a date next fall at the earliest. He would have to contact all of his witnesses, and hope that they would recommit to taking time out of their schedules and again appear to testify on Dickson's behalf.

". . . and I would like to exercise my 170.6 challenge."

Richard's eyes whipped forward in time to see a black cloud form and then cross Marwick's face. Under a "170.6" challenge, either party could object to being sent to a particular judge, and did not even have to identify the reasons for the challenge. Because of the absolute nature of the right, each side could only make a 170.6 challenge once during a proceeding. In this case, the attorney who made the challenge, besides looking uncomfortable under the sharply held stare of the Judge, had only to recite under oath a standardized statement to the effect that the he or his client had reasonable grounds to believe that the particular judge assigned would not be fair to his cause. Most attorneys are very reluctant to use the challenge, as the judges tend to take it quite personally and remember the affront to their impartiality and dignity long after the particular case is over. Richard could even remember one judge telling an attorney that the attorney and his entire firm might as well plan on challenging him in the future any time he should be so unlucky as to be assigned to his courtroom. But of most immediate importance to Richard, the challenge meant that a tance to Richard, the challenge meant that a judge was now free to be assigned to hear Dickson's case immediately and not some months down the road.

Richard stood and walked forward before the court clerk could finish calling out the entire name of Dickson's case. In an attempt to rein himself in, he glanced over at Stucky only to bark his shin on the last chair in the row. The sharp pain actually was a welcome distraction for the short moments it took to reach the counsel table. He then looked up to the realization that Marwick was waiting not so patiently for his attention. Mumbling a hasty apology, Richard again turned slightly to glance at Stucky. His opponent stood comfortably, as if somewhat bored by the whole process. Richard tried to dismiss his suspicion that Stucky's appearance was designed solely to make Richard uncomfortable. Marwick cleared his throat and looked over at Richard without apparent recognition. He then looked over at Stucky, who stood straighter in deference to the court. Then, without further hesitation, Marwick intoned the assignment.

"Judge Jamison, Department 4."

~ ~ ~ ~ ~

The more comfortable appearing seats in the jury box filled quickly, followed by the first three rows in the spectator section behind the rail, as the stream of individuals self-consciously entered the courtroom. Judge Jamison always requested fifty people from the jury commissioner for the jury selection process. The commissioner normally sent only thirty people to all of the other judges sitting by assignment in the Napa County Superior Court, and the battles he had with Judge Jamison over the issue, which both saw as representative of the larger question of control over courthouse administration, were a source of secret amusement among court personnel. Although only fourteen jurors would be selected, twelve to deliberate on the possible verdict and two alternates to act as backups in case of illness or absence of the others, Judge Jamison hated any delays that might be encountered if he had to request more people from the commissioner in the middle of the proceedings.

The pool of prospective jurors was truly a cross section of the community. They were picked primarily from voter registration lists, which were thought to help guarantee a moderate level of literacy. The differences in background and experience were immediately apparent, if clothes alone were any guide. A small number of business suits consistently looked at their watches as if to convey the fact that they had more important places to be than serving on a civil jury. Others, students mostly, wore a combination of jeans, tee-shirts and similar casual dress. Scattered within the group sat more traditional blue-collar types wearing work clothes that included overalls and heavy workboats. To a person, however, they all looked as if sitting in this courtroom was the last place that they would choose to be on a Monday morning.

At this point in the process the potential jurors did not know one another, and sat like the fifty strangers that they were. To offset the physical intimacy of chairs being spaced fairly close together, most of the women in the group sat in the exact center of their seats, erecting invisible barriers to define their own space in this new and uncomfortable setting. In general, the men tended to extend the established borders of their space by stretching legs beyond their limitations of the separate seats, and placing arms over armrests. This conduct would soon be replaced by a period of bonding, as the individuals began to recognize each other, or catch each others eye, and develop a more considerate "we are in this together" mentality. Richard had to remember to keep an eye on who became friends with whom, as this process shaped how the individuals viewed one another. Resentment could occur rapidly if he were to excuse from the jury pool an individual with whom others had become friendly.

Richard knew that first impressions on a new jury were critical. Most of them had never been in a courtroom before and were clearly uneasy about the entire jury process. He could certainly emphasize with that feeling. This was the first time that he had faced selection of a jury as lead counsel and, between himself and Stucky, he would be the first to address the pool of potential jurors during the selection process. He could see several of the individuals scanning the courtroom to get their bearings, and as the last few entered the doors in the back of the courtroom he pushed his chair back with a loud scrape on the hardwood floor. Striding confidently to the clerk, who looked up in surprise from her reading, Richard quietly asked her if the Judge Jamison would be breaking from noon to one or one thirty. The prospective jurors, those who were paying attention for lack of anything better to do, did not hear the question or the response. They did, however, see the clerk answer and Richard smile in positive response. Apart from giving Richard an excuse to move out of his seat and release some of the nervous energy that was building to an explosively high level in his chest, the intended purpose of the exercise was to get the jurors to identify him with the courthouse ritual, to look at Richard as part of the process so that when the trial began they might give his statements a slightly greater degree of deference. Richard walked back to were Dickson was sitting and nodded confidently. As planned, each of the potential jurors who were watching assumed that the entire interaction meant something positive for Richard and Dickson.

To complete the picture of positive confidence, something he still did not necessarily feel, Richard walked back to his counsel table and pulled out a clean legal pad. Drawing out and uncapping two pens, one with red ink and the other with black, he made a quick note on the pad and then underscored the note to highlight its importance. The pad and pens were then returned to one of the two large leather brief bags that sat on the floor next to the end of the table.

The brief bags contained Richard's trial notebooks as well as all summaries of the evidence that he intended to present to the jury. The trial notebooks, meticulously prepared by Gayle, contained an outline of the case and the notes for Richard's opening statement as well as notes on the applicable law. They also held a list of questions that he could choose from in conducting his selection of the jurors. They were a tremendous help, even more so than if he had prepared the materials himself, as Gayle was very particular about the notebooks and required neatness above all else. The information was precisely printed out, with Richard's handwritten notations appearing in the margins to reflect ideas that occurred to him during periodic reviews of the materials. Time permitting, the portions with the handwritten notations would also be typed and the new sheets exchanged for old. Although the notebooks had been put together by Gayle without his input or direction, he had reviewed them so many times that there was nothing in them that he could not find within several seconds.

The bulk of the materials to be used as evidence, as well as copies of the deposition transcripts, remained in his office as they would not be needed during the jury selection process. These materials filled several large brown storage boxes, and Richard wanted to appear as uncluttered as possible. To this end nothing sat in front of him on the counsel table. Gayle, sitting next to him, kept her materials to a minimum to complete the effect. In front of her appeared two pencils, tips sharpened to a razor point, a pad of yellow paper and a graph that reflected two rows of seven boxes. She would be filling in the boxes with the names of the prospective jurors as they were selected, along with pieces of information from their background that may later become helpful in deciding the manner of presentation and points to stress during the closing arguments.

While waiting for Judge Jamison to appear in the courtroom through the side door that lead directly to his chambers, Richard reviewed in his mind the questions that he would ask during the selection process. Jury selection in a civil trial always holds less excitement for prospective jurors than criminal trials.

Whether it is the lack of sensationalism or the public perception that business disputes simply aren't as voyeuristically meaningful as murder cases, Richard knew that it is hard to get, and harder to hold, the attention of civil jurors. Judge Jamison apparently wasn't concerned about cooperating with Richard's rising stress level, and the door to his chambers remained shut. Turning to Gayle, Richard engaged her in mock conversation, hoping to appear as if exploring issues of tremendous legal significance while they waited. Out of the corner of his eye he could see the fidgeting in the jury box become more noticeable. Richard wanted the few potential jurors who were still paying attention to perceive him as ready to proceed immediately and therefore not responsible for the length of time that it was taking to get matters started.

Time continued to pass without the judge's appearance, so Richard again got up and this time walked over to the bailiff, a deputy sheriff happily on rotation from the more stressful assignments of street patrol, domestic disturbances and other assorted duties. Circling the bailiff's waist was a customized black leather belt, spit polished to a mirror finish, with a silver buckle edged with 14 caret gold trim. Hanging from the left side of the belt were two sets of handcuffs, chrome chains loose, and a large ring of keys on a clip. On the other side of the belt hung a large black revolver next to a separate container that held extra bullets. The handle of the revolver stood clear of the holster, gleaming black walnut grips well polished and reflecting the owner's pride in his equipment. Richard understood guns, and when he was a boy had often gone target shooting with his father, but was still impressed by the sheer size of the 357 Magnum—basically a small cannon—strapped to the bailiff's waist. The bailiff looked up from his newspaper, which he had been reading to pass the time, and nodded pleasantly. Richard commented that the gun was certain to stop any of the potential jurors from getting out of line, evoking a small chuckle in response. The bailiff was pleased that his pride and joy had been noticed, and Richard suddenly found himself enmeshed in a discussion of stopping power, muzzle velocity and related mind numbing pieces of gun trivia. Richard tried to close the conversation with a lame joke about shooting blanks, only to receive a glare from the bailiff that reflected a sudden suspicion that Richard was merely pumping him. With eyes locked on Richard's, the bailiff reached down with his right hand and thumbed open the leather catch on the holster. Reaching across with his left hand he gripped the handle backwards and slowly withdrew the revolver from the holster. Without looking down he then pulled the holding pin that locked the cylinder to the barrel. Snapping the cylinder free from the gun, he then withdrew a large bullet and held it in front of Richard's face between a callused thumb and forefinger.

"Take it." He stated in a monotone.

Richard complied quickly, mind temporarily distracted from the potential jurors, and hefted the bullet in his hand. The large black head of the bullet, with prongs bent inward, was distinctive in its architecture and he recognized the deadly design without having to be told more.

"I thought that these were not allowed . . ." he suggested involuntarily, but stopped in mid-sentence in response to the bailiff's lopsided and unfriendly grin. Clearly pleased with the reaction the bailiff shrugged, casually took the bullet out of Richard's hand and replaced it into the open cylinder. Then, swinging the gun into the flat of the open palm of his free hand he snapped the cylinder shut and replaced the gun in his holster with one smooth motion. Richard forced a smile and dropped any pretense at further conversation in favor of moving back to the table near Dickson.

In the back of the courtroom, in the last row of the spectator section, sat Davis. From her vantage point she could see clearly the entire jury pool and watched them carefully for any hints that would help in the upcoming selection process. By design she sat on Stucky's side of the courtroom, as far as possible from Richard or Dickson. At this point there were so many people sitting in the spectator section that she just appeared to be another potential juror. Since the group would shrink during the next day or so, as individuals would either be excused from serving on the jury by the court or challenged from serving by Richard or Stucky because of potential problems due to conflicts or similar reasons, she wanted to avoid the impression to the remaining jurors that she was assisting Richard. By maintaining the appearance that he was assisted only by Gayle, in contrast to Stucky's fairly large group of associates and assistants, Richard wanted to reinforce the impression that the dispute involved the "local boy" against the large out-of-town corporation. Terri had arranged to leave on breaks and quickly run down to the pay phone on the lobby floor. Richard had written down that phone number earlier and, time permitting, would call her for any quick insights developed from her perspective.

Almost twenty minutes after the last potential juror was seated the side door near the bench swung outward with a loud bang as it opened fully against the wall of the courtroom. With black robe billowing Judge Jamison practically jogged into the courtroom and raced up the three steps to his raised bench. Throwing himself in the high-backed swivel chair behind the bench he simultaneously reached for and slammed down with a sharp crack a large wooded gavel. Silence was complete as everyone came immediately to attention.

With the selection pool of prospective jurors settled Judge Jamison turned and smiled at the jury box. Richard had never appeared or tried a case before him and was concerned with Judge Jamison's background as a former prosecutor. Prosecutors, to Richard's experience and way of thinking, were often more concerned with making sure that someone paid for the crime that had been committed, regardless of the particular defendant's actual involvement. For the public demands that someone be punished when a crime is committed, and often society's interest in punishment is served even if the interests of justice is not. Prosecutors tend also to be more conservative than most lawyers and as judges are therefore prone to be defense oriented in civil trials. Judge Jamison certainly looked the part of the conservative jurist. Tall and clean shaven, his sharp clear eyes quickly gave the impression that he missed nothing that took place in his courtroom. His head was held straight and tall, and was topped by closely cropped gray hair in a style that reflected his early training as a lieutenant in the United States Navy Judge Advocate Generals. During his tour of duty with the JAG, Judge Jamison had prosecuted the military equivalent of civilian criminal violations. He had earned a reputation as a stiff-necked, no nonsense, prosecutor. This reputation had served him well in his post-military practice and his ability to catch the eye of a Republican governor who desired to appoint the type of judge who would help him project his platform of being tough on crime.

The opening remarks came with no preamble, no slight clearing of the throat or tapping on the microphone. In fact, Judge Jamison never used his microphone. Although his distinctive rumble could be heard in all corners of the courtroom, and sometimes into the hall when confronted by a particularly dense lawyer on the law and motion calendar, he often described his aversion to microphones as reflection of his belief that everyone appearing before him should be interested enough in the proceedings to pay attention and listen without the need for mechanical devices.

"All right. Bailiff, please select the first twelve."

The bailiff hitched his gun belt over his ample stomach and headed over to a five gallon canister mounted on either end so it would rotate on its axle. The names of each person in the entire jury pool had been placed in the container on separate pieces of paper. Without ceremony the bailiff pulled out the first name and handed it to the clerk, who took the slip of paper and read it out loud to the courtroom.

"Elizabeth Dedra."

All heads swiveled around to watch a matronly looking woman, casually attired in a light gray polyester pantsuit, gingerly stand in the spectator section.

"Please approach," commanded the bailiff, "and take the first seat in the jury box."

All eyes followed her as she stepped past the other people in her row and then walked toward the jury box. Richard watched her intently, trying to pick up clues to her personality and background from her style of dress, her walk and how she dealt with being the center of so much attention. Turning to Gayle he whispered "write down 'sensible shoes.' " Gayle quickly complied, and in the chart under the name "Dedra" appeared the words "sensible shoes."

Richard had a personal theory that a person's shoes tended to reveal a lot about that person's personality. Although the style of dress may change at a relatively rapid rate with fashion trends, people tended to keep and wear their shoes until they had worn out and had to be replaced. Under his theory, spiked heels on a woman tended to reflect a person who would want to be noticed, but might be insecure about her abilities. Cowboy boots on a man otherwise dressed in a business suit might indicate someone who wanted to reflect their feeling of independence and unconventionality. Someone, hopefully, who could empathize with Dickson as an individual fighting against a faceless corporate bureaucracy.

His hand poised while he waited for the first selection to become situated, as soon as the first juror sat down the bailiff immediately pulled another name. He continued in the same manner until the entire box was full with the first twelve prospective jurors. During the calling of their names, Richard continued to whisper comments to Gayle after each name was announced and the graph paper now was full of short buzz words on each person.

"All right, ladies and gentlemen. Those of you that paid attention in your high school civics class know that jury duty is one of the honors that our society provides." Judge Jamison's head whipped around, immediately stifling a giggle that had broken out among the spectators. "My comments are made with the utmost seriousness. And I trust that each of you will take them and this entire process in the same manner." Noting with satisfaction the offender's meek but affirmative nodding he continued.

"Good. Now this case promises to last at least a week and maybe the better part of two."

Although the second part of the statement was met with light groans, Judge Jamison ignored this response as he ignored the response of every jury panel to this particular portion of his opening remarks. He understood that nobody could legitimately be blamed for not wanting to spend more than a few days on jury duty. Merely not wanting to attend, however, was definitely not a sufficient reason for being excused in his mind.

"I want a show of hands of those people that cannot commit to serving for that length of time."

Almost all hands shot up, to be reluctantly lowered as Judge Jamison firmly continued without acknowledging anyone.

"And I will consider as proper excuses only the need to provide care for children or the nonambulatory and those who are the sole wage earners for their family and who get paid solely on commission. All right, who fits into either of these two categories?"

Now only two of the potential jurors in the jury box raised their hands. As this stage of the process Richard listened out of one ear while looking at Gayle's graph. Noting that the first juror, Elizabeth Dedra, had not raised her hand to be excused, he thought about how she would fit into the profile he had written out the night before. She was older, which generally was considered to be a negative from the plaintiff's point of view as older jurors tend to be more conservative. A point buttressed by the 'sensible shoes' Richard had first noticed. In this case, however, Richard had written on the positive side of her profile "older." He felt that his pitch on the damage to Dickson's reputation would fly better with an older, more conservative, juror who could empathize with Dickson's concerns over how he was perceived by others in the community.

Judge Jamison finished his questioning of the two jurors who had asked to be excused, and during the process dismissed and replaced one of the two. As soon as an open spot on the panel had been refilled and the potential jurors again settled down, Judge Jamison glanced back at the clock and continued.

"The attorneys will now ask you some questions about your background and experiences. And please remember my earlier comments that, while this case involves a civil dispute, you must give the proceeding the same attention and solemnity as if someone's life or liberty was at stake."

From the back row of the juror box a hand went up. "Yes?"

"May I ask a question, your honor?"

"Certainly." Judge Jamison smiled in what he alone thought to be a fatherly and encouraging manner. "Go ahead."

"I would like to discuss a problem with you. Privately if possible."

At this comment Richard, Stucky and everyone else in the courtroom gave the speaker their undivided attention. He was heavy set, well built and tall, and was dressed completely in black with a large quartz crystal dangling from around his neck on a slim silver chain. Richard noticed Judge Jamison nodding thoughtfully at the request and quickly stood up.

"We have no objection to an in camera discussion in your chambers your Honor."

Stucky, mad at being beaten to the punch, scrambled to his feet and cleared his throat.

"Nor do we, your honor."

"All right, everyone please stay in the courtroom. Sir, please join me through here."

The in camera hearing, essentially a private meeting between the prospective juror and Judge Jamison and without the court reporter present, lasted all of ten minutes.

The door to Judge Jamison's chambers reopened and the prospective juror walked back into the courtroom followed halfway by Judge Jamison, who stopped at the doorframe and motioned to Richard and Stucky. They immediately rose to join Jamison in his chambers. Neither said anything as they walked across the courtroom, and remained silent upon entering the Judge's office. Jamison closed the door behind them and wearily rubbed his right hand across his weathered face. Looking up he chewed his lower lip for a moment.

"We have an individual who says that he believes only in 'natural law'."

"What's wrong with that, your Honor." Stucky, with characteristic insolence, leaned back against the wall frame. "Can't say that I think what Mr. Magnus is claiming in this case is natural."

Richard fought back the urge to respond in kind, knowing that the Judge probably would not be terribly interested in an exchange of quick repartee. He instead choose to consider the comment thoughtfully, having previously noted a number of books in Judge Jamison's office that dealt with the history and origins of the law. Shaw had mentioned that Judge Jamison thought of himself as something of an amateur legal historian and scholar, with several articles to his credit. Richard also had an affinity for the obscure and now might be a time to align himself with the Judge on a personal level.

"Does that mean that this guy believes in the Roman senate's method of resolving disputes?"

"Close, Mr. Magnus. Very good. But should you be referring to the Roman jurists of the Antonine Age," came the thoughtful reply, "involving analysis of a dispute along the lines of the philosophical speculations developed during that time period, then for our individual here the answer is no."

Judge Jamison looked at both counsel and continued in a very professorial tone.

"He says that he was raised by the Klamath Indians along the North Coast. From his upbringing, he claims that the only law that should be followed is law that is natural to the environment and not the laws that the civilization of any man may make."

"Then let's get rid of him." Stucky's undiplomatic interruption earned him a baleful glance from Judge Jamison.

"Of course you can 'get rid of him' Mr. Stucky. I merely wanted to bring this matter to your attention. I strongly suggest, however, that you give some thought to the respect that other beliefs are entitled to. I called you back in here so that I could get your stipulation to excuse him, politely, for cause so that he does not need to be embarrassed by having his private beliefs examined in open court. Is that procedure acceptable to you Mr. Stucky?"

Stucky was smart enough to merely mumble "yes sir" in response and Richard avoided all further comment other than acknowledging his agreement to Judge Jamison's suggestion. The three then filed back into the courtroom and retook their respective places. With a few well chosen words the man was thanked for his time and excused. Judge Jamison, his patience and good humor suddenly worn thin, turned his head to Richard and snapped out "proceed."

Selection of the jury continued without further notable event over the balance of the morning. When it was finally concluded, and the individuals all selected, Richard tried to focus solely on his opening statement—the next stage of the trial—but still was not overly comfortable with the composition of the panel. He had used up all of his peremptory challenges in an attempt to find the right mix of backgrounds and opinions, but the random selections from the jury pool after each challenge seemingly resulted in a new individual who appeared worse than the one just excused. Finally, after a long pause so the clerk could complete the paperwork portion of the selection process, as a single unit the twelve jurors and two alternates stood to take the oath of their new and transient office. Each of them looked appropriately solemn as the court clerk dispassionately read the oath of their new position off of a worn index card. Richard glanced up from the notes of his opening statement and watched each of them in turn, seeking additional clues to their individual personalities. At the same time his mind still wrestled with the finer points of the theme of the case that he would lay out as soon as the jury was seated.

For the last several days he had gone over the central question of his focus. He had wrestled with the decision whether to depict Wine House as an uncaring and evil multinational corporation whose deeds had global consequences, and thus try to inflame the jury against Wine House, or to disregard the harm being done globally and instead direct the jurors to consider solely how Dickson had been treated and hope that they saw the events his way. As with many difficult strategic decisions, he had fully discussed the choice with Michael Shaw the night before.

They had been sitting in Michael's corner office going over how Richard expected the trial to go, including a discussion that centered on a witness by witness analysis to confirm for the last time how and what Richard hoped to be able to prove over whatever length of time that the trial might last. Richard selected a fine thin cigar from Michael's large collection and reached out for the brass clipper to snip the end off the cigar. Usually he would have just torn the end off of the cigar with his teeth, but he was still sufficiently intimidated by his mentor that he refrained from giving in to the impulse and instead dutifully used followed Michael's example.

"So why do you want to put Alexander on the stand?"

Michael blew out a long slender stream of blue smoke from a cigar that dripped ashes across the gray plush rug while he waited patiently for an answer.

"Because these guys approved the use of hazardous wastes all over the United States. Even if the use at other sites was not illegal, he had to have at least been aware of what went on. And I can make the argument to the jury to show what slime balls these guys are."

"Now wait, Richard. Think about your focus."

"What do you mean?"

"You have gotten too close to the case. You aren't thinking clearly, what with the threats and the pressure you think Wine House has applied to the District Attorney to hassle you."

"Thanks a whole hell of a lot, Mike. Just the encouragement I need the night before trial."

"Look, Richard. You have lived with this case—and too damn closely if you were to ask me—for the last four months. Ultimately, this case is not going to get decided on what actually took place. There is no way to send the jury back in time, nor will they have the full context of the history between Dickson and Wine House. No, Richard. This case—like all cases—will be decided based on the jury's *perception* of what took place. A perception created by the witnesses that you decide to put on the stand, by the questions that you ask, and by the arguments that you make throughout the trial. The jury will decide the case based on what they perceive to have occurred, and you must focus on how best to shape that perception. You have a good case on how Dickson was treated. You don't need to correct all of the evils in the world. Just go out and get the best damn award from that jury you can for Dickson."

"Yep, and let Wine House get away with business as usual."

"Look, Rich. You need to worry only about Dickson. Any award, even one dollar, will at least keep the District Attorney from thinking that he can get a quick indictment and conviction. He has political aspirations, but he won't chance them with an iffy conviction if you can get the jury behind you."

"Thanks for adding to the pressure."

"Just keep in mind what your goal is. It should be to win for Dr. Dickson. And not to cure the evils in the world in one fell swoop. Don't get too greedy. You can ask the jury for a fair award and let them do justice. They will anyway, even if you ask for millions. In fact, if you ask for too much you can piss off the jury. As my father used to say, 'pigs get fat, but hogs get slaughtered.' "

Now, with these thoughts still echoing in his mind, Richard set himself for the battle to finally begin.

CHAPTER ELEVEN

APPROACHING THE LECTERN Richard smiled and took a small sip of water from the paper cup Gayle had thoughtfully poured for him while they were on the break. Placing his notes down gently he paused and made eye contact with each of the jurors.

"Thank you, Ladies and Gentlemen for your patience. You have been selected to sit on what may be a very long trial. And although it is your duty to sit as jurors I appreciate the effort that it will take and the time that you are giving up from the rest of your lives." Richard paused and took another sip of water. Nervousness was drying his throat faster than he could wet it and made his tongue feel like it would stick to the roof of his mouth. "Because this trial may last several weeks I want to take this opportunity to provide an overview of what you will hear from the witnesses and what will be read from the documents presented. An introduction, if you like, to the people that were involved."

At the end of each sentence Richard hesitated long enough to make further eye contact with each of the jurors. Some, in turn, smiled back, expecting to be entertained: others leaned forward slightly, unconsciously reflecting their intention to take their new job as a juror seriously. One elderly man in a tattered plaid sports coat already appeared ready to go to sleep. Richard mentally adjusted the mechanics of his presentation to reflect the responses of the jury panel and in his mind's eye picked the two individuals from whom the foreperson would likely be selected.

"In April 1994 Dr. Dickson was employed by Wine House as the Winemaster and President of Winery Peak under a contract that was to last through 2009. Winery Peak is a start-up winery and vineyard, owned and operated by Wine House, that was set to release its first vintage in spring 2005.

On April 10, 2007, after several employees of Winery Peak became ill from an unknown cause, the Napa County Health Services discovered evidence that someone had intentionally used the remote acreage in the mountains surrounding the winery property to discharge large amounts of toxic residues. On April 14, 2007, Dr. Dickson was fired unceremoniously, without any investigation and without any cause for termination. On April 15, 2007, the corporate press department at Wine House conducted a well orchestrated press conference to address the problem. During the conference the corporate spokesperson stated that Dr. Dickson had been let go, and created the clear impression the Dr. Dickson was responsible for the toxic dumping."

Richard paused, his head down.

"In one week, one short week, Dr. Dickson's reputation, built over thirty years in the wine making industry, was destroyed."

Richard continued, slowly raising both his head and the volume of his voice.

"During this trial we will present evidence that this corporate Defendant had no reasonable basis to claim that Dr. Dickson had any part in the dumping of the toxics, but knowingly, willfully and intentionally fired him based on his supposed 'role' in the dumping. And this Defendant then blamed Dr. Dickson so that it could shift the public's attention and focus from the fact that chemicals had been dumped on its property whether or not Dr. Dickson was involved. A planned campaign was then designed by its media specialists, its spin doctors, so that they could rush to the press with appropriate sound bites."

"Look at Dr. Dickson." The jurors obediently followed his demand. "You will hear from Dr. Dickson. You will be the judges of his credibility—his believability."

Dr. Dickson smiled self-depreciatingly at this comment.

"You will hear that Wine House fired him—without regard for his involvement—so it could have a scapegoat. Wine House fired him, and attempted to destroy his reputation, even though it had no reason to claim that he played any part in what was being done behind his back and without his knowledge."

As he finished, Richard overtly shot a heated stare in the direction of the designated representative of Wine House sitting at counsel table, a man whom Richard had never seen before the trial, and held it for several long moments. Even as he turned to continue, however, he saved a special look for Stucky. Stucky did not acknowledge Richard's look. He instead carefully continued to pen his notes of Richard's comments. Stucky wanted to capture, as accurately as possible, the exact words and phrases used. During closing argument he would try to characterize the words and phrases as promises made, but not kept, by Richard to the jury. Promises not kept as they were not—hopefully from Stucky's standpoint—supported by any credible evidence. Stucky's assumption that Richard knew that this risk existed did not diminish his desire to record what the jury had heard. Should the Judge decide to keep some of the proffered evidence from the jury, or should a witness deviate from expectations, Stucky would still characterize in a pejorative fashion the difference between what Richard had promised and what he had finally delivered. Finally, notes complete, Stucky placed the top back on his pen and then carefully set the pen back on the table next to his pad of paper with the top of the pen perfectly aligned with the edge of the notepad. Pursing his lips in apparent contemplation, he nodded his head to himself twice and then rose to face the jury box.

Richard watched anxiously and a small heavy ball formed in the pit of his stomach as he waited for Stucky's presentation and rejoinder. He comforted himself with the thought that Stucky was basically a cold bastard, and not to his mind particularly good looking. Stucky had a habit of wearing raw silk suits, tailored without pockets to make sure that the jackets would lie flat and smooth.

He had that type of ego, which should come across as soon as he addressed the jury. With what Stucky thought passed for an endearing smile, but looked more to Richard like a sickly grin, he began without preamble.

"I won't waste your time."

Stucky did not move from where he stood, immediately behind the counsel table.

"My name is Patrick Stucky. I represent Wine House and it is my style is to present my client's case directly, without"—looking at Richard—"confusing the issues and in the most efficient amount of time possible. None of us should have to have our time wasted by a case that presents such a straightforward case of wrongdoing by Dr. Dickson."

Without breaking oratorical stride he turned and now walked three steps to a group of placards that had been previously placed behind the lectern. The top placard reflected a timeline that covered the history of Winery Peak and Dickson's employment period through the day on which he was fired.

"In early 2007 vineyard workers at Winery Peak began to fall seriously ill. Horrible illnesses that were the result of substantial overexposure to chemicals and toxic materials that are used in winery operations. Our investigation has revealed that the chemicals had been dumped. Dumped, presumably, to avoid the expense of having to properly dispose of the materials."

"During this trial you will hear from the representatives of Wine House. They will describe for you how they were contacted by representatives of the State of California. And that they were told that areas of the property that makes up Winery Peak was quickly on the road to being so full of dumped toxics that the entire vineyard would have to be closed so it could be handled as a superfund cleanup site. You will hear from vineyard workers who are still bearing the scars of their exposure to dangerous chemicals. And you will hear evidence that suggests that the use of and dumping of the chemicals was part of Dr. Dickson's plan for improving the profit ratios at Winery Peak *and thereby protect his own job*."

"When you have heard all of the evidence we believe that you will find Dr. Dickson knew about the use of the chemicals, that he knowingly and intentionally allowed the chemicals to be dumped. And you will agree that Wine House was completely justified in terminating Dr. Dickson from the important position of President of Winery Peak."

As Stucky turned and sat down Richard slowly and deliberately gathered his notes and rose from his chair. He wanted the jury to switch their attention off of Stucky as quickly as possible, to instead watch him go through the mechanics of his presentation and hopefully let slip from their minds Stucky's last comments, especially the one that suggested a compelling motive for Dickson to allow the chemical to be dumped. When he was sure that he held their complete attention he turned and called Dickson to the stand.

Richard had thought long and hard over the order in which he would present the witnesses. He really did not have that many to choose from, and wanted to make sure that he leveraged the greatest amount of impact out of all of them. But he knew that his opening witness could only be one person, as the case would be largely won—or lost—through Dickson himself. If the jury were to bond with Dickson, or at least find his position somewhat sympathetic, Stucky would have a much more difficult time taking on Dickson during cross-examination.

During their practice session the night before Richard had walked Dickson through question after potential question, fine tuning the answers. Nothing so rehearsed that it would sound staged or from a script, but instead a gentle reminder of particular word choices that might sound better than others. When they were done with the direct examination, Michael Shaw joined then to rehearse areas of the anticipated cross-examination. Michael played the role of Stucky and Gayle, with a smile, pretended to be Judge Jamison. Michael began slowly, letting Dickson relax into the tempo of the questions before turning the heat up with a series of particularly bothersome inquiries. To Richard's concern Dickson became rattled and, in response, began to argue his position with Michael. They broke the exchange to let Dickson cool off, and Michael carefully explained to Dickson how he must relax on the stand and trust in Richard to either object or re-explore the areas when it was his turn during redirect examination. Both Richard and Michael could see Dickson tiring and Richard, understanding the suggestion in Michael's eyes, had finally called it a night.

All of the frustrations of waiting and preparation suddenly seemed to fall away as soon as Richard called Dickson to the stand. Dickson had been sitting with his wife in the spectator section immediately behind Richard. With an unintentionally nice touch, Dickson's wife had given him a good luck type half hug as he stood. A touch hopefully not lost on the home town jury. Dickson took the stand without incident and Richard, following Michael's suggestion, remained sitting behind the counsel table. Michael had reminded Richard that during direct examination the witness must be the object of attention, with Richard merely acting as the director of the process of the question-answer format. On cross-examination, however, Richard was to stand and take control of the proceedings—telling his story through the placement and timing of the questions. Questions that only allowed the witness enough room to answer either "yes" or "no" and thereby confirm the points that Richard was trying to make.

To ease the jury into the difficult process of actively listening to evidence, and acquaint them with Dickson, Richard began with a series of questions that called for a fairly detailed description of Dickson's thirty-five plus years in the wine industry. Long years spent in the fields, and not just behind some desk in a sanitized and aloof office. He guided Dickson to relate time spent working in relative obscurity until his experience level began to match his natural gift for wine making, and eventually resulted in successes that propelled his reputation in the industry into the rarified air of a wine master. Although the number of winemakers in the United States had grown substantially in the late 1980's and early 1990's, as it had become trendy for successful stockbrokers, doctors and other professionals to buy acreage and produce a few hundred to several thousand cases of wine a year, only a handful of individuals were recognized internationally as masters of their craft. Dickson was one of the few and, as he described for the jury his experiences in the industry, the lines in his face eased to reflect the keen pleasure that he took from his life's work. His response to Richard's questions took on a narrative form, almost professorial in tone, as he described the early years at Winery Peak. Heeding both Michael's advice and the manner in which the jury seemed to be enjoying the story, Richard remained in the background with questions interspersed just enough to keep the narrative on tract and moving forward from the early days of his relationship with Winery Peak, including the negotiation of the terms of his employment, through to the present.

To help the jury visualize Dickson's words, Gayle had blown up some photos Dickson had taken during the early development of the site. As Dickson described various aspects of creating a winery from scratch, such as blasting a reservoir or staking the young vines, Richard would quietly change one poster board for another. They finally finished with the background information and Richard let the jury think about the testimony in silence for a moment while he moved the easel that held the poster boards against the far wall. He made sure to leave the last poster board on the easel, a flattering blowup of Dickson and one of the fieldworkers working together to place a new vine into the ground, positioned in a manner that it faced the jury from behind Stucky's chair. At the very least Richard hoped that the poster would irritate Stucky.

Taking his seat again, Richard asked Dickson to explain how grape growers dealt with the need to fertilize the vines and control pests. These were the only reasons that a grower could possibly have for using chemicals in the field. They had gone over this area extensively during their preparation stage and Richard first used Dickson's testimony to educate the jury on the general use of chemicals in farming and then specifically on the use in grape growing. During one point Dickson began unexpectedly to go off on a tangent about organic grape growing, but Richard quickly reeled him back on track. They then turned to a discussion on the staffing of wineries, particularly the use of documented and undocumented aliens by the various valley wineries. After describing historic conditions, Dickson detailed the programs that he had tried to implement over the last fifteen years. Richard hoped to argue to the jury that Dickson's demonstrated concern over his workers, coupled with his detailed knowledge about the proper use of chemicals, made it improbable that Dickson knew about the use of the chemicals located in the old quarry, much less would have permitted the acts to have occurred upon which Wine House was now claiming the right to have terminated Dickson's employment.

The day was growing late as the questions continued. Richard had done a good job timing Dickson's testimony to last the entire day. Although Stucky would have the night to review his notes of the day's testimony, the jury would also have the entire night to ponder and absorb not only what Dickson had said, but how he had said it. Hopefully some of what occurred during the day would stick in their minds. Now, with the afternoon drawing rapidly to a close, to shake the jury from the sometimes numbing routine of the question and answer format of the proceedings Richard stood and walked purposefully towards Dickson. With voice now raised, in direct contrast to the somewhat subdued tone he had used throughout the day, he squarely addressed Dickson.

"Dr. Dickson. Have you ever used organophosphates?"

"No, sir."

"Have you, or anyone on your behalf, ever dumped chemicals of any type into the old quarry?"

"Absolutely not."

"Would you have allowed anyone to dump chemicals anywhere at Winery Peak?"

"No way!"

"And did Wine House have cause to fire you?"

"No, no they did not."

Richard now paused meaningfully to look directly at the jury, every juror in turn, attempting to convey the strength of his convictions. He then turned towards Judge Jamison and acknowledged that he was done with his questions for Dickson. The day had certainly taken its toll, for when Judge Jamison excused the jury it was all Richard could do to stand outwardly strong while the jury slowly filed past him and out of the courtroom.

~ ~ ~ ~ ~

That night sleep came slowly for Richard. Nagging self-doubt worked on his mind, keeping sleep from providing him much needed rest. He had not even turned in to bed until after 1:00 A.M., even though he knew that the next day would require his full concentration. Between 1:00 and 3:00 A.M. he had gotten up no fewer than four times to jot down thoughts and ideas as they came to him in sporadic bursts. Adding to his discomfort was the gnawing thought of Allen Rose, who had appeared unannounced in the back of the courtroom. Richard had not seen him enter the courtroom, although it must have been after he had resumed his examination of Dickson. There had simply been a moment between questions when Richard had turned to select an exhibit to show to Dickson from the tidy pile on the table, and instead caught a glimpse of Allen out of the corner of his eye. The pending question had flown out of his head, to be momentarily replaced by anger at the thought that Rose would care so much about his goddamn power play at the Firm that he would want to try to unnerve Richard by his presence. Although the thought had passed quickly, and the pace of the questioning resumed without too much difficulty, he could not shake the feeling that the jury had wondered about the cause of his clear misstep.

As the night wore on he tried every position possible on the bed in an attempt to find a comfortable spot, without luck, until he had finally dozed off around 3:30. He actually managed three full hours of uninterrupted sleep before waking on his own, minutes before the alarm would go off.

~ ~ ~ ~ ~

"It was important for you to show Wine House that you could make Winery Peak a financial success. Correct?"

Dickson looked at Stucky warily, pausing just briefly enough to repeat the question in his own mind to make sure that he understood what was being asked. Stucky had been going at him all day, and the pace was wearing at his ability to concentrate. For the last half-hour he had wondered where Stucky had been headed with his questions, and tried to remember Richard's admonition not to try to out guess Stucky's intentions. Dickson nodded his head in the affirmative.

"That was a 'yes', Dr. Dickson?"

"Yes, Mr. Stucky."

"And you had definite ideas how to further develop Winery Peak. Correct?"

"Well . . . we discussed several ideas."

"Now, Dr. Dickson." Stucky's tone now sounded like a teacher, calmly directing a particularly slow student. "You did more than merely 'discuss' your ideas. You went so far as to hire an architect."

"We hired an architect at the beginning of the project."

"But sir, you had him continue to develop plans after the first phase was complete. Yes or no?"

"Yes."

"And you had him design Phase 2, before you had approval for Phase 2 from Wine House."

"We wanted to have . . ."

Stucky held up his hand, like an irritated traffic cop, and cut Dickson off in mid-sentence before turning to Judge Jamison.

"Your Honor, may the Court please admonish the witness to just answer the questions and not argue."

Richard started to rise to his feet, only to be pre-empted by Judge Jamison.

"Dr. Dickson. Please listen carefully to the questions. Your counsel can ask you further questions if he feels that it is necessary during his re-examination."

Richard grimaced inwardly, hoping that Dickson would take the not so subtle hint from the Judge to answer the questions directly. Too many witnesses, thought Richard, think that they can control the pace and outcome of the cross-examination through their answers, but Stucky was too experienced to let that happen.

"Now Dr. Dickson. Please listen carefully to my questions. You had the architect design Phase 2 before there was approval from Wine House."

"Yes."

Stucky moved across the courtroom to a table against the side wall. The table was covered by a brown linen tarp, through which could be seen the outlines of a large rectangular box approximately five feet long and almost two feet high. Standing at one end, Stucky quietly requested the bailiff grab the other and between the two of them the table was lifted and placed immediately before the witness box. Slowly, delicately, Stucky removed the cover from the box. On the table sat a clean Plexiglas box. Inside the box sat a scale model of Winery Peak. The model included both the buildings that had already been constructed as well as two substantially larger structures that did not yet exist at the site. Stucky waited long enough for the jury to become acquainted with the model before taking a slender silver pen-like object from his front shirt pocket. He then extended the end, in a phallic way, until the entire pen was now a three foot long pointer. Waving the pointer generally over the entire complex, Stucky half turned towards Dickson.

"This model represents your grand scheme."

"That would be the finished project."

"But only these three small buildings presently exist."

"That's correct."

"You did not have permission to build the remaining two structures before you were separated from employment."

"That's correct, but we have not yet asked for approval of funds."

"Please, just answer my questions, Dr. Dickson."

Stucky confidently continued, clearly enjoying himself and ready to bring closure to this area of questioning.

"And each of these two buildings alone could house all of the operations that are currently located in all three of the existing buildings."

"That, Mr. Stucky, is incorrect."

"Incorrect?"

The word slipped out of his mouth before he realized it, so intent was Stucky on establishing a motive for Dickson to have dumped the chemicals. He planned on establishing motive by showing that Dickson had in mind a grandiose plan of development. Before he could say anything further, however, Dickson sharply pressed on as if Stucky's slip of the tongue was a request for clarification.

"Incorrect, Mr. Stucky. I worked on that model myself. Your Honor, may I demonstrate?"

Interested at the turn of events, Judge Jamison simply nodded his assent. Dickson extracted his lanky frame from the narrow confines of the witness chair and stepped over to the table. With powerful forearms knotting from the effort, he lifted the entire piece of Plexiglas off of the table by himself and set it gently down on the floor. Then, with the rock steady hand of someone who knows what he is doing, Dickson reached across the length of the table. With a sharp tug the building shell was lifted cleanly off of the larger of the two proposed structures. Underneath the shell sat six tall cylinders, now exposed in two neat rows of three, connected together with steel pipe.

"You see, Mr. Stucky, these buildings are really just shells to enclose the steel wine tanks that are used to store the wine before the wine is placed into French oak barrels. The tanks are perfectly happy to sit outside all day and night. We factored the cooling costs and determined that we can amortize the costs of shell construction well within acceptable levels based on the energy savings without any extra capital expenditure. The walls and roof will be a nice touch, but since corporate already approved installation of the tanks themselves, we could do the rest at any time without additional increase to our basis."

Dickson calmly handed the shell to Stucky and turned back to the witness chair. As he turned, with his back to the jury, Dickson allowed himself one brief grin in Richard's direction, whose stomach was doing flip flops from Dickson's extemporaneous demonstration. Mercifully, Judge Jamison looked up at the clock and, noting the time for the record, called the day finished.

~ ~ ~ ~ ~

"Don't argue with me, I just think you were lucky and don't want you to push your luck!"

Dickson turned angrily from the window to face Richard before replying.

"Sometimes I think you don't believe me."

"Sit down, Pete." Richard snapped back wearily. He got up and crossed the room towards Dickson. "You have got to realize that arguing with opposing counsel is like wrestling with a pig in shit."

Dickson stopped short in his pacing, puzzled at the reference.

"Sooner or later you realize that while you both are getting dirty, only the pig, and not you, is enjoying himself."

Richard paused long enough to allow Dickson to cool off and, although he did not get a smile or similar acknowledgment in return, decided to continue in the lighter vein.

"You have to come to terms with the fact that you are going to hear a lot worse things said about you over the next two weeks."

Dickson interrupted. "But I don't have to hear it from you." Richard nodded and picked up a legal pad.

"All right, all right, fair enough. Remember when we first got together? I asked you to tell me why I should believe you. You were mad then too. And I told you then as now, that if you couldn't convince me you would never be able to convince the jury. You did a good job then, but only because you focused on the objective. Now, when we argue the case to the jury I want them to know you, to be able to stand in your shoes and ask themselves why would you have trashed a project in which you put so much effort using means that are inconsistent with your approach to this business."

"I still just can't figure why in hell they would claim that I dumped the stuff. Blaming me can't do any good. I sure as hell don't have enough money to clean it up even if Wine House was able to prove that I did do it!"

"You have to remember that this game is being played on many levels. First, this has been a public relations nightmare for Wine House. They have every left-wing fruitcake in California boycotting all of their wine brands as environmental exploiters. If the marketing department can pin the responsibility on you as a rouge employee, then they can claim the role of white knights of the environment." Richard rubbed his face wearily. "Secondly, they have got to have the State of California as well as the EPA regulators breathing down their necks. Someone at Wine House must have known about the dumping. That much stuff doesn't just magically appear. And that someone is facing a long stretch of unemployment as well as possible criminal liability unless you become the fall guy. It's really pretty Machiavellian."

"You don't have to sound so damn impressed." Dickson injected bitterly.

"I am impressed. They would have succeeded in their plan if the field workers had not been using the quarry for a pool. Obviously, when the shit hit the fan and those field workers got sick, someone moved quickly to make sure that the situation exposure could be minimized. Given the time constraints, their decision was well thought out. And Wine House is going to make damn sure that its plan comes together."

The phone rang a welcome interruption to the discussion. Waving Dickson to silence Richard picked up the receiver with one hand and downed the tails of his drink using his other hand. Which resulted in a fairly wet sounding "hello." While Richard spoke quietly on the phone Dickson turned back to stare out at the world outside of the window. His stomach turned and boiled, the acid and stress dissolving away the lining. On the other side of the glass, life seemed to be progressing pretty much as was normal for the small town. Various nondescript cars passed intermittently, making their way slowly through the intersection. The sun would flash at Dickson occasionally as the chrome of a random bumper would catch the light. Coming from a life formally free of lawyers, at least as far as his personal life was concerned, Dickson could not shake the heavy feeling that he was helplessly ensnared in the judicial process, and was more of a victim than a beneficiary of its protections. The days before the lawsuit now felt like a distant memory, as if they had involved someone else altogether, and the end was something that could not be pictured in the slightest. Relations with his wife, although supportive on the surface, had grown strained and their sex life was certainly at an all time low.

Clenching his eyes, he drew a deep breath in exasperation and to help ward off the onset of yet another stress attack. The attacks had been coming more frequently, to the point of waking him up in the middle of the night in a cold sweat. The last thing in the world that he needed right now was to alienate Richard, who was clearly pulling out all of the stops, and with that thought turned back from the window to wait patiently while Richard concluded the phone call. Dickson then nodded affirmatively, as if their conversation had not been interrupted by the call.

"All right, Richard. Whatever their agenda may be, I don't care. Just kick their ass."

~~~~~

For Richard and Dickson the next three days of the trial passed rapidly. On the second day Stucky had quickly finished his cross-examination of Dickson, scoring no major points or being scored upon in return. After Dickson left the stand Richard had then called three individuals who had
~~~~~

worked with Dickson over the years, in an attempt to establish Dickson's pattern and practice of concerned involvement when it came to his workers and the environment. Their testimony was not terribly exciting and was not challenged by Stucky. Next in order appeared an expert in the use of the agricultural application of chemical agents, to testify about the available alternatives to the use of organophosphates. This witness responding favorably to the questions posed by Richard during direct examination, only to then fall apart during Stucky's cross-examination after he had to admit, in the face of insistent questioning, that organophosphates were still readily available outside of California and were significantly cheaper to use. These were points that both Richard knew would support Stucky's argument that Dickson illegally used the chemicals to improperly boost the bottom line profits of the fledgling winery's operations.

Reaching near the end of his list of witnesses, Richard gave another name to the bailiff to summon from the hallway. Within a few moments the attention of the entire courtroom turned to the rear as Rebecca Stewart entered and gracefully walked towards the witness stand. She walked purposely with head held high, eyes straight and true towards her destination. Neither looking at Richard nor Stucky as she passed by the counsel tables, she seemed oddly detached from the proceedings. Richard was not troubled by her mannerisms as he did not expect or want any greeting or other overt sign of recognition. As they had discussed previously, Terri had served her with an updated trial subpoena and now, because her presence was judicially compelled, she would be able to state truthfully that she was not taking sides nor was voluntarily present on anyone's behalf. As she straightened her skirt to take her seat in the witness chair, Richard glanced over at Stucky to see his reaction to Stewart's appearance. Stucky was whispering urgently to his paralegal, and they both plainly had trouble placing Stewart's name or relevance to the issues being tried. Now, thought Richard, now it was time to drop a bombshell on Wine House.

With carefully phrased short questions Richard began to lay a foundation for Stewart's substantive testimony and her personal knowledge of events. Stewart responded smoothly, her well honed skills in making presentations to the members of the press evident as she spoke. Richard continued by having her describe her educational background and work experience before her involvement with Winery Peak. She spoke in a way that was most intriguing to watch, each word leaving her mouth perfectly formed, vowels molded effortlessly by rounded lips. Although all of the jurors were paying close attention, the sixth juror in the front row was clearly the most interested by either what she had to say, or at least by the manner in which she seemed to be saying it. He seemed enraptured, hanging on to every word, almost to the point of tipping forward in his chair. As she continued with a short narrative answer, Stewart shifted slowly in her seat and, perhaps by reflex alone, smoothed with one untroubled hand the crease in her short skirt above her right thigh where it crossed over her left. Juror Six sighed audibly, provoking both a giggle from the juror immediately behind him and a rose colored flash in Stewart's cheeks as she demurely blushed. Richard also noticed the interaction and, to avoid any further distractions, plunged ahead into the substance of her testimony.

"Were you asked to put together a public relations response to the press reports involving the discovery of the chemicals?"

"Yes."

"And what was the response that you put together?"

"Wine House had built itself a strong reputation in the marketplace for mid-range varietals. The company had made a point of placing itself in that market position by suggesting that its wines are particularly appropriate for family occasions, friends over to dinner or what not. The `snob appeal' approach that is used for super premium wines was to be carefully avoided for the wines to be produced at Winery

Peak. And there was a terrific concern that the situation with employees becoming ill from exposure to chemicals at Winery Peak would have a negative effect on the theme of 'family values.' After all, look what the threat of benzene contamination did to the sales of Perrier a few years back."

"And were you asked to do anything to help protect the 'family values' theme?"

"Objection."

Richard wheeled in surprise as the interruption was called out, turning so quickly that he nearly caught the toe of one foot on the heel of the other. Judge Jamison himself raised a bushy eyebrow in anticipation, which Stucky took as an invitation to proceed, although in somewhat calmer tones than before.

"We object to this question, Your Honor. There is no relevancy to the marketing strategy of Wine House to this case. Dr. Dickson was fired for . . ."

"Stop right there, Mr. Stucky," Judge Jamison interrupted, "I do not want any long speeches this afternoon. Mr. Magnus, your response please."

"If Wine House claims that it fired Dr. Dickson to protect its corporate reputation, a point that it has previously stated, then the development of that reputation is relevant."

"All right, Mr. Stucky, I am inclined to allow the line of questioning to continue for the moment subject to a motion to strike. Madam Reporter, would you read back the last question for the witness?"

As the court reporter busied herself with the process of searching through the paper tape for the beginning of the last question Stucky nodded his understanding to Judge Jamison and sat down. He knew that he had to be careful at this point, as he had been caught unprepared by the appearance of Stewart. Even though she still worked on Wine House accounts, he could not believe that Richard would have called her as a witness, subpoena or not, unless he felt that her testimony would be favorable to Dickson and, therefore, unfavorable to Wine House. At least, Stucky rationalized, he had not acted completely as if he had been caught with his pants down. His objection must have clued the Judge into the possibility that the testimony should not be presented to the jury, and may help in his attempts to limit additional damaging testimony.

Stewart listened carefully to the court reporter as the question was read from the transcript. As soon as the reporter had replaced the tape in the stenographic machine Stewart calmly answered the question in the affirmative.

"And what were you asked to do?"

Stewart at first sat back in response to this question, and gazed upwards in silent contemplation as if mentally preparing her answer. With a short toss of her head, in a manner that seemed to say that she had made up her mind on some personal issue, she looked directly at the jury and began to explain in minute detail the steps involved in creating a marketing and public relations campaign. Although leery of the narrative form of her response, Richard did not interrupt as he wanted to avoid the perception that he had any part in the preparation of her testimony. In truth, he had very little to do with the nature and extent of her testimony and now could only but hope for the best.

As she addressed the jury, Stewart described the decision-making process leading to the program to set monies aside to assist the families of the workers whom had suffered adverse reactions to the chemicals. Looking at the jury while she spoke, Richard could not decide whether the testimony—in the eyes of the jury—was portraying Wine House as a company that truly cared about its workers, or as a company that was quick to coldly calculate the best possible public relations angle to be gained from the tragedy. One thing, however, was certain to Richard. Juror Six was so mesmerized by Stewart that he was sure to fall out of his chair if he were to lean any further forward.

Stewart paused in her testimony and delicately poured a glass of water from the carafe that sat on the edge of the table next to the witness chair. No one spoke as the water flowed into a small paper cup that she had lifted from a short stack that had been placed in that specific location so as to be available for use by the witnesses. Although fairly bursting to ask the next question, Richard waited patiently while she slowly sipped the water. She finished the cup and drew a small embroidered handkerchief out of her purse to pat dry the corners of her mouth. All eyes in the courtroom watched this process with rapt attention, so elegant was her movements. When he was sure that she was done with the cup of water, and that he had her full attention, Richard again rose to his feet and addressed her as if there had been no interruption.

"And did Wine House follow through with the campaign?"

"Objection."

Stucky's objection was quicker this time, but not so quick that Stewart was unable to commence her response. Stucky was not about to let her continue, however, and in a louder voice pointedly repeated the word "objection" to drown out her voice. This time Judge Jamison immediately motioned both counsel to approach the bench, and Stucky moved forward approvingly. Richard hastened forward from his position behind the counsel table, moving stiffly on Stucky's heels and angry with the interruption. The conference was interfering with his timing, and the issue of timing could be critical to his plan to gain momentum and get the jury angry at Wine House. At least, he noted to himself, in a conference at the bench the three could discuss Stucky's position outside of the jury's hearing, and therefore avoid any further problem from Stucky's penchant for speechmaking. The jury needed to view Wine House as simply another huge company that would do or say anything to sell its products. Showing that Wine House had not followed through on its highly publicized promises to fund relief for its workers could go a long way in painting that picture. If possible, he had hoped to stretch the point during closing argument and ask the jurors to consider the probability that if Wine House cared so little for its workers on this issue then it was more than likely that Wine House, and not Dickson, was the one responsible for the chemicals being in the quarry. With

Stucky's objection, however, he faced the possibility that he would never get the testimony before the jury on this point and be hampered in his ability to later make that argument.

The conference with Judge Jamison took only a short minute. With heads bowed together, positions were exchanged in muted voices. Judge Jamison listened first to Stucky's whispered concerns regarding the relevancy of the information and then to Richard's rejoinder. To Richard's dismay and disbelief Judge Jamison then noted that the prejudice to Wine House—should it have to explain it marketing position in the context of its fiscal and tax reporting position because of the disbursement of the funds—outweighed the remote relevance of the information to Richard's case. Without further comment Richard turned and walked back to the counsel table, looking as if steam should be appearing from his ears, unaware of the interest that Juror Six had taken in the entire discourse. When they were all back in their places, and ready to proceed, Richard stated quietly that he had no more questions for Stewart and thanked her for her appearance. Stucky then rose and remarked lightly that he also had no questions and therefore no use for this witness. As Judge Jamison excused Stewart, Stucky failed to notice the look on the face of Juror Six, reflecting a person decidedly unhappy with the manner in which Stucky had interfered with Stewart's ability to relate what she had come to the trial to say.

~ ~ ~ ~ ~

"You look pretty down in the mouth."

Frank Walsh had to repeat his observation loudly to be heard over the din of the customers at the roadside diner where he had met Richard for dinner. The diner was housed in a squat gray building which, from the outside, was generally indistinguishable from the auto body shop next door. The diner was furnished with a mixture of cheap wooden chairs that did not fully match one another, grouped around a number of chipped linoleum tables and was efficiently run by two whitish gray haired waitresses who had the habit of treating everyone like children. The food was filling, if seldom more than merely passable, and was inexpensive enough that Frank and Richard had become regulars back when they had both been fresh out of law school with nothing more to show for their advanced education other than ten years of future loan payments to the government for their student loans. Although their respective finances had changed significantly since those early days, force of habit kept them coming back when they wanted an opportunity to talk freely.

Richard did look much as Frank described. The case was going badly from Richard's point of view, and there was no real relief or magic testimony in sight. At Frank's prompting Richard described how the last several days had gone. Uncomfortable the way that Stewart's testimony had ultimately turned out, and the Judge's decision to exclude her key testimony, Richard had strained to put the episode behind him and had next called an economist to the stand to explain the economic losses suffered by Dickson because of the loss of his job. The testimony had been simple enough, and there had been no unexpected hitches or stumbles, but the information came across as dry as listening to Congressional budgetary testimony on C-Span. For his next witness he had intended on reading selected portions from the deposition transcript of Montgomery Arthur Alexander III in lieu of live testimony. Although this deposition testimony was important in order to establish his theme of the case, because of the jurisdictional limits on a subpoena it was impossible to compel Alexander's actual attendance at the trial. Since reading testimony from a transcript was a tedious process that involved reading the questions and answers into the record, and often lost everyone's attention during the process, Richard asked Judge Jamison for permission to have Michael Shaw sit in the witness chair and read the answers from the transcript after Richard read the questions. The portions read to the jury focused on Alexander's preoccupation with image, a theme that Richard hoped to establish as a motive for the need to use Dickson as the fall guy. With the exception of Stucky's sole objection that Michael was adding improper inflection to the answers, making the answers sound snooty, and Richard's concern that the jury simply was not interested in listening to a transcript being read, the testimony from Alexander's deposition transcript was presented without incident.

After finishing with the reading of Alexander's transcript Richard had rested his case in chief. All of the witnesses that he had planned to call on behalf of Dickson had been presented and had testified on both direct and cross-examination. His exhibits had been presented, and as to each one Judge Jamison had ruled whether or not they would be entered into evidence. Now that the jury had heard Dickson's side of the dispute it was Stucky's turn to present Wine House's defense case through the witnesses that would testify against Dickson. As he waited for Stucky to begin Richard had considered the possibilities open to Wine House. He had a general idea who Stucky would put on the witness stand, and he was ready to cross-examine those individuals. But he could not be sure that there was no one else, previously unknown to Richard or Dickson, who would appear and testify. There was no requirement to identify rebuttal or impeachment witnesses before they were called to the stand. He expected Stucky to roar to the offensive with a witness who could immediately shift the jury's perception of Dickson, and was instead surprised when Stucky first took the step of requesting leave to approach the bench. When they both were in front of the Judge, Stucky simply indicated that he had a motion to make to the court, and requested that the jury be excused from the courtroom. The request was stated too comfortably, and Stucky appeared too self-assured, for Richard's liking. To his further alarm, Judge Jamison appeared to know exactly what Stucky had in mind, and motioned for both counsel to return to their respective tables. Judge Jamison then instructed the jury that there was some business that the court needed to consider with counsel outside of their presence, and that they were being excused early for the lunch break. The jury did not have to be told twice that they could leave early, and within a few moments the courtroom was almost completely empty. As he watched the individual jurors file past, Richard searched his mind but could not think of a valid reason for Stucky's request, which was made all the more troubling by the fact that the Judge had excused the jury almost forty minutes before the normal lunch break.

Even after the last juror had cleared the courtroom Judge Jamison waited until the bailiff closed both of the courtroom doors before asking Stucky to proceed. Stucky reached into his briefcase, withdrew a thick sheaf of papers and handed a copy to Richard and the original to the clerk. Before Richard could even skim the heading in the document, Stucky began to address the court by describing in summary fashion the evidence presented on behalf of Dickson, his client's view of the case, and his own belief that to allow the case to go forward would result in a both a waste of court's time and a travesty of justice.

"We have now sat here, your Honor, for several days listening to Mr. Magnus parade a number of witnesses before this court. We have listened carefully, waiting to hear exactly why Mr. Dickson should be able to go forward with this case. Even giving Mr. Magnus the benefit of the doubt, the best that has been established is the fact that Mr. Dickson truly loved Winery Peak. He apparently loved it so much that he looked on Winery Peak as his own personal project to care for and nurture. So much so that he would do anything to protect against the possibility that Wine House would take it away from him. But Mr. Dickson has not presented any evidence that even remotely suggests that he was fired because he discovered something wrong was taking place. And the memorandum which we have just handed you sets forth in great detail the legal authorities that support the extensive discretion vested in Wine House to make employment decisions concerning its managerial level employees—especially an employee that was acting as the president of one of the operating divisions. This brief sets forth all of the legal authorities necessary for the court to grant our request to end this charade now by entering judgment in favor of Wine House."

Stucky paused for a moment, filling a paper cup with water from the carafe sitting on the corner of his table. After taking a small sip he continued.

"There is no reason for this case to proceed any further. No need to take up the time of your Honor, the time of the jurors, or the time of Wine House. There is a complete absence of evidence from which the jury could find against Wine House and, therefore, I request that the Court now enter a judgment of non-suit against Mr. Dickson and let us all go home."

As soon as Stucky finished talking Judge Jamison looked sharply over at Richard and in biting words asked for his response to Stucky's request for non-suit. With a shock Richard realized that the Judge was being asked to dismiss the entire case. Worse yet, clearly Judge Jamison was taking the request seriously, and thereby telegraphed his opinion that the request had some merit at a minimum. Although he should have anticipated the move by Stucky, Richard's mind spun so quickly that for a brief moment he could not concentrate on anything other than the weight of Stucky's brief in his hands. In essence, Stucky was suggesting to Judge Jamison that the court could make a finding that there was no legally cognizable evidence on which the jury could base an award against Wine House and in favor of Dickson. Feeling his heart continue to pound Richard tried to quickly formulate a response, but a million disparate thoughts instead prevented him from thinking clearly. A stray thought finally broke free from the rest and then gripped his mind so hard that, for a terrifying moment, he feared that he would not be able to articulate a rejoinder and Judge Jamison would indeed grant Stucky's request. Fortunately that feeling passed in a flash and Richard looked upwards from Stucky's brief towards an obviously impatient judge.

Time seemed to slow and almost stop as Richard's mind continued to race. His senses seemed to expand and heighten in response to the adrenalin that was being pumped into his system. Every word that had been uttered by Stucky seemed to still resonate against the old glass panes in the small leaded windows above his head and into Richard's ears. Each syllable enunciated so precisely that Richard could almost feel Stucky's tongue click against his front teeth as he flicked out the word "non-suit." With one part of his mind he wondered at how his eyes seemed to be in special focus, and could easily discern the raised grain on the wood molding that framed the pale faux silk wainscoting that covered the bottom third of the side walls. To make matters even more distracting, he was also acutely aware that the bailiff was slowly rotating one of his prized black bullets between his fingers in that same irritating fashion. The bailiff had been watching Richard closely and, when he was sure that Richard was looking his way, with deliberate movements placed the bullet on its side with the talon point facing directly at Richard. Instead of rattling him further, the bullet served as a necessary catalyst for his attention by allowing anger to displace uncertainty as his dominant emotion. He knew that the case was in dire jeopardy, but he could now argue against that possibility in a calmer and more orderly fashion.

Quickly Richard regrouped and began to talk, recapping the testimony from the last several days and particularly stressing the agreement that Dickson had made when he had first agreed to join Wine House. When he noticed that he was repeating some of these points, Richard then pointed out the inferences that the jury could find from the testimony that had been presented, even where the points had not been stated directly. Finally, and to his own ears lamely, Richard concluded his remarks with a request that he be allowed to brief the issue should the court be inclined to grant the motion. As he sat down he realized, in the back of his mind, that the case could be over in seconds and the jury would never be asked to render a decision in judgment of the facts. Should that be the result, he would surely be asked by Allen to explain to the entire partnership the process that he followed in determining that this case was good enough to take on a contingency in light of the court's conclusion that it was not even good enough to submit to the jury. Should the court enter a judgment of non-suit as requested by Stucky, it would mean that he had miscalculated enormously, and that he should have realized that there was no case before taking up the precious time of the jury, the court and Wine House. An order granting non-suit could also be interpreted as a finding that Richard and Dickson lacked probable cause to file the lawsuit. This finding, if made, would satisfy one of the elements necessary to support the previously threatened claim by Wine House that it was the victim of malicious prosecution by Dickson and could also expose the firm to the same claim.

Judge Jamison had first looked bothered at Richard's explanation, and then spent a long moment looking at his own notes in silence. He fianlly put his notes to the side, and began to skim through Stucky's brief. After a few moments, which seemed like hours to Richard, he then put Stucky's brief to the side and removed his glasses, apparently satisfied—but looking no happier—with the decision that he had reached.

"Please stand, Mr. Magnus."

Now Richard really knew that he was in for it. As he stood he could almost feel his knees knocking together with concern. He turned and also motioned Dickson to stand before turning his full attention back to the front of the courtroom. Stucky also stood, although as quietly as possible. He knew when things were going his way and did not want to attract any attention at this moment.

"I have carefully considered what you have said on Dr. Dickson's behalf, and I obviously have heard all of the testimony presented in this case. Mr. Magnus, I do not like to take cases away from the jury—they serve an important function in our judicial system."

With those words Richard braced himself for the worst.

"I do not like to take cases away from the jury," he repeated, "and I am as close as I have ever been before."

Judge Jamison paused, hoping his words were sinking in. Although the philosophical import of what he just said was lost on Richard, who just wanted to hear the bottom line ruling, Stucky frowned as he was quick to grasp the significance of the last phrase.

"Mr. Stucky, while your arguments are well stated, I do find that there is at least a scintilla of evidence from which the jury could rule in favor of Dr. Dickson . . ."

"That's all I need . . ." Richard in his relief undiplomatically interrupted, understanding immediately the narrowness of his reprieve, but stopped in mid-sentence as Judge Jamison growlingly continued.

" . . . and, for the moment, I am going to allow the case to proceed."

Waves of relief broke over Richard, and he barely paid attention to Stucky's protestations over Judge Jamison's decision. Judge Jamison testily admonished Stucky that he had made his ruling and diplomatically posed as a rhetorical question the undisputable decision that perhaps they should also take the opportunity to adjourn for the lunch break.

~~~~~

After the hour long hiatus, during which Richard had done nothing other than dwell on his close escape from the motion for non-suit, Stucky had appeared well-rested and refreshed, almost as if he had won the motion. Showing no outward signs of disappointment with Judge Jamison's ruling, Stucky had immediately called his first witness, a financial analyst for Wine House who had the primary responsibility of maintaining the economic forecasts and determining the financial viability of each of the several wineries under the Wine House corporate umbrella. The analyst had testified that Winery Peak, as a stand alone start up operation, was expected to operate under a zero based budget as soon as it had expended the sums originally allocated to the preliminary expenses. Without missing a beat, he went on to testify that the projections for Winery Peak reflected substantial hurdles in the way of achieving its financial targets, and that the sub-
~~~~~

stitution of an organophosphate enriched fertilizer for any of the fertilizers on the California Department of Agriculture's approved list would result in a substantial positive impact to the operation's financial bottom line. Although unstated, implicit in the testimony from the analyst was the presumption of a negative impact on Dickson's career should Winery Peak have failed to meet its fiscal goals, thereby establishing Dickson's motive to first use the chemicals and then dump the unused residue to avoid detection.

On cross-examination Richard had scored some minor points, and even forced the analyst to admit that the same econometric model applied with similar force and effect to any of the several wineries operated directly by Wine House. The net effect was not overly helpful to Dickson, however, and Richard could not help but dwell on the negative testimony elicited by Stucky. Making matters worse, he could see that the trial was clearly going to last longer than he had anticipated, and Richard's other cases were going to suffer as a result of the restrictions on his time. Allen Rose had pulled the help he had been receiving from his fellow associates, explaining to the other partners that the prosecution of a contingency fee case should not interfere with Richard's duty to the Firm or to the other clients of the Firm. Knowing that Allen's true intent was focused solely on furthering his own position within the power structure of the Firm, and was not based on any legitimate concerns for the overall well being of the partnership, made Allen's sanctimonious pronouncements even more difficult for Richard to swallow. Allen's tactics were successful within the Firm and had the effect of significantly increasing the need for Richard to win. Yet with the mounting pressure to be on top of all of his responsibilities, he could feel his grasp on the case slipping unwillingly out of his hands.

~ ~ ~ ~ ~

When Richard had finished describing what was happening at the trial, Frank tried to give him something lighter to think about by changing subjects by discussing the current state of office politics at the D.A.'s office. Since Richard knew most of the people that worked there from the days when he was a newly sworn assistant district attorney, this type of gossip usually was an area of conversation that he found entertaining. On this occassion, however, he just continued to morosely pick away at his chicken fried steak while Frank went on about the not so private affair between one of the senior investigators and the receptionist.

In the middle of looking around to wave down the waitress for more coffee he suddenly froze and then looked down at the table. Frank noticed Richard's particular reaction and paused in mid-sentence, then completely stopped his graphic description of one of the more intimate details of the office romance. When he was sure that he had Frank's attention, without looking up Richard motioned his head across the room towards the counter where a number of men sat on metal stools while they chowed down on their dinners. At the far end, apart from the others, a slender pale man with thinning brown hair sat alone. Before Frank could turn his head back to ask for an explanation of Richard's sudden interest in that end of the diner, Richard scraped his wooden chair back from the table and began rapidly threading his way past the other tables towards the slender stranger. As he tried to maneuver around two tables pushed together to accommodate a rather large family, one of the two toddlers at the table picked that moment to suddenly cry out "Mommy—I got to go potty . . ." causing the mother to drop her fork and scoop the child into her arms in a single fluid movement towards the restroom. The mother and Richard, heading in opposite directions, did a version of the two step tango as they each hurriedly tried to get past one another.

This commotion did not go unnoticed by the slender stranger, who calmly placed some bills on the counter before stepping lively out the front door. Richard finally made his way past the mother, in time to see the front door swing closed on its automatic hinge. Anger born of frustration at the last few days of trial sent adrenalin surging into his body and he bolted after his prey through the door and down the stairs outside into the gravel parking lot.

At the edge of the parking lot the stranger had already stepped into a gray sedan and was pulling the door closed behind him. As Richard broke into a full out sprint the engine roared to life and the car was immediately put into gear. As the distance closed Richard's intense concentration on reaching his goal before it pulled out of the parking lot almost caused him to fail to notice an old blue van that was starting to back out of one of the diagonal parking spaces. With a last second swivel hips move that would have made any all star halfback turn green with envy, he dodged past the left rear corner of the van's oversized chrome bumper. The quick sideways move threw off his stride, however, and he hit the edge of a depression in the gravel with the outside edge of his foot. The impact caused his knee to hyperextend and sent him sprawling hands first to the ground. Though he was able to tuck and roll, the sharp chunks of gravel bit into his palms and then sliced through his slacks and across the exposed skin on his kneecaps. Rolling to his feet without paying any attention to what had just happened, he could only watch helplessly as the gray sedan pulled out into the traffic and drive off down the street. The van also continued to pull out of the parking lot, its driver oblivious to Richard's condition, and then also drove off into traffic.

Richard stood still for a moment, and then desolately began picking the larger pieces of gravel out of his scraped hands. After a moment he cast a quick glance through the hole torn in his pants, but with a resolute shake of his head simply decided to ignore his bloody knee and instead stiffly walked back to the front door of the diner to where Frank was standing.

"What the hell was that all about?"

"It was the weirdest thing, Frank. I know that I must be getting paranoid, but I looked up and knew that I had seen that guy several times in the last few weeks."

"So what? You know that this ain't the biggest town in the world."

"It's just too much of a damn coincidence. And why the hell did he bolt like that?"

"You mean apart from the fact that a crazy man like you was suddenly coming after him? I would bolt too! Look, Richard, you are wired tighter than a drum. Loosen up guy, this is only one case."

"Its not 'just one case.'" Richard flared his response. "And I am not about to let those assholes at Wine House scare me off of it."

"You really think that the guy you just chased has some connection with Wine House? Boy, you are getting paranoid. Look, if it will make you feel any better I will look into it. I will also call Bondi and ask him to have some of his patrol officers keep an eye out for you over the next couple of weeks until this thing is over."

Richard looked over at his friend and realized how stressed out he must sound. The last thing he needed now was to blow off the people that were on his side. With a guilty nod he accepted Frank's generous offer.

~ ~ ~ ~ ~

"Objection!"

All eyes of the jury turned to Richard as he rose slowly to his feet.

"I know that I have never seen the letter that Mr. Stucky has handed to this witness. And the letter is clearly one that I should have received from counsel during pretrial discovery."

The Judge looked expectantly at Stucky, his interest in the explanation greater than his irritation at Richard's little speech.

"Response, Mr. Stucky?"

"Certainly, your Honor. Mr. Magnus never asked for this specific letter. Had he asked then we could have considered whether his request was reasonable."

"And there was no request for this specific letter?"

"Correct, your Honor."

Stucky looked serenely over at the jury and waited. "And your specific objection, Mr. Magnus?"

Knowing that the judge had made his mind up, and not in his favor, Richard inwardly cursed but made a tactical retreat.

"I am objecting on the basis of fundamental unfairness. Wine House apparently does not wish this trial to be fairly presented to the jury, but would rather play games with the evidence."

"Counsel, that is not a legal objection." The Judge interjected flatly, now irritated at what the jury was hearing.

"Sorry, your Honor. That's the one I'm making."

"Objection overruled."

As Richard sat down he attempted to hold his head up, to take on the appearance of the unbowed defender of the underdog, and as Stucky continued to mark the letter for introduction into evidence Richard had the small satisfaction of noting that three of the jurors had nodded their heads in apparent sympathy for his position.

"All right, Mr. Stucky, call your next witness."

Richard hunkered down as he listened to Stucky call Dr. Louis Rosenblum to the stand. Rosenblum had an extensive background in pathology and years of experience in forensics. Stucky had disclosed Rosenblum during the pretrial proceedings as one of his expert witnesses. After receipt of Stucky's written disclosure of expert witnesses, Richard had sought and taken each of their depositions. In contrast to normal percipient witnesses, who can only testify about matters on which they had personal experience or knowledge, an expert witness can testify to his or her opinions as long as the opinions are outside of the general knowledge or experience of a lay person and are based on the expert's general area of expertise. In contrast to the depositions he took of the people associated directly with Wine House, during which Richard attempted to gain admissions against the interests of Wine House, the depositions of Stucky's expert witnesses sought a detailed identification of every opinion to be offered at trial as well as the factual underpinning for each of the opinions. These witnesses were paid professionals, and the depositions failed to provide any earth-shattering information to be used during cross-examination.

In fact, the deposition of Rosenblum had not lasted very long at all. His role, as stated in the disclosure statement, was simple and the opinions were well-defined by Stucky. In essence, Rosenblum had been asked to review the autopsy report on the fieldworker who had died after exposure to the chemicals in the quarry waters. Based on that review, and a review of the analysis performed on the water samples obtained by the County Health Department, Rosenblum had reached the opinion that the fieldworker would not have died but for the exposure to the chemicals. After concluding the deposition, Richard had asked a local doctor to review Rosenblum's opinions for errors or discrepancies. This review had not taken very long either, and to Richard's dismay the doctor concluded that Rosenblum's testimony was generally accurate and well-reasoned. With growing concern over the impact of the potential testimony on the jury, Richard had sought out Michael's advice. In his characteristically blunt fashion, Michael had responded to the request by grilling Richard with questions.

"What is the relevancy of this testimony to the issue of whether Dickson was properly fired?"

"When I brought the matter to the court's attention out of the presence of the jury Stucky claimed that it reflects on the exercise of managerial privilege by Wine House in firing Dickson. He claims that the degree of harm was so great that Dickson should have taken steps to better protect the workplace from this type of event. I asked Jamison to exclude the testimony because it avoids presentation of any link between how the workers were exposed and the result of the exposure, and it implies that Dickson is to blame for their illness. Jamison said that he would instruct the jury that they could only consider the testimony for the purpose of whether wine House acted reasonably, and were not to consider the testimony on the issue of who was involved in how the chemicals got into the quarry in the first place. But that limited instruction does not seem like it will help."

"You're right. Once the jury hears the testimony, telling them that they can only consider it for a limited purpose does you no good at all. Well, you better figure out some way to limit the testimony before he answers any questions, or at least figure out some way to discredit Rosenblum in the jury's eyes during your cross-examination. Sounds like Stucky really wants to confuse the issue of the right to terminate Dickson with the unfortunate fact that people have actually suffered from exposure to the whole mess. And I am sure that he would like to be able to then act as if it were a given that Dickson was responsible. Then you are on the defensive to show that Dickson was not only not responsible for the spill, but also not responsible for the impact on the farm workers."

"So I should still try to exclude the testimony."

"You sure as hell have to try. Although it probably will not be easy. Sounds like Stucky was smart enough to tell Rosenblum not to sensationalize the testimony. That he will do himself during the closing arguments. Just make sure you have Terri check Rosenblum out before he testifies. Even if you can't attack the message, at least try to be able to attack the messenger."

Richard looked at Michael quizzically. "What do you mean?"

Michael smiled wolfishly, thinking back over the years to expert witnesses that he had confronted.

"How much is he being paid to testify? Probably more for the day than the average juror makes in a week. How much time has he spent on the case? If too little, then he can be portrayed as a mere hired gun who will say anything for Wine House. If he has spent too much time given the limited nature of his assignment, then argue that the issue is not as clear as Stucky will attempt to convey. Does Rosenblum have a former relationship with Stucky or his firm or Wine House. How good are his credentials? Not just the most recent ones. Look at them all. Are they all relevant? Are they all accurate? Don't make the mistake of always trying to take witnesses head on. If you can argue that the testimony should not be trusted because of who the witness is, and not because of what exactly was said, you can distract from the problem of what the jury hears."

Richard had followed Michael's advice, and instructed Terri to conduct a complete background check on Rosenblum. The report provided some interesting reading, but nothing earth shattering. Rosenblum had led a fairly normal life, with the first half of his career after college devoted to a short stint in the army followed by the rigors of medical school, residency and internships. The second half of his career had focused on a successful private "hands on" practice that included some forensic consulting. Not much for Richard to work with.

Stucky began to ask his questions of Rosenblum while Richard waited patiently for an opening. As he testified Gayle took detailed notes while Richard leafed again through Terri's report. Listening through one ear while he read, at times he would make a star in the margin of the report. The testimony came in just as he feared and directly along the lines that he had heard during the deposition. Following Michael's suggestion he refrained from making too many objections, to avoid giving Rosemblum's testimony too much credence, and had his request for a limiting instruction given on one occasion so that he could later argue the point to the jury during closing arguments. Overall there was little to object to, either as to the form of the questions or in the content of the answers, and the jury's interest only added to his mounting frustration. One or two minor answers created some potential for points to be made on cross-examination, but his greatest hope lay in having the witness simply finish before he could do too much damage to Dickson's case.

Mercifully, Stucky finished before Richard exploded from having to sit so still for so long. He flipped through his notes, and then Gayle's, before deciding that he had nothing to ask about the substantive areas of the testimony. He had heard over the years that the most difficult decision in cross-examination is when to sit still and not to ask any questions at all, and that questions should be asked only when there is a definite game plan to the examination. Yet conventional wisdom was not much help in the face of twelve jurors who were looking at him to proceed. At the very least he felt that he had to ask something of the witness. As he stood Gayle pulled sharply on his sleeve. He looked down at a note that she slid to him across the table and then glanced again at the first page of Terri's report.

"Dr. Rosenblum . . . It is 'Doctor' is it not?"

"Yes. Doctor of Medicine."

"It takes a long time to become a 'doctor of medicine', does it not sir?"

"Why yes, yes it does. Including premed education, medical school, residency, it takes many years."

"And you spent those 'many years' studying to be a doctor, did you not?"

Stucky rose to his feet before Rosenblum could answer, and Rosenblum settled back into the witness chair at the first indication of Stucky's intentions. Rosenblum was not new to the role as a testifying witness, and knew that he was to stop in place whenever Stucky stood to make an objection in order to assist Stucky so far as was possible.

"If you please, Your Honor, we submitted Dr. Rosenblum's résumé to Mr. Magnus and the Court. There is no need for Mr. Magnus to insult Dr. Rosenblum while he reviews those credentials."

"Your point is noted, Mr. Stucky. Do you have a copy of the résumé, Mr. Magnus?"

"Thank you, yes I do your Honor. And I would like it to be marked as an Exhibit and handed to the witness."

"Well, I assume Mr. Stucky that you have no objection, having raised the issue yourself. Go ahead Mr. Magnus. But watch the sarcasm in your voice to Dr. Rosenblum or I will sustain Mr. Stucky's objections that you are being argumentative even if he does not make them."

Richard nodded his understanding and quickly handed a copy of the résumé to the clerk, who marked it as an exhibit and then handed it to the witness. He chanced a glance at the jury, and was unsettled by the look on the face of the woman sitting fourth from the back. A juror by the name of Sager, whom he had considered to be one of "his" jurors during the selection process. The expression was decidedly unfriendly. He decided to cut directly to the chase.

"Dr. Rosenblum, did you prepare this document?"

"Yes." Rosenblum smiled handsomely and crossed his long legs.

"It is very impressive."

"Thank you."

"You consider this to be an important document?"

"Well . . . I do not know if I would call it 'important' . . ."

"You knew it would be used in the course of your business and that it represented yourself to others including this jury."

The question was really a statement, which suddenly made Stucky uncomfortable.

"I suppose that is true, yes."

"And as you sit here now you are telling the jury that it is accurate."

"Yes."

The witness now appeared slightly defensive, uncrossing his legs to sit forward in the witness chair, and Richard knew instinctively that it now was time to pull the plug before Stucky could ruin his momentum.

"The résumé says that you studied at Monte Clair Army Hospital. You do see that entry on the first page of your résumé under the heading 'Medical Experience'?"

Hearing no answer, Richard walked over to the jury box and faced the jury.

"Let me read it aloud. 'Medical Experience. Trinity Medical School; Internship, Holy Oak Hospital; Intensive Care Unit, Monte Clair Hospital. Do you see that entry?"

"Yes, Mr. Magnus, but you should know . . ."

"Excuse me, Sir, but I just want you to answer my questions. You were not a doctor at the time that you were at Monte Clair, now were you."

"No, but there is nothing that is not true about that entry . . ."

"Only that it is a tad, bit misleading until someone points it out. In fact, you were not even a medical corpsman. You were assigned to the mess detail for the Army unit assigned to the ICU, isn't that true. What else about your testimony has been designed to create misleading appearances?"

As Richard turned away from the witness he did not even bother to listen to Stucky's half hearted objection that the last question was argumentative, and neither did the jury.

~ ~ ~ ~ ~

Richard sat and stared at the television set in front of him. He knew that he should be looking at his notes, or organizing the exhibits, but the mental strain and physical exhaustion kept him pinned to the couch. A half empty beer, now nearing room temperature, lay loosely in his left hand. Although the trial was taking much longer than he had anticipated, he was glad that the weekend was providing a short respite from the rigors of the courtroom. The afternoon session earlier that day had been particularly brutal, as Stucky had scored some good points establishing how the difficulties in the wine industry required more flexibility by management when making decisions to change their team to try different approaches. One of the most damning moments involved introduction of a memo written by Dickson several years earlier. In the memo Dickson has directed his immediate staff to review all transactions involving independent contractors, and to terminate the relationship if the cost benefit analysis indicated that the work could be done by onsite staff at a reduced cost to the winery. Without saying so directly, Stucky has implied that the same philosophy that was applied by Wine House to Dickson had previously been applied by Dickson himself to others, and he now should not complain about the impact of his own policies. Richard knew he would have to deal with the issue soon, but simply could not muster enough energy to concentrate on anything at the moment.

When the phone rang Richard noted that it was almost 10:30 P.M., and at first thought with irritation that Dickson could at least wait until the morning to call with his latest idea or question. Remembering quickly that Dickson would not likely be the caller, as he had earlier agreed to Richard's suggestion to relax and clear his mind by having his grandchildren over for the night, Richard leaned over to pick up the phone.

"Hello?"

"Is this Nathan Magnus?"

"This is Richard Magnus."

"Is your middle name Nathan?"

"Yes."

"You are a lawyer."

"Yes. What can I do for you?"

Richard put his beer down on the coffee table and began to sit up. The call did not feel right.

"I want to know if you would have some time to meet with me this weekend. I have a small legal problem and I need to get some answers to a few questions."

Richard reached over to the end table and picked up a pad of paper. He quickly began to jot down the time and what had been said so far by the caller.

"To whom am I talking to?"

"I would rather not say. I have been reviewing the qualifications of many attorneys and I want to ask you some questions about a probate matter."

"Who referred you to me?"

"Well . . . I am self-referred. But your reputation is well known. Are you free tomorrow?"

"I am sorry, but the firm has a policy not to handle matters where the client won't give his name."

"Well, perhaps I'll just drop by. Goodnight, Mr. Magnus."

The line went stone dead with a click. He could feel his heart pounding double-time against the wall of his chest as he tried to play the conversation back over in his mind. There was no good explanation for the call, just as there had been no good explanation for the slender man in the diner. Richard fought against his imagination, trying to rationalize that this case was not big enough to generate this sort of interest, but he also knew that he did not have the type of reputation that would result in people calling him out of the blue. It also made no sense for someone to call him this late at night. Richard felt a surge of paranoia as he looked over his notes of the call. The caller had referred to a "probate" matter, which are those types of cases that involve the estate of someone who had died. Although there were attorneys at the firm that handled those types of matters, Richard certainly was not one of them. He tried to dismiss the thought that caller meant something ominous by the reference to "probate," as it seemed unlikely that anyone would use such a heavy handed approach. Nonetheless, Richard quickly went around the house and made sure that all of the windows and doors were closed and locked tight. As added security, he took his old wooden Little League bat down from the rafters in the garage and laid it next to the side of his bed. Richard did not believe in having a gun in his house, and he still felt that the decision had been a sound one. He felt so jumpy that he probably would grab the gun and shoot in the direction of every little sound in the night. Feeling wide awake, and his mind definitely not thinking about the case, Richard retired to his room for the long sleepless night ahead.

CHAPTER TWELVE

RAIN HAD BEEN FALLING intermittently the entire morning. Not enough of a weather system to be described as a true storm, but certainly enough to be an irritation to anyone who had business outdoors. Earlier in the week the weather had been angrier. Clouds had massed against the lip of mountains that circled the valley, and then broke in waves that travelled above the valley floor. Rain had fallen in furious bursts, obscured the horizon and alternating with a hint of sleet as the temperature dipped down in sun sheltered areas. But overnight the worst of the front had passed through, leaving the tail end as a gray smudged sky that in turn misted and sprinkled.

Richard kept the wipers on the intermittent cycle, slow enough to avoid the squeal of rubber rubbing against the window but fast enough to keep the window from being smudged. The repetitive buildup of mist on the glass caused Richard and Dickson to squint in intervals with the wiper action, and the force of their concentration had kept their conversation to a minimum. They remained silent, even though the truck had shed its speed as soon as they turned off of the firm asphalt of the main road. As he drove on the dirt access road that headed towards the quarry, Richard kept thinking about the testimony from the afternoon before.

Stucky had returned from the lunch break full of energy and accompanied by Stewart Charles. Charles was an expert witness hired by Wine House to testify about the use of chemicals in the wine and grape growing business. Before the trial, after Stucky had disclosed the general nature of the testimony expected from Charles, Richard had also taken his deposition and elicited his opinions in exhaustive detail. The deposition had lasted several hours, but had resulted in nothing more than dry recitation of the historical use of chemical fertilizers and insecticides. Neither Richard nor Dickson had been terribly impressed about his potential testimony, as Dickson had assured Richard that the historical perspective was not relevant to a new winery like Winery Peak. When Charles actually took the stand, however, both Richard and Dickson had received an unexpected shock.

The courtroom had been hot all morning, decidedly so, as the old furnace system struggled to keep up with the falling temperatures outside. The entire building was on the same forced air heating system. Since Judge Jamison's courtroom was closest to the main vent from the furnace room, his courtroom would fry while people occupying the offices at the far end of the building would still be wearing their sweaters. As the day wore on the heating system continued to pump hot air through the vents and began to permeate the questions as it had already done with the participants. The bailiff, at the Judge's direction, had already called down to custodial services for some relief. The only response was reflected in the fans coming on and simply stirring the hot air. Since the windows were painted shut, from past attempts the staff knew better than try to pry them open. They had better methods of wasting their time than trying to obtain relief that way. The jury suffered most from the heat due to the fact that the jury box was raised up above the floor to give the jurors an unobstructed view of the courtroom and especially the witness box. The heat added to their inattention, which was always bad during the late afternoon sessions. Stucky knew that immediately after the lunch break the jury would be somewhat fresh from their lunch break, at least for an hour or so, and he wanted to take advantage of the situation before the stale air could again play a role.

Stucky had established the tempo for Charles' testimony by first asking a series of questions that elicited his qualifications as a chemist and viticulturist. Charles had then run though the background of the use of different agricultural fertilizers and insecticides in United States and European wineries. He had come across as somewhat technical and dry, and the jury had not appeared either terribly excited or skeptical. Even the ones who had been taking notes assiduously during earlier stages of the proceedings were now simply listening as he went on. The testimony, while credible, was to Richard and Dickson uneventful and tracked much of what had been said by Charles during his deposition.

Having established a reason for the jury to conclude that Charles was knowledgeable and credible about what he had to say, Stucky then directed him through a description of the nature and history of organophosphates. This testimony had perked the jury's attention, especially when he described the effects of similar molecular combinations that had been used in chemical warfare and which were now classified as illegal because of the use of the components in the manufacture of nerve gas. With his foundation carefully laid, Stucky moved in for the critical testimony.

"Mr. Charles, have you reviewed the tests conducted of the water from the quarry?"

"Yes sir, I have."

"And do you have an opinion regarding the information you reviewed?"

"Yes. From my review it is clear that there are quantities of organophosphates in the waters; that the chemical is not a naturally appearing compound, and; that the type of compound has not been approved for use in the United States since the mid-1970s."

"Why was it banned from use in the United States?"

"The particular chemical compound has an acute toxicity level. Studies at the National Cancer Institute have shown that this compound is an extremely strong carcinogen. Independent studies conducted for the United States Department of Fish and Game and the Department of Agriculture determined that the residue from this chemical and field runoff where it was used was having a substantially negative effect on local wildlife populations."

"Would it have a negative effect on people?"

Richard almost jumped to his feet to make an objection, and then thought the better of it. Although Charles was not a toxicologist, even if granted his objection would serve mostly to draw attention to his concerns with the testimony.

"Absolutely."

"Why was it even used commercially in the first place?"

"It worked. Plain and simple. And it was relatively cheap to buy and simple to apply in the fields. Because of its soluble nature, it would not stay in the soil and cause buildup problems. Someone who might have a very small profit margin would be attracted to use this compound as safer compounds cost substantially more to use."

"Somebody like a startup winery?"

"Objection." Richard felt that he could not just let that question be asked without stating his concerns. "Your Honor, the question calls for speculation by the witness regarding operations at Winery Peak."

"Overruled, Mr. Magnus. The witness stated his qualifications as a viticulturalist. And the question did not call for application to a specific winery. Proceed Mr. Charles."

"A startup would find this compound most attractive. Startups have to look very closely at the expenses, as it takes several years before they even have a product to sell from the grapes."

"And what else did you determine from the water samples?"

"First, from the relatively small amount of molecular breakdown it appears as though the compound has not been in the quarry for more than several years."

"Almost as long as Winery Peak has been in operation." Stucky helpfully noted directly to the jury.

"Well, I don't have any personal knowledge of that fact, but that is the general length of time in my estimation."

"Do you have an opinion regarding how the chemicals found their way into the quarry?"

"Excuse me, your Honor."

This time Richard knew he had to say something. This witness was suddenly scoring major points for Wine House. The give and take between Stucky and the witness was achieving maximum effect, for Stucky was drawing the undivided attention of the jury as he asked the questions by pacing back and forth across the width of the courtroom. This constant movement, which was in stark contrast to Richard's habit of sitting quietly at counsel table when it was his turn to ask the questions, had to be stopped.

"Your Honor, Mr. Stucky's pacing is very distracting. Without being too picayune, could he please be asked by the Court to stay in one place?"

"Well Mr. Magnus, clearly counsel have very different styles. But, Mr. Stucky, please do not wander."

Stucky shifted his eyes at Richard, full of quiet irritation, but out of sight of the jury, and promised himself retribution before the case was over. He forced a smile as he returned to the area behind his station at counsel desk and tried to pick up the momentum where it had been interrupted.

"Thank you your Honor. You can answer, Mr. Charles."

"Well, from my review of the local topography and the physical layout of the winery, especially the vineyards that sit on the surrounding ridgeline, I could easily chart the flow of irrigation water along the lines of the watershed. Because of the natural flow patterns, runoff—particularly rain runoff—would collect in the two small steam beds that channel surface waters into the quarry. Any residual chemicals would be washed down these channels and collect in concentrated forms in the quarry waters."

Stucky selected a topographical map from his folio of exhibits, asked and received permission from Judge Jamison to approach the witness and handed the map to Charles. Richard waited a moment, and when it was clear that Stucky did not intend to provide him a courtesy copy cleared his throat just as Stucky was about to ask Charles to identify the document.

"I'm sorry, your Honor, I have not seen the exhibit and was not provided a copy."

Judge Jamison nodded and directed Stucky to show the document to Richard. To comply, Stucky took two steps backwards and, without looking, thrust the document into Richard's face so that it almost brushed his nose. Judge

Jamison was not amused, and sharply directed both counsel to approach the bench. To ensure that the conversation was out of the hearing of the jury, the Judge cupped his hand over the microphone and leaned across the bench towards counsel with his admonishment.

"All right, both of you are getting far too close to being out of order. I know that emotions can get high in a case like this, but you two are supposed to act like professionals. And Mr. Stucky, you jam a document in counsel's face again and I'll sanction you so fast that your head will spin. Now, step back and behave yourselves!"

A moment passed while Richard and Stucky resumed their respective positions, neither daring to look at the jury. Stucky skimmed through his notes head down, checked off a number of areas, and then readdressed the witness.

"Last question, Mr. Charles. You own your own small winery. Would you use this chemical?"

"No, Mr. Stucky, definitely not. The compound was banned for good reasons. And I would fire anyone working for me in a second if I found out that they had used it."

"Thank you, Mr. Charles, no further questions at this time."

Apart from the last interruption, Stucky knew that his direct examination had finished exactly as planned. Judge Jamison had indicated, immediately after the lunch break, that he would let the jury go for the day after the mid-afternoon break. Richard knew better than to argue, as short afternoons were customary on Friday, and he needed the time to think. He was concerned that the jury would be able to slowly digest the testimony for the entire weekend without hearing any contradictions Richard hoped to elicit from Charles during cross-examination. As the jury fidgeted in their seats and waited for the Judge to say what was to next take place, Richard knew that he should say something to place some doubt in the jury's mind regarding Charles' testimony. Richard stood to get the attention of Judge Jamison, who had just finished a note on the pad on his bench and was beginning to rearrange carefully the papers in front of him. Before Stucky could interrupt, Richard took the initiative.

"Excuse me, your Honor. I want to make sure Mr. Charles does not disappear over the weekend. There are some things that he has yet to tell the jury."

Stucky was on his feet immediately, his face tight in light of Judge Jamison's earlier admonition.

"That is totally out of order, your Honor . . ."

Judge Jamison cut him off with a peremptory wave of his hand.

"The jury is instructed to disregard the comments of counsel. We will begin Monday at 9:00 A.M. with Mr. Charles. You are again instructed not to discuss this case during the weekend, conduct any independent investigation or form any conclusions until all of the evidence is in. You are now excused. Counsel will wait."

The jury filed out, grateful for the opportunity to have the balance of the afternoon off. Some cast sideways glances at Dickson, who stood stoically with his arm around his wife. Richard nodded to a few as they passed, in an attempt to silently have them acknowledge each other as a person and therefore someone against whom it would be harder to vote. When they were all gone, Judge Jamison cleared his throat to get everyone's attention.

"Okay, you two. I do not want any further interruptions, and I want you both to cool off. Do not make me consider either a mistrial or an instruction to the jury about your conduct that one or both of you will not like." Judge Jamison appeared ready to stare them down, but neither was interested in saying anything. "Anything further?" The Judge paused briefly, and with satisfaction that his point had been made continued. "I thought not. Good. I will see you promptly on Monday at 8:30."

A large muddy pothole snapped Richard's attention back from his thoughts over events in the courtroom to the task at hand. Driving along Richard could feel the impact on the road conditions from the rain over last several days. At first he had barely noticed the loss of traction, as the road's base rock had offset the muddy clay underneath. Where the gravel had worn thin, however, the mud first sucked in the tires and then refused to provide anything solid for the tires to grip. Richard knew from discussions with Dickson that the clay was adobe, and set like concrete when dry. When saturated with rainwater, the microscopic particles of clay silt expanded and gave way to any pressure. On downhill sections of the road Richard merely let the weight and momentum of the truck carry him forward until he could feel resistance against the tires. On the uphill portions he simply tried to maintain a consistent forward speed and thereby avoid spinning the tires loose. Along the way Dickson had been signaling from time to time to pull over, and each time had stepped out into the muck and drizzle to snap off several shots of the road bed with his 35mm Nikon. Since Dickson would have to testify that the photos accurately represented the road conditions as they existed at the time that he was fired, at Richard's direction he continued to make careful notes of the steps he followed before and after each shot.

The entire process had already lasted over an hour, and they were quickly losing the afternoon light. Richard felt himself getting irritated with the amount of time Dickson was taking with each shot, as they were still a long way from the quarry gate. He kept quiet, however, as he knew that they were making good enough use of the time spent on the trip. Another hour passed before they finished the task. Richard motioned Dickson back into the cab to head back to Dickson's place just as a fresh cloudburst began in earnest. Throwing the truck into low gear, Richard turned the truck around on the narrow road by climbing the bank of the far side of the wall cut into hillside. With front end clear, he shifted out of low and accelerated. In contrast to the relatively slow speed Richard maintained on the way into the quarry, he allowed the truck to pick up speed on the way out. His mind was on the pictures, hoping that they would turn out as well as Dickson seemed to think, and knowing that he would consider the time well spent if they would help Monday morning with the cross-examination of Charles. Richard was also anxious to get back to his notes from Charles' testimony on direct examination, while the sound of Charles' voice was still clear in his mind.

Although the road was mostly downhill from the quarry to the main road, Richard could see a fairly steep uphill section ahead. Only a few hundred yards long, the stretch appeared to exceed a 17% uphill grade and had ruts worn deep into the clay base where trucks had passed that way before on other rainy days. On the way in, coming downhill, Dickson had captured the entire stretch on film as an example of a portion where the road had been torn up by large truck wheels. Dickson had remarked that this condition appeared strange. With the quarry having been closed for several years prior to construction of Winery Peak, in the absence of any legitimate use for the quarry the uphill portion of the road bed should have been worn relatively smooth of tire tracks by the passage of time and the insistence of the winter rains.

As he approached the slope Richard shifted into deep low with a jarring shift of the clutch. On the bottom of the hill, where the water splayed across the road evenly before pooling on the northern side, large amounts of muck and mud sucked at the tires before being flung through the air in ropey bands as Richard stomped on the accelerator. The truck continued to jerk forward, tires biting then slipping in the soil, and Richard fought to maintain control over their direction. The nose of the truck began to slip sideways as the front tires followed the rutted surface of the road. As the road ascended the ruts became deeper with sides now polished from the action of spinning tires. He tried to jam the steering wheel sideways and climb up the side of the deepest rut while maintaining the position of the truck relative to the direction of the roadbed, but instead managed only to jam the clay into the tire treads causing them to act as if they were racing slicks. The truck slowed and, momentarily, stopped before sliding backwards for several feet until the tires anchored sideways into the rut. Richard tried to maneuver forward but only succeeded in spinning the tires in place.

With a big sigh he turned the ignition off to let the engine, and his super tensed-upper body, rest. Until this point Dickson had been watching silently but now, in the new quiet, broke out in a gentle laugh.

"And just what, may I ask, is so goddamn funny?" Richard demanded in response. His forearms ached from the effort of keeping the steering wheel in a strong grasp, and he was in no mood for joking.

"Sorry, Richard. No offense intended. Just that—well—sometimes getting stuck in the mud can change your perspective on the problems you face in the world."

Richard leaned back and rested his head against the rear glass window of the cab. Dickson was right, he grudgingly realized, and with a groan swung open the door and dropped out of the cab to the ground. His boots sank instantly into the mud up to the tops of his laces. Lifting his foot made a sour sucking sound as the mud reluctantly released its hold. With a grimace Richard headed to the rear bumper. Dickson slid over behind the wheel and then stuck his head out the window to watch Richard's progress.

"Looks like we need something for traction before you start to push."

Richard bit off a smartass response and instead looked around for something, anything, to help. The bed of the truck was disappointingly empty. The sides of the road were not any more comforting. They did not present anything immediately useful like old boards or large tree limbs to jam under the rear wheels. The wintery undergrowth of small brown plants, dried leaves and small twigs, however, was plentiful and could be mixed with the mud to provide some support. Tossing his jacket into the bed of the truck, as this looked like messy work, he stretched arms wide and scooped a large bundle of the native mixture to his chest. Walking back to the rear of the truck he then stuffed the armload under and around the wheels. Dickson nodded his approval and, with Richard against the rear bumper to push, turned the key in the ignition. The engine roared to life and a cloud of bluish gray smoke belched out of the exhaust as Dickson raced the engine. With a drop of the clutch the engine engaged and the wheels began to spin furiously. At first the truck merely rocked forward as the rear wheels first bit into the mixture of mud and leaves and spit the remains into Richard's face and chest. With Dickson alternatively easing off and gunning the engine the truck finally jerked to a solid purchase and pushed the front wheels out of the rut. From there on it was clear, although slippery, sailing up the remaining portion of the slope. Dickson continued for forty yards until he had completely crested the hill before easing off the gas and pulled over to wait for Richard to walk, now mud encrusted, up the slope. With a grin he hopped from the cab to watch Richard try to wipe the mud from his face and arms. First frowning at the situation, Richard finally caught Dickson's eye and infectious good spirits. Breaking into a sheepish grin, Richard finished wiping his hands and good-naturedly waved Dickson back into the truck.

~ ~ ~ ~ ~

Since pulling the bags from the trash Terri had been concentrating nonstop on her attempts to piece together the jumbled strips of shredded documents in the hope of finding something, anything, which would be useful to Richard. At first the job felt like a giant jigsaw puzzle, with its secrets held tightly against all efforts to discover clues. To help the process, every square inch of available space in her living room was quickly covered with the thin strips of paper. Several of the pages had been deceptively easy to configure. Even though now fully shredded, the individual strips had remained together in the garbage in the same position as they had occupied before shredding. With these pages Terri had merely to carefully remove them from the trash bag and insert the collected strips together between clear sheets of plastic. The plastic and paper sandwich was then heated in Terri's oven to form a laminated shield to protect the product of her efforts. As time passed Terri finished the easy sheets. But as the job grew more exacting her motivation level wore down, even though she continued to attack the jumbled pile with slow but methodical effort.

Taking a break from an unfinished page that did not promise to reveal anything exciting, Terri pulled out the telephone number she had written down from the side of the garbage bin and telephoned the waste management company to determine the date and time of the next pickup. This information was carefully noted in her daytimer, along with a notation to revisit the winery before the pickup to pull any other bags of shredded documents. Pushing the unfinished page away Terri turned to a new stack of strips. At first nothing significant appeared from the jumbled strips and she concentrated more on matching the strips than the contents of the page. Then, suddenly and with a sense of relief, Terri realized that she had finally produced something interesting.

Written on Wine House letterhead, the multipage document was a photocopy of an earlier fax transmission setting forth a detailed chronology of Dickson's employment. Scrambling now, Terri worked feverishly to find all of the matching strips. Thirty minutes passed before she realized that she was unable to find more than a portion of pages two and three, but nothing of the remaining balance of the document. With a renewed sense of accomplishment and energy, Terri placed the fax transmission aside and continued to take the various strips around to several partially reconstructed documents rather than concentrate of any one document to the exclusion of all of the others.

As the hours passed and gray morning light began to ease the darkness of night Terri pressed on, always with an underlying concern that she would miss something in her need to finish the project quickly. A loud smacking sound outside announced the arrival of the early morning paper on her driveway and broke her concentration long enough for her stomach to grab her attention for a change. With a large fistful of strips in hand she headed back from the living room into the kitchen to stir up some eggs for breakfast. The strips were set on the counter while eggs, milk and cheese were taken from the refrigerator. With one hand she began to mix the ingredients together, and the other hand continued to idly play with the strips. Although the paper had been fed into the shredder vertically, the Wine House letterhead made the search for clues amid the strips easier. When the butter browned to the point of spitting in the pan Terri scooped the raw eggs into the heat to cook while she concentrated on another promising group of strips. These strips had somehow stayed together in the bag even though they had been jumbled apart from their original order. With excitement growing Terri ignored her breakfast and shifted all of her focus to the emerging page. Three more strips were added before she stopped to review her handiwork. She stared so hard at the completed page that she did not notice that the butter was now blackened and had started to give off an acrid smelling smoke. There on the page was a notation to the chronology that spelled out more than the remainder of Dickson's career. At the top of the page was the handwritten instruction "D. McKenna to attend Dickson press conference," followed by a date. The date was the same as the morning of the press conference where Dickson's name had been first publicly linked to the chemicals. More important, the name "D. McKenna" matched the first and last initials on the monogrammed cuff of the mysterious stranger.

~~~~~

Richard woke up slowly from his dream feeling heavy and stiff. The night before, after watching Dickson develop the film, he had gone home to relax on the sofa with a cold beer. The sofa had seemed to be as good a place as any to crash and he had fallen asleep with the 11:00 P.M. news flickering in his face. He now felt like he must have slept in the same position all night, on his side with his face buried into the thinly padded armrest. Rolling over seemed only to increase the pressure on his eyelids and cheekbones, throwing him momentarily off balance. Not for the first time did Richard wonder why he was too cheap to buy a decent sofa to replace
~~~~~

the one he had salvaged years ago from the family room in his parents' house.

With an effort he moved off of the sofa and, with bare feet slapping on the tiled hallway, walked into the dark bathroom. Squinting his eyes in anticipation he flicked on the florescent lights, which bounced off of the wall mirror behind the sink and directly into his face. As his eyes slowly adjusted to the light he looked into the mirror and gasped aloud. The left eyelid was swollen noticeably, and the skin on his forehead was blotched and irritated. Richard leaned towards the mirror for a closer inspection and, upon confirming his original reaction, began to swear silently, slowly and steadily. Where, he asked himself, where could he possibly have picked up a case of poison oak at this time of the year? The blisters were immediately recognizable and from past experience he knew that the condition would get much worse before it got better. How much worse would depend on the type and extent of exposure. His mind flashed on his brother's experience years before when, during the process of burning fall leaves, he had been accidentally bathed in the smoke of a burning poison oak bush. After inhaling some of the smoke he had to be hospitalized for over a week when blisters formed in his throat and sinuses. Richard could not remember being near any piles of burning leaves in the last week, which left direct contact in the last few days as the only possible cause of his condition. With a flash he realized what had happened. In the hills around Winery Peak poison oak tends to run rampant. During the spring months the leaves are dark green and glisten with the clear, but highly concentrated, oils. In fall the leaves turn bright red and slowly fall off of the branches to mix with pine needles and leaves from other plants in a pile at the base of the bush. Until the process repeats itself in the next spring the bush simply appears as another lonely tangle of bare branches. When he had gathered material from the side of the road to stuff in the mud under the truck's tires he had unthinkingly grabbed handfuls of loose leaves and twigs from the ground. He had been too absorbed in the immediate problem of getting unstuck to have even given any thought to what he was grabbing, and his face and arms were the worse for it.

He sat on the toilet seat to collect his thoughts and idly scratched. Appearing in front of the jury in this condition could be somewhat risky. Although he probably could count on the sympathy vote from some of the jurors, he did not want his condition to distract from the presentation of his case. Fortunately he had the entire day and Sunday before he had to appear and, if lucky, the swelling would go down somewhat. There was clearly not enough time for the swelling to go away completely, as the symptoms usually took at least a week to pass. He stood up, while continuing to think the problem through, and stepped into the bathtub. It took a conscious effort of will to stop scratching, even though he knew that he would tear the skin if he continued. Knowing that the rash was a reaction to the oils in the plant, and that the rash would spread as long as the skin maintained contact with the oils, he had learned through experience to wash the effected areas thoroughly, but gently, with soap.

The shower head distributed the hot water in a pelting spray, and the individual beads of heat had the significant benefit of stimulating the skin without the danger caused by prolonged scratching. Exposing portions of his arms slowly to the shower head produced an incredibly sensuous feeling, accompanied by deep warm shivers from the line of his scalp to his toes. He lowered the water to a lukewarm temperature to avoid heating and spreading the oils to the open pores. Then, with arms and face completely rinsed, he grabbed a bar of soap and began to build up a double handful of lather which was then spread carefully over his entire body. When he was completely lathered from head to foot, almost as if on cue the phone in his bedroom began to ring.

Under usual circumstances he would have ignored the phone, slowly finish his shower and later pick up the message from his answering machine. The answering machine had been a birthday present years ago from his mother, who could not stand the fact that he would go for days without returning phone calls and was still uncomfortable with the concept that there were people who did not drop everything and jump when the phone rang. But today was not a usual day, as too much was happening and this case was too important to take the chance of missing an important call. Irritated with the thought that his mother would approve of his response Richard stepped out of the shower and, with soapy water dripping, walked across the floor to answer the phone on the fourth ring.

"Jesus, Richard, I thought you would never answer the damn phone."

"Good morning, Terri . . . Its good to hear from you too. Only I'm dripping all over the floor."

"As much as that makes an interesting picture, I have got something better that will blow you away. We got them, Richard . . . we really got them."

Terri quickly described her work and what she had found in the pile of shredded documents. Shit, he thought, now I've finally got them by the short hairs. With this information I can force Wine house to produce McKenna at trial. Then let him explain why he was acting as a shill at the press conference. And, Richard suddenly realized, I can ask the Judge Jamison to continue the trial for a few days because Wine House failed to properly produce McKenna as a witness. By then this damn poison oak will have gone away.

His feeling of elation suddenly plunged as fast as it had arisen. All Terri had was a document that she had taken from the trash. A shredded document at that. The Judge might even say she had stolen it, even though it had been put in the public domain when the Winery Peak employees had placed it into the commercial garbage bins. He had a sinking feeling that this idea was going nowhere fast.

"Terri," he interrupted her story rudely "do we have any way of verifying this information? I mean, the fact that this guy's monogram matches the initials of the name of the guy on the document is good, but given the source I would like to go to the Judge with a little more."

"No problem," she answered triumphantly. "After piecing together the document I logged on to the Wine House

WAN—the wide area network that links all of their computer systems among all of the various sites. I was able to log on as if I was also linked to the local area network at Winery Peak."

"Can they trace it?"

"Not a chance, but not a problem. They set up access through the Internet for people with questions about the Company as a public relations ploy, but left wide open an easy way into their system. Pretty unsophisticated, whoever is in charge of designing their information technology systems. But nothing illegal about my access. Finding the information, however, was not so easy. I tried accessing the personnel lists in the Human Resources Department. When I entered 'D. McKenna' I kept getting a restricted field notice in response. So I then accessed the software program on which they operate their online calendar system. The data base includes the calendars for all of the top executives. When I located Alexander's calendar I scrolled back to the day that you took his deposition and bingo! The same morning had an earlier entry showing a meeting with Stucky and our friend D. McKenna. I have a printout that I'll bring by later with the other documents."

Richard quickly thanked Terri and made arrangements to meet later at his office. He had a lot of thinking to do as there were a lot of obstacles in the way of bringing the information to the attention of Judge Jamison. But best of all, thought Richard as he gently pressed a towel against his skin, he had not thought about scratching for at least ten minutes.

~~~~~

Monday now could not have come soon enough for Richard. Although furiously busy all of Saturday preparing witness testimony and cross-examination outlines, and most of Sunday planning Monday's maneuvers, the time had seemed to crawl by. He had explained his strategy the night before to Dickson, who did not quite follow the ins and outs of the
~~~~~

tactics involved but had given Richard the go ahead to pursue whatever Richard had in mind—as long as he used, in Dickson's words, his best judgment.

They had arrived early at the courthouse and went straight to the courtroom, which was empty except for the bailiff who was calmly reading the morning paper while sipping an oversized Styrofoam cup of coffee. Richard made a beeline to the bailiff and quietly informed him that there were some matters that he wanted to discuss with the Judge before the jury was called. This was not an unusual occurrence during a trial, as there are many procedural matters that arise during a trial that should not be discussed in the presence of the jury, and the bailiff casually nodded his understanding before excusing himself to go into chambers to notify Judge Jamison about the request. Ten minutes later, when Stucky strode confidently into the courtroom, Richard walked over to advise Stucky of what he had told the bailiff. Stucky's smile faded rapidly, his eyes narrowed and he listened intently to Richard before peppering Richard with a number of questions concerning the details of his request to see the Judge. Richard clenched his jaw in response, stared stonily at Stucky and then turned on his heel to walk back to where Dickson stood without otherwise acknowledging that Stucky had even spoken at all.

All rose quickly when Judge Jamison entered the courtroom precisely at 8:30. Richard had been warned by Shaw that Judge Jamison hated to keep the jury waiting once the trial commenced, so he stayed on his feet even after the bailiff sang out the very customary "be seated." During the entire trial the jury was instructed to appear each morning at the courthouse by 8:45 A.M., fifteen minutes before the proceedings began, in order to avoid delays because of stragglers. The jury members would congregate and wait downstairs in the main jury room until summoned to the courtroom by the bailiff. Because of Richard's request this morning, however, today they would have to stay downstairs a little longer.

"If it please the court . . ." Richard began only to be cut off by Judge Jamison.

"What happened to you?"

It's pretty clear, Judge, thought Richard wryly, I ate a fan for breakfast.

"Poison oak, Your Honor."

"Well, you look like hell . . . You should go see a doctor." Judge Jamison waved at the court reporter. "Dora, that's not on the record. All right, let's proceed. All counsel are present outside the presence of the jury. Proceed, Mr. Magnus, proceed."

"Thank you. Over the weekend we were able to corroborate the identity of a material witness to the decision to terminate. We request a short continuance and an Order that Wine House produce this witness immediately."

"Seems like you should have 'corroborated' earlier, Mr. Magnus." Jamison responded pointedly. "Explanation?"

"We would have, your Honor, but Wine House intentionally failed to disclose his identity."

Richard triumphantly pulled a large sheaf of papers from his briefcase, handing a copy to Stucky and a copy to the clerk who in turn handed the papers to Judge Jamison. Included in the bundle were written answers from Wine House signed under penalty of perjury, submitted in response to written interrogatories from Richard that requested an identification of all of the individuals that were involved in the decision to terminate Dickson. The answers conspicuously failed to mention, or make any reference to, a "D. McKenna." Also included in the papers was a copy of the document that Terri had pieced together from the Winery Peak trash. Richard had agonized over whether to present it to the court with the other documents, but finally had decided that the small risk of the court finding that the document had been obtained improperly was outweighed by the need to fully support his request. And presenting the printout of Alexander's calendar was unthinkable, as there was no way to support or explain Terri's electronic investigation in a manner that Judge Jamison was likely to understand. Besides, he had rationalized, trash is trash when everything else is all said and done, and Winery Peak can hardly complain about him having in his possession what they voluntarily threw away.

"Let's hear the explanation, Mr. Stucky."

Thankfully to Richard, Judge Jamison's tone in asking for an explanation was decidedly unfriendly. In response Stucky held up his left hand while he quickly flipped through the pages with his right. Stucky had practically grabbed the pages out of Richard's outstretched hand, with the jury downstairs the need for his outward courtroom cool had lessened in the heat of the moment. When he reached the previously shredded document he stopped short.

"Your Honor," Stucky sounded ponderous, "we have a serious problem."

Richard took a sharp breath, Stucky's tone of voice immediately set off all of his alarm bells. Stucky lifted the entire stack, clipped together at the top, by the single page between thumb and forefinger as if it were too offensive to have too close to his body.

"This is a Wine House internal memo, subject to the attorney-client privilege. It has never been produced to Mr. Magnus, by accident or otherwise, and I demand an explanation of how it came into his possession."

Richard's stomach sank somewhat. He could tell from the look on Judge Jamison's face that Stucky was close to having masterly turned the tables on him. Richard knew that he better say something fast to regain control of the morning.

"First, your Honor, this document was obtained from the public domain. Second, the fact that counsel's client does not have good document control in no way relieves them of the fact that they have played games with the identity of their witnesses. Thirdly . . ."

"All right, counsel. I have heard more than enough for now." Richard listened intently, waiting for the decision, but could not help but think with a small part of his mind that Judge Jamison's face was beginning to resemble a dark and angry cloud.

"No continuance. I have the jury to think about, and there is no reason while they should sit while this issue is being thrashed out. Mr. Stucky, I want an explanation by 8:30 A.M. tomorrow. Mr. Magnus, I want an explanation from you too at the same time regarding that document. I am not, however, going to let this case end in a mistrial and force the taxpayers to pay for a retrial of this case. But that does not mean I will have any reservations about holding you both in contempt! Now we are going to call the jury back in, and I want both of you ready to start in fifteen minutes."

Richard steeled himself against his acute disappointment. He could deal with giving an explanation about the document came into his possession. Without a great deal of effort he was also able to rationalize that the worse possible case facing him would be a simple trespassing fine. But he knew, and it was more important, that he had to figure out a way to bring to the attention of the jury the fact that Wine House had gone to such great lengths to make Dickson appear to be a bad guy. Unfortunately, with the jury about to come back into the courtroom in minutes, he simply did not have the time to figure out how he was going to accomplish that goal.

CHAPTER THIRTEEN

MRS. SAGER had not been very truthful. Since her husband had died several years earlier her life had become more than merely quiet. With her adult children ignoring repeated attempts to be involved in their lives, and with little in the way of outside interests or hobbies, she had grown resigned to the realities of solitude and boredom. One of her more consistent vices, an avid interest in the supermarket tabloids, was the favorite of her few remaining contacts with the world at large. The glossy pages made her convinced that interesting events only happened to other people. This depressing status quo would continue in place, she often thought, unless something significant was to change in her life. But the possibility of remarriage, or even a significant relationship with a man, had grown increasingly unlikely as the years rolled along. Completely oblivious to her own shortcomings, over the years she had slowly formed the opinion that men in general were to blame for their inability to see her obvious—to her—attractions.

When she received the summons to jury duty in the mail the official envelope had appeared as a dignified and exciting white and gray invitation amid the colorful clutter of the junk mail. The summons had even been addressed to her by name, instead of the impersonal salutation of "Dear Occupant." Always irritating, felt Mrs. Sager, as if the senders of the junk mail did not know her name after sending mail to the same person at the same address for nearly twenty years. During the jury selection process she had appeared withdrawn and quiet to her fellow members of the pool of potential jurors. Matronly in appearance, the others had been respectful and kept their distance during the long wait to be called to the courtroom. A few of the other ladies made friendly overtures, but from the response generally thought her to be aloof. She had been one of the original twelve called to sit in the jury box, and felt elated—if also a little flustered—at finally having someone pay her the attention that she felt she so clearly deserved. Because of the apparent deference in which she was treated by the other potential jurors, Richard had incorrectly assumed that she had made friends among the other individuals and might even play a leadership role during deliberations. Normally a potential juror that appeared to have too strong of a personality would be excused by one side or the other fairly rapidly, as strong willed jurors tended to fix their position quickly and could overwhelm the deliberations of the other jurors. Care had to be exercised, however, when the potential jurors started to become friends, as hard feelings could result if friends were separated during the selection process.

Her responses to Richard's questions directed at eliciting information regarding her general background and beliefs had resolved his decision in favor of her remaining on the jury, as the information she provided matched sufficiently his desired juror profile. In describing herself as a widow, she had implied strongly that she had enjoyed a happy and well rounded relationship with her former husband and a healthy attitude towards men in general. Unbeknownst to Richard, who took her remarks as favorable towards the generally attractive Dickson, Mrs. Sager had already developed a strong but well-hidden dislike towards his client. Dickson, to her way of thinking, was a prime example of the type of man who should have been interested in her. Through her ability to pass judgment on Dickson's case, she felt with satisfaction that she finally had been given the opportunity to show all of those unnamed and unidentified men the mistake that they had made in ignoring her for all of these years. Richard, trying to focus on the big picture, had simply misread cause of her satisfaction. At the end of the selection process neither he nor Stucky had bothered to consider her further as someone to challenge and strike from the jury.

From the very beginning of the trial the eventual outcome of her vote was certain in her mind, and not favorable to Dickson, although she had affirmatively promised—in response to the Judge Jamison's question to the entire panel—that she would and could keep her mind open until all of the evidence was in. She had expressed complete ignorance of the case, although she had followed the entire dispute from the original television reports of the first press conference at Winery Peak through the most recent newspaper articles. As the trial progressed, and the days passed one after another, she had grown uneasy with the thought that some of the other jurors might not share her views. Judge Jamison had also admonished all of the jurors at the beginning of the case, and repeated himself at the beginning of every break, that they were not to discuss the case with the one another until all of the evidence was in and the case submitted to them for deliberations. This admonition consistently frustrated her attempts to lead any of the other jurors in conversation concerning the case or her ability to learn how the other jurors intended to vote. Over the weekend she had contemplated calling a friend who knew the mother of one of the other jurors to see if she could learn anything, but her fear of being removed from the jury for inappropriate behavior had stayed her hand from calling.

For her the weekend had passed slowly. As soon as the jury had been excused the previous Friday she had been eager to get back to court, back to the trial and the attention. At least at the trial she was somebody. People acknowledged her, asked her to join them in their activities and waited until she was comfortably seated in the jury box before beginning testimony after the breaks. She took pride every morning at her own punctuality in arriving exactly at 8:45 A.M., a trait that her late husband had often unsuccessfully urged her to adopt. This morning the delay had turned her pride first to annoyance and then frustration as 9:00 A.M. had come and gone. She was sure that it was a trick by Dickson, or certainly his lawyer, used in an attempt to avoid allowing her to pass judgment. As the minutes continued to pass without any explanation her feeling became more difficult to hide, but she was rebuffed when she tried to complain to one of the other jurors and she was reduced to fuming quietly in her seat.

~ ~ ~ ~ ~

Although Judge Jamison usually was a stickler for punctuality, for a change he did not seem inclined to voice his concern over the failure to start on time. The short delay did not matter much in the context of the amount of time Richard had available during this morning to cross-examine the witness before the mid-morning break. But he was glad for the extra time to review his notes while the witness waited tensely, remembering Michael's advice that the moments of anticipation before the first question was asked could help unnerve the witness as much as a timeout helps to unnerve a place-kicker before the field goal is attempted. By the time that everyone finally was ready Richard was prepared to pounce on the heart of the testimony.

"You are trained as a chemist, are you not?"

"Yes. Actually as a chemical engineer."

"Thank you for the clarification. As a chemical engineer it is very important that you be precise in your written work. Correct?"

"Yes."

"And you wrote a Field Analysis Report for Wine House."

Charles nodded affirmatively at the folder Richard held in the air.

"And you knew when you wrote the report that Dr. Dickson was going to be used by Wine House as the fall guy . . ."

"Objection, your Honor!" Stucky was on his feet in a flash. "I'm tired at the continued slams at Wine House."

"Withdrawn, your Honor."

Richard smiled inwardly at Stucky for falling into his gambit. Nothing wakes a jury up faster than the possibility that there may be something said that one side believes that they are not supposed to hear. Rather than take the chance that Judge Jamison would sustain the objection, he decided simply to rephrase the same point as a new question.

"And you knew when you wrote the report that Wine House was taking the position that Dr. Dickson was responsible for the dumping at Winery Peak."

"Well . . . I'm not sure I knew that."

Charles hesitated and looked over at Stucky for help, but he should have known that none was forthcoming from that direction. Richard, alert to his discomfort, followed his gaze over at Stucky.

"I am over here, Mr. Charles, not over with Mr. Stucky. Now then. You were careful when you wrote the report, were you not?"

"Well, yes."

"And it is your practice to make sure that you are accurate and precise, is it not?"

"I do try to be accurate."

"And you make sure that you understand your assignment before you begin, don't you?"

Again on his feet, Stucky interrupted the questioning.

"Objection, this is simply badgering the witness."

"I'll allow it."

The Judge's interest was growing as he watched Richard try to set and then tighten the noose.

"And you knew that your work would be used by Wine House—and more particularly by Mr. Stucky—in this trial. Isn't that true."

"Well, I don't think I knew so . . ."

"But the cover letter of your report indicates a copy was sent to Mr. Stucky. Correct?"

"Yes . . ."

"And you knew that Mr. Stucky was representing Wine House in this trial. But your testimony on direct was that you did not think he would be using it in this trial."

"I, I don't know . . ."

"Of course you don't."

Richard stared stonily at Charles and then turned to look knowingly at the jury to make sure that they understood his point—that the report was expressly manufactured for the purpose of the trial—before he continued questioning this witness. Satisfied with what he saw, Richard next looked at the Judge who was now looked at the witness with unfriendly eyes. To avoid any unnecessary loss of momentum he launched into his next question.

"In your report, Mr. Charles, you note that the concentration of the chemicals is very high."

"Yes sir. I believe that from the concentrations there must have been a large amount that leached its way into the quarry."

"And if the chemicals had been dumped directly into the quarry, not used for several years on the fields as you have speculated, how much would have had to have been dumped at one time to reach the concentrations that you measured?"

"But . . . but I did not say that the chemicals were dumped."

"Humor me sir, and assume that the chemicals were directly placed into the water—how much?"

"Well, given the amount of water in the quarry, I would say several truckloads."

"What size of truck?"

"Well, I was referring to a standard dump truck." Charles looked thoughtful, unmindful of the point of the question. "You would need a special permit to carry this type of chemical in larger quantities, and I do not think that a truck any larger than the size of a standard dump truck would have been able to navigate the quarry access road in its present condition. But a regular dump truck could have carried enough to reach that level of concentration if it made several trips."

"Have you heard of anyone on behalf of Winery Peak stating that they drove one of these trucks to the quarry?"

"No."

"To the best of your knowledge has anyone from Winery Peak been identified as driving one of these trucks to the quarry?"

"No."

"So, to your knowledge, if someone drove a truck to the quarry, and dumped it in, they would have acted on behalf of someone other than Dr. Dickson."

"I don't know . . ."

"And, as far as you know, they could have been working directly for Wine House without Dr. Dickson's knowledge."

Stucky's objection to the question, on the basis that it assumed facts that were not in evidence, was quickly sustained by Judge Jamison. Richard did not care, for he assumed that Charles would not have given a helpful answer, and having achieved his goal of placing the suggestion before the jury he continued without acknowledging the minor interruption.

"And from the concentration levels, do you have any idea of the coverage from the chemical?"

"I'm afraid that I am not following you."

"Isn't it true, Mr. Charles, that, based on the size of the vineyards at Winery Peak, your report reflects concentration levels so high that there must have been several years worth of the chemicals dumped into the quarry.?"

"It was a surprisingly high ratio, but Dr. Dickson has been at Winery Peak for five years."

Richard ignored the last comment and bored on.

"And from the decomposition of the chemicals in the water it is your position that the chemicals had been in the water more than one year. Correct?"

"As I said, I do not think it has been more than several years."

"But at least one year."

"That is a fair estimate."

"At least two years."

"Possibly, but I did not explore that matter."

"A critical issue, but you did not explore it."

Richard shot back, then briefly paused to avoid the objection that he was being argumentative. Surprisingly, it did not come.

"And did you take into account the fact that Winery Peak has been producing wine quality grapes for only two years?"

"Winery Peak has been in operation," came the satisfied reply, "for five years, Mr. Magnus."

"You have made a mistake, Mr. Charles, in your calculations. Although the vines were planted five years ago, because of the length of time for the vines to mature the wine quality grapes, and the need to use any insecticides, are only something that has occurred in the last two years. And—according to your report—from the level of decomposition no chemicals were added to the quarry in the last year. Leaving, again by your calculations, only one year for the runoff to have leached "several years" worth of chemicals into the water. So where did the additional volume of chemicals come from?"

Charles looked confused, and finally—reluctantly—conceded that he did not know. Richard decided he would not do much better with this witness.

"No more questions of this witness, your Honor."

Stucky shook his head to indicate that he had nothing further to ask Charles, who was then excused by Judge Jamison. Charles exited from the witness chair, head down and in a hurry, which clearly reaffirmed the point Richard had tried to make regarding Charles' purported neutrality. But his happiness at having dulled the thrust of the testimony from Charles could not keep his concentration from drifting. As Stucky called his next witness he simply looked forward to the end of the trial, regardless of the outcome. With pangs of guilt he knew that his feelings were not fair to Dickson, but the grind of the repeated sixteen hour work days and sleepless nights was finally taking its toll. He could only feel glad when Stucky advised Judge Jamison that he had one witness left before resting the defense.

Richard knew, when Stucky called the next witness to the stand, that he had heard the name before during one of the several Wine House depositions that had been taken in either California or New York. A quick review of his witness notebook confirmed that the witness was the lead staff auditor who had been assigned by Wine House to prepare the financial records of Winery Peak for the company-wide annual audit process. Arriving last year at Winery Peak with several other staff accountants, the auditor and his staff had spent three weeks reviewing the operation's books and records. Dickson had described their role to Richard in extremely mundane terms and as casually dismissed their involvement as without importance. As a result of Dickson's description, Richard had concluded that the auditor had minimal potential of testifying. That conclusion, buttressed with the need to cut some corners in response to the pressure from Allen, resulted in his decision not to take the deposition of this particular witness before the trial. He now had literally no idea what the witness would be testifying about, nor did he have any idea what he could ask on cross-examination. Strangely enough, even in light of the threat posed by this witness, he could not seem to muster enough energy to do much more than flip to a fresh sheet on his legal pad. Noticing that he was down to one of his last few sheets he bent down to pull a fresh pad from his briefcase, but then checked even that impulse as a waste of time. Surely, he thought, this witness will not require a lot of note taking. In retrospect Richard later realized that he should have realized that Stucky would not have selected for his last witness someone who did not have something important to say.

Stucky's direct examination was somewhat dry, reflecting the subject matter of the audit portion of the testimony, but was very thorough when evaluated on the technical merits of the information presented. The examination focused on the winery's pro formas, cost escalators and budget considerations. Each point was laid out in precise fashion, designed to establish the existence of a legitimate business reason to terminate Dickson. The witness was one of those individuals who loved mathematical precision, and happily walked the jury through some fairly complicated spreadsheets. The jury did not seem to share his excitement and, as the testimony continued, appeared generally listless and disinterested as the time wore on. Stucky was not completely oblivious of the effect of this testimony on the jury, but knew that he had to present the economic information to establish the factual basis for the arguments that he intended to make to the jury during the closing presentations before deliberations. Using two charts and a few quick questions that in ten minutes effectively recasted and summarized the information presented over the last hour, Stucky concluded his examination and turned the witness over to Richard. Although the overall testimony had lasted longer than the general attention span of his audience, the colored charts and graphs had interjected enough of a different approach to the information that Stucky was comfortable that he had been successful in gaining the jurors' attention to the last ten minutes of the presentation.

Glancing at the wall clock behind the bench Richard hurriedly calculated the time remaining until the lunch break. Although there were a number of questions that he could ask generically about the witness's background in order to stall, and phrase them in a manner that might convey something wrong with the witness's qualifications, he did not think that he could legitimately stretch the cross-examination long enough to cover the time remaining. Remembering Michael Shaw's admonition to do whatever was possible to end on some semblance of a high point with the last witness before the closing arguments, he desperately needed a few moments to clear his head and find some opening in the testimony the auditor had just given. Mastering himself, he turned towards Judge Jamison.

"If it please the Court, I would like to request a short break."

"Why, Mr. Magnus?"

Great, thought Richard sarcastically, he knows what I want but does not want to give me the slightest goddamn break. Stucky was silent, knowing this time to fade as far as possible into the background of this discussion. Richard asked to approach the bench, in an attempt to waste some time with a side bar conference, was quickly rebuffed when Judge Jamison tersely ordered him to get on with his examination of the witness. Richard's eyes partially widened in disbelief. He simply had to find a way of covering the time remaining until the lunch break, and knew he was in danger of looking foolish in front of the jurors. Stalling with the background questions, long enough to think of something—anything—that would let him end by making one point on Stucky's last witness, was the only remaining option. In his brief bag was the outline of questions that he had used for Rosenblum. The first page of the outline listed questions designed to cast doubt on the qualifications Rosenblum had listed in support of his ability to opine on the substantive areas of his testimony. The same questions would also now have to serve as an outline for this witness. Without looking down more than briefly, he reached down for the manila folder that contained the outline and pulled forth a fistful of documents that included several folders including the one he was after. As he separated the folders, he noticed that he also had plucked the folder that contained the results of Terri's recent investigations.

Intuitively reflecting on the contents of Terri's folder in the time necessary to place the other folders on the table, he mentally switched gears and with a long shot in mind addressed the witness.

"You described yourself as lead supervisor for your audit team."

"Yes, Mr. Magnus."

"And that is a senior executive position at Wine House."

"More precisely, it is a manager 3 position."

"Whatever. You have worked in that position for approximately ten years."

"Actually, twelve years, sir."

"And in the performance of your duties you have met with and interacted with other members of senior management at wine House over the years."

"Yes."

"Including Mr. Alexander."

With a flourish Richard drew a folded newspaper out from the materials pulled together by Terri. It was an old copy of the New York Examiner, boasting on the front page of its business section a large picture of Montgomery Alexander III surrounded by several other individuals in dark business suits. After showing the picture to Stucky, who grudgingly had no comment or objection for the moment, he handed it to the clerk who obligingly marked it with a number for identification. Richard then handed the newspaper to the witness.

"Do you recognize anyone in this picture?"

"Yes."

"Please identify the individuals whom you recognize by stating their names and positions."

Stucky was mystified by this line of questions, but they were not improper enough to outweigh the appearance of concern that could be created should he object and be faced with Judge Jamison overruling his objection. The witness, with a short glance at Stucky, then turned to the paper and began to identify several of the individuals in the picture in addition to Alexander. One was the executive vice president of marketing, another as a senior manager in the corporate division, and a third identified by the witness simply as a direct report to Alexander.

"Do you know all of the 'direct reports' to Alexander?"

"Well . . . I'm sure that I do not. But I do know most of them, at least by sight. We pride ourselves . . ." said the witness smugly, in an attempt to ad lib some points for Wine House, "on our feeling of family and interest in one another. And you do not work as an auditor for corporate for long without learning who reports to whom."

Please, Richard prayed to himself, please let this happen. Reaching into the folder that contained Terri's investigation, he selected a second photo. This photo was an enhancement of the still image that Terri had reproduced from the tape of the press conference. The photo was a head and shoulders shot, without caption or description, and it was impossible to tell its location or background simply by looking directly at it without the benefit of the cropped background. Richard tried to quell his excitement and showed the picture to Stucky, who apparently did not recognize the picture or grasp the significance of the trap Richard had hopefully set, and voiced no objection. After being marked for identification, Richard placed the picture on the tray in front of the witness. He tried to play down his emotions, as the witness could easily disclaim any knowledge of the man in the photo, leaving the entire line of question for naught.

The witness picked up the photo with both hands, edges held between thumbs and forefingers, and looked at the face only briefly before addressing Richard.

"Okay, I know him. This is one of Alexander's direct reports. I do not know his exact title or responsibilities, but I have seen him on several occasions in meetings chaired by Alexander."

Richard reached for the picture, obviously pleased with the result, when the witness pulled the photo back from Richard's outstretched hand to look again at the face that stared out in the direction of the camera.

". . . and his name is McKenna."

~ ~ ~ ~ ~

Michael drained his glass in an attempt to mask the extent of his frustration. Without thought to the napkin sitting on the table, he wiped the foamy residue from his upper lip with the back of his hand. Time had come for Richard to close the door on the trial. Although they agreed that Dickson had to take the stand one last time for rebuttal testimony, Richard refused to commit that he would follow Michael's pointed advice to first proceed by putting Tom Murphy on the witness stand. Their difference in opinion, on what Michael viewed as a relatively simply strategy decision, served as the kindling for the smoldering sense of frustration that had been building in Michael's chest for some time relating to a more personal matter. While he had been happy to take the heat from his partners for Richard while the case progressed, he had still expected some consideration and deference to his judgment. He had, apparently, misjudged the sentiments of his partners. Most of them now appeared to be falling in line behind the position taken by Allen Rose, and were focusing greedily on the net profit analysis as the only measure of the firm's success. They seemed to care little for the ethical obligations involved, at least insofar as those obligations interfered with their personal net worth. He had argued for hours about the overall benefit to the firm to be able to market Richard as a skilled trial lawyer, and had pointed out the need for Richard to actually try cases to satisfy the promise of that marketing statement. Support for Michael's position had faded as Richard had given up any pretence of trying to attend to his other cases while he fought this one.

Thinking painfully of the shortsightedness of his partners, and the growing divergence between their respective business philosophies, he raised his glass slightly. Noticing with surprise that the glass was empty as the rim came close to his lips, he then brought it down sharply on the glass topped table. Nearby heads turned slightly as a loud crack snapped off from the table and ricocheted through the room, and as quickly turned back to their own conversations in the busy restaurant. Michael blushed slightly from the attention and drew his thoughts tighter together.

"Damn it, Richard," he continued in exasperation, "you can't expect everything to fall into place as if by magic. This is not some prearranged puzzle, set solely in place for your enjoyment."

"Look, Michael, I'm sorry that you have been taking a lot of heat for me at the firm, but I cannot go back on my word and require Tom Murphy to testify."

The two continued to eat in morose silence, neither tasting what should have been an excellent meal of fresh pasta topped with caramelized onions and tomatoes sautéed in garlic and olive oil. Richard's unwillingness to call Murphy to the witness stand had been a constant sore spot to Michael, who felt that his testimony would be credible and critical due to his role as an impartial third party witness. Michael was also well aware that Murphy had conducted the initial investigation into the situation on behalf of the County and knew from Richard that Murphy had spent time reviewing the Winery Peak files in the dusty Quonset hut with Terri. At the end of that day, months before, Terri had conveyed Murphy's offer to testify to the fact that he had reviewed the files and that he had determined from the records that nothing improper was used, nor was there any mention in those files of the chemicals that had been found when the water in the quarry had been tested. Although this investigation of the records would not rule out the possibility that chemicals had been used at Winery Peak in the past, since they could and probably would have been deployed without any record keeping at all, this type of testimony certainly would be a positive boost to the case at this critical juncture.

Although originally listed as one of their witnesses during the pre-litigation strategy sessions, three weeks before trial Terri suddenly advised Richard that Murphy had developed cold feet about the idea of testifying. Since it was so close to trial, Richard had been powerless to simply subpoena Murphy for his deposition and thereby force the testimony. When he pointed this problem out to Terri, and suggested that he was entitled to some explanation for Murphy's change of heart, he had only received an unknowing shrug of her slender shoulders in response. In truth, Terri suspected that her friend was under some kind of pressure from his boss concerning the entire investigation, but she did not want to cause Murphy further trouble on the basis of her educated guesses. Michael had attacked the situation head on when he had first been apprised of the change in plans, and had advised Richard to simply subpoena Murphy to appear at the trial to testify. Now that Stucky had rested his defense case, Michael wanted to revisit the issue and have Richard call Murphy as a potential witness to contradict some of the points raised by Charles. Not being as sanguine about the ability to compel a straight answer from Murphy under the circumstances, and based upon his own experiences with people who had a special interest in the case, Richard maintained that he simply could not call Murphy unwillingly to the stand. Reluctantly, he maintained that he would have to rely solely on Dickson during the rebuttal stage of the trial.

In an attempt to act nonchalant in the face of the tension existing between them, Richard stretched his arm across the table for more bottled mineral water and succeeded only in knocking over the bottle when he took his eyes off the bottle to look down for his own glass. They both jumped out of their chairs as the water splashed and fizzled across the white linen tablecloth, and were quickly shooed aside by an efficient blond waitress in tight fitting pants who came to their rescue. While they stood self-consciously behind her, waiting for the table to be cleared, Michael silently took the opportunity to make amends by wrapping his long fingers around Richard's neck in a strong but friendly grip. Richard tensed at first, then relaxed his neck muscles and let his head roll slowly to acknowledge the silent offer of peace between them.

"Well, Michael, I know I should accept what you are saying . . ."

"Don't worry, Richard. What you are doing, given the pressure you are under, shows a lot of character. . ."

"Thanks. I was told once that character is what you end up with when you don't get what you really wanted."

Michael smiled in response to hearing his own observations being repeated back at him by Richard, but did not bother otherwise to answer. What Richard said may be true, he thought, but if Richard does not win big we both will be able to see how much character my partners truly lack.

~ ~ ~ ~ ~

"Do you have any rebuttal witnesses, Mr. Magnus?"

Judge Jamison was superficially solicitous enough in his inquiry, although he had expressed in chambers to counsel his impatience with the fact that the trial had now lasted longer than the estimates given by either Richard or Stucky at the pretrial conference. Richard was quick to acknowledge that he did indeed have testimony to present in rebuttal and waved Dickson back to the witness stand. While Dickson was getting settled in the witness chair, Gayle aligned the overhead projector with the whiteboard that hung on the wall to the side of the jury box and set a color transparency on the top of the viewfinder. The transparency was a duplication of one of the photographs Dickson had taken during his drive with Richard to the quarry. When the system was warmed and ready she nodded to Richard, who had been waiting impatiently. Finding to his surprise that he had been holding his breath in anticipation, he drew a breath and turned to Dickson and began.

"You are familiar with the site characteristics around the old quarry, are you not?"

"Yes. We took a long look at that area of the property when we first laid out the winery in relation to the vineyards. Because of the remote nature of the property, we knew that we would have to do something to guarantee a fresh and constant supply of water. There was a possibility that we could convert the old quarry into an irrigation reservoir instead of having to build one from scratch. However, because of the logistics, we abandoned that idea very early into the planning stages of the project."

"What were some of the logistical problems?"

"There were a number of concerns including the placement of the pumping station and the feasibility of placing appropriate access roads."

"What was wrong with the road that had been used by the original operator of the quarry."

"That road had not been maintained since the quarry had been closed years, in fact decades, before we began to conduct our evaluations. Among other problems that were encountered, we would have had to spend a lot of money to bring the road up to current county standards. This made use of the quarry prohibitively expensive."

"After you decided not to use the quarry was the old road used for any other purpose?"

"No sir. We accessed the fields that were being cultivated on the two main ridges from the other side of the property using the existing roads."

Richard nodded, thinking so far so good, and stepped over to the overhead projector. He reached over to turn it on and paused with his hand on the switch.

"Has there been any reason that you can think of for trucks to have been driving over the quarry access road during the last couple of years?"

"No, absolutely not."

His fingers snapped the on switch and an unfocused beam of light shot out of the overhead and bounced off of the whiteboard. Gayle quickly adjusted the lens. All eyes in the courtroom watched as the picture of a rutted dirt road appeared and then sharpened into focus.

"Did you take this picture?"

"Yes. It is a photograph I just took of the access road." Dickson reached over to the side of the stand and lifted a slim metal pointer. He waved the tip of the pointer towards the left side of the projection.

"You can see the deep ruts on the uphill stretch in the foreground."

"What is the significance of the depth of the ruts?"

"These ruts were made by truck tires—larger than we use on our pickup trucks and, by the depth of the ruts, the trucks must have been fully loaded. There was no traffic from Winery Peak that could have produced those tracks, and they were not there when we first evaluated the quarry several years ago."

"Are you suggesting that someone intentionally dumped truckloads of chemicals into the quarry?"

"There is no other way that the chemicals could have gotten there."

"If that chemical compound works so good, why would anyone throw it into a quarry where it would get all wet and be worthless?"

"Well, Mr. Magnus, this chemical is banned in California. Based on the concentrations we have heard, disposal costs in an EPA sanctioned site is very expensive—potentially in the millions. If someone who did not care for the land thought that they might otherwise have to incur the fairly significant costs for proper disposal . . . Well, I guess that they might think—erroneously—that they had a pretty good reason to get rid of their remaining stores by dumping them in the quarry."

"Thank you, Dr. Dickson. No more questions. Thank you, your Honor."

Stucky stood, too quickly and confidently to Richard's liking, and solemnly buttoned the front of his coat before walking directly over to stand facing Dickson. Stucky's voice then whipped out against Dickson, startling in its contrast to his outwardly calm demeanor of moments before.

"You expect us to believe that somebody, out of the blue, directly dumped organophosphates into the quarry?"

Without allowing time for a response he continued in an unrelentingly barrage.

"And even if it happened as you say, it clearly happened while you were in charge of Winery Peak, did it not? And you were supposed to be the one ultimately responsible for everything that took place at the winery, were you not? But you had no idea—not a clue—that these mystery trucks were using the access road?"

Stucky shook his head slowly from side to side, but his eyes remained locked on Dickson's, who in turn looked helplessly over at Richard. Damn it, Richard thought, say something—anything—but do not let him conclude on that point without some response.

The sweep hand on the wall clock swung from the one to the nine before Stucky made another move. The forty long seconds seemed like an eternity to Richard, yet Dickson did not have anything to say. Finally Stucky threw his hands up into the air and turned to Judge Jamison.

"No more questions, your Honor."

~ ~ ~ ~ ~

Richard had been the first to present a closing argument to the jury, and had immediately asked them to focus on the question of motive, pointing out the fact that Dickson could not possibly have been motivated to poison that which he had devoted years trying to develop. After a discussion of motive he then presented an analysis of the credibility of the witnesses, a point that he felt strongly to stand in Dickson's favor when compared to the witnesses put forth by Wine House. From there he ran through the evidence, paying particular attention to the fact that, from the chemicals tested and the concentrations in the quarry, it was unlikely that the chemicals could have been from field runoff considering the number of years that the fields had been in production. At times he deviated from his notes, extemporizing on points that seemed to have caught the attention of one or more of the jurors like sunlight flashing off of glass. Winding to the conclusion of his remarks almost drove the breath from his body, so much effort did he put forth. Yet when he was done, notwithstanding all of his attempts to fire the jury's imagination and enthusiasm for Dickson and indignation against Wine House, all he had was twelve faces staring in his direction without expression or clue to their thoughts.

Stucky, true to the form that he had displayed throughout the trial, had wasted no time in addressing the jury in his determination to drive Richard's arguments from their minds. He first spoke of "Dickson's dream," described as an attempt by Dickson to build an edifice to his massive ego. Using Dickson's own testimony to buttress his arguments, including Dickson's almost boastful description to the long hours and weekends spent in building the project from scratch, he wove the theme that Dickson would let nothing stand in the way of making the winery a success. If using banned chemicals would make the economics better, reasoned Stucky, then it was consistent with "Dickson's Dream" to make use of any and all means available to make his dream come true. To Richard's dismay, as Stucky continued with his comments two of the jurors seemingly displayed outward approval of this argument by nodding their heads almost every time Stucky jabbed his finger into the air to emphasize a point. At least, he rationalized, Stucky was sure to be done soon, and their roles in the process would be over as soon as the case was turned over to the jury.

Finally, mercifully, Stucky had finished and Richard knew that his rebuttal would be the last chance to address the jury before it commenced deliberations. He had to get his point across, but he had to also be short and sweet. Without any notes to guide him, and nothing but his feelings to fall back on, the words just began to tumble out, first slowly and then with more speed as his frustrations propelled his thoughts.

"The question you must decide is whether Dr. Dickson was wrongfully terminated. The answer to that question lies in whether the reason for terminating his position was a pretext for some other activity. So . . . who was really behind the dumping of those chemicals, and who had the most to gain—or lose? To conclude that Dr. Dickson had any involvement one would first have to decide that Dr. Dickson either authorized or knew about the use of those chemicals at Winery Peak—but the evidence shows that that is not a viable conclusion—and not one that Wine House can legitimately claim to have reached. Did Wine House have a motive not to tell the truth? Absolutely! Wine House's motive was an exposure in the millions of dollars in charges to transport and process the sludge, the chemicals that *it* dumped on what it considered to be an unused portion of *its* property—but without telling Dr. Dickson. But once the word got out the dumping had occurred they had a public relations nightmare on its hands."

"Remember Rebecca Stewart's comment how Wine House carefully, meticulously, shapes the public's perception of its wines? It has tried to pull the same stunt here; tried to shape your perception so that you would ignore what it is trying to do to one good man. But in the final analysis, Wine House cannot hide from its attempt to blame Dr. Dickson as a shield for its own wrongdoing—you cannot let it slip its responsibility by saying that Wine House was 'exercising its prerogative'."

Richard paused and took several short breaths. The last three weeks of trial had worn him down physically and emotionally and he was dangerously close to pushing the jury too hard. Between the long days in the courtroom and the preparation every evening for the next day of trial he had been averaging no more than three hours of sleep per night. He was done, running on fumes, and he had to close the loop with one last plea.

"Before you carefully consider the testimony that you have heard and the documents that you have seen I want to remind you—once again—to think about credibility, believability, motive. Because everything you have heard and seen must be measured by these factors. And when you consider all of the information, I know that you will find for Dr. Dickson."

~~~~~

Richard felt like he was wearing a path in the carpet in his office, but could not relax long enough to stop his incessant back and forth pacing. Since waiting at the Courthouse for the jury to reach its decision was as easy as waiting outside an operating room for the surgeon to report on the outcome of a particularly difficult surgery, Richard, Gayle and Dickson had left for Richard's office to sit out the wait and stare at the walls as soon as the jury had been sequestered. When the balance of the first day had passed without resolution, they had agreed to meet again in Richard's office the next day to wait out the call.

He glanced over at Dickson, sitting across the room engrossed in a magazine, just as the phone rang on his desk. Dickson grimaced and turned towards the phone before looking questioningly at Richard. They both stared at each other for a moment before the second ring jolted Richard into action. Before lifting the receiver he steeled himself for a repeat of yesterday afternoon's call from the court clerk. That call had come only a few hours after the jury had begun their deliberations. During the short conversation the clerk
~~~~~

had indicated only that their presence was required in the courtroom. Believing from her comment that the jury must have reached a verdict, Richard had reacted with the same sense of calm typified by someone on the way to the hospital in anticipation of the delivery of their first child. Gayle, with many trials under her belt, had provided both a slightly more balanced approach to the news as well as the keys to the car after Richard's frenzied search failed to locate their whereabouts on the lip of one of the bookshelves.

Trying to make time, they had immediately swung past Dickson's house to pick up his wife and then sped to the Courthouse in nervous silence. Upon their arrival the bailiff had asked them to wait, which they did for almost fifteen minutes until Stucky finally joined them. As soon as everyone was accounted for they were ushered into Judge Jamison's chambers. Once seated, they were quietly informed of a problem with the jury, who was far from reaching a decision. To the acute disappointment of everyone in Judge Jamison's chambers, the jury was in a state of uproar over comments by one of their members. The foreperson, not knowing how to proceed, had sent a written message to Judge Jamison asking for his guidance, and the Judge in turn had summoned the parties to outline the situation.

It appeared that Mrs. Sager, identified simply as "juror number 4," was patently refusing to discuss the evidence that had been presented and was instead insisting on redirecting the discussion in a manner that prevented the rest of the jurors from any objective analysis of the issues. Two of the jurors, Mr. Williams and Mr. Kennedy, had become so incensed at her comments that they had threatened to completely withhold their votes unless she was removed from the jury. Three other jurors had taken vocal exception to this ultimatum and one was now in tears in the hallway restroom.

Richard knew that he only needed nine of the twelve jurors to vote in Dickson's favor to win, but was troubled by Sager's apparent intransigence. Judge Jamison was circumspect in his description of the topical areas that Sager had insisted on discussing, alluding simply to a general fanaticism against "men in power." Richard reflected that, although this reference could as equally be directed at the men that dominated the corporate power structure at Wine House as at Dickson, the latter was more likely given the nature of the witnesses that had been presented by both sides. Whatever it meant, Sager had apparently alienated the remaining members of the jury to such an extent that the possibility of her opinions dominating the jury's decision seemed quite small. Judge Jamison did not ask for Richard's opinion, however, but had instead curtly informed them that he would entertain a motion for a mistrial—and start from scratch—unless Stucky and Richard simply stipulated to replacing Sager with one of the alternate jurors. Stucky, who thought that he had gained an upper hand during the presentation of the evidence and—unbeknownst to Richard—was under ever-mounting pressure from Alexander to gain closure, rapidly assented to replacement of Sager. Richard was not as sanguine about the alternative presented by Judge Jamison and desperately wished that he could discuss the situation with Michael before committing himself. This was impossible, given the situation, and he instead asked for a moment alone to discuss the alternatives with Dickson. They had stepped into the now empty courtroom where Dickson grudgingly admitted replacement was the only viable choice as he could not, would not, voluntarily put his family through a retrial of the case. Within minutes of communicating this decision to Judge Jamison the entire jury was reassembled in the courtroom and, after going through the mechanics of thanking an overtly angry Sager for her participation in the process, replaced her with one of the alternates to the obvious relief of the remaining jurors. Fortunately for Richard's state of mind, as Sager left the courtroom he was in sole position to see the baleful glance that she directed towards Dickson, confirming his suspicions over the direction of—although not the reasons for—her ill will.

~ ~ ~ ~ ~

"The jury has reached a verdict."

The voice of Judge Jamison's clerk, flat and unemotional across the phone line, brought his thoughts back to the present. After yesterday's incident involving Sager the jury had again retired to a separate room to deliberate and almost six hours had passed by Richard's informal calculations. Conventional wisdom suggested that the longer the jury took to deliberate the more likely it was that they would find in favor of the plaintiff. That morning in his office, as each additional hour had ticked off of the clock, Richard had tensed in anticipation for the phone to ring with the announcement that a verdict had been reached. Six hours was somewhat of a twilight period, during which it was all too easy to rationalize how the jury had spent its time finding in favor of either Wine House or Dickson.

"We will expect you in the next fifteen minutes."

Richard stomach knotted, but his voice tried to match the clerk's neutral tones. "That's fine," he replied, knowing that it was now show time for sure.

As soon as he put the phone down Richard felt a surge of adrenaline and practically grabbed Dickson to hustle out the door. Action and activity, no matter what kind, was better than sitting still. Seven minutes later they pulled to the courthouse, this time having called Dickson's wife to meet them. As they walked up the courthouse stairs Richard turned to Dickson and paused.

"No matter what happens in there make sure you remain stoic. No matter what decision the jury reaches, it is unlikely that this case will be over without a few more fights with Wine House." Shifting his briefcase in his hands Richard took Dickson gently by the arm. "And you should feel comfortable that there was not a damn thing that you could have done or said differently in there."

When they made their way into the courtroom Stucky was already standing behind counsel table. As they placed their briefcases next to counsel table entered neither Richard nor Dickson acknowledged his presence, nor did he acknowledge theirs. Instead, still angry from Richard's comments during closing argument, he looked purposefully the other way. The lack of any exchange between the two did not go unnoticed by the court clerk, who made it a habit to keep an eye out for the manner in which the parties interacted and kept Judge Jamison advised at all points during the proceedings. One never knew when an opportunity might arise during the trial, at which time the parties could be interested in discussing settlement of their dispute. Even at this late point in the trial settlement was not unheard of, for until the jury came back with its verdict the uncertainty of the result lent itself to the possibility of a compromise. With an inaudible sigh, however, the court clerk recognized that there were too many hard feelings between these folks, that there would not be any letting down or willingness to concede any points, and there definitely would not be a settlement before the jury announced its verdict. Someone had definitely touched a nerve, perhaps two or three, and only the jury's verdict would close out this stage of the case.

Once everyone was present and seated the court clerk buzzed Judge Jamison in chambers. He quickly came out, as if he had been waiting at the door for his cue, and asked the clerk to call the jury from the deliberations room across the hallway. Within moments they filed through the twin doors of the courtroom, collectively looking self-conscious at being the obvious center of attention. Richard immediately stood, as he had done throughout the trial as a gesture of respect whenever the jury entered the courtroom, and motioned by slightly pointing his finger for Dickson to also stand. Stucky knew much better than remain sitting by himself and also stood while the jury quietly reclaimed their seats in the jury box.

As each of the jurors had filed past the counsel table Richard had attempted to make eye contact, searching for some clue to the decision that would be announced in the next few minutes. None of the jurors seemed eager to look his way. He reluctantly but optimistically took this as a good sign. Michael had suggested that jurors tend to look away from the party in whose favor they have decided, as a subconscious reflection of the desire to appear impartial. Had the jury gone against him, cautioned Michael, they would probably look at him directly in an attempt to convey understanding or ease the guilt they might feel at the upcoming news. Either way, at this stage it really did not matter if Michael's theories were correct. The jury had already reached its decision and nothing could now change that particular outcome.

In response to Judge Jamison's request the foreperson silently handed the multipage verdict form to the bailiff, who unfolded the long white form and checked the bottom of each page for the foreperson's signature. He then refolded the form and handed the entire package up to Judge Jamison. Without a word Judge Jamison slowly unfolded the pages and silently began to read the information as it appeared in front of him. The verdict form was comprised of a long series of questions that had been answered collectively by the jury. Most of the questions required a simple yes or no answer. If the jury answered "yes" to a question, it reflected a determination that Richard had presented sufficient evidence to have satisfied that particular element of one of the claims and they could then proceed to the next question on the form. If the jury answered a question concerning a particular element of any one of the claims in the negative, then as to that entire claim the jury would skip the rest of the questions and find in favor of Wine House before addressing the next claim.

At first, no expression crossed Judge Jamison's face as he read to himself and Richard could only sit helplessly and follow Judge Jamison's eyes as they traveled back and forth across each page of the form. Halfway through the third page Judge Jamison looked up briefly, without moving his head, and stared somewhat disbelievingly at Richard over the tops of his bifocals. Not quite knowing how to react in response, Richard merely looked down at the top of the table and pretended to write himself a note on the yellow pad that sat by itself on the table in front of him. Judge Jamison looked back to the words on the form and continued to read until he finished with the last page. He then signaled that he was done by emitting an audible sigh. Handing the entire verdict to the clerk, Judge Jamison then looked sternly over at the jury.

"Madam Foreperson, is this the verdict of all of you?"

"It is, your Honor."

"Then, Madam Clerk, please read the verdict."

Now, finally, the moment that they had worked towards for months was at hand. Richard, by force of habit and to conceal his nervousness, prepared himself to take detailed notes of the verdict even while knowing in his heart that his notes would not really be needed.

CHAPTER FOURTEEN

IT DID NOT TAKE LONG for word of the jury's tremendous verdict to spread through the halls of the Firm. A constant stream of the curious, including members of the office staff, some well wishers from the corporate and transactional departments at the Firm and several others simply too nosey to stay away came by the desk of Richard's secretary to ask for information. She did not have much to add to the verdict itself, having spoken only briefly to Richard when he called from the courthouse for his messages and to tell her the basic details, but she knew how much he valued her contribution and was happy to bask in the glow of his success. Towards the end of the afternoon, immediately before her normal quitting time, Richard made his way into the office and past her desk to drop off his trial notes before rendezvousing with Dickson for a celebratory drink or three. Although he tried to slip unnoticed into his office, he did not even make it halfway down the hallway past the receptionist's desk before those in the immediate vicinity of the lobby broke out into spontaneous applause. He grinned and blushed deeply before waving off the unexpected recognition.

Finally making his way through the gathered crowd, past several litigation associates who gave him high fives, he reached his office feeling like he was now in a welcome sanctuary. From the moment the verdict had been read out to the courtroom he had not fully trusted his ability to control his emotions. The clerk had read the entire form, page by page, question by question, response by response, until they were through with the entire document. After each question he would pause, somewhat dramatically, before reading the response. Richard's concentration had grown so strong that he did not notice how hard his fingers were clenched, or that nail of his index finger dug far enough into his skin to cause a blood blister to form the next morning. When the questions were all answered he had a clean sweep in Dickson's favor. Richard was flooded with relief so strong that he did not quite hear the bailiff read the amount awarded, but the look of astonishment on Gayle's face caused him to ask to have the sum stated again. Even hearing the amount twice did not help make the numbers quite understandable, given that the amount was almost twice what he had asked the jury to award.

Settling into his chair Richard looked at the massive pile of pink telephone slips stacked in the in box on his desk. He could only imagine what his voice mail must be like, not to mention the status of his email in-box notwithstanding the extended absence greeting that he had left on the former and the "out of office assistant" function he had used on the latter. All of those messages could be ignored for the time being, but relief from the physical onslaught of people was not to be had as his friends in the Firm began wandering into his office to hear the blow by blow description from the trial. Knowing that he was not going to get anything done while he was in the office that day, he started to enjoy himself, with feet propped on his desk, when Allen Rose suddenly appeared in the doorway like an unwelcome apparition. The room emptied fairly quickly at his arrival, associates leaving like started pigeons before a hungry cat. They were all well aware of the political situation within the Firm involving Allen and this case, and no one wanted to be seen as too closely aligned with Richard should Allen need someone upon whom to take out his anger. Allen stood for a moment, lips pursed together, as if still evaluating Richard. In turn Richard dropped his feet heavily to the floor and sought to stay calm, the stunning nature of his victory tearing at his penchant for diplomacy like strong drink. The hell with him, thought Richard, unless he is here to apologize for the grief he has been handing out over this case. Neither spoke for a moment, dramatically escalating the electricity in the air as each second passed. Against his own desires, but unable to stomach the test of wills, Allen broke the tense silence between them by speaking first.

"I suppose congratulations are in order."

Allen paused delicately, waiting for some type of conciliatory response. He did not get one from Richard, who just sat and stared noncommitantly. Allen did not like the attitude reflected on Richard's brow, and plunged forward in a vain attempt to demonstrate both his control over the conversation and his superior position within the Firm.

"Have you given any thought to how much of a surcharge that we can add to the fee in light of the result that we achieved for Dr. Dickson?"

Richard did not wait to think whether or not Allen had meant his remark seriously in light of all of the grief that he had given himself and Michael over the contingency nature of the lawsuit. Instead, without hesitation or thought to the consequences of what he was about to say and devoid of his typical inhibition against saying exactly what was on his mind, he simultaneously began to bark out a response while vaulting out of the chair from behind his desk.

"You son of a bitch! You sanctimonious asshole! Have you never given a good goddamn thought to honesty—integrity? How dare you come into my office and talk about the result that 'we' got for Dr. Dickson . . ."

Before he could continue to express the strong feelings of injustice that had been pent up throughout the trial, a very wide eyed Allen backed quickly out of Richard's office and moved down the hallway towards the opposite end of the building.

~ ~ ~ ~ ~

The morning sky was electric. Piercingly cobalt blue heavens to the west were giving way reluctantly to pinkish orange shafts of light from a hungry sun that had yet to spring over the horizon to the east. At this time of the morning, while temperatures remained steady for the next hour or so until the sun could send warm currents to stir the air, only a slight breeze drifted evenly from the north end of the valley to the south. A number of hot air balloons already rose gently on the lazy currents into the sky from the fields surrounding Calistoga to the north of Napa. They would take advantage of the natural guidance system that the breezes presented, and ultimately landing in the fields slightly south of Napa after an hour in the air. Each balloon was brightly colored, most with a rainbow of stripes against the sides, all followed closely on the ground by a separate chase car. The balloons could be controlled for height, and the experienced balloonist would maneuver higher or lower to catch the small western or southerly cross-currents to orient themselves within the center of the valley. The end of the flight was the most delicate part, as the vineyard owners were not very forgiving about the damage that the large balloons could do to the vines during the somewhat uncontrolled descents.

As he drove alone in the early morning traffic Richard was oblivious to the splendors of the picturesque setting that surrounded him. He was headed to a meeting that he gladly would have avoided. The euphoria from the trial was still running through his blood and he hated to let anything interfere with his tremendous feeling of accomplishment. But stalling the meeting any longer, as attractive an option as it was, would not work, nor would a simple refusal to attend. This meeting, although unavoidable, had been finally scheduled by Frank Walsh for this morning as a courtesy to Richard's schedule.

Frank, who had curiously been present during the reading of the verdict, had not waited long after the announcement to sidle up to Richard at the Courthouse and advise him that the District Attorney's interest in the larger picture had not waned. He cautioned Richard to avoid extensive post-trial publicity, and particularly to avoid any discussions with Wine House that did not relate directly to the few procedural matters remaining in the lawsuit. At the time, although Richard had been told by Stucky to expect various post trial motions by Wine House during which Judge Jamison would be asked to reverse, or at least modify, the jury's verdict and award of damages, he had agreed to Frank's request as he saw no reason to initiate any discussions with anyone from Wine House. Knowing how careful the District Attorney was to gauge public sentiment before taking any action, in order to solidify Dickson's public persona as a man vindicated for a grievous wrong he purposely had not understood Frank's admonition to apply to questions from the press. During the week following the trial Richard was approached by several newspapers and two trade publications interested in the story. Unprepared for the extent of the sudden limelight, he had given several interviews during which he had expressed his opinion on several wide ranging topics including those that did not touch directly on the subject matter of the trial. When the stories eventually appeared in print Frank again made contact, this time with a no option request from the District Attorney for a face to face meeting to discuss the fact that "more serious" issues remained unresolved. Richard quickly assumed that this was the opening ploy of the District Attorney to get Dickson to agree to a plea bargain, along the probable lines of which he would asked to plead guilty in exchange for being sentenced to a lesser charge, instead of having to endure a long and complicated criminal trial in connection with the deaths of the two farm workers.

To give himself time to prepare for the negotiation over Dickson's fate, Richard suggested to Frank that he meet with the District Attorney in two days in order to give himself time to finalize his trial notes while his memory was still fresh. Frank countered with meeting the next morning, as soon as the Criminal Courts Annex opened at 9:00 A.M., implying that the District Attorney would have to otherwise immediately take Dickson into custody. Apparently unwilling to let any further delay challenge the fickle nature of public sentiment, which could castrate him for not acting soon enough—or attack him for taking any action at all after the civil verdict had been handed down in Dickson's favor, it was clear to Richard that the District Attorney simply wanted to move forward—the open question remained, however, whether he also simply wanted closure.

The afternoon before the meeting Richard had called Dickson to advise him of the developments with the District Attorney. To his surprise, Dickson did not seem terribly concerned about these developments or the ongoing interest in his life by the criminal justice system. With blunt sentences Richard tried to convey a sense or urgency and concern, but Dickson was still too buoyed by the recent vindication of his honor and name to allow Richard too continue along those lines. He shrugged off Richard's suggestion that a specialist in criminal defense be retained, stating that Richard was certainly lawyer enough to handle all of his needs. This comment served only to depress Richard, who now knew more than ever the true extent of his own inadequacies and inexperience and wisely avoided the ego trap of assuming that he was sufficiently qualified to handle the potential charges that could be levied against Dickson. A year ago he might have charged ahead, his lack of experience a buffer to a more cautious approach. If he had learned but one thing in the past year, however, it was to avoid trying to appear as an expert in all areas and to instead be comfortable and confident about the areas in which he did have some experience and exposure. Somehow the closeness of the victory on Dickson's behalf gave him a better perspective of the difference between being a lawyer, a title attained solely by virtue of having gone to law school and passing the bar exam, and finally attaining the level of knowledge tempered by years of experience to be able to call legitimately oneself a "trusted advisor." He now understood Michael's familiar observation that the seemingly unbending black letter rules of law could be tempered to shades of gray in almost every case by their actual application to people and events.

The approach to the Criminal Courts Annex, where the District Attorney had his office, felt like a new and somehow difficult experience although he had been there many times before. On prior occasions, when he had spent countless hours at the complex at the very beginning of his career, the role he had been asked to play was on behalf of the People of the State of California, a basically faceless, and to some seemingly soulless, client. Like most of the young interns and Assistant District Attorneys, he had been overly impressed at the time with his own position. Between the sense of power and privilege that automatically came with the job, and the sense of invulnerability that arose from the nature of the civil service classification, he had not given much thought to the lives that he had touched. The various defendants, as the party line ran within the Department, were always guilty sleazebags or they would not have been arrested in the first place and their attorneys, the "despicable" defense bar, were always engaged in every trick imaginable to thwart the progress of obtaining convictions. To the young Assistant District Attorneys, the victims, when they were even acknowledged at all, were looked on as handy witnesses who could be used effectively to shape the decision of the jury. Success was not measured on the basis of whether justice was done. The most important indication of success focused on whether the attorney had a high conviction rate. Anything less than an 80% conviction rate was entirely unacceptable within the Department and most of the young hotshots posted "scores" that averaged in the low nineties.

Much of the conviction rate was attributable to the combination of good police work at the arrest and investigation stages and overall sloppiness from an entirely overworked public defenders office. Most of the public defenders were newly out of law school and highly idealistic. They had to be idealistic to compensate for the long hours, inadequate staff, unresponsive clients and incredible low rate of pay. The burn out rate was high, resulting in constant turnover with the more successful ones going into private practice where they could charge substantial sums to insure equal justice for the fortunate few who could afford to pay their rates.

As a new Assistant District Attorney fresh out of law school, Richard's conviction rate always had been near the top of his class. Even though he had been entirely too junior to handle felony matters, and was not battle-tested against significantly experienced adversaries, he had enjoyed the challenges in the courtroom without once considering the social significance of the process. He now recalled those feelings with a sense of remorse as he mounted the steps of the building, considering for the first time the extent to which the lack of any restraints on prosecutorial discretion could have a negative effect on society. Fortunately for Dickson, after the recent victory he could afford his services with plenty to spare. Richard morbidly thought about all of the others that the government was able to steamroll, too middle class to qualify for the public defenders' office but too poor to be able to afford quality private defense counsel without having to commit most of their worldly possessions.

As was his habit, he arrived in the parking lot 15 minutes early for the meeting. The doors to the multi-story building did not open to the public until precisely 9:00 A.M., and he knew that he would have to wait. But better to wait there than worry about being on time because he went first to his office. Already a crowd gathered in front of the building, waiting patiently to go inside. Some were prospective jurors, identifiable generally by an outward sense of boredom and most prepared for the long wait with various forms of reading materials. The balance of the crowd appeared to alternate between friends or family of the defendants or the victims, identifiable by their outward showing of insolence and hostility towards each other. Seemingly long ago, when he had called this conservative gray building his office, the morning crowd was simply something to avoid as he passed through the side door on his way to work. The side door was manned by a deputy sheriff, stationed at that location for the sole purpose of allowing certain people to enter quickly and without the hassle of going through the main entrance. Now that he had to wait in front like everyone else the crowd became something for him to study to pass the time, although he made sure to view his neighbors covertly as there were several who could clearly ask him for free legal advise if they thought that they could catch the attention of one of the "suits." Richard finally grew bored of this pastime and began to pace back and forth across the gray concrete slabs that led from the sidewalk to the front door. Near the far end, where the concrete ran under the metal overhang, he had to walk carefully in order to avoid the accumulation of pigeon dropping. Turning around to walk back he looked over at the main doors in time to see movement behind the glass and decided to make his way over to join the line deployed in front of the doors.

He was not alone in moving towards the doors and the line quickly queued up behind him. Feeling like he stood out in his dark gray suit, at least in comparison with the others in line, he self-consciously lowered his eyes and waited his turn patiently as the deputy sheriffs at the door slowly admitted the waiting throng. The process took considerable time due to the extensive security features that had been installed in the past year. Immediately inside the doorway was a waist high counter, behind which ran a short conveyor belt. As each person entered the building they laid all of their belongings on the counter. The deputy sheriff conducted a visual inspection and then placed the items on the belt where they were quickly whisked under an airport x-ray machine. The next deputy handed out small plastic baskets, similar to the baskets used in fast food restaurants for fries, to hold pocket change or other small items while each individual walked through a metal detector. On the side of the metal detector was a sign, in English and Spanish, warning in red letters against a black background that no guns, weapons or drugs were allowed inside of the building. Although the sign stated an obvious point, considering the nature of the building and the presence of so many deputies, without fail each year several arrests were made when the warning was ignored.

When Richard finally reached the inside of the building he flashed his business card at the deputy, who waved him through without all of the formalities pressed upon the other visitors. Rank still hath its privileges, thought Richard, as he nervously scanned the hallway to see if there was anyone who he recognized. He did not expect to see anyone in particular, but it was a long standing habit that he had developed and used every time he was in a setting that was potentially adversarial. This habit allowed him to feel like he could exert a small degree of control over his surroundings by being able to approach or avoid others before they could approach him, and he felt better having gotten his bearings rather than simply walking directly into the meeting. Because he was especially nervous about this meeting, and its unknown agenda, he decided against using the elevator to the second floor and walked down to the staircase at the end of the rather featureless hallway.

Richard pushed the door open without much effort and entered the stairwell. Just as he was about to mount the stairs he heard the door open at the top of the stairs. Pausing in mid-step he listened carefully as two voices drifted down to his ears. The stairwell served as an unofficial smoking area as the landing at the second floor was open to the outside air above the balustrade. Although the blood pounding in his ears made it difficult at first to hear what was being said, he recognized one of the voices immediately. The speaker had a very distinctive Brooklyn accent, graveled by a long history of smoking. Richard had met him before on two occasions, the most recent time some six months before when he and Michael Shaw had traveled together to the federal building in San Francisco to discuss the alleged participation of one of their clients in an insider trading scheme. With a start he heard Dickson's name mentioned and wished again that he had brought Michael along for an added show of strength, not to mention his greater knowledge and experience in dealing with these types of negotiations. As he again debated the merits of delaying the meeting until Michael could attend, the voices faded as cigarettes were stubbed out against the concrete wall. Waiting an extra few seconds after hearing the door above open and close, he slowly backed up and moved out into the first floor hallway. He turned and walked towards the elevators next to the front entrance, his wingtips clicking against the polished floors. By the time that he had reached the front entrance his confidence had returned enough to turn and firmly press the already lit button for the elevator. The doors slid open even before he could release the button and he stepped inside with several others.

When the elevator reached the second floor he wasted no time in making his way down the hallway to the office of the District Attorney. When he entered the reception area was empty except for a lone receptionist who sat at her desk reading the morning paper. In stark contrast to the rest of the building, which was decorated with prints of dead presidents and framed copies of various documents including the Declaration of Independence and the U.S. Constitution, the reception area was plushly outfitted with new furniture and rather expensive appearing pieces of modern art. The receptionist folded her newspaper and placed it carefully in a drawer in her desk, clearly having spent her time so far this morning waiting for his arrival. She confirmed his identity without distraction or embarking on an unnecessary tangent, stood and then led the way to the conference room. Stopping in front of the closed door she knocked twice and then turned the handle to open the door before stepping out of the way for Richard to enter. As she moved out of his line of sight he could see four middle aged men in narrow conservative ties sitting around a square wooden conference table that was cluttered with several piles of papers and files.

As soon as he stepped through the door the conversation stopped, all four simultaneously slide their chairs back from the table and stood to greet him. Closest was Frank Walsh, who looked sheepishly at Richard for a moment before self-consciously offering his hand.

"Congratulations, Richard."

Frank's outstretched hand took Richard somewhat by surprise. Looking around at the other faces was no help in deciphering the mood of the meeting. The District Attorney maintained the same toughened visage that he had perfected during several election campaigns and the remaining participants wore pleasant yet noncommittal expressions. Each in turn after Frank offered their hands in congratulations and made polite noises about his success at the trial. Still, the underlying feeling in the room remained somewhat somber, making Richard more uncomfortable than ever. After everyone was seated Richard waited patiently, and silently, until Frank finally took the lead.

"You know that this office has been following your case rather carefully."

He just nodded his head in the affirmative, determined to say as little as possible. If they wanted to make a deal, then he was prepared to sit and force them to do all of the talking. Michael, the night before, had suggested to Richard that any precipitous comments that he might make could change the terms of the deal before it was even offered, and probably for the worse. If they were truly anxious to close the matter, at least so far as Dickson's involvement was concerned, then he could afford to make them sweat out their position. Frank waited for a verbal response in addition to the nod of Richard's head just as Michael had suggested that he would. Having Frank take the lead in the meeting bothered Richard, although from a logical point of view it should not have surprised him terribly given the nature of their past friendship. Supposedly they could "talk" to one another and he might be expected to agree to something that he otherwise would never accept if it were to have been proposed by anyone else in the room. From an emotional standpoint Frank's participation angered him, as he felt that they were trying to manipulate his friendship, but he knew that anger was a dangerous emotion in negotiations as it could cloud his better judgment. Silence, as Michael had advised, was the best response while the presentation played itself out.

"What you do not know," Frank continued, "is the fact that we have been working now for some time with Dr. Dickson."

Richard frowned incredulously at this plainly offered statement, dumbfounded by the news. Frank had to have a higher opinion of his intelligence than to make what would be so obvious of a lie, not to mention the ease with which the statement could be verified or refuted, leaving truth as the only reasonable description of this otherwise incredible statement. Richard could not now sit silently and merely nod in the face of such news.

"All right, Frank, I'll bite at your statement. Explain what is going on."

He hated to see the satisfied looks on the faces of the others around the table, so he turned his chair slightly so that he only had to look in Frank's direction. Noticing his discomfort, Frank began to explain how the FBI had been monitoring the activities of the regional director of the EPA for sometime when, in the course of the investigation, they had discovered that a number of the investigations of the Agency had been terminated earlier than standard operating procedures would reasonably have allowed. And the terminations often had been accompanied with a recommendation against any further action by the office of the United States Attorney. A wiretap had been put in place, and had tapped into a number of calls between the director and a line that was registered to an operating subsidiary of Wine House. When further records indicated that calls had also been placed directly from Winery Peak to the director, Dickson had been added to the list of possible suspects. The FBI had commenced planning a sting operation that would have involved one of the Wine House facilities in the Sonoma Valley twenty miles to the north of Winery Peak when news of the problem at the old quarry had hit the news wire. A jurisdictional battle between the federal authorities and the District Attorney's office, created when the farm workers had fallen ill, had been narrowly averted after the phone tap had revealed the desire of Wine House to frame Dickson for the presence of the contaminants.

Dickson had gone from being classified as a suspect to a valuable resource. Not only did he have detailed information about the inner operations of Wine House, but his trial also served to divert any attention that might otherwise have been focused by Wine House on the FBI investigation. To maintain the proper level of authenticity, Dickson had been persuaded in believing that he could not confide in Richard concerning these developments as Richard might change his trial strategy and accidentally tip off Wine House to the criminal investigation.

Richard began to feel a slow boil as he thought through the information. He hardly knew with whom he should be the angriest. Frank had clearly lied to him on during their prior conversations, including the night at the diner when he had ended up picking gravel splinters out of his hands.

"So Frank. Who was that guy at the diner? One of your investigators checking me out in case I had been bought out by Wine House?"

"No," replied Frank, cautiously reading the anger in Richard's eyes. "In fact, for your information he is an officer who was assigned to keep a protective eye on you in light of some of those phone calls that you were getting. We felt that you were doing well enough at trial that you could have been putting yourself at risk. I told you that night not to worry," he added defensively, "but you were not about to listen to anyone."

"You just try to ignore somebody staring at you," he shot back coldly.

Richard checked himself from adding anything further, mad at having risen to the bait, and remained silent. His grandfather had warned him often about his explosive temper, suggesting constantly through his youth that winning a fight through patience and logic—without physical displays of emotion—was the ultimate success in battle. But right now he would rather win the argument by head-butting Frank in the face, so keen was his anger at being kept in the dark by his friend. Frank recognized the pain he had caused Richard, and seemed at a temporary loss for words due to his embarrassment at what his friend had been put through. To hide his discomfort he began to trace with his pencil the lines of grain on the wooden arm of his chair.

Oblivious to Frank's unenviable position, Richard struggled to focus on the point of all of this information. He figured that Frank was being used solely for the introduction, to soften him up as a lead-in for the real reason for the meeting, and he needed to keep attention focused on the others around the table. Sooner or later the pitch would come, he reminded himself, although he could not envision what it would be in light of the news that they were already working directly with Dickson.

The older man at the far side of the table, the one who had been introduced as the representative from the feds, cleared his throat and gruffly began by confirming that he was the Agent In Charge from the FBI. In a blur of information he went through, in clinical detail, the background of the investigation of Wine House and the tie in with Winery Peak. Without a pause he set forth the true reason for the meeting as an informal request for his cooperation and the turn over of all of his working papers and files. Richard listened patiently, now that he knew what was expected of him, to the line of patriotic fervor from the Special Agent and the listing of all of the reasons why he should jump at the opportunity to help. According to the Special Agent, with his assistance in extracting further information from Wine House the investigation could be quickly concluded. He nodded to acknowledge the fact that he was following the presentation, but was still too emotionally strung-out by the revelations to cogently reply. His reserve must have been all too apparent, for the Special Agent's tone suddenly shifted and became harsher.

"Your cooperation is a small price to pay for us to ignore your own little version of 'self-help"

"What are you talking about?"

"Cut out the innocent bullshit, Mr. Magnus. Dr. Dickson followed your instructions to get rid of the two bags of organophosphates that he claims was put in his well house. What he did not tell you was the fact that he delivered them to us. You should have contacted the County yourself."

So this was it, thought Richard. He knew that he had been on solid ground when he gave his instructions to Dickson to get rid of the chemicals. Private ownership was not illegal, only commercial use, and he had not instructed Dickson to dump the stuff. But he was not so naïve as to believe that they could not create enough of a cloud that he would have to spend a lifetime just trying to clear his name. A neat trap, and quite an eye-opener for someone who had vainly held on to an idealized belief in right and wrong.

~ ~ ~ ~ ~

The meeting had not lasted much longer. In truth, they had not wanted Richard to do much other than merely stay out of the way of their investigation. The documents in his files could have as easily been pulled together independently by the government from its various sources, and they really did not need his permission as the materials ultimately belonged to Dickson. Once Dickson had given his consent, preferably in writing from Richard's point of view, he really had no room to complain.

True to his word the General Counsel of Wine House had consummated the settlement along the lines that they had discussed at the Courthouse. Within three weeks a cashier's check arrived, made payable to Richard in trust for Dickson in a staggering sum. As a show of "gratitude" for securing the 33% contingency fee, the firm had given Richard the underwhelming bonus of a mere $5,000. Richard knew that he had a lot of decisions to make, not the least of which was where he wanted to practice and with whom. But he had no trouble deciding how to spend his bonus. With no hesitation he had booked a flight direct to New York and to Lynn. All of the other decisions that he had to make could wait until he returned.

As he drove alone to the airport he reflected on what Frank had told him about Dickson's involvement. After the meeting he had curbed the desire to drive directly to Dickson's house and confront him in person. Instead, Richard called Dickson from his office. During the conversation he had waited agonizingly for Dickson to make some mention of the work he had been performing for the Feds. But Dickson did not say anything, or even hint about his cooperation, and Richard stewed but kept the conversation cordially directed at resolution of some minor points in connection with closure of the file. He knew that he should not dwell on the issue, that it really was none of his business, but he could not help from feeling somewhat betrayed.

With a wry smile he remembered one of Michael's many seemingly prescient admonitions about his role and relationships as an attorney. A witness—or even a client for that matter—should never be totally trusted to tell the truth or completely confide the entire story; that anything from a small "white" lie to a large series of intentional falsehoods should not be unexpected even when it may be surprising. Both memory and exigent circumstances changes memory of even the most honest person, and serves as a handy excuse for inconsistent positions from those who are less than honest. And yet, even with all of this terrific advice and logic, he knew that for the rest of his career he would only be able to puzzle without answer over the question of where Dickson fit into that spectrum.

THE END

RAMBLE HOUSE's

HARRY STEPHEN KEELER WEBWORK MYSTERIES

(RH) indicates the title is available ONLY in the **RAMBLE HOUSE** edition

The Ace of Spades Murder
The Affair of the Bottled Deuce (RH)
The Amazing Web
The Barking Clock
Behind That Mask
The Book with the Orange Leaves
The Bottle with the Green Wax Seal
The Box from Japan
The Case of the Canny Killer
The Case of the Crazy Corpse (RH)
The Case of the Flying Hands (RH)
The Case of the Ivory Arrow
The Case of the Jeweled Ragpicker
The Case of the Lavender Gripsack
The Case of the Mysterious Moll
The Case of the 16 Beans
The Case of the Transparent Nude (RH)
The Case of the Transposed Legs
The Case of the Two-Headed Idiot (RH)
The Case of the Two Strange Ladies
The Circus Stealers (RH)
Cleopatra's Tears
A Copy of Beowulf (RH)
The Crimson Cube (RH)
The Face of the Man From Saturn
Find the Clock
The Five Silver Buddhas
The 4th King
The Gallows Waits, My Lord! (RH)
The Green Jade Hand
Finger! Finger!
Hangman's Nights (RH)
I, Chameleon (RH)
I Killed Lincoln at 10:13! (RH)
The Iron Ring
The Man Who Changed His Skin (RH)
The Man with the Crimson Box
The Man with the Magic Eardrums
The Man with the Wooden Spectacles
The Marceau Case
The Matilda Hunter Murder
The Monocled Monster
The Murder of London Lew
The Murdered Mathematician
The Mysterious Card (RH)
The Mysterious Ivory Ball of Wong Shing Li (RH)
The Mystery of the Fiddling Cracksman
The Peacock Fan
The Photo of Lady X (RH)
The Portrait of Jirjohn Cobb
Report on Vanessa Hewstone (RH)
Riddle of the Travelling Skull
Riddle of the Wooden Parrakeet (RH)
The Scarlet Mummy (RH)
The Search for X-Y-Z
The Sharkskin Book
Sing Sing Nights
The Six From Nowhere (RH)
The Skull of the Waltzing Clown
The Spectacles of Mr. Cagliostro
Stand By—London Calling!
The Steeltown Strangler
The Stolen Gravestone (RH)
Strange Journey (RH)
The Strange Will
The Straw Hat Murders (RH)
The Street of 1000 Eyes (RH)
Thieves' Nights
Three Novellos (RH)
The Tiger Snake
The Trap (RH)
Vagabond Nights (Defrauded Yeggman)
Vagabond Nights 2 (10 Hours)
The Vanishing Gold Truck
The Voice of the Seven Sparrows
The Washington Square Enigma
When Thief Meets Thief
The White Circle (RH)
The Wonderful Scheme of Mr. Christopher Thorne
X. Jones—of Scotland Yard
Y. Cheung, Business Detective

Keeler Related Works

A To Izzard: A Harry Stephen Keeler Companion by Fender Tucker — Articles and stories about Harry, by Harry, and in his style. Included is a compleat bibliography.

Wild About Harry: Reviews of Keeler Novels — Edited by Richard Polt & Fender Tucker — 22 reviews of works by Harry Stephen Keeler from *Keeler News.* A perfect introduction to the author.

The Keeler Keyhole Collection: Annotated newsletter rants from Harry Stephen Keeler, edited by Francis M. Nevins. Over 400 pages of incredibly personal Keeleriana.

Fakealoo — Pastiches of the style of Harry Stephen Keeler by selected demented members of the HSK Society. Updated every year with the new winner.

RAMBLE HOUSE's OTHER LOONS

The End of It All and Other Stories — Ed Gorman's latest short story collection
Four Dancing Tuatara Press Books — *Beast or Man?* By Sean M'Guire; *The Whistling Ancestors* by Richard E. Goddard; *The Shadow on the House* and *Sorcerer's Chessmen* by Mark Hansom. With introductions by John Pelan
The Dumpling — Political murder from 1907 by Coulson Kernahan
Victims & Villains — Intriguing Sherlockiana from Derham Groves
Evidence in Blue — 1938 mystery by E. Charles Vivian
The Case of the Little Green Men — Mack Reynolds wrote this love song to sci-fi fans back in 1951 and it's now back in print.
Hell Fire — A new hard-boiled novel by Jack Moskovitz about an arsonist, an arson cop and a Nazi hooker. It isn't pretty.
Researching American-Made Toy Soldiers — A 276-page collection of a lifetime of articles by toy soldier expert Richard O'Brien
Strands of the Web: Short Stories of Harry Stephen Keeler — Edited and Introduced by Fred Cleaver
The Sam McCain Novels — Ed Gorman's terrific series includes *The Day the Music Died, Wake Up Little Susie* and *Will You Still Love Me Tomorrow?*
A Shot Rang Out — Three decades of reviews from Jon Breen
Mysterious Martin, the Master of Murder — Two versions of a strange 1912 novel by Tod Robbins about a man who writes books that can kill.
Dago Red — 22 tales of dark suspense by Bill Pronzini
The Night Remembers — A 1991 Jack Walsh mystery from Ed Gorman
Rough Cut & New, Improved Murder — Ed Gorman's first two novels
Hollywood Dreams — A novel of the Depression by Richard O'Brien
Seven Gelett Burgess Novels — *The Master of Mysteries, The White Cat, Two O'Clock Courage, Ladies in Boxes, Find the Woman, The Heart Line, The Picaroons*
The Organ Reader — A huge compilation of just about everything published in the 1971-1972 radical bay-area newspaper, *THE ORGAN*.
A Clear Path to Cross — Sharon Knowles short mystery stories by Ed Lynskey
Old Times' Sake — Short stories by James Reasoner from Mike Shayne Magazine
Freaks and Fantasies — Eerie tales by Tod Robbins, collaborator of Tod Browning on the film FREAKS.
Six Jim Harmon Double Novels — *Vixen Hollow/Celluloid Scandal, The Man Who Made Maniacs/Silent Siren, Ape Rape/Wanton Witch, Sex Burns Like Fire/Twist Session, Sudden Lust/Passion Strip, Sin Unlimited/Harlot Master, Twilight Girls/Sex Institution.* Written in the early 60s.
Marblehead: A Novel of H.P. Lovecraft — A long-lost masterpiece from Richard A. Lupoff. Published for the first time!
The Compleat Ova Hamlet — Parodies of SF authors by Richard A. Lupoff - A brand new edition with more stories and more illustrations by Trina Robbins.
The Secret Adventures of Sherlock Holmes — Three Sherlockian pastiches by the Brooklyn author/publisher, Gary Lovisi.
The Universal Holmes — Richard A. Lupoff's 2007 collection of five Holmesian pastiches and a recipe for giant rat stew.
Four Joel Townsley Rogers Novels — By the author of *The Red Right Hand: Once In a Red Moon, Lady With the Dice, The Stopped Clock, Never Leave My Bed*
Two Joel Townsley Rogers Story Collections — Night of Horror and Killing Time
Twenty Norman Berrow Novels — *The Bishop's Sword, Ghost House, Don't Go Out After Dark, Claws of the Cougar, The Smokers of Hashish, The Secret Dancer, Don't Jump Mr. Boland!, The Footprints of Satan, Fingers for Ransom, The Three Tiers of Fantasy, The Spaniard's Thumb, The Eleventh Plague, Words Have Wings, One Thrilling Night, The Lady's in Danger, It Howls at Night, The Terror in the Fog, Oil Under the Window, Murder in the Melody, The Singing Room*
The N. R. De Mexico Novels — Robert Bragg presents *Marijuana Girl, Madman on a Drum, Private Chauffeur* in one volume.
Four Chelsea Quinn Yarbro Novels featuring Charlie Moon — *Ogilvie, Tallant and Moon, Music When the Sweet Voice Dies, Poisonous Fruit* and *Dead Mice*
Five Walter S. Masterman Mysteries — *The Green Toad, The Flying Beast, The Yellow Mistletoe, The Wrong Verdict* and *The Perjured Alibi.* Fantastic impossible plots.
Two Hake Talbot Novels — *Rim of the Pit, The Hangman's Handyman.* Classic locked room mysteries.
Two Alexander Laing Novels — *The Motives of Nicholas Holtz* and *Dr. Scarlett*, stories of medical mayhem and intrigue from the 30s.

Four David Hume Novels — *Corpses Never Argue, Cemetery First Stop, Make Way for the Mourners, Eternity Here I Come*, and more to come.

Three Wade Wright Novels — *Echo of Fear, Death At Nostalgia Street* and *It Leads to Murder*, with more to come!

Eight Rupert Penny Novels — *Policeman's Holiday, Policeman's Evidence, Lucky Policeman, Policeman in Armour, Sealed Room Murder, Sweet Poison, The Talkative Policeman, She had to Have Gas* and *Cut and Run* (by Martin Tanner.)

Five Jack Mann Novels — Strange murder in the English countryside. *Gees' First Case, Nightmare Farm, Grey Shapes, The Ninth Life, The Glass Too Many.*

Seven Max Afford Novels — *Owl of Darkness, Death's Mannikins, Blood on His Hands, The Dead Are Blind, The Sheep and the Wolves, Sinners in Paradise* and *Two Locked Room Mysteries and a Ripping Yarn* by one of Australia's finest novelists.

Five Joseph Shallit Novels — *The Case of the Billion Dollar Body, Lady Don't Die on My Doorstep, Kiss the Killer, Yell Bloody Murder, Take Your Last Look.* One of America's best 50's authors.

Two Crimson Clown Novels — By Johnston McCulley, author of the Zorro novels, *The Crimson Clown* and *The Crimson Clown Again.*

The Best of 10-Story Book — edited by Chris Mikul, over 35 stories from the literary magazine Harry Stephen Keeler edited.

A Young Man's Heart — A forgotten early classic by Cornell Woolrich

The Anthony Boucher Chronicles — edited by Francis M. Nevins
Book reviews by Anthony Boucher written for the *San Francisco Chronicle,* 1942 - 1947. Essential and fascinating reading.

Muddled Mind: Complete Works of Ed Wood, Jr. — David Hayes and Hayden Davis deconstruct the life and works of a mad genius.

Gadsby — A lipogram (a novel without the letter E). Ernest Vincent Wright's last work, published in 1939 right before his death.

My First Time: The One Experience You Never Forget — Michael Birchwood — 64 true first-person narratives of how they lost it.

A Roland Daniel Double: The Signal and The Return of Wu Fang — Classic thrillers from the 30s

Murder in Shawnee — Two novels of the Alleghenies by John Douglas: *Shawnee Alley Fire* and *Haunts.*

Deep Space and other Stories — A collection of SF gems by Richard A. Lupoff

Blood Moon — The first of the Robert Payne series by Ed Gorman

The Time Armada — Fox B. Holden's 1953 SF gem.

Black River Falls — Suspense from the master, Ed Gorman

Sideslip — 1968 SF masterpiece by Ted White and Dave Van Arnam

The Triune Man — Mindscrambling science fiction from Richard A. Lupoff

Detective Duff Unravels It — Episodic mysteries by Harvey O'Higgins

Automaton — Brilliant treatise on robotics: 1928-style! By H. Stafford Hatfield

The Incredible Adventures of Rowland Hern — Rousing 1928 impossible crimes by Nicholas Olde.

Slammer Days — Two full-length prison memoirs: *Men into Beasts* (1952) by George Sylvester Viereck and *Home Away From Home* (1962) by Jack Woodford

Murder in Black and White — 1931 classic tennis whodunit by Evelyn Elder

Killer's Caress — Cary Moran's 1936 hardboiled thriller

The Golden Dagger — 1951 Scotland Yard yarn by E. R. Punshon

A Smell of Smoke — 1951 English countryside thriller by Miles Burton

Ruled By Radio — 1925 futuristic novel by Robert L. Hadfield & Frank E. Farncombe

Murder in Silk — A 1937 Yellow Peril novel of the silk trade by Ralph Trevor

The Case of the Withered Hand — 1936 potboiler by John G. Brandon

Finger-prints Never Lie — A 1939 classic detective novel by John G. Brandon

Inclination to Murder — 1966 thriller by New Zealand's Harriet Hunter

Invaders from the Dark — Classic werewolf tale from Greye La Spina

Fatal Accident — Murder by automobile, a 1936 mystery by Cecil M. Wills

The Devil Drives — A prison and lost treasure novel by Virgil Markham

Dr. Odin — Douglas Newton's 1933 potboiler comes back to life.

The Chinese Jar Mystery — Murder in the manor by John Stephen Strange, 1934

The Julius Caesar Murder Case — A classic 1935 re-telling of the assassination by Wallace Irwin that's much more fun than the Shakespeare version

West Texas War and Other Western Stories — by Gary Lovisi

The Contested Earth and Other SF Stories — A never-before published space opera and seven short stories by Jim Harmon.

Tales of the Macabre and Ordinary — Modern twisted horror by Chris Mikul, author of the *Bizarrism* series.

The Gold Star Line — Seaboard adventure from L.T. Reade and Robert Eustace.

The Werewolf vs the Vampire Woman — Hard to believe ultraviolence by either Arthur M. Scarm or Arthur M. Scram.

Black Hogan Strikes Again — Australia's Peter Renwick pens a tale of the outback.

Don Diablo: Book of a Lost Film — Two-volume treatment of a western by Paul Landres, with diagrams. Intro by Francis M. Nevins.

The Charlie Chaplin Murder Mystery — Movie hijinks by Wes D. Gehring

The Koky Comics — A collection of all of the 1978-1981 Sunday and daily comic strips by Richard O'Brien and Mort Gerberg, in two volumes.

Suzy — Another collection of comic strips from Richard O'Brien and Bob Vojtko

Dime Novels: Ramble House's 10-Cent Books — *Knife in the Dark* by Robert Leslie Bellem, *Hot Lead* and *Song of Death* by Ed Earl Repp, *A Hashish House in New York* by H.H. Kane, and five more.

Blood in a Snap — The *Finnegan's Wake* of the 21st century, by Jim Weiler

Stakeout on Millennium Drive — Award-winning Indianapolis Noir — Ian Woollen.

Dope Tales #1 — Two dope-riddled classics; *Dope Runners* by Gerald Grantham and *Death Takes the Joystick* by Phillip Condé.

Dope Tales #2 — Two more narco-classics; *The Invisible Hand* by Rex Dark and *The Smokers of Hashish* by Norman Berrow.

Dope Tales #3 — Two enchanting novels of opium by the master, Sax Rohmer. *Dope* and *The Yellow Claw.*

Tenebrae — Ernest G. Henham's 1898 horror tale brought back.

The Singular Problem of the Stygian House-Boat — Two classic tales by John Kendrick Bangs about the denizens of Hades.

Tiresias — Psychotic modern horror novel by Jonathan M. Sweet.

The One After Snelling — Kickass modern noir from Richard O'Brien.

The Sign of the Scorpion — 1935 Edmund Snell tale of oriental evil.

The House of the Vampire — 1907 poetic thriller by George S. Viereck.

An Angel in the Street — Modern hardboiled noir by Peter Genovese.

The Devil's Mistress — Scottish gothic tale by J. W. Brodie-Innes.

The Lord of Terror — 1925 mystery with master-criminal, Fantômas.

The Lady of the Terraces — 1925 adventure by E. Charles Vivian.

My Deadly Angel — 1955 Cold War drama by John Chelton

Prose Bowl — Futuristic satire — Bill Pronzini & Barry N. Malzberg .

Satan's Den Exposed — True crime in Truth or Consequences New Mexico — Award-winning journalism by the *Desert Journal*.

The Amorous Intrigues & Adventures of Aaron Burr — by Anonymous — Hot historical action.

I Stole $16,000,000 — A true story by cracksman Herbert E. Wilson.

The Black Dark Murders — Vintage 50s college murder yarn by Milt Ozaki, writing as Robert O. Saber.

Sex Slave — Potboiler of lust in the days of Cleopatra — Dion Leclerq.

You'll Die Laughing — Bruce Elliott's 1945 novel of murder at a practical joker's English countryside manor.

The Private Journal & Diary of John H. Surratt — The memoirs of the man who conspired to assassinate President Lincoln.

Dead Man Talks Too Much — Hollywood boozer by Weed Dickenson

Red Light — History of legal prostitution in Shreveport Louisiana by Eric Brock. Includes wonderful photos of the houses and the ladies.

A Snark Selection — Lewis Carroll's *The Hunting of the Snark* with two Snarkian chapters by Harry Stephen Keeler — Illustrated by Gavin L. O'Keefe.

Ripped from the Headlines! — The Jack the Ripper story as told in the newspaper articles in the *New York* and *London Times.*

Geronimo — S. M. Barrett's 1905 autobiography of a noble American.

The White Peril in the Far East — Sidney Lewis Gulick's 1905 indictment of the West and assurance that Japan would never attack the U.S.

The Compleat Calhoon — All of Fender Tucker's works: Includes *Totah Six-Pack, Weed, Women and Song* and *Tales from the Tower,* plus a CD of all of his songs.

Totah Six-Pack — Just Fender Tucker's six tales about Farmington in one sleek volume.

RAMBLE HOUSE

Fender Tucker, Prop.

www.ramblehouse.com fender@ramblehouse.com

228-826-1783 10329 Sheephead Drive, Vancleave MS 39565

www.ingramcontent.com/pod-product-compliance
Lightning Source LLC
LaVergne TN
LVHW091021080826
845145LV00002B/318

* 9 7 8 1 6 0 5 4 3 3 4 0 0 *